T0318183

Praise for the Novels
of Joanne Rendell

Crossing Washington Square

"For every reader who has ever wondered why nineteenth-century novels about women are called 'the canon,' but contemporary novels about women are called 'chick lit' comes a charming, witty and cerebral novel about Rachel Grey, an Austen-worthy heroine fighting for love and respect in the academic shark tank."

—Nicola Kraus, *New York Times* bestselling coauthor of
The Nanny Diaries

"Joanne Rendell has done it again! *Crossing Washington Square* is a book that will stay with you long after you turn that final page. Curl up on a park bench somewhere, watch the leaves fall, and spend some much beloved time with Rachel and Diana. These are the kinds of characters you'll wish you could invite over for tea."

—Jessica Brody, bestselling author of
The Fidelity Files and *Love Under Cover*

continued . . .

Written by today's freshest new talents and selected by New American Library, NAL Accent novels touch on subjects close to a woman's heart, from friendship to family to finding our place in the world. The Conversation Guides included in each book are intended to enrich the individual reading experience, as well as encourage us to explore these topics together—because books, and life, are meant for sharing.

Visit us online at www.penguin.com.

"In *Crossing Washington Square*, Joanne Rendell creates a fascinating, fictional academic world complete with a cast of smart and funny female characters. While supremely entertaining, Rendell's novel also encourages readers to interrogate some long-standing biases against women's popular fiction, ultimately proving that chick lit can be a good beach read plus so much more."

—Professor Caroline Smith, George Washington University, author of
Cosmopolitan Culture and *Consumerism in Chick Lit*

"Austen, Plath, Jennifer Weiner, Emily Giffin . . . it's all good when you're crossing into Washington Square with an unlikely friendship between two professors of literature. Joanne Rendell's *Crossing Washington Square* brings the love of women's fiction—whatever kind— into sharp focus as her characters navigate the often murky waters of love, literature, and love of literature."

—Robin Kall, host of *Reading with Robin*, WHJJ, Providence radio show

"Once I started reading Joanne Rendell's new novel, *Crossing Washington Square*, I had a hard time putting it down. This gripping book . . . is intelligent chick lit, an engaging story beautifully told with multiple layers that touch some of the major issues relevant to the experience of women: relationships between friends, family, colleagues, and lovers."

—Dr. Irene S. Levine, The Huffington Post

The Professors' Wives' Club

"As an NYU alum, I enjoyed the behind-the-scenes escapades at the fictional Manhattan U. in *The Professors' Wives' Club*. Joanne Rendell has created a quick, fun read about a wonderful group of friends."

—Kate Jacobs, #1 *New York Times* bestselling author of
The Friday Night Knitting Club

"The four women in *The Professors' Wives' Club* who risk it all in pursuit of life, love, and green space in New York City are smart, funny, and real—friends you'd want for life. Rendell doesn't shy away from tough issues, but her light touch and readable prose make this charming first novel a delight."

—Christina Baker Kline, author of *The Way Life Should Be*

"Alternately amusing and serious, with a little literary mystery thrown in for good measure, Rendell's smart and pleasing tale of friendship and self-actualization has broad appeal." —*Booklist*

"Joanne Rendell's irresistible debut novel is a captivating look at an ivory tower Peyton Place filled with intrigue, heartbreak, and hope."

—Michelle Yu and Blossom Kan, authors of *China Dolls*

"As a self-absorbed undergrad I never realized that the really juicy stuff was going on outside of the frat parties and late nights at the library! The women of *The Professors' Wives' Club* are a force with which to be reckoned. Joanne Rendell's debut novel is smart and suspenseful with an intriguing Edgar Allan Poe backstory. I cannot wait for Joanne's second novel."

—Robin Kall, host of *Reading with Robin*, WHJJ, Providence radio show

"Joanne Rendell has created characters who will inspire, entertain, and keep you hooked from the very first moment you meet them. I loved spending time with these ladies and only wish *The Professors' Wives' Club* were a bit longer so I could have more time with these wonderful women."

—Yvette Corporon, senior producer for *Extra* and author of
Peeing in Peace: Tales and Tips for Type A Moms

ALSO BY JOANNE RENDELL

Crossing Washington Square

The Professors' Wives' Club

OUT OF THE SHADOWS

Joanne Rendell

NAL
ACCENT

NAL Accent
Published by New American Library, a division of
Penguin Group (USA) Inc., 375 Hudson Street,
New York, New York 10014, USA
Penguin Group (Canada), 90 Eglinton Avenue East, Suite 700, Toronto,
Ontario M4P 2Y3, Canada (a division of Pearson Penguin Canada Inc.)
Penguin Books Ltd., 80 Strand, London WC2R 0RL, England
Penguin Ireland, 25 St. Stephen's Green, Dublin 2,
Ireland (a division of Penguin Books Ltd.)
Penguin Group (Australia), 250 Camberwell Road, Camberwell, Victoria 3124,
Australia (a division of Pearson Australia Group Pty. Ltd.)
Penguin Books India Pvt. Ltd., 11 Community Centre, Panchsheel Park,
New Delhi - 110 017, India
Penguin Group (NZ), 67 Apollo Drive, Rosedale, North Shore 0632,
New Zealand (a division of Pearson New Zealand Ltd.)
Penguin Books (South Africa) (Pty.) Ltd., 24 Sturdee Avenue,
Rosebank, Johannesburg 2196, South Africa

Penguin Books Ltd., Registered Offices:
80 Strand, London WC2R 0RL, England

First published by NAL Accent, an imprint of New American Library,
a division of Penguin Group (USA) Inc.

Copyright © Joanne Rendell, 2010
Conversation Guide copyright © Penguin Group (USA) Inc., 2010
All rights reserved

 REGISTERED TRADEMARK—MARCA REGISTRADA

LIBRARY OF CONGRESS CATALOGING-IN-PUBLICATION DATA:

Rendell, Joanne.
  Out of the shadows/Joanne Rendell.
  p.   cm.
  ISBN 978-0-451-23112-3
  1. Female friendship—Fiction. 2. Genealogy—Fiction. 3. Shelley, Mary Wollstonecraft,
1797–1851—Fiction. I. Title.
  PS3618.E5747098   2010
  813'.6—dc22   2010016231

Set in Fairfield
Designed by Alissa Amell

Without limiting the rights under copyright reserved above, no part of this publication may be reproduced, stored in or introduced into a retrieval system, or transmitted, in any form, or by any means (electronic, mechanical, photocopying, recording, or otherwise), without the prior written permission of both the copyright owner and the above publisher of this book.

PUBLISHER'S NOTE
This is a work of fiction. Names, characters, places, and incidents either are the product of the author's imagination or are used fictitiously, and any resemblance to actual persons, living or dead, business establishments, events, or locales is entirely coincidental.
  The publisher does not have any control over and does not assume any responsibility for author or third-party Web sites or their content.

The scanning, uploading, and distribution of this book via the Internet or via any other means without the permission of the publisher is illegal and punishable by law. Please purchase only authorized electronic editions, and do not participate in or encourage electronic piracy of copyrighted materials. Your support of the author's rights is appreciated.

147204767

For my mum, Kate Matthews

Acknowledgments

To my wonderful editors, Kara Cesare and Kerry Donovan. Kara believed in this book from the start and Kerry nurtured it, offered her keen editorial insights, and encouraged me to take it to the next level. As always, I'm deeply grateful for the friendship, guidance, and support of my agent, Claudia Cross.

To my first readers, Yvette Manessis Corporon, Dina Jordan, and my mother-in-law, Jana Lewis. The three of you were incredibly supportive through the writing of *Out of the Shadows* and kept me moving forward with your cheerleading.

To those biographers and writers whose works inspired and informed *Out of the Shadows*. Emily Sunstein's *Mary Shelly: Romance and Reality*; Miranda Seymour's *Mary Shelly*; Anne Kostelanetz Mellor's *Mary Shelly: Her Life, Her Fiction, Her Monsters*; and John Williams's *Mary Shelly: A Literary Life* were invaluable sources of information regarding Mary Shelly. And for details on genetic science and testing I'm indebted to Lenny Guarante's *Ageless Quest: One Scientists Search for the Genes that Prolong Life*; Lennard Davis's *Go Ask Your Father: One Man's Obsession with Finding His Origins Through DNA Testing*; and Carl Elliot's *New Yorker* article "Guinea Pigging" (January 7, 2008).

To readers of *The Professors' Wives' Club* and *Crossing Washington Square*, I thank you. Hearing how much you enjoyed the books keeps me writing and I love how my characters seem to speak to so many of you in different ways. Thanks to the bloggers and reviewers who have given kind and enthusiastic shout-outs for my books.

To Phil Treble, Web designer, photographer, postcard creator, and friend. I owe you many more Twinkies than I can fit in a suitcase to England.

To all my friends and family, who were such great sports and helped make the *Crossing Washington Square* readings so much fun: Kendra Gahagan, Leanna Renee Heiber, Ron Hogan, Merla and Ron Lawruk, Alan and Jana Lewis, Janine Lewis, Elin Morgan, Kevin O'Neely, David Pattillo, Annie Robinson, Maya Rodale, Ken Scarsborough, Caroline Smith, and Ruth Weston.

To the rest of my family and friends who have supported me and made me smile. A special mention to all the wonderful homeschool parents I know. You allow me to do the crazy but fun "homeschool-writing" juggle!

To Brad and Benny. You are my shining stars and the loves of my life. You inspire me every moment of every day.

Out of the Shadows is about lost mothers, but it's also about the enduring power of a mother's love. Therefore, I dedicate this book to Kate Matthews. I'm so glad I get to call this kind, strong, adventurous, and endlessly loving woman "my mum."

OUT OF THE
SHADOWS

February 1803—Somers Town, England

"When the electricity was first applied to the face, the jaws of the corpse began to tremble. The muscles in its cheeks twisted, contorted, and clenched. Then"—Dr. Anthony Carlisle paused for a second and looked around at the family assembled in the small study—"then one eye opened!"

"Opened?" William Godwin cried out.

"I swear, good man, the eye opened. It bulged and pulsed as if it were going to leave the cadaver's head completely." Carlisle's own eyes flashed with excitement.

There was a horrified hush. William Godwin stared up at the doctor, his mouth gaping. Godwin's wife raised a silk handkerchief to her cheek and looked ready to swoon. The four children gathered in the room were wide-eyed and speechless. Standing by the fireplace with one hand propped on the mantelpiece, Carlisle once again scanned his captivated audience.

"When Professor Aldini applied electricity for the second time," he went on, his voice now descending into a dramatic whisper, "the dead man's hand shot up in the air and formed a fist. Then his legs started to kick and flail."

Godwin shook his head with vigor. "It cannot be so."

"On my honor. I saw it with my own eyes," Carlisle responded, placing his hand over his heart.

Young Mary stared up at the doctor and then, shifting her head, she looked up at her father, whose knees she sat upon. Her wide eyes traced the creases of wonder and dismay etched on his brow. Her father's clear astonishment served only to make Mary more horrified by what she was hearing, and she burrowed herself tighter against him.

At five and a half, Mary was too old to be sitting on her father's knee. But she was small for her age and William Godwin didn't seem to mind her being there. Indeed, he had been in a jovial mood all day, and it was he who had invited his daughter, with a wink and a tap of his hand, onto his lap in the first place. Without a moment's hesitation, Mary hopped onto her father's knees and snuggled back against his chest. Her wild golden hair nestled itself under Godwin's chin and she tucked her feet behind his stocky calves. Her stepmother looked over with a disapproving glare and her younger stepsister, Jane, frowned with apparent envy. But Mary ignored them both and instead turned her attention to the man by the fire.

Anthony Carlisle had been a guest in the Godwin house many times before and Mary knew well his long, polished cane, his velvet tailcoat, and gleaming white cravat. Even at five years old, she knew that Dr. Carlisle was in attendance the day she was born. She also knew that the doctor was with her mother in the ten days of sickness that followed her birth: the same ten days of pain and fever that her mother endured before she died. Sadness tugged in Mary's small chest when she looked at this man. He had nursed her dying mother, but in the end he couldn't save her. Mary forgave him, though, because the doctor always brought with him such astonishing stories— and young Mary adored nothing more than a thrilling and intriguing story.

On this dark February night, with the fire roaring in the hearth and the candles flickering in the old candelabra above, Carlisle was presenting his newest tale: a gruesome account of a medical experiment he recently witnessed on the other side of London.

"And you say the dead man was a murderer?" Godwin was now asking.

"Indeed. George Foster was his name." Carlisle nodded. "Before Aldini proceeded with his experimentation, Foster was convicted and hanged for the murder of his wife and child, whom he drowned in Paddington Canal."

Godwin's wife, Mary's stepmother, gasped as she heard this. "A monster!" she cried out.

"Perhaps," the doctor said, lifting one eyebrow. "He was convicted on circumstantial evidence alone. No corroborating evidence was brought forth."

"Are you saying the man may have been innocent?" Godwin asked.

Carlisle looked at Godwin. "That we will never know, my friend. But onlookers at Foster's execution did remark on his sorrowful countenance in the moments before his death and took it as evidence of a guilty conscience."

There was another silence in the room. Meanwhile, Carlisle looked about him, and, clearly noticing that some of his audience's earlier horror had waned, he raised his fist with a jerk into the air. Everyone flinched at the sudden movement.

"But when Foster's corpse raised his hand, like so," Carlisle announced, his tone forceful and animated, "and with his eyes bulging, a monster he most surely was!"

His words had the desired effect. Every person in the room was wide-eyed once more.

"Some witnesses said that the corpse was nearly brought back to life," the doctor went on.

"Back to life?" It was now Mary's turn to ask a question. Her voice was small and a little shaken.

"Yes, sweet child," Carlisle said, looking down at her. "Some bystanders believed the man was nearly returned to the living."

There was another gasp from Mary's stepmother.

Carlisle then gave a small smile. "But I do not believe that was so."

"No?" Godwin asked.

Carlisle returned his gaze to Mary's father. "As you know, Professor Aldini's foremost concern is with galvanism, an area of knowledge established by his uncle, the great Luigi Galvani. It is an area of knowledge that seeks to explain the activation and movement of animals." Carlisle added, "Bringing a corpse to life was not Aldini's purpose; neither was it the outcome of his experiment. The experiment, in fact, was of a better use and tendency . . ."

Mary could no longer concentrate on what the doctor was saying. His words surpassed her comprehension. However, his tale of the jerking, quivering corpse did not. Even if she closed her eyes, which she did as Carlisle continued to talk, she could not shake the image of the dead man with a bulging eye, flailing legs, and a sinister fist thrust in the air. Mary buried herself deeper into her father's chest but still the image would not disappear.

Only much later, after the doctor left and after many hours staring into the darkness of her bedchamber, did Mary finally manage to shut out the image of a shuddering cadaver from her mind.

One

It was Anthony who suggested the DNA test, although Clara knew he wasn't particularly interested in the results. The quest was what he desired. He craved the search, the act of stripping away every shred of doubt, every veil and hindrance, to uncover the truth. The fact that Clara may or may not be related to the nineteenth-century writer Mary Shelley was almost irrelevant to Anthony. He proposed the test because this painstaking work of peeling back nature—layer by layer, cell by cell, gene by infinitesimal gene—was what drove him every day in his laboratory.

When they first fell in love, he marveled at the way Clara took pause to watch the world. This surprised her, because Anthony himself was always so precise, so focused, and rarely distracted. He never stopped to take in a sunset or to watch a flight of swallows darting in the wind. There was always too much to do or something more important playing on his mind. But on occasion, when he caught Clara staring up at a stormy sky or gazing down at a procession of ants burrowing into the earth, he would pull her into his arms and say, "Those eyes of yours see everything, don't they?" Then he would laugh and add, "You really should stop reading all those crusty history books about long-dead scientists and come work in the lab with me. Come where the action's happening now. The secrets of the double helix would never be safe with you around. Not with your eyes gazing on it."

Anthony was wrong, though. The secrets of the double helix would always be safe with Clara. She had a keen and studious eye; it was true. She also loved the stories of scientists. She was fascinated by what drove them, what made them study the great mysteries of the world and turn their gazes onto the tiny details of life. But when Clara gazed upon nature and the world it wasn't with a scientist's eye. She did not to try to strip away or expose or understand. Instead, her eyes saw only beauty and mystery; they marveled at the very magic and unknowability of all they took in.

Indeed, the night Anthony suggested the DNA test, Clara dreamed of a double helix floating, shimmering, and dancing, its helices twining and intertwining with each other. It was like the images on Anthony's screen saver, although much more beautiful. At first, Clara's dream seemed so magical and joyful, but then the helices suddenly broke apart and shattered into a million tiny pieces. Clara woke up with a start and stared into the darkness as she remembered Anthony's proposal from earlier that evening. She wanted the genetic test, but part of her was scared, too: scared that her own quest to find out her family's history would end so abruptly, perhaps with disappointment. Fear nagged low in her stomach, but there was excitement as well. The two feelings were laced together like the helices she'd just dreamed of.

Clara could not sleep after that. Anthony's slow breathing beside her was not soothing. His presence only made her apprehension and excitement twist tighter together. It was better to get up, she decided, and soon enough she was padding barefoot across the wooden floor toward her tiny study just off the bedroom. As she passed the window, she paused for a moment. Manhattan twinkled and rumbled in the April night outside. The city, which was still so new to Clara, was like the double helix, too, its beauty and thrills wrapped so tightly with its aggression, its unceasing roar, and those darker elements that Clara could always feel lurking not far from the surface. She rubbed her bare arms and moved on from the window.

In her study, Clara flicked the switch on her desk lamp. It blinked a few times and buzzed, and then cast its yellow glow across the various piles of paper, books, and, to the left, her slumbering laptop. Some of the papers were student assignments awaiting her grades. Another pile, covered with a thin layer of dust, were notes for her next academic book on Charles Darwin. Most of the paperwork and books on the desk, however, concerned Mary Shelley.

Clara sat down at the desk and shuffled through some of these papers. Finally, she found the one she was searching for, the one that bore a portrait of the author. Clara's copy of the nineteenth-century painting was in color, but it was of poor quality and rather grainy, so she had to pull it close to study it. She'd looked at this portrait a thousand times, but she never tired of it. She loved the wide-open arc of Mary Shelley's forehead, her thin yet inquisitive lips, and the delicate slope of her porcelain shoulders that were revealed by the low-cut bodice of her dark velvet evening dress.

Most of all, Clara was enchanted by Shelley's large hazel eyes. They appeared so infinitely thoughtful. It was as if, in her eyes, you could see the richness and vivacity of her mind. In spite of the properness of Shelley's dress and her delicate pose, the eyes in the portrait spoke of something deeper, much more complex and dark. They revealed the kind of imagination that could conjure up a story like *Frankenstein*: a tale of a monster so frightful and yet so pitiful that it would live on in the popular imagination much longer than Mary Shelley was remembered for being its creator.

Clara kept hold of the picture and wheeled her desk chair back a few feet until she was in line with a long, antique mirror that hung in her office. She looked at herself in the gloomy light and then down at the picture. She glanced up again and back at the paper a second time. She'd done this many times before: studying her reflection, and then the portrait, searching for a family resemblance. She and Shelley shared the same pale skin and the same small frame. Clara's eyes were blue, not hazel like Shelley's, yet they were similarly wide. It was hard to see in this particular portrait, but Mary Shelley's hair was always described by family and acquaintances as golden and wispy, budding and tumbling in radiant splendor from her high, pale forehead. Clara's own hair was a similar reddish gold, although she doubted that the chaotic curls she saw in the mirror tonight would ever be described as radiant or splendid.

Clara wheeled herself back to her desk, and under the glow of the lamp she focused intently on Shelley's hair in the picture. This hair could hold the secret. It might reveal the truth of their possible blood tie, their shared DNA. Clara's mother was always adamant that there was a link between their family and Mary Shelley's. She didn't have any evidence to support the claim, no document to confirm the connection. It was just something she was told by her mother and in turn her mother had been told by her mother. It was a tidbit of family history passed down from generation to generation.

And now it seemed Shelley's hair might confirm—or not—this story. Clara had found out just the previous morning that a lock of Shelley's hair still existed. Not only that, but the hair was housed only forty blocks from her own apartment, at the New York Public Library.

She was still reveling in the discovery when Anthony had returned home, late as always, from his lab at the university.

"They said I can come and view it," she told Anthony with an excited grin.

She was in the kitchen and he was standing in the doorway, the top button on his shirt undone and his hair slightly rumpled. He smiled back at her, but the smile faded somewhere below his eyes.

"That's great." Her fiancé's tone was flat and she could tell he was tired.

Clara's excitement immediately began to wane. Anthony wasn't interested in this new journey of hers; she knew that. But sometimes, if his mood was right, if he hadn't worked too many hours at the lab, he would at least show enthusiasm, even if it was faked.

Tonight clearly wasn't one of those times.

"How was your day?" she asked, changing tack.

Anthony yawned. "Long."

Under the tiny track lights that ran the length of the kitchen, the gray hair at his temples shimmered. Anthony hated that his hair was beginning to betray him and show his forty years so visibly. His face was lean and handsome still. His body was tight and toned, thanks to his rigorous exercise regimen and his unrelentingly healthy diet. But his hair he had no control over. The pesky silver strands kept sprouting. Clara thought they just made him more striking, but for Anthony they signaled he was aging.

"I'm going to turn in," Anthony said. But then, clearly seeing the disappointment that flickered across Clara's face, he added, "I'm happy for you, Clara. About the lock of hair, I mean."

Clara felt relieved yet sad all in the same moment. She was thankful he was trying to make amends. But his indifference was real and palpable. Anthony had other much bigger, more pressing concerns to consume his time and thoughts these days. His work, his lab, the drug he was creating—these were the things that cycled through his mind almost every minute of every hour of every day. And now that the media was taking an interest in his work, he was dealing with perky publicists, too, calls from CBS and *The Charlie Rose Show*, e-mails from science reporters at the *New York Times*. He even had to worry about his wardrobe.

"Thanks," Clara said finally in a quiet voice.

Anthony flashed an apologetic, tired smile and then headed out of the room. Clara returned to the sink, where the dishes awaited. But before she even turned on the faucet, Anthony was back.

"A lock of her hair, you said?"

Clara looked over her shoulder to see Anthony completely changed. His eyes, which had looked so flat and tired just seconds ago, now glistened. They always glimmered like this when he spoke about his work, but picked out by the kitchen lights their sheen was even more intense.

"Yes," Clara said, stunned by this sudden change in countenance. "Why?"

It wasn't just his eyes; his body, too, now seemed more upright and taut, as if some key had turned, tightening every nerve and sinew inside him.

"You know what this means?" he asked, walking toward her.

"What?"

He rolled his eyes. "Think about it, Clara."

She shook her head. "I'm lost. I have no idea—"

"A DNA test." Anthony laughed, almost shouting.

"What? I—"

Anthony cut her off again. "At last, you can put this whole Mary Shelley stuff to bed. You can prove once and for all whether you're related."

Clara stared up at Anthony, who was now right next to her. For a second, she was still confused. But then it began to make sense.

"Her hair. DNA from her hair," she said with a gasp.

Anthony gave a laugh and a clap. "By George, she's got it."

The pieces were tumbling into place now, but questions soon followed.

"Would it work?" Clara asked. "With hair that old, I mean."

"It will be a challenge." Anthony's gaze became serious. "There's a lab in Philadelphia that specializes in extraction of DNA from hair. In fact, extracting DNA from hair samples is all the lab does. Their clients are mostly law enforcement agencies. The oldest hair sample they ever managed to extract DNA from was forty-three years old."

Clara shook her head. "Mary Shelley's hair is nearly four times that old."

"As I said, it's going to be a challenge, but I think we can do it."

More pieces clattered into place in Clara's mind. "You would do it? In your lab?"

Anthony shrugged. "Of course."

Clara was silent for a few moments as she took all of it in. A DNA test could offer the answer—the answer she'd yearned for these last months. But the test results could also lead to disappointment, maybe even humiliation. Anthony and his lab would put in all this work and maybe the result would turn out to be negative. She would be disappointed and she would have wasted valuable lab time.

Before these doubts could fully take hold, however, something occurred to Clara.

"I'm not a direct descendant, though. Mary Shelley had only one son who made it to adulthood and he didn't have any kids."

The glimmer in Anthony's deep blue eyes was beginning to fade. He yawned and replied, "Testing your mitochondrial DNA will confirm whether you and Shelley share maternal ancestry."

"You mean if Shelley's grandmother was also my great-great-something-grandmother, the test would confirm it?"

Last week Clara had found out from letters she wrote to the archive offices in Maryland that a woman way back in her mother's family had the maiden name Dickson. From her research, she knew that Mary Shelley's grandmother was a Dickson, too. She hadn't allowed herself to get too excited by this discovery, though. Dickson was a common name, after all, and she knew the trail might lead nowhere.

Anthony was nodding. "Yes, it will confirm that. Definitely."

A million more questions jostled in Clara's mind, but Anthony spoke again before she could ask even one.

"We can look into it tomorrow," he said. "For now, I'm beat. I need to sleep." He then gave her a swift, firm kiss on her forehead and left the kitchen.

Hours later, in the middle of the night, Clara continued to look at the portrait of Mary Shelley under the light of her desk lamp. She scanned Shelley's face and wondered again whether she and this woman really shared DNA and whether a test could prove it to be so. She thought, too, of her dream and the dancing double helix, so beautiful yet so delicate. In a sterile laboratory, under the harsh glare of fluorescent lights, could such unfathomable grace really be read and understood and decoded?

Clara was about to flick off her lamp and return to bed when the framed photo of her mother toward the back of her desk caught her eye. In the picture, her mother stood in front of the small-town library where she worked for nearly four decades. She held a book under one arm, and a floppy sun hat almost obscured her wide, smiling eyes. Clara found herself smiling back at her mother.

"Maybe you were right," she whispered.

Clara's mother was always the believer. She'd lived for books. She devoured and treasured them, and revered their authors. She had fiercely believed that they were, in some way, related to Mary Shelley. Clara's younger sister, Maxie, on the other hand, was an ever-vocal skeptic. She thought their mother was clutching at a dream, a fantasy born out of her bookish mind. Clara didn't really know what to believe, and up until a few months ago she hadn't thought too deeply about the possible family connection. Occasionally she would read

Mary Shelley's name in a book or on the pages of a newspaper and she'd wonder—but only vaguely.

Then, seven months ago, not long after Clara and Anthony moved to New York, her mother died suddenly and everything changed. Clara's halfhearted interest in Mary Shelley turned into a consuming passion.

Two

Clara shivered. She'd been sitting on this bench in Washington Square Park for twenty minutes and she was starting to get cold—and angry. Her sister, Maxie, had called at the crack of dawn demanding they meet here at eight a.m., and now Maxie was late.

"Typical," Clara grumbled under her breath as she pulled her Windbreaker tighter across her chest.

The April morning was colder than Clara had expected and her flimsy coat was not enough to keep out the bite in the air. Fortunately, though, as she scanned the park one more time, she spied her sister. She was trotting along in skintight indigo jeans and scuffed cowboy boots, her dark hair flapping in the breeze. She was smoking, too; the telltale smoke rose in a curling trail behind her.

"You look terrible."

These were Maxie's first words as she approached. Clara's sister was never one for tact.

"What do you expect? It's cold. It's nearly eight thirty in the morning," Clara retorted. She glared as Maxie slumped down beside her on the bench. "And you're late."

Maxie just gave Clara an amused look and then took a long drag on her cigarette, probably her second or third of the morning. She puffed out the smoke and watched it flutter and twist into the crisp spring air. Maxie could make even smoking look beautiful. The delicate symmetry of her face, her dark, watchful eyes, the pucker of her rose red lips, and then the smoke shimmering upward; it was all like a choreographed dance, so graceful and effortless.

This morning, though, her sister's smoking just made Clara more irritated.

"What is it, then? Why are we here?" she demanded. She didn't bother to ask why Maxie was late. Maxie was always late, and her excuses were usually vague and not worth listening to. "What's so important that you dragged me out this early?"

Clara had been awake half the night thinking about the DNA test, only to have Maxie call her at seven and demand they meet. The park was a short walk from Clara's apartment and not far from her office at Manhattan University, where she would head later, but it was still hard to get up and out so early.

Maxie let out her gravelly twenty-Winstons-a-day laugh. "I thought you liked early mornings."

Clara glared in silence.

"Okay, okay," Maxie said, waving her cigarette between her long fingers. She knew she was testing Clara's patience. "You're in a bad mood, so I will get straight to the—"

Maxie was cut off by a warbling sound coming from her purse. She reached into the bag, under the folds of its soft blue leather, and pulled out her cell phone. Clara sighed. Of course, the cell phone. Maxie was never without it, and conversations with her were always punctuated by its presence.

"Hel-loo," Maxie singsonged into the phone. "Oh, hi . . ." she said, as her face unfolded into one of her dazzling smiles.

She sprang to her feet, giving Clara a customary apologetic shrug, and paced away from the bench. Clara, meanwhile, sat back and watched her sister. She couldn't hear what was being said, but she could tell Maxie was excited. Her sister's free hand waved and gestured in the air, and every now and then the same hand would flick her long black hair over her shoulder, a sure sign that Maxie was excited about something.

Clara was exasperated by the phone interruption, but in spite of all this, watching her sister by turns fascinated and soothed her. Her sister's beauty intrigued Clara. Maxie and she couldn't be more different. A friend of their mother's once described the sisters as the "yin and yang of loveliness." Where Clara was petite, softly curved, and with a head of golden curls that would never be tamed, Maxie was olive-skinned, of towering height, and with the sinews and angles of a dancer. Her hair was even darker than her deep brown eyes, and it was so infinitely straight it shone like polished marble.

Their father was a tall man with a shock of glossy black hair. At least, that was what the photographs told. He died thirty years ago, when Clara was four and Maxie just a baby. Their mother was much more like Clara, small and golden. Clara often thought of how incredible it was that she and her sister shared these same parents—and thus came from the exact same commingling of genes. How could this blending of DNA create such remarkably different outcomes?

Today, with the prospect of a genetic test still hovering in her mind, Clara found herself pondering the link to Mary Shelley again. In the stark morning light, she realized how ridiculous it was to try to find resemblances to a woman separated by numerous generations and gene pools, when Clara bore almost no resemblance to her very own sister.

"No way?"

Maxie's shriek echoed across the park. It caused Clara to jump, and then, in the next moment, it reminded her that she and her sister's differences were not only on the outside.

"I'm getting cold," Clara shouted out to her sister.

"I'm nearly done," Maxie snapped back.

Clara almost laughed. Nothing ever changed between them. They were like magnetic poles: so opposite, often at odds, but always pulled inescapably toward each other.

"Okay, I'm done," Maxie said finally, as she closed her phone and headed back toward the bench.

"Out with it, then," Clara said as her sister sat down and started to light up another cigarette. "What did you want to talk to me about?"

Maxie took a drag. "I met this guy. . . ."

Clara groaned. She couldn't help it. "Don't tell me I left the house at seven forty-five to hear one of your guy stories."

"It's not that kind of guy story."

"So was he your type?" Clara's tone was somewhere between mocking and bored.

Maxie nudged Clara with one of her pointy elbows. "You're not listening. I said it wasn't that kind of guy story. Although"—she paused—"he is cute. But not really my type. Too much of a nice-guy, hippie type. *Although*"—she paused again and winked—"apparently his brother is some big shot. A journalist for the *New Yorker* or something. I might need to get a look at him."

Clara rolled her eyes.

"But that's beside the point," Maxie went on. "Daniel came into the restaurant last night. He knows Jack, one of the bartenders. Anyway, after we closed up, we all got to talking: me, Jack, a couple of other waitresses, and this guy Daniel. . . ."

"Max." Clara sighed. "Get to the point."

She didn't mean to sound so irritable, but she was chilled and tired.

"I am getting to the point," Maxie barked, but then she took another annoyingly long drag. "So we somehow got to talking about that whole six-degrees-of-separation thing. You know, how everyone is just six steps away from being connected to Kevin Bacon or, say, the pope . . ."

Clara raised an eyebrow. "Kevin Bacon or the pope?"

"I'm trying to get to the point," Maxie jibed back. "I was trying to come up with my own connection to someone, so I told them about Mary Shelley and our family."

"I thought you didn't believe—"

Maxie cut across Clara's words. "This Daniel guy got really interested. Apparently he works for some old woman who writes about Mary Shelley. . . ."

"He does?"

"Aha." Maxie laughed. "Now I have your attention!"

"Who's the woman?" Clara demanded. "What did she write? Is she a professor or something?"

"I think she wrote some biographies. He said her name was . . . Now, what was it?" Maxie gave an agonizing pause. "Kathy? No, Katie." She paused again. "No, Kay. That was it, Kay."

"Kay McNally?" Clara blurted out.

Maxie snapped her thumb and finger and then pointed at Clara. "That was it. Yes. I kept thinking of those car maps. Rand McNally . . ."

"Kay McNally's biographies were the first ones I ever read." Clara was talking more to herself than to Maxie. "They were amazing."

Maxie was now searching in the deep recesses of her blue purse. "I told him that you were on this whole Mary Shelley jag. You're still on it, right?"

"Yes, I am."

Clara's reply was terse. Mary Shelley jag? Her sister made it sound so adolescent, so irrational and irrelevant. Six months ago, Clara came across a copy of *Frankenstein* when she was sorting and boxing all the books in their mother's house after she died and it kicked off a sudden, deep yearning to know more, to see if the family connection was true. Once she began the search, it became a sort of obsession for her. Over the next months, Clara read every book by Mary Shelley and every biography about her. She wrote countless letters to the archive offices in the United States and in London, trying to flesh out her family tree. Crisscrossing Manhattan and visiting myriad libraries and bookstores, she chased articles, papers, and out-of-print books that told of the author's life and the lives of her famous parents, William Godwin and Mary Wollstonecraft.

But in just a few words, Maxie made all this seem insignificant— silly, almost.

Maxie was pushing a small white card toward Clara.

"So this Daniel guy gave me his card. He said you could call and he would put you in contact with the woman." Maxie was back to smoking her cigarette. "He said she'd love to meet you. She lives near here somewhere. Washington Square, I think. She's a real live wire, apparently, even though she's, like, eighty or something. You could tell he really likes her."

Clara took the card and fingered its square edges. Then, from nowhere, she shared, "I'm going to have a DNA test."

On the walk to the park just a while ago, she had decided she wouldn't tell her sister about her plans. Maxie would just dismiss the idea as a waste of time. So Clara had utterly stunned herself by blurting out those words.

She clearly surprised Maxie, too, who was now looking over at Clara, wide-eyed.

"What? What do you mean?" Maxie then paused and chuckled. "Has Anthony persuaded you to be a guinea pig for some new experiment of his?"

"No . . ."

Maxie was laughing more heartily. "Is he going to use your DNA sequence to finally help him concoct an age-defying potion?"

Clara frowned.

"Are you going to be a lab rat for his Peter Pan wonder drug?"

Clara frowned harder. "Are you finished?"

Maxie held up her hands in mock surrender, but still she was grinning.

"The test is going to see if I am—if we are," Clara corrected, "related to Mary Shelley."

Maxie let out a puff of smoke too fast and had to cough a few times before she could speak. "You what? You're kidding, right?"

Clara now regretted mentioning the test. Nonetheless, she'd come this far; she might as well explain the rest. She told Maxie about the lock of hair at the library and Anthony's idea last night.

When she was finished, Maxie just stared at her for a few moments.

"What?" Clara prompted, beginning to feel slightly uncomfortable under Maxie's scrutiny.

Maxie's earlier smiles and chuckles were gone. "It's not going to bring her back, you know. This test, all this reading about Shelley . . ."

"Bring who back?"

"Mom," Maxie replied in an almost-whisper.

For the first time since she arrived, Clara could hear the breeze kicking at the nearby trees and the rumble of cars on Fourth Street not far away. Neither of the sisters spoke; neither knew what to say next. The word hung in the air between them like a heavy cloud, unmoving and ominous.

They'd talked about their mother since she died, but not often. If her name came up, it was always awkward and jarring. For Clara, there was so much to say, still so many questions to ask Maxie. But, at the same time, she didn't really want to go there. The fight they had after Maxie turned up late for their mother's funeral was heated and furious. It was charged with grief and shock, of course, but it was also as if the fight had been brewing for months, even years. Every pent-up resentment and old hurt between the sisters came out that day in an angry torrent of shouts and tears.

It was surprising to Clara that they found their way back from the fight. Perhaps it was because they both said such hurtful things that they both felt guilty enough to forgive. Probably, though, it was their inability to break free from each other; it was the magnetic pull they could not escape.

Anthony never had much time for Clara's sister, but after Maxie's late showing at the funeral, he felt too disgusted to have anything to do with her. He was bemused that Clara still did.

"First off, she shows up at the end of your mom's funeral because she decided a callback for some off-Broadway play was more important," Anthony would point out when the subject of Maxie came up. "Then, every time you arranged a trip to Pennsylvania to pack up your mom's house, she didn't show or came up with some flaky excuse." He would then laugh bitterly. "But she sure turned up on time to pick up her inheritance check."

Anthony was right in many ways. Yet there was a lot he didn't understand about Maxie. There was a lot Clara herself didn't understand, and, in spite of everything, she just couldn't quite give up on her sister yet. Moreover, if Clara was honest with herself, she'd been lonely since she arrived in New York City last fall. Anthony worked all hours these days, and because Clara's mother died not long after they moved to town she hadn't really settled in. Having Maxie nearby filled the gap where new friends should be.

And that was why, at eight thirty a.m. on a brisk April morning, she was sitting on this park bench next to her sister.

"You called just to give me this guy's card?" Clara said finally, purposely changing the topic from their mother. She waved the business card still in her hand. "Was that it?"

Maxie smiled, clearly relieved to change the topic. "Well, no . . ." She then gave a sheepish shrug. "There's something else."

Clara knew there would be something else.

"Anthony," Maxie said.

"What about Anthony?"

As much as he had no time for Maxie, Maxie didn't have much time for Anthony either. Mostly, she liked to make jokes about his work and that was about all.

"He's doing really great, isn't he?"

Clara's eyes narrowed.

"He seems to be onto something with those old-age genes."

"Longevity genes," Clara corrected.

"He reckons they're going to cure cancer, doesn't he?" As Maxie said this, she looked at the almost-finished cigarette in her hand, let out a small laugh, and then threw it on the floor. She stubbed out the glowing ember with the pointed toe of her cowboy boot.

Clara gave a sigh. "If you want to talk about Anthony's work, go call on him at the lab. . . ."

"Yeah, he'd love that," Maxie scoffed.

"Why don't you get to the point, Max?"

"He's going to be on *Charlie Rose*, isn't he? Like, this week or something?" Maxie was flashing one of her bright white smiles.

"Yes, and . . . ?" Clara began, but already the answer to why Maxie should care about Anthony's television debut was becoming clear.

"He must have a killer publicist or agent or something. . . ."

Clara held up a hand. She didn't need any more explanations. "His lab has a publicist; you're right. And yes, okay, I'll ask him who it is and whether they can help you," she said. "But Anthony is not your biggest fan, so don't expect much."

Maxie lunged across the bench and swept Clara into a hug. "Thanks, C. You're an angel," she gushed.

"Like I said"—Clara wriggled free of her sister's long, thin arms— "don't expect much."

But Maxie wasn't listening. She was now riffling through her purse and pulling out a manila envelope. "My head shot and résumé," she explained, pushing the envelope into Clara's hands. "Maybe he can get it to someone . . . his publicist, an agent he might meet at *Charlie Rose*, anyone. "

Clara took the envelope but didn't look inside. Instead, she stared over at her sister. "So this was really why you dragged me out at eight a.m., isn't it?"

Maxie gave another coy shrug. "Well, I gave you the card, too, right? Now you and that old woman can whoop it up talking about Mary Shelley."

Clara had lost count of the times when her sister would call her up and demand they meet because matters were "urgent," only to find that matters weren't really urgent at all. To anyone looking in on their relationship, Clara knew she must look like the fool, the sap, the placid sister putting up with a whole lot of bother. Yet an outsider could not know all the complexities. Maxie was self-absorbed most of the time; there was no denying it. But she also struggled in ways that Clara—with her PhD, her successful fiancé, her nice apartment— never struggled. Maxie strived but mostly failed as an actor, and now that she'd turned thirty she was finding, to her horror, that the fateful words "too old" were being whispered at auditions and callbacks. Clara's sister lived on the fluctuating tips from the restaurant where she worked, and her tiny apartment was a noisy sixth-floor walk-up in the East Village. Men loved Maxie but too often they let her down. In the face of all of this, Clara could not shake the deep-seated urge to protect her younger sister, and, ironically, the urge seemed to grow stronger with their mother gone.

Even now, with the envelope in her hands, Clara couldn't help feeling slightly sorry for Maxie. Anthony would do nothing with the résumé. If Clara even gave it to him at all, it would go straight in the trash. She didn't have the heart to tell Maxie this, though. It was easier to let her sister believe that a faceless agent or publicist did what most agents and publicists did best: never call.

"You're the best," Maxie was now saying, still beaming over at Clara.

"I—" Clara began, but she was cut off, as always, by Maxie's ringing phone.

Maxie peeked at the screen on her cell and then turned to Clara. "I have to take this. Thanks so much, C. I'll call you later, okay?"

Then she got up, opened her phone, and moved away. Clara watched her sister's long legs as she strode off toward Washington Square's fountain. When Maxie was almost out of sight, Clara shook her head, and then, in spite of the chill working its way into her skin, she sat back and looked up at the trees for a few moments. New buds were growing full on the branches, pregnant with their imminent blossom. Clara found herself thinking of her mother's garden with its carefully planned springtime blooms. As she remembered the colors, the smells, and her mother's proud smile, a familiar sadness tugged hard inside her.

Helena Fitzgerald, Clara and Maxie's mother, was healthy and full of life one week and by the following week she was gone. Last fall, the stroke took her from her beloved garden in the sleepy Pennsylvania town where she lived to the emergency room at a nearby hospital. She spent six days surrounded by beeping, pulsing machines and with tubes snaking their way around and beneath her pallid skin. On the seventh day, with Clara by her side, Helena simply slipped away. Her eyelids gave a final flutter, her heart ebbed to a halt, and her chest wheezed one last time. The flatline beep from the ECG machine rang in Clara's ears for days afterward.

The shock hit hard, but the unfairness of it all lasted longer. At thirty-four Clara felt too young to have lost her mother. Her mother, at sixty-five, had been too young and seemingly too healthy to die. This thought would take Clara by surprise every now and then and leave her feeling winded and utterly bereft. She'd lost her mom. How could that be?

This morning, though, she was determined not to let the sadness take hold. Her day was set to be a busy one filled with meetings, student appointments, and class preparation. Then, as Anthony instructed, she would go over to his lab later this afternoon and have a swab taken. A cotton tip would trace the inside of her cheek, gathering the secrets of her DNA—DNA that may or may not echo that of Mary Shelley.

Whatever the result turned out to be, Clara thought, as she finally pushed herself up from the bench, she was sure her mother would have been pleased. Helena Fitzgerald was a devoted librarian, a reader with hundreds of well-thumbed books lining every wall of her home. Thus she delighted in the story of Mary Shelley, and to know one of her daughters finally shared this delight would have made her happy.

April 1805—Somers Town, England

The skies outside were a vivid blue and the spring sun shone on the meadows behind the town house. Inside, William Godwin's study was gloomy, and dark shadows clung to the furniture. The drapes at the window were always left partially closed to protect the hundreds of books lining the walls. When Godwin was in his study, a collection of candles together with an oil lamp on his desk would give just enough light for him to work by. And when all the family gathered in this room after lunch or in the evenings when Godwin received guests, the fire would be stoked high and the study would be bathed in a cheery glow.

But this afternoon the master of the house was visiting friends in Camden Town, and his study had receded into shadows. The gloom didn't frighten Godwin's seven-year-old daughter, though. Nothing about her father's study could ever frighten young Mary. Whether it was empty and dark, as it was now, or bursting with firelight, people, and conversation, she loved it here. In the study Mary felt cocooned, surrounded by books she loved to look at, even if she couldn't read and understand them all yet. The room's stillness made her feel peaceful, content, and a long way from her stepsister and stepmother, with their unending chatter and bossy demands.

Mary liked to sneak into her father's study when she knew she wouldn't be missed. She would creep up to the desk and let her small fingers glide over Godwin's papers and opened books, his ink pots and strange ornaments. She would then retreat to one of the armchairs by the door, where she would hitch up the skirts of her housedress, curl her legs beneath her, and then stare up at the portrait of her mother that hung above the fireplace.

A slice of sunlight fell to the left of the painting today and Mary could see the portrait well enough in spite of the gloom. Her eyes traced and retraced every inch of the canvas. She studied the pink flush on her mother's otherwise pale cheeks. Her gaze traversed the burned-gold wispiness of her mother's hair that was so like her own. Mary would stare for a while at her mother's thoughtful hazel eyes that, instead of looking straight out from the canvas, looked off to the side in some unreadable gaze. Her mother's pretty muslin dress, which dipped down at the neck toward a high waistband, would always hold Mary's attention the longest. In particular, her gaze would linger on the soft curve of her mother's stomach just below the waistband.

The portrait was painted when her mother was pregnant—pregnant with the daughter who now studied the picture, and the same daughter whom she would never know. Whenever young Mary gazed at her mother's burgeoning belly, her eyes would prick with tears. But she would smile, too. She missed her mother every day, and even at the tender age of seven she'd begun to blame herself, and her own birth, for her mother's death. At the same time, though, when she looked at the gentle rise under her mother's dress, she felt excitement and reverence.

To think that she was born from this great and beautiful woman: this woman called Mary Wollstonecraft, a woman for whom she heard nothing but praise, respect, and adoration. It made Mary's chest swell with pride. Her father, although now remarried, still spoke of Wollstonecraft in adoring tones and always kept the portrait of his first wife in pride of place above the fireplace in his study. Mary was convinced that her mother was his one and only great love. Wollstonecraft's beauty was unquestionable, and her sharp and powerful mind made her Godwin's true equal. Even though Mary couldn't really understand her mother's writings at this young age, she knew of their importance. She'd heard visitors in her father's study arguing over her mother's famous book about the rights of women. The debates would rage into the night, and Mary would hear voices agreeing that women should be allowed an education, just as her mother argued they should. Other voices would fiercely disagree.

The only person who said little when it came to Wollstonecraft was Mary's stepmother, Mary Jane Vial. Whenever conversations turned to Wollstonecraft, Godwin's new wife would slip from the study or retreat into an unfamiliar silence. Her eyes would always carefully avoid the portrait, too. If Mary's stepmother felt inferior, then she had every reason to be—at least, according to young Mary. The woman was plain in comparison and her chatter and gossip were incessant. She was nothing like Mary imagined her own mother to be.

Now, as Mary stared up at the portrait and thought about her stepmother, her smile began to wane. Sometimes she felt so alone in this house, even though it was always filled with people and children and noise. If her mother were still here, it wouldn't be this way. Her mother would listen to the stories that Mary liked to spin in her head. She would take her into London and to the theaters, like Mary's father did when she was very small and before her stepmother came along. Mary Wollstonecraft would read books to her young daughter and take time to explain them. She would wake her with warm words, and put her to bed with kind smiles. Mother and daughter would orbit each other like two bright golden moons.

"Mary!"

The shout came from the hallway and jerked Mary from her thoughts. She had no time to move, let alone hide, before the door burst open and her stepmother was standing over her.

"Why are you in the master's study?" her stepmother asked. Her tone wasn't hostile, just flat and monotone, like it always was when she spoke to Mary.

"I . . ." Mary began, but she didn't finish.

Mary's younger stepsister, Jane, pranced into the room behind her mother.

"Mary, Mary!" she squealed. "Why were you hiding?"

Jane's ringlets bobbed on each side of her small face as she jiggled up and down and her black eyes flashed with mischief.

"I wasn't hiding," Mary lied in a quiet voice, rising to her feet.

"Let's go to the meadows," Jane said with a high giggle.

"You're going nowhere, young lady," Mary's stepmother cut in. She cast a stern glare at her daughter. "You have not finished this morning's lessons."

Jane was then herded from the room, her shoulders grasped in her mother's large hands. Mary followed behind, relieved that Jane provided a distraction. So quick was she to get Jane back to her studies, Godwin's second wife seemed to have forgotten about finding Mary in her husband's study.

Before Mary left her father's room entirely, however, she leaned down and picked a book from one of the lower shelves. She knew exactly which book she was after. She'd retrieved it from this shelf countless times before. When the book was in her hands, she shuffled it quickly under the folds in her skirt. Then, out in the hallway, she moved in the opposite direction from her stepmother and stepsister and headed for the parlor door and toward the meadows outside.

Three

Clara often left the door slightly open to lessen the stuffiness in her tiny and windowless office at the university. But a door ajar was often seen as an invitation to colleagues on the prowl for conversation or a distraction from their academic affairs.

"Clara? Hello!"

Clara looked up to see Professor Douglas Martin standing at the threshold. His eyes were wide, as if he were startled to see her, when of course there was no surprise at all. She had heard someone pacing by her office twice already. He was probably deciding whether to disturb her.

"Hi, Douglas."

Her colleague was still at the doorway, tugging at the gray hairs of his beard just under his chin. Clara had been in this department only since the beginning of the academic year, but she already knew that this hair-pulling tic meant Douglas was excited about something. And Douglas's excitement probably meant a long conversation was imminent.

A sinking feeling tugged low in Clara's stomach. She had nine more student papers to grade before her class started in an hour. Then there were the department evaluations to complete and the three letters of recommendation she'd promised to write. Mary Shelley had been stealing every moment of her time in recent months and she'd let administrative tasks slide.

Since Anthony had proposed the genetic test more than two weeks ago, however, she'd become more focused and determined to tackle all these forgotten tasks. The results of the test would put the Shelley matter to bed, just as Anthony said. Writing more letters to the archive offices seemed pointless. Reading more biographies and articles seemed beside the point. Soon Clara would know once and for all the truth of their connection. Books and letters were irrelevant now. Science would offer the clear and unequivocal answer.

"Can I help you, Douglas?" Clara asked, after a few moments of her colleague saying nothing.

"Ah, yes, there is something. . . ." Douglas trailed off as he moved into the room and slipped into the chair on the other side of Clara's desk. He stared through his small spectacles at Clara.

"So I saw the article," he finally told her.

Clara was confused for a second. "Sorry?"

"The article in *Nature*."

She was still lost.

Douglas nodded with a vigor that made Clara worry his glasses might tumble from his nose. "The article about Anthony," he persisted. "Your Anthony."

"Of course, yes." A flush of pink bloomed on Clara's cheeks. She was embarrassed that she had to be reminded of her fiancé's recent accomplishment.

"I saw him on *The Charlie Rose Show*, too," he added. "Fascinating, truly fascinating."

Frustration kicked inside Clara. This was clearly going to take some time. It was moments like these when Clara wished she weren't a historian of science. If she were in the business school or the department of music or even in the regular history department, her colleagues would be less likely to read *Nature* during their lunch breaks.

"Longevity genes," Douglas was now saying. "They really are

intriguing. I went to the library and read a couple of journals about them. It seems there are two key longevity genes; one of them governs the cell's ability to convert nutrients into energy and . . ."

Clara began to tune out. She wasn't like her colleagues. For the most part, historians of science were as fascinated with the details of science as were the true scientists. They reveled in the minutiae and the intricate facts about cells and genes, atoms and particles, elements and compounds. Although Clara would have admitted it to no one, the details didn't interest her much. Instead she was intrigued by the people involved: the scientists themselves. She'd ended up a historian of science because Charles Darwin—the curious boy, the passionate man, the loving husband and devoted father—fascinated her. His theory of evolution held her interest, too, but only because it was the product of such an intriguing person.

"Ha!" Douglas's loud laugh snapped Clara from her thoughts. "Just a few years ago, scientists looking at all this aging stuff were seen as crazies, weren't they?" He gave another yelping laugh. "A bunch of age-phobic nuts who want to be cryogenically preserved when they die!"

Clara nodded. "Anthony still has to fend off that stereotype."

"But now he's found that these longevity genes might stop cancer." Douglas's eyes were wide. "Amazing."

"Anthony and his colleagues have seen this in test mice, yes." Clara then slipped into the familiar spiel. People asked about Anthony all the time these days and she had her answers perfected. "When the longevity gene SIRT1 is activated it can slow the development and growth of certain tumors."

She smiled and said nothing more, hoping this might be the end of their conversation.

Douglas didn't move.

"You must be proud of him," Douglas said.

"I am."

And she was immensely proud, of course. Anthony's work was incredible, groundbreaking, revolutionary, just as Charlie Rose and the reporter from *Nature* described. Over the past eight years, Anthony's career had soared. He'd moved from university to university, garnering more respect, more breakthroughs, and more promotions along the way. Now, at Manhattan University, he was the principal investigator of a generously funded state-of-the-art laboratory.

Clara's career, meanwhile, had puttered along in the slow lane. In fact, she'd become what she'd never intended to become: a trailing spouse. It was such a pathetic term, conjuring images of floppy-eared dogs dutifully lolloping after their masters. Nonetheless, it was the term used in academia for people like Clara who followed their sought-after partners to whichever university was offering a new job. Clara had been trailing Anthony's meteoric rise in the world of aging genetics for seven years now and she'd moved between four different universities and four different cities.

"You're not even a trailing spouse," Maxie once pointed out, as she laughed her gruff laugh. "You're his trailing fiancée."

"Well, at least I have a fiancé," Clara bit back.

Her response was adolescent and embarrassing, mostly because she knew her sister was right. Clara had worn an engagement ring for years now, yet wedding plans had long since floundered. Anthony and she were too busy moving and adjusting to new homes, new cities, new jobs to even think about bridal gowns, wedding cakes, and guest lists.

"The article in *Nature* said that Anthony's lab has found a compound that can activate this gene." Douglas was nodding at an alarming rate again.

"Correct," Clara replied. "The compound, the drug, should be going into phase-one trials soon."

As she said this, she smiled. Clinical trials were good for Anthony, but they were also good for her. When the trials began, there would be no more uprooting, no more new apartments, no more new universities or cities. Anthony would have more time and they would start focusing on her career. That was the deal they made years ago. As soon as clinical trials of the new drug began, Clara's trailing life would come to an end. Anthony would help her settle down and focus. She wrote a book about Darwin just after she finished grad school that was well received, but it was high time she finished her next project.

"Do you think Anthony would be interested in coming to talk to the department?" Douglas was leaning on Clara's desk now.

Clara thought for a second and then said, "I'm sure he'd love to."

It was a lie. Anthony would not have time, and even if he did, her small department with its eight full-time faculty didn't offer the right kind of audience. Any time away from his lab these days was strategic. Potential funders, people in the media, other important geneticists—these were the people Anthony was willing to speak to nowadays.

"Great!" Douglas slapped the desk, making Clara jump. "Well, let's set something up soon."

Clara immediately regretted lying. Now Douglas would be sure to hound her about Anthony's talk every time they met. She didn't know him well, but she did know he had that kind of persistent nature. She'd seen it at work in faculty meetings.

"I will ask Anthony, but—"

"Wonderful, wonderful," Douglas interrupted.

He pushed himself up from the chair and looked as if he was going to turn and leave. But something caught his eye and he faltered. Clara followed his gaze. He was staring at the stack of Mary Shelley books perched on the end of her desk.

"Mary Shelley, eh?" Douglas barked out. "I thought you were more of a Charles Darwin girl."

A bolt of anger shot through Clara. "I'm not a Charles Darwin girl, Douglas." But then she added in a calmer tone, "It's a personal project."

Douglas's eyes moved from the books to Clara and he cocked his head. "I see." He then paused and Clara held her breath, wondering what he would say next. Only a few weeks ago she'd overheard Douglas talking to a young grad student in the hallway.

"Mary Shelley is responsible for a whole lot of hysteria and ignorance about science," he'd said. "We can happily leave her to folks in the English literature department. Historians of science take science too seriously for all that *Frankenstein* nonsense."

Clara didn't have the time or inclination to pick over this argument with Douglas now, and she was thankful his mind seemed to be elsewhere, too.

"I'd better get going," he said, backing toward the door. "But let me know when Anthony can come to the department and give a talk."

Clara gave a half nod and a wave, and, as Douglas pulled the door shut behind him, her shoulders slumped with relief. She leaned toward her desk and pulled a student paper from the pile. She began to read, but soon her mind was wandering. She was thinking of Shelley, of course, for as much as she told herself that she was now recharged and refocused on her academic work, at the same time she was missing Mary Shelley. For months she had lived and breathed the author—and now she felt her absence.

She reached out to pick up one of her books, one of the ones that Douglas had spied. It was her favorite biography, the one by Kay McNally. Clara felt a kick of disappointment as she read the author's name. The day Maxie gave her the small white business card Clara had called and asked about Kay McNally. Daniel was kind and friendly, with a low, singsong voice, but he told her that Kay was under the weather and probably wouldn't be up for visitors for a while. He took Clara's number and said that Kay would call when she was back on her feet. That was almost two weeks ago and still Kay hadn't called.

Clara looked at the book again and stroked its glossy cover. Kay was in her eighties apparently, and it occurred to Clara she might never get back on her feet. She wondered if she would she ever get to meet this woman. As she considered this, her office phone let out a ring. The yelp of the phone felt like a reprimand for getting distracted from her paperwork.

She slapped down the book and picked up the receiver.

"Hello?"

"Great news." It was Anthony and his voice sounded tight, breathless, and definitely excited. "We will have the results by the end of the week."

A lump caught in Clara's throat. "My results?"

"Of course, your results." Anthony laughed.

For a second, Clara was too stunned to speak. She didn't think it would be this fast. She figured she had weeks—months even—to prepare herself. But now the results were just a few days away.

"Are you pleased?"

"Yes, yes," Clara replied. "Of course."

But was she?

"And there's more good news."

"There is?"

Excitement kicked in Clara's chest. Perhaps Anthony had some preliminary data. Maybe he already had reason to believe that the results would be positive; that she would be found to share DNA with Mary Shelley.

"NPR is coming to interview us about the test. The reporter wants to be there when you open the results."

"What?" Clara slammed back against her office chair. Her swift movement prompted a gust of air to flutter and kick at the loose papers on her desk.

"The reporter wants to—"

"I know; I heard you." Clara couldn't help being terse. She was reeling. "But why? Why are they interested in this?"

Anthony gave a low chuckle. "It's a great story, Clara. Can't you see that? Woman who thinks she's related to Mary Shelley has genetic test to finally prove it." He gave another laugh. "It's a newspaper headline."

"But I don't want to be a headline," Clara said in a quiet voice. Unlike her sister, Clara never liked limelight of any kind.

"You know, we have put a lot of other important work on hold for this, Clara. I thought you'd be pleased." Anthony was now the terse one.

"I am pleased, but—"

"Besides, this NPR interview is a great opportunity. We discovered a pretty groundbreaking DNA extraction technique while we were working on this, and the radio interview is going to bring some nice attention to the lab."

Clara struggled to hold her tongue. She didn't want her personal journey, her family story, being used as some sort of funding vehicle for Anthony's lab. She wanted Anthony to call NPR and cancel the interview straightaway. Having some reporter from a national radio station—a radio station that all her friends and colleagues listened to—witness her opening the results just sounded agonizing . . . and possibly humiliating.

But Clara knew she couldn't say any of this. Anthony had put important work on hold, and even if his motives went beyond just helping Clara, she should still be grateful. She must acquiesce.

"Can I bring Maxie?" she asked. "When we get the results, I mean."

"Maxie?"

Anthony sounded shocked, and Clara was shocked herself. Her question had come, it seemed, from nowhere.

"Why would you want to bring her?"

Why, indeed? She knew that guilt played a part. Clara never gave Maxie's résumé and head shot to Anthony before he went on *The Charlie Rose Show*, and every time she saw the manila envelope on her desk—it was sitting there right now—she regretted this decision. It wouldn't have hurt to pass them along, and if Anthony did nothing with them that was his prerogative. This interview might make amends, though. It was unlikely that Maxie would garner any real connections (NPR reporters were a long way from the Hollywood inside), but at least it would show that Clara was trying.

There was more to it than just guilt, though. In spite of everything, in spite of their fights, their differences, her sister's flip dismissal of the whole Shelley topic, Clara wanted her sister to be there. She needed her there. They could face this together.

"Okay, fine," Anthony was saying, "but just make sure she doesn't start shooting her big mouth off. This isn't Maxie Fitzgerald showtime."

"I will. She won't."

Clara and Anthony said their good-byes soon after, and when she hung up the phone, Clara realized the twin feelings of excitement and fear were back, mingling, and intertwining like helices inside her once again.

Later that day, after her class was done and her paperwork almost completed, Clara took a walk. She needed the fresh air to clear her head. Under overcast skies, she found herself wandering the puzzle of streets in Manhattan's West Village. May had just begun, but there was still a nip in the air, and Clara pulled her light jacket tightly around her as she walked. Her pace was slow and meandering, though.

This neighborhood was her favorite part of the city—at least, so far it was. She still felt a stranger to New York in many ways. But in the West Village she wasn't an outsider. The place felt oddly familiar, like a hometown she'd always known but never actually been to. The neighborhood reminded her of Cambridge in England, where she spent her four years of grad school. It was something about the mishmash of streets, the old sash windows, and the trees popping up from uneven sidewalks. And just like the English town, there was always something to look at, some window to peer into, or an interesting hundred-year-old cornice to gaze up at. There were the people, too: the dog walkers, the students, the gay guys, the old Puerto Rican men who sat on a crumbling bench near Hudson Street. Clara could spend hours here, wandering, peeking, and looking around.

Eight years ago, Clara spent many hours in Cambridge doing the same. Indeed, it was on one such wandering that she first met Anthony. Clara was just starting the final year of her doctorate and most days she could be found in the university library looking at their extensive collection of Charles Darwin papers, or she would be in her room at St. Catharine's College typing away on an old desktop computer.

But the day she met Anthony, she'd had enough of dingy library lighting and the dull glow from her computer screen. She went out into the world to refresh her mind and to take in the last traces of early October sun. She ambled from her college down one of the town's narrow streets and then stopped on an old bridge to watch tourists and students grapple with punting boats on the river below. She laughed at their poor attempts to propel themselves along the twinkling water with their long and cumbersome poles. When she was through watching, she slowly headed north across the grassy meadows beside the river. The meadows were known affectionately

as the Backs, because they backed onto a number of colleges, including the grand, enigmatic, and almost otherworldly King's College.
Clara stopped a number of times to take in the beautiful sight: the
green meadows, the small group of grazing cows, the billowing leaves
in the trees, and the peaks and arches of the majestic King's College.
Every so often, a bike would squeak, click, and whir past her on the
pathway. Other than that, Clara was blissfully alone.

But just as she was heading to another small bridge that would
take her across the river and back to town, a shout and a loud clattering noise came from behind her. Startled, she whirled around and saw
a man on a bike a few feet away, careening in her direction. Her re-
flexes were quick and she leaped onto the grass. Meanwhile, the man
and his bike clattered to the ground on the other side of the path.

Clara was swift to help the man up—and fast to berate him.

"You were going way too fast!" she snapped, her pulse thudding
from the shock.

The man pushed back his thick dark hair and flashed a sheepish
grin. "And you were going too slow," he said with an accent that was
distinctly American.

She frowned at him. She felt mad at his words, and doubly mad
at his accent. It was brash, fast-wheeling Americans like this guy
who made it hard for Clara in Cambridge. The English loved to hate
Americans, and she'd spent a long time learning to be demure, not
loud; polite, not brash, so as not to confirm all their stereotypes. This
jerk on the bike was every Yank stereotype rolled into one.

Yet even through her anger, she couldn't help noticing his eyes.
They were the color of the sky, with the same intensity as the late-
afternoon sun. They were remarkable.

"Are you okay?" the man was saying as he dusted off his chinos
and pulled his bike back up to standing. His expression was now serious, concerned.

Clara would not be won over, though. "Yes," she grunted, before turning on her heel and beginning to move away.

"I'm sorry," the guy called out. "You're right: I was going too fast. . . ."

But Clara kept walking. She didn't want to look back. There was something so captivating about those blue eyes, she realized, and it was best to keep moving away from them.

The problem was, the same evening, the very same pair of eyes turned up to dinner at her college. Clara didn't often attend the formal dinners for grad students and professors. She found them a little stuffy and pompous. But she had signed up for the dinner because Professor Becker insisted she come along. Ernest Becker was an esteemed geneticist and a don at the college. He was also a very sweet man who had taken a liking to Clara, particularly to her work on Darwin, and treated her rather like a grandfather would a favorite granddaughter.

It turned out that his insistence that she come to dinner wasn't only about desiring her company. It seemed he also wanted to test out his skills as a matchmaker, and therefore he'd also invited Anthony Greene, a young single postdoctoral researcher working in his lab.

"Clara," Professor Becker said in a chirpy voice. "This is Anthony Greene. He's with us for the next year. Quite the rising star in his field, I might add."

Clara was almost unable to move or speak when she realized she was being introduced to the same brash American who nearly mowed her down earlier.

Anthony spoke first. "We meet again," he said.

Professor Becker looked confused—and a little disappointed. "You already know each other?"

Clara finally found her voice. "We ran into each other once before," she quipped, although she wasn't smiling.

Anthony was smiling, though, and his blue eyes sparkled, too.

Clara tried to stay mad at him, but even in that instant she knew she was going to fail miserably. There was something about this Anthony Greene that would be hard to shake off—she knew it already.

Professor Becker made sure Clara and Anthony were seated next to each other at the end of the table and then busied himself for the rest of the evening talking to other diners. It was awkward at first, mostly because Clara tried to maintain her aloofness. But Anthony soon broke through, and before long their conversation flowed as freely as the college red wine. They talked about Cambridge, they talked about home, and they talked about the places where they would love to study in the future. He told her about his research; she told him about hers.

"Why Darwin?" Anthony asked, when they were deep into the main course.

"Short answer: the Galapagos."

Anthony raised one eyebrow, prompting her to go on.

"I went there in the summer between my junior and senior years at college. I'd always wanted to go since I was a kid." Clara paused. "My dad loved nature and wildlife and our house was full of books and magazines about places like the Galapagos, places that offered a smorgasbord of fascinating creatures and plants."

"A smorgasbord?" Anthony chuckled. "I like it." He then paused and added, "Did your dad go with you? When you visited, I mean?"

"He died when I was four." Clara gave a small shrug. "Maybe that was part of why it was such a big dream for me. I wanted to go to the place he read so much about but never got to go." She was quiet for a moment and then let out a laugh. "I worked my butt off doing double shifts at the student cafeteria all through my junior year so I could pay for the trip."

Anthony smiled a slow smile. "And let me guess. You went to the Galapagos and you saw all those creatures that Darwin wrote about. . . ."

"I saw the giant tortoises with their stubby necks on one island . . ."

". . . and the giant tortoises with their long necks on another island where the vegetation grows taller," Anthony said, finishing her sentence.

Clara grinned, delighted he knew the story about the tortoises and how they showed Darwin so graphically how species adapted to suit their different environments. "Yep. It was all there in front of me. Everything that prompted *The Origin of Species*." She took a sip of wine. "Then our tour guide loaned me a book about Darwin and I ate it up. Every part of his life was so interesting, even his childhood. As a boy, he was surrounded by all these women—his sisters, his mother—and he loved them all intensely. But he was also a loner who loved to just go off into the countryside and look at things, collect things. The world was one big, intriguing specimen for him."

Anthony watched her for a moment and then said the Latin words, "*Cave et aude.*"

Clara's pale eyebrows shot up in surprise.

"*Cave et aude,*" Anthony repeated. "'Watch and listen.' That was the Darwin family motto, wasn't it?"

"It was," Clara said with a slow nod. She was shocked he knew this. Who but a Darwin scholar would know such a fact?

He chuckled a little at her obvious surprise. "I remember reading that somewhere."

As clear as her shock was to him, it was obvious to Clara that Anthony did not want to appear full of himself. She'd thought him the ugly American earlier, but the more they talked, the more she realized there was actually a gentle modesty about him. His sharp mind was evident, his intellect was keen, but he wasn't a show-off. Not by any means.

She looked across the table and into his crystal blue eyes and found herself thinking, for the first time, how pleased she was that Becker had brought Anthony along to dinner. Anthony looked back at her and for a few moments they said nothing. It was as if a new understanding were flowing between them—and a river of new feelings.

Stirred by this moment, Clara leaned forward and whispered, "I have a secret."

Anthony leaned in, too. "Yes?"

"I think 'Watch and Listen' is going to be the title of my thesis."

He let out laugh and then leaned even closer toward her and whispered, "I thought you were going to tell me a really juicy secret."

Clara shrugged and tried to hide a smile.

There was flirtation in the air, and she was enjoying it. Heat radiated up from her stomach, tingled at her neck, and made her cheeks flush.

When she next looked over, Anthony was gazing at her. "I can see why you're a Darwin scholar," he said.

"You can?" Clara cocked her head.

Anthony took a sip of wine and then added, "You're like him."

Clara gave a laugh. "Like Charles Darwin?"

His eyes twinkled in the candlelight. "You're a whole lot prettier, of course. . . ."

Clara shook her head, but a smile was still on her face. She couldn't help taking pleasure in the compliment. Clara was a bookish and petite twentysomething with untamed golden curls and wide blue eyes. Men liked her, but they were usually bespectacled guys who were intelligent yet neurotic, attractive yet unkempt. Anthony was in another league entirely. He had good looks, grace, and charm, but he had passion and intensity, too. It radiated from him like heat from a furnace, and it captivated her.

Anthony was now waving his fork in her direction. "Hear me out, hear me out," he pleaded. "Darwin was an observer, a keen and meticulous observer, as you said. And you seem like that, too." He paused and then added, "I have a feeling the world is a specimen for you, too."

Clara was speechless for a moment. No one ever talked about her in this way. No one had ever summed her up so quickly, so succinctly.

Before she could respond, Anthony added with a chuckle, "And that's why you got in the way of my bike today. You were too busy gawking."

Clara chuckled, too. "If you were around on your bike in Darwin's time, no doubt you would have mowed him down when he was out collecting bugs. . . ."

"And the theory of evolution would never have come into being," Anthony said as he finished her thought.

"Exactly," Clara said, poking her own fork back in his direction.

The rest of the night played out in the same flirtatious, bantering way, and it ended with Anthony asking Clara on a date for the very next night. More dates followed, and before long Clara and Anthony were inseparable—and in love.

Now, years later, as Clara stood on a street corner in the West Village, she thought about those early days and smiled. They seemed such a long time ago; so much had changed since then. In Cambridge, when they weren't studying, they were always together. On drizzly days during the English winter, they would snuggle by a fire in a cozy pub and laugh, talk, and drink wine. When spring came, they would cycle to country villages outside the town and picnic in meadows along the way.

These days, she was lucky to see Anthony for an hour before he would crash into bed, exhausted from another long day at the lab. The last vacation they took together was more than three years ago. She had to remember clinical trials were on the horizon, though, and before long she would have Anthony back; her blue-eyed, smart, and laughing Anthony whom she'd missed so much of late.

Then, as if conjuring him with her thoughts, Clara saw him. At least, she saw a figure who looked a lot like Anthony. She was looking down West Tenth as she waited to cross the street and the man was walking in her direction, although she couldn't really make out his face from this distance.

"Anthony?" she said aloud, surprised and confused.

His stride looked very much like Anthony's: confident, wide, and speedy. But it didn't make sense that Anthony would be here. His lab was on the other side of Washington Square, and as far as she knew there were no Manhattan University offices on this block. A group of tourists gaggled around Clara on the edge of the sidewalk, and by the time she moved out from among their backpacks and flapping maps, the figure was darting up some steps. Clara started to move across the street, but before she even got to the sidewalk, he disappeared inside a building farther up the block.

Clara stopped for a second on the other side of the road, still bemused. She struggled to remember what Anthony was wearing this morning. The figure she saw had on a dark jacket and beige pants. Anthony wore such a combination most days. It must have been him. She started to trot down the street. She just had to check to see which building it was. Maybe it was some other lab or office she didn't know about.

When she finally reached the building she looked up. Unlike the rest of the pretty old town houses on the block, this building was modern and a little run-down. The brown paint on the door was peeling and some of the windows were cracked. Clara crept up the steps and peered at the small sign to the left of the door. JOHNSON MCGUIRE SHELTER, it read. She then noticed a piece of paper tacked below this sign that read, HOT SHOWERS 7–7:30 A.M. ONE NIGHT ONLY. Clara stepped back and looked up at the building again. This time she noticed the windows with their uniform drab blinds. She also spotted an old and battered sign stuck to the glass in a first-floor window that read, A HOME FOR ALL.

The place was a homeless shelter. But Clara had no idea what Anthony would be doing here. He didn't do any charity work. He simply had no time. And there was no other reason she could imagine why he would need to come to this place. As she continued to stare up at the building, Clara began to convince herself that the person who disappeared inside was not her fiancé. It was impossible.

Clara looked up at the shelter one more time and then turned away. But just as she was about to head back down the steps, the door banged open behind her. She spun around, but instead of Anthony she saw an old man shuffling down the steps wearing a torn overcoat, a fraying purple fedora, and a pair of mismatched shoes. As he passed Clara, she noticed he was inspecting a small pill bottle in his left hand. He was so engrossed in the bottle's label he appeared not to notice her. Only when he reached the bottom step and he began pushing the bottle into the pocket of his dirtied coat did he look up. Then he saw Clara.

"A beautiful day," he said. His lips parted into a smile, revealing yellowing and broken teeth.

Clara was distracted at first by these unkempt teeth, but then she noticed the man's eyes: brown as chocolate, glimmering and dancing amid the wrinkled paleness of his skin.

"It is, isn't it?" she responded.

"Ah!" the man exclaimed with his smile growing even bigger. "A beautiful smile from a beautiful lady. Just what I needed."

Clara gave a laugh that seemed to delight the man even more.

He laughed, too, a deep, rolling laugh, and said, "You've made this old man—Georgie Worth's my name—you've made my day." The man tipped his hat, causing the weather-beaten feather in its brim to bob up and down. "Good day to you, beautiful lady." He chuckled and then shuffled off along the sidewalk, humming as he went.

Clara's smile lingered as she watched him leave.

"Good-bye, Georgie Worth," she found herself murmuring under her breath.

Four

Anthony came home later than usual that night. Clara was already in bed and sinking into sleep.

"Hey," she mumbled from under the covers.

"Sorry I'm late," he whispered back. "It was a long one today."

He headed to the bathroom. When he finally came back and slipped into bed beside her, she turned to face him. She couldn't see his face in the darkness, but she spoke to his shadowy outline. She asked the question that had nagged at her all evening.

"Were you in the West Village this afternoon?"

She could have sworn she felt him flinch as she said this, but his reply was cool and unruffled. "No, why?"

"I just thought I saw you." She paused and then added tentatively, "At a homeless shelter?"

Anthony let out a laugh and reached over to squeeze her waist. "I have a place to live, Clara."

"I know, but it really looked like you. Are you sure? I mean . . ."

"I was not in the West Village today," he snapped.

"But—"

Anthony cut across her, barking out, "And I definitely was not at some homeless shelter."

Clara was taken aback by his harsh tone. Anthony was tired a lot these days, and he sometimes took an exhausted and irritated tone

with her. But he never snapped at her like this, not with such unabashed annoyance in his voice.

In her shock, she couldn't help hissing back, "There's no need to
be so testy, Anthony."

"I'm sorry," he muttered, although he didn't sound very sorry. He
followed with a strained chuckle. "You clearly need your eyes tested,
because it wasn't me."

Clara didn't laugh. Instead, she rolled away from him, still stung
by his snappish behavior.

"Come on, Clara. Don't be like that."

Anthony's arm slid around her and she thought he might try to
pull her close. But he didn't. His arm just lay there, weighing heavily
on her side. In no less than a minute, he was asleep. His slow and
deep breaths whispered against Clara's neck. Meanwhile, Clara lay
awake, trying to sort out her jumbled emotions. Anthony's words, his
angry tone, still stung. His tiredness was also frustrating. She couldn't
help wondering if she would ever again see him bright eyed and not
desperate to slump into bed after another grueling day at the lab.
Most of all, though, she felt a gaping, gnawing loneliness deep inside
her. Clara and Anthony were skin to skin. Yet suddenly, she felt a million miles away from him.

The next morning, Clara rose first, but as she was getting out of the
shower she heard the front door creak open.

"See you later," Anthony called out.

Clara hadn't heard him get up, let alone get dressed and ready to
leave. Before she went into the bathroom, he was still in bed, barely
stirring. Clara loved to take long hot showers and Anthony was never
one to let the grass grow under his feet. Most mornings he sprang out
of bed and left for the gym first thing, stopping only to grab his bag,

his papers, and the clothes he would change into after his workout. But his departure this morning was quicker than ever. She wondered if he was avoiding her. They didn't go to sleep on the best of terms, after all.

Pulling a towel around her, Clara padded out to the hallway, leaving a trail of damp footprints on the polished floor behind her. She was about to head into the kitchen to switch on the coffee machine when the front door made another clicking noise. She turned around to see Anthony walking back in.

"Oh, hi," he said, catching sight of Clara.

"You're back?"

"I forgot to take . . ." he murmured, and then, seeming to compose himself, he added, "Someone called when you were in the shower. I took down the number." He pointed to the notepad on the small hallway table.

Clara shifted from foot to foot, feeling chilled with her wet skin and small towel. "Thanks."

"You're welcome." Anthony shrugged. The air between them was still brittle. "It was a woman called Kay McNally."

"It was?" exclaimed Clara. She couldn't hide her excitement that Professor McNally had finally returned her call.

Anthony nodded. "She sounded . . ." He paused and thought for a moment.

"English?" Clara offered. She'd read in the back of Kay's books that the woman was born and raised in Oxford.

"Yes, that. But she also sounded"—he screwed up his nose a little—"well, old."

"She's a retired professor. She wrote a couple of biographies on Mary Shelley."

But Anthony didn't hear. He was busy rifling through a pocket of one of his coats that was hanging on the coatrack. He finally pulled out something small and transferred it to the pocket of the track pants he was wearing. Clara didn't see what it was, but she could hear it rattle as Anthony started moving out the door once again.

"You're in a hurry today," Clara said. Then, not wanting him to get away without her asking what was on her mind, she added, "You're not avoiding me, are you, Anthony?"

Anthony halted and turned to look at her. "Don't be ridiculous, Clara," he said, rolling his eyes. "I've just got a lot on my plate at the moment. Your DNA test is taking up a lot of time," he added, before bustling outside and pulling the door shut behind him.

Clara sat at the kitchen counter a short while later. Her hair still hung wet around her ears and neck, but she was dressed and had finished sorting through the day's mail. The piece of paper on which Anthony had scribbled Kay McNally's number lay on the counter in front of her. Clara reached over and picked up the cordless phone.

"Hello?" A whispery and slightly shaky female voice answered after Clara punched in the numbers.

"Dr. McNally?"

"Speaking."

"This is Clara Fitzgerald. . . ."

"Ah, yes," the woman said, her voice now stronger, "Dr. Fitzgerald!"

"Call me Clara," Clara immediately responded.

The woman laughed down the line. "And please call me Kay. Aren't we silly? We academics, I mean. We're always being so formal with one another."

Clara didn't quite know how to respond, but luckily Kay was talking again, so she didn't have to.

"Daniel, my friend, well, he . . ." She paused and then said, "Well, he said you left a message and you were interested in talking with me about Mary Shelley."

"I did. I am," Clara said, all in a rush. "I've read your books, Dr. Mc—I mean Kay. I've learned so much from you about Shelley."

"Oh." Kay let out a chuckle. "How kind you are!"

"It's true. I especially loved the book you wrote about her years in London, after Percy Shelley died. So much has been written about their elopement and the days when they were first together, when she wrote *Frankenstein*. But much less is written about her widowed years."

"Exactly. And what an interesting and unique widow she was. That's why I wanted to write the book." Kay was silent for a few moments. "Can I ask why you are interested in Mary Shelley? Is it for an academic project?"

"No, no," Clara said, leaning forward onto the counter and propping her elbows on the cool granite countertop. "It's personal."

She went on to tell Kay about her mother's family and the claim that they were related to Shelley. She told her about the books she read, the articles she chased, and the letters she wrote to the archive offices.

"How long have you been working on all this?" Kay asked.

"Just over six months."

"Six months?" Kay chimed down the phone line. "All that in six months?"

Clara smiled, but it was a sad smile. "Since my mom died," she confessed.

"Ah, I see," Kay said in a quiet tone. "I'm so sorry for your loss, dear."

"Thank you," Clara replied.

The words caught in her throat. The kindness of this woman stirred something within her, and suddenly a memory shimmered into

Clara's mind. She was no older than five and she was snuggled under her childhood comforter, the one with the lighthouses hand-stitched in light blue and dusky pink cotton threads. Her mother was sitting in bed beside her, the comforter pulled over her legs, too. One-year-old Maxie, zipped up in a scarlet sleep suit, was curled up in her mother's lap, fast asleep. The soft light from the globe lamp next to Clara's bed lit up her mother's pale face and made the golden strands in her hair glitter. Her face was animated. She was telling a story of Mary Shelley.

Throughout Clara's childhood her mother told stories about this smart and feisty young woman who wrote many books, who traveled all over Europe, and who fell in love with a wild-eyed poet named Percy. Clara's favorite was always the tale of the stormy night in Lake Geneva, when Mary and Percy shared ghost stories with a famous and flamboyant lord named Byron.

"The very next day," her mother would say, "nineteen-year-old Mary sat down and began to write a book called *Frankenstein*, the tale of a man who creates a monster."

Clara would listen, enthralled, captivated, and never wanting the stories to end. They always did, though. But before her mother would kiss her on the forehead and switch off the lamp, she would whisper into Clara's small ear, "We share Mary's blood. Our ancestors are hers."

Soon enough Clara grew up and her mother's nighttime stories faded into a patchwork of other memories. Mary Shelley would come up now and again. But in the face of her daughters' disinterest and their preoccupied lives, Helena Fitzgerald no longer talked about the writer so much. She had no reason to tell those beautiful bedtime tales, and she died too soon to pass them on to grandchildren. Clara would have given anything for one more moment snuggled close with her mother, listening to her stories.

"Lost mothers." Kay's soft voice whispered down the phone line, pulling Clara from her memories.

"Sorry?"

"Losing our mothers. It's the hardest thing, isn't it? But it can change us, too, sometimes in profound ways. It can shape our direction and who we will become." Kay paused and then went on. "Think of little Mary; she lost her mother so young and she must have felt her absence so keenly. We don't know much about what she really thought as a child. Her diaries were lost, of course. But we can guess that she consoled herself with her mother's books. If her mother had been around still, if she hadn't died after giving birth, perhaps Mary's interest in her would have been much less. Maybe she'd never have become a writer like her mother."

"It's true," murmured Clara.

"Think of Victor Frankenstein, too. It is his mother's death of scarlet fever that sets him off on his journey to try to create life."

Clara nodded and said, "And I suppose it's true for the monster as well. Frankenstein creates him. He gives birth to him, in a way. But then he abandons him. . . ."

"And the sorry creature goes on to wreak havoc in the world." Kay gave a chuckle. "A lost mother doesn't always change us in the best ways, but it does change us."

Both women said nothing for a few beats.

"I was getting close, I think," Clara said finally. "In my search to see if the family connection was true, I mean."

"How close?"

"I traced lots of birth and death records, and I discovered that Dickson was once a family name on my mother's side. . . ."

"And Mary's grandmother was a Dickson, wasn't she?"

Clara smiled at Kay's sharp memory. "Exactly. Elizabeth Dickson was Mary Shelley's grandmother and Mary Wollstonecraft's mother."

"So, do you know if your Dicksons are connected to theirs?"

"The truth is, I haven't followed up with the archive offices yet."

"Oh?"

"I found all this out recently, and then a couple of weeks ago, Anthony—my fiancé," she clarified, "he had an idea about a DNA test."

It was then that Clara told Kay about the test and the upcoming results.

Kay let out a breathy whistle when Clara was finished. "My, oh, my, the wonders of modern science." Her tone was upbeat, but there was a hint of something else, too. Irony, perhaps. "I wonder what our Mary would have made of this," she then added with a light laugh.

Clara had never asked herself this question. She had so readily handed over her own DNA for the test, but she'd never stopped to consider whether Mary, across time and space, would have been happy to give up hers. Taking one of her fragile hairs—stripping it down, plucking out the secrets of its DNA—was such an intimate act. Would she have approved?

"When you find out the results"—Kay was talking again—"I must be the first to know. You hear?"

"Of course," Clara said with a nod. "Anthony thinks it won't be long now, maybe just a few days."

There was a long pause at Kay's end. "I'm afraid, dear, I must get going. The tiredness just pounces on me these days."

"Oh, I'm so sorry. I didn't mean—"

Kay cut Clara off. "No need to be sorry. It has been a delight talking to you, Clara." She added, "There's one more thing before I go. It's about those lost journals, the ones from Mary Shelley's childhood. . . ."

"The ones that got left behind, with all her letters, when she first eloped to France with Percy?"

Kay laughed. "You've done your homework. Yes, that's one theory of how they disappeared." She paused and Clara thought she heard a small yawn. "There's something about those lost letters and journals I want to share with you. Could we meet in person?"

"I'd love to."

"I'm not too mobile these days, so . . ."

"I can come to you," Clara offered right away.

There was something about this woman that made Clara want to meet her immediately. It wasn't just the shared love of Shelley. There was a gentle sparkle in the old woman's voice that was both enticing and infinitely soothing.

"How about this weekend?" Kay suggested.

"Perfect."

April 1805—St. Pancras, England

After escaping her stepmother and slipping silently outside the house, Mary didn't stay in the meadows long. She was soon moving along the sandy, winding pathway that led toward St. Pancras and the church-yard where her mother was buried. Usually she made this trip with her father and her older sister, Fanny. In fact, if her father knew she was coming alone, he would be very angry. St. Pancras was considered too far from their home for Mary to come unescorted. But Mary had made this trip alone before, and she would do it again—in spite of her father's wishes.

Along the way she picked wildflowers that were newly bloomed in the warm spring weather. She bunched them into one hand and with the other kept a tight grip on the book she'd taken from her father's study. Her curling hair flew out behind her as she trotted onward. When Mary reached the churchyard, she let herself through the heavy iron gate and moved quickly toward her mother's grave. Once there, she set about her usual routine: placing the flowers at the foot of the grave's pedestal and then tracing her mother's name on the headstone with one finger. This was how her father first taught Mary to read. He brought her to the grave and guided her tiny fingers along the rough, deeply carved letters.

Mary completed her ritual and then turned, sat down, and leaned back against the grave. She pulled the book she'd been carrying onto her lap. "Mary Wollstonecraft's *Original Stories*," the cover read, "with Five Illustrations by William Blake." Mary had looked at this book so many times before. She knew every inch of its battered outer cloth and every blemish on the yellowing pages within. But it never grew old. It was a story written by her mother for children, and now that Mary read it easily on her own, now that she'd grown into a child whom her mother might have imagined when she wrote it, the book just seemed to get richer every time.

Wollstonecraft's book was many books within a book, many stories within a story—which made it all the more compelling for Mary. The connecting narrative was about a kind woman, Mrs. Mason, who took it upon herself to educate two young girls. In the course of this education, she tells her young students stories of people she knew: stories that she hopes will guide them toward becoming rational, thoughtful, and kind young women.

As Mary read, she would always cast herself as one of the young girls and she would imagine Mrs. Mason just like her mother. She saw the two of them walking through meadows, sitting in the flickering candlelight of a study, or nestled beside each other in a cozy bed-chamber, and her mother would tell her the very same stories Mrs. Mason imparted in the book.

Even at her young age, Mary was certain that this was what her mother would have desired, if she'd lived. She would have wanted to educate Mary and her older daughter, Fanny, just as Mrs. Mason did her wards. She would have desired to see her girls getting an education equal to that of boys. Wollstonecraft would have accepted nothing less than watching her girls flourish into young women who would be as astute and learned as any young gentleman.

Daughter and mother were bonded through this book. Mary could feel it in every word and every story. She never felt lonely when she was caught up in its pages. And on days like this one, when she managed to escape the house and sneak away to Wollstonecraft's graveside, she felt as if her mother were everywhere. In the shade of the two willow trees planted by her father on either side of the grave, Mary would carefully open the book, start reading, and revel in her mother's love, which she could feel all around her. Loneliness was nowhere in sight.

Today she would stay and read until the sun dipped behind the nearby church, signaling that it was time to return home.

Five

Clara's hand trembled as she held the envelope in her hands. The microphone with its round black head was perched on the lab bench just a foot away. With the mic so close, Clara was all too aware that every word she uttered, every sound she made, would be recorded for countless radio listeners to hear. This made her all the more nervous. After studying the unmarked and unopened envelope for a few seconds, Clara looked up at Anthony, who sat close by. He was dressed in a spotless navy suit.

"We managed to extract DNA from Shelley's hair sample," he was saying. "But it was a long and very intricate process."

"Because the hair sample was so old?" the interviewer asked.

The interviewer sat across the bench from Anthony. She had introduced herself as Ellen Smythe ("with a y") just a short while ago. She was a tiny woman with sharp features, heavy square glasses, and graying hair cropped closely around her ears. She seemed intensely serious, the kind of person who clearly let little frivolity into her life.

"Correct." Anthony nodded. "The hair was very fragile and damaged by age. But we managed to extract the DNA and it was worth the work. We have pioneered a new extraction technique in the process."

Anthony went on to describe this new process. His tone was cool and measured. There was a slickness and poise about him these days, something he'd been working on since the media started taking an interest in him. Clara watched him now, just as she'd watched him being interviewed by Charlie Rose a couple of weeks ago, and once again she was impressed by his erudite manner, the polished and compelling way he explained his work. The old Anthony was still there, too, though. His tone might be cool, but Clara knew his eyes well, and at the moment they were sparkling with excitement—bursting, almost.

"The technique might prove useful for genetic research well beyond this one case," Anthony went on. "It may pave the way for future breakthroughs." He then started to list the specific scientific arenas where his new technique could be used.

Clara's gaze shifted from Anthony to Maxie, who was sitting on his other side. She wished her sister were next to her at this moment. She wanted to nudge her or warn her with her eyes to quit with the dazzling smile. Maxie had been grinning since they all stepped into the lab a short while ago, even though it was clear (at least to Clara) that a pristine white-toothed smile would be the last thing to impress this austere interviewer. Her sister's desperation to be noticed was making Clara even more anxious.

"So, Clara, how did all this come about?"

The interviewer's words startled Clara, and she found herself momentarily lost for words.

"Why did you decide to have these tests done?" Ellen asked.

Clara was still struggling to find her voice, which really wasn't like her. This was her opportunity to talk about Mary Shelley, and her mom, and the family connection she'd spent so much time thinking about. Yet holding this envelope unnerved her. All she could think about were the results inside.

A flicker of disapproval crossed the interviewer's face. "Do you have good reason to believe Mary Shelley might be an ancestor of yours?" she prompted.

Clara finally opened her mouth to speak, telling herself it was time to focus, but she was cut off by Maxie.

"Our mother was a librarian for nearly forty years. She loved books and stories, and she was a wonderful storyteller herself," Maxie began. "Every night, when we were girls, she would snuggle into bed beside us and read books she'd brought home from the library. After she read the books, she would tell a beautiful tale conjured up from her own imagination. She never failed to have a new story, and her stories told of wondrous lands peopled with princesses and dragons, heroes and villains. Each night we were riveted to our pillows for those twenty precious minutes before bedtime, and every night we were sad when her stories ended. Without fail, we would beg for more. But each night our mother would smile kindly, wave her fingers, and say, 'It's time to sleep, girls.'"

Maxie paused at this point and looked across at the interviewer to see if she had her full attention—which she did. She had everyone's attention, in fact, including her older sister's. Part of Clara was annoyed, of course. She couldn't believe Maxie would just jump in like this. It was Clara's journey that had initiated the test and this interview, and now Maxie was stealing the limelight. At the same time, though, Clara was in awe. Their mother wasn't the only great storyteller in the family. Maxie was, too. She might be struggling to make it as an actress, but it wasn't because of a lack of talent. She struggled because she was incapable of turning up for auditions on time, and when she finally did get a role in some play or other, she too easily lost her temper with pushy theater directors. But there was no doubt that Maxie was a gifted performer. She exuded a glow, an energy, a graceful composure; and this coupled with her paradoxically gruff but feminine voice and her dark beauty made people want to look at her, listen to her, gaze at her.

Maxie was performing now, and everyone was captivated.

"We knew we could have only one story a night," Maxie was saying, "but it didn't stop us from trying for another. When our mother would remind us of the rules, one of us would then try a different tack. We would ask about her childhood, her parents who died before either of us were born. We begged to hear about her family and her ancestors. Anything to keep her beside us. Sometimes she would answer our questions. Other times she would yawn, smooth our cheeks, and say, 'Not tonight.' But whenever we asked her to tell us about Mary Shelley, she would always give in."

While Maxie went on to explain their mother's claim about the family connection, Clara found herself biting back tears. Hearing Maxie talk this way about their mother made her chest tighten and her eyes prickle. Maxie was performing; there was no doubt. But these stories didn't come from nowhere. They were true. In spite of losing their dad when they were little, Clara and Maxie were happy children. They skipped and snuggled and laughed through their early years, bathed in the glow of their mother's seemingly endless love.

Clara still could not fathom what had gone so wrong between her sister and her mother. Maxie was never as close to their mother as Clara was; it was true. The two of them were so different. Helena Fitzgerald had been a quiet and bookish woman. She was unhurried, steadfast, and always polite. Meanwhile, her youngest daughter was a fiery child, a ball of exuberance, color, and life. She was never scared, always loud, and she flitted like a beautiful butterfly from one friend to another, one interest to another, one unfinished book to another. Maxie was a tumultuous teenager, too, and she was the cause of many rows and slamming doors. But it was nothing out of the ordinary—no worse than any other adolescent girl fighting with those who loved her most. Or so it seemed to Clara.

But by the time Maxie left home and headed to New York, she and Clara's mother rarely saw each other; they hardly ever spoke. Maxie certainly never visited for Thanksgiving or Christmas, which Clara did dutifully every year. When Clara tried to talk to her mother about it one time, her mother looked so sad, so confused, so unable to fathom it for herself, Clara regretted ever bringing it up.

Perhaps Anthony was right and it was simply Maxie's narcissism that drove an invisible wedge between them. But for Clara that explanation felt too straightforward, too clear-cut. And as she looked over at her sister now, with her deep chocolate eyes and her shining black hair, Clara was reminded of all the questions left to ask and the sea of feelings that remained unspoken.

"Clara has been tracing our family tree, trying to find what the actual link might be," Maxie was now saying, still smiling her million-dollar smile. She then paused, leaned forward, and added, "My sister loves to chase the unchasable. When she was in grad school, she spent eight months searching for a lost letter from Charles Darwin to his wife. She was convinced it existed, even though her professors said it didn't." Maxie gave a gruff laugh. "She never found it."

Clara's jaw dropped. She was appalled that her sister had just told this story. It was true, of course. She had chased that letter for too long, only to turn up nothing. But she didn't want this shared with millions on national radio. Suddenly Clara found herself thinking how hard it must have been for her quiet and unassuming mother to have such a brash and tactless daughter. No wonder they fought.

She glared over at Maxie, but Maxie refused to look in her direction. She just kept grinning her ridiculous grin over at the interviewer.

Ellen Smythe, however, had turned her attention back to Clara. "And what have you found out so far, Clara?" she asked.

Clara took a deep breath. This was her second chance. It was now her turn to speak. Maxie couldn't be trusted to speak for her anymore.

"I wrote a series of letters and requests to the U.S. archive offices and discovered that our own great-great-grandmother was named Elena Dickson," she began. "I also learned that Mary Shelley's grandmother was called Elizabeth Dickson. She was the mother of seven children—including the early feminist Mary Wollstonecraft, who was, of course, Mary Shelley's mother. . . ."

Ellen cut in, "Of course. Yes. If you are related to Mary Shelley, this also means you are related to Mary Wollstonecraft."

Clara was about to go on with her story, but Anthony interrupted.

"The truth about Clara's link to Shelley—or Wollstonecraft, for that matter—will be written in their mitochondrial DNA," he said.

Clara felt a kick of annoyance. First Maxie, now Anthony. When would she get to speak?

"Mitochondrial DNA is inherited through the maternal line," Anthony continued. "In other words, it is passed down from great-grandmother, to grandmother, to mother." His eyes were twinkling again. "We have sequenced the mitochondrial DNA from Clara and from Shelley's hair sample. I don't know the results yet. I asked my colleagues to keep them from me until this moment." He waved toward the envelope in Clara's hands. "But if we see a match in the mitochondrial sequence, it looks like Clara won't have to waste her time contacting any more archive offices." He followed the last comment with a chuckle.

Clara's annoyance was now usurped by the tug and wrench of fear. The time to open the envelope was here, and she wasn't sure if she was ready. Her heart was beginning to thud behind her ribs.

"It seems like a good time to open the results," the interviewer said, looking back at Clara. "What do you think, Clara?"

Clara looked down at the envelope and said nothing for a moment.

"Come on, Clara," Anthony prompted.

Clara looked over at her fiancé and then across at Maxie. Her sister was still smiling, but it was a different kind of smile. It was one that spoke of love, excitement, and encouragement, and one that made Clara forget for a few seconds all their differences. Clara was no longer the exasperated older sister, always nagging, always disappointed. Maxie was no longer the flaky younger sister, always aware she was letting Clara down but forever unable to stop herself. Instead, in this moment, they were two young girls again, caught up in some big adventure, rooting for each other and conspiring together.

Maxie's smile gave Clara the strength she needed. Her gaze dipped back to the envelope and she turned it over in her hands, pushed back the loose flap, and pulled out the single sheet contained inside. She looked down at the page and was confronted by a dizzying jumble of numbers and letters: the codes used by geneticists that Clara had no clue how to decipher. She felt like her high school self looking down at a long and impossible calculus problem.

Before she knew what was happening, Anthony whipped the sheet out of her hands. At first she felt nothing but shock that her results, her precious results, had been snatched away from her so fast. But then, as she looked over and watched Anthony scanning them and nodding knowingly, she felt another jolt of annoyance.

"Hmmm, yes, yes," Anthony was now saying as his eyes continued to move across the page.

The interviewer leaned in. "What does it say, Professor Greene?" Her voice was tense with anticipation.

Anthony didn't reply at first. He carried on nodding and reading. It occurred to Clara suddenly that he might have already seen these results, in spite of what he said. In fact, now that Clara thought about it, of course he'd seen the results. Anthony always liked to be prepared. There was no way he would appear on a national radio show without deciphering the results of the test beforehand.

"Well, well," Anthony boomed out finally. "It looks like Clara and Mary Shelley do share common maternal ancestry after all."

"We do?" Clara blurted out.

At the same moment, Maxie also blurted out, "They do . . . ? We do?"

"The mitochondrial DNA sequences of the two samples match," Anthony said with an efficient nod.

"They match perfectly?" Clara whispered while her heart beat like a hammer against her ribs.

"Yes." Anthony nodded. "They do."

Clara fell back against her chair. "I can't believe it." After a moment she began to smile. "But it's true," she then murmured under her breath.

Six

"There's ivy crawling all over the brickwork," Kay had said about her building. "You won't miss it."

Clara had called Kay just an hour after getting the results. The older woman hooted with delight at the news and then insisted that their meeting should be moved forward a day.

"Come tomorrow," she insisted, before giving Clara directions to her apartment.

The next morning Clara stood in front of a four-story town house just off Washington Square. The walls, just as Kay described, were carpeted in glossy green ivy, and as Clara skipped up the short flight of stairs to the front door, she marveled at the dexterity of the climbing plant and how it managed to seek out every nook and crevice on the building's facade. She even had to push back a dangling stem so she could press the buzzer for Kay's apartment.

"Hello?" a deep male voice crackled through the intercom.

Clara was taken aback and looked down again, confused, at the button she'd just pressed.

"Hello?" the voice asked again.

This time Clara recognized the low, lilting voice. It was Daniel, the man Maxie met and the person who had put her in contact with Kay in the first place.

"Hi," Clara spoke up finally. "This is Clara Fitzgerald. I'm here to see Dr. McNally."

"Of course. Come on up."

There was a loud buzzing noise, after which Clara pushed open the door and stepped into the dark hallway. Once inside she climbed three flights of steep stairs. Clara was relatively fit, but even she was breathing hard when she reached Kay's apartment. She took a few moments to catch her breath, and then, just as she lifted her hand to knock, the door swung open. A tall man with dark eyes stared down at her. He was probably in his late thirties and his hair was brown, flecked with gold strands here and there and the occasional streak of gray. It was also longish and curled haphazardly over the collar of his black linen shirt. The thing Clara noticed most about this man, however, was his hands. One lay casually across his chest. The other held the door. They were huge hands, wide, with long fingers. His fingernails were similarly wide and long, the moons at their base perfect white crescents.

"Clara," the man said in his quiet, deep voice, "I'm Daniel."

Before she knew what was happening, one of Daniel's hands, the one that was resting on his torso, reached toward her. She put up her own hand and he enclosed it in his. Her fingers and palm felt tiny—minuscule.

"Nice to meet you, Daniel," she said, finally remembering she must speak and not simply stare down at their contradictory hands.

"You, too," his voice rumbled. "Please come in," he added, as he let go of Clara's hand and waved her inside.

For the briefest of moments, her hand tingled as if a glove had been removed and a sharp wind had caught it. Her hand felt suddenly exposed, cold and naked. Clara flexed her fingers a couple of times, wanting to shake the feeling but also, inexplicably, to savor it, too.

"Kay's in her bedroom," Daniel was saying as she followed him into the apartment and across the small, book-lined living room.

Daniel didn't stop walking. He seemed to be headed for the bedroom, and Clara was unclear whether she should keep following. "Should I wait here?"

"No, no," Daniel said, and as he turned to face her, Clara noticed how even though his eyes appeared a uniform brown when she first saw them, with the light from two long windows shining into them, they now seemed to contain a whole palette of browns and greens.

"Kay's having one of her lazy days, as she calls them. She wants to talk with you in her room. She's decent, of course," he added with a wink.

He put one of his hands on the door handle in front of him and pushed open the old oak door to Kay's room. At the same moment, he placed his other hand on Clara's shoulder to guide her inside. As soon as his fingers left her, the tingling feeling returned. This time, though, the tingling was coupled with a rise of heat from her abdomen to her chest. It was a heat that signaled only one thing: desire. Caught by surprise, Clara almost stopped in her tracks. She hadn't experienced such heat, such a spark of new lust, in years, and she immediately felt a ripple of embarrassment, and then guilt. She was an engaged woman—engaged to a handsome and brilliant man. She could not have feelings like this. It wasn't right.

But Clara's gaze then met Kay's, who was sitting upright in bed among a rainbow of plump cushions. She urged herself onward into the room, trying to shut out Daniel and the brush of his fingertips.

"Clara!" the old woman exclaimed. "I'm so happy you made it."

"I'm happy to be here," Clara replied as she moved toward the bed and shook Kay's hand. Afterward she stepped back and took in the woman's snow-white hair pulled up into a twirled knot on the top of her head, and her delicate half-moon specs over which peered dark blue, almost violet eyes. Kay's skin was smooth yet lined. It also held a pallor so gray and translucent that Clara knew instantly Kay wasn't just old or infirm; she was unwell, too.

But whatever it was, Kay was not letting her pain or her illness defeat her. The twinkle in her eyes and the depth of her smile made that abundantly clear.

"Please," Kay was saying, as she waved toward a pretty ottoman beside the bed. "Take a seat."

"Would you both like a drink?"

The voice was Daniel's, and instantly Clara was reminded of his hands and the heat that had burned in her chest. For some reason, at this memory a knot of annoyance formed beneath her ribs and she found herself frowning up at Daniel.

He caught her look and flinched with surprise.

"Or shall I just leave you to it?" Daniel offered, his voice even quieter than before.

"No, no." Kay laughed. "I'd say we both need a long, cool glass of lemonade. Wouldn't you, Clara? Daniel makes the most delicious lemonade."

Clara simply nodded and tried to offer Daniel an apologetic smile to make up for the frown she had inadvertently just delivered to him. But he was already moving out of the room. She watched him leave, noticing again what a tall man he was. She also noticed for the first time that his feet were bare. He moved on those feet with the grace and light-footedness of a dancer.

"Delicious, isn't he?" whispered Kay.

Clara's eyes moved back toward the bed, and, as she spotted Kay nodding at Daniel's retreating back, she found herself flushing.

"I suppose," she mumbled, still embarrassed.

Kay's fine white eyebrows shot up. "You suppose?" she hissed, grinning. "Did you not take a good look? The man is a god. Long, lean, handsome . . ."

Clara couldn't help laughing. The sparkle in Kay's voice and eyes was infectious.

"And he has those amazing hands," Kay added, leaning over and tapping a finger on Clara's own hand.

"They are a fine pair of hands," she conceded in a conspiratorial whisper.

"He's a massage therapist, of course," Kay said. "With hands like that, he'd have to be. That's how we met, you know. He was my massage therapist. He did wonders for my bad back. But now he does more lemonade making for me than massage." She gave a short laugh and waved toward herself. "These old bones can't take much contact these days. Even Daniel's amazing hands are sometimes too much."

"So does he work for you now?" Clara asked, confused as to why Daniel would be here if he was no longer giving Kay massages.

Kay shook her head. "No, no. He's just a very kind and sweet man. He comes for a couple of hours a day. Sometimes he helps around the apartment. You know, replacing bulbs, fixing a leaky faucet, that kind of thing. And sometimes he makes me lunch—and lemonade, of course. Most of the time, though, we talk or read books together, or we sit just here." Kay patted the bed. "And look out there." She nodded toward the window, where Clara could see the tops of two trees blowing in the breeze. "There's a nest in the tree on the right. We've been watching the baby birds grow and take their first cautious flights."

Kay's eyes moistened. Then, after gazing at the trees for a few seconds, she shook her head again and looked back at Clara.

"But no, Daniel doesn't work for me. Although, Lord knows, I should probably pay him for all his hard work. He claims he enjoys being here, helping me out. And how can I say no to having such a young, attractive man in my house?"

The mischief had returned to Kay's eyes.

"I agree." Clara chuckled. "It would be hard."

Just then there was a tinkle of ice cubes against glass and Daniel was back in the room. After he passed them both their drinks and they said their thanks, Clara looked up at him. She wanted to apologize for the look she gave him earlier, but she had no idea how she would even begin.

"I'm going to take the trash and recycling out," Daniel was saying. "I'll leave you two Shelley fans to talk."

As he backed out of the room, Kay blew him a kiss, which he caught and slapped to his cheek.

"I don't know what I'd do without him," Kay muttered in a dreamy tone once he was gone. She then turned her gaze to Clara. "But Daniel's right: We Shelley fans need to talk." She paused, raising an inquisitive finger, and asked, "So tell me about yesterday. I want to hear it all—the test, what it was like opening the results. Were you nervous?"

"I was terrified," Clara admitted with a puff of laughter. "I was so scared the results would be negative. I couldn't help thinking how ridiculous it would make me look."

Kay waggled her head. "Nonsense. It wouldn't have made you look ridiculous. Science doesn't always have all the answers," she said, and then added, "Although it often thinks it does. But that's a whole other discussion." Kay smiled. "So how does it feel? How does it feel to finally know?"

"To be honest, I'm not sure yet. I thought I would feel ecstatic, delighted. But instead I just feel numb. Shocked, I guess."

"I'm sure it will take a little while to sink in."

Clara was silent for a second. "I think I'm kind of sad, too," she said finally in a quiet voice.

Kay pulled off her half-moon specs and her deep blue eyes stared over at Clara. "Sad?"

"Sad that it's all over. Does that sound absurd? I mean, I should be pleased, right? Pleased that I now know the truth . . ."

"That doesn't sound absurd to me." Kay paused and then waved a finger. "Do you remember what it was like when you finally finished grad school?"

Clara nodded.

"It felt so wonderful to finally be done, didn't it? But it was also followed by an emptiness, a void where all the books and words and worries about when you would finish used to be." Kay gave a laugh. "It was the same with me and the Shelley biographies. When they were done, my pleasure at the completed manuscripts was always mixed with the ache of absence."

Clara nodded vigorously. "You're right. It's exactly that." The two women said nothing for a short while, until Clara added, "I'm sad, too, that I can't tell my mom."

Kay simply looked over at Clara, her eyes prompting her to say more.

"All her life, she believed we were related to Shelley. And it was only when she died that I started taking an interest." Clara sighed. "Just seven months after we lost her, we finally find out that it is true and we can't even share it with her." The last words caught in her throat.

"She believed, though," Kay said as she reached forward, across the bed, and laid her hand on Clara's arm. "She always had her belief, and that, I'm sure, was enough."

"Perhaps," Clara murmured. Then, not wanting to suck Kay into her own sadness, she changed the subject. "So you said you wanted to talk about Shelley's childhood letters and journals—the ones that were lost?"

Kay studied Clara for a second. "That's right." She smiled before saying, "Maybe we can do something else in memory of your mother. . . ."

Clara cocked her head, her curiosity now piqued.

"As we said on the phone," Kay said, "one theory is that Shelley's journals and letters were left behind in a trunk when Mary and Percy first eloped. But nothing has ever been unearthed to corroborate this. None of the papers have ever been found. At least, none that were made public." Kay shifted in her bed and winced a little. The small movement clearly caused some pain. "However, I have reason to believe there might be some childhood letters in existence. . . ."

"You do?" Clara exclaimed, her eyes wide with excitement.

Kay nodded and repositioned herself in the bed again. "Nearly ten years ago, I was at a conference in London. I met an old man." She winked at Clara. "Older than me, would you believe?"

Clara simply smiled.

"I met the man not at the conference, but in a coffee shop nearby. Somewhere on the Strand, if I remember correctly. He worked at Sotheby's, the auction house, all his life. He was an art specialist who researched all kinds of artworks that came up for auction. Somehow we got to talking and he told me some amazing tales of trips he'd taken to Rome, Tokyo, Honolulu, you name it, investigating famous artworks or treasures. He told me about paintings and statues and obscure little objects, and the otherworldly prices they sold for. He was a fascinating man. So soft-spoken, but so animated and alive, too. He had this soft tuft of silver-gray hair. . . ."

Kay looked up to the ceiling, as if trying to recall the man once again.

"I told him why I was in London and described my research on Mary Shelley. I remember, as I talked, he started to scratch his head and seemed to ponder something. Finally, he barked out, 'Mary Shelley, of course!'" Kay paused for a second and laughed. "He made me jump. Up until that moment, he was so quiet and whispery. He went on to say he had once heard of some rare documents that were supposed to have been written by Mary Shelley as a girl, and that most of the scholarly world believed they had vanished. He seemed to think some of the letters and journal entries were written while young Shelley was on board a ship. . . ."

"When she was sent to Scotland? To the Baxters?"

Kay nodded, her eyes glinting. "You do know your Shelley, don't you? Exactly. She sailed alone from Ramsgate to Dundee when she was just shy of fifteen. She stayed with the Baxter family for two long visits, almost a year and a half altogether."

Clara had read a lot about this period of Mary Shelley's life and about her stays in Scotland with a family she wasn't related to. Most biographers suspected that the uneasy and possibly fiery relationship between young Mary and her stepmother was the reason Shelley's father sent her away from their home in London. In a letter sent to the Baxters when Mary left for Dundee, Godwin described her as a difficult girl who shouldn't be indulged.

"Alone on a ship for six days with not a penny to her name," Kay was saying, as she shook her head. Then, reading Clara's thoughts, she added, "A high price to pay for acting up in front of a stepmother she never liked—a stepmother who was a poor replacement for the beloved mother she never knew."

The women nodded at each other in agreement.

"Anyway," Kay went on, "the man explained that the Shelley documents were never auctioned. In the Sotheby's world, though, everyone knows about private collections and who collects what, where, and how much they paid for their pieces. He was pretty sure what he heard about Shelley's documents was true and they existed somewhere in a collection."

"Whose collection?" Clara asked, an excited breath catching in her throat.

"That's exactly what I asked him, of course. He couldn't remember. He had a feeling it was someone in the United States, but about any more than that, he drew a blank." Kay shook her head. "I pressed him further, trying to jog his memory, but nothing. He did remember writing something about the Shelley pieces in a journal, though. But he confessed that his own papers and journals were in disarray. When we parted, he vowed he would try to look through them for me."

"And did he?" Clara was now leaning forward on the ottoman with her elbows propped like an eager schoolgirl's on Kay's bed.

"He took my address and he wrote me a letter a few months later saying he hadn't forgotten and that he was still searching his archives. I then didn't hear from him for a long time, almost a year. I didn't want to pester, of course, but I was desperate to know whether he found anything. Eventually I wrote to him. I didn't hear back for a long time until a letter arrived from his nephew saying that the man— Gerald Darrach was his name—saying that Gerald's Alzheimer's had progressed and that he was no longer well enough to respond to my letter." Kay shook her head again and sighed. "I didn't even know he was ill."

Clara frowned. "How sad."

"He died six months ago," Kay went on, also frowning. "I heard about it only when those arrived by mail."

Clara followed Kay's pointing finger. In the corner of the room was a stack of boxes. Each of them seemed to be straining with their heavily stuffed contents.

"His papers," Kay explained. "Gerald didn't have much family, apparently. And his nephew, remembering my letter from years ago, sent me these, hoping I might find what I was looking for."

Excitement instantly kicked in Clara's chest. "Did you?"

Kay gave a quick frown. "The irony is that the boxes arrived just as I got sick myself. I managed to look through some of Gerald's papers. But he was right: They're in disarray. It's not just his journals in those boxes. There's also a mishmash of notes and research on the various artifacts he dealt with at Sotheby's. It also seems he was trying his hand at fiction writing. There are all kinds of short stories and first drafts of book chapters." She stopped and sighed. "Nothing is typed; everything is written by hand, and his handwriting is very small and spidery. It's tiring work just getting through a page, let alone a whole box." Kay shook her head. "Very tiring indeed. Especially when I don't have a lot of energy."

Scanning Kay's gray face, Clara wondered about her sickness. She was clearly in pain and weak, but—and as the next thought struck her, a lump formed in Clara's throat—was Kay dying? Clara was with her own mother when she died. But it was all so sudden. Her mother had been healthy and strong, living on her own. Then the next week, she was gone.

Clara's eyes teared up at the memory, but she didn't have time to dwell on any of this, because Kay was talking again.

"I was wondering if you'd be interested in helping me." She pointed at the boxes. "Helping me look through Gerald's papers, I mean. This is an imposition, I know. But when I spoke to you on the phone I liked you, and I just had a feeling you might be interested in learning more about Shelley."

Clara opened her mouth to respond, but Kay held up her hand.

"Now, please, please, don't feel obliged to say yes. From my own years in academia, I know how busy life can be as a professor. People think you have these long, carefree summers. They don't understand how you have to spend all those hot, beautiful months slaving over books you don't have time to write when school is in session!" She winked at Clara. "I'm sure you have a book to slave over this summer, but I was hoping, wondering, if you might have some time to look through—"

This time Clara couldn't wait. She blurted, "I'd love to."

Kay clapped her hands with clear delight, but then narrowed her eyes. "Are you sure? I don't want to take up your time. There's a lot of paperwork in those boxes, and Gerald's handwriting is terribly small, as I said. It could be a lengthy process." She paused and added, "You and your husband—"

"Fiancé," corrected Clara.

"You and your fiancé have summer plans, I'm sure."

Clara shook her head. "Anthony only has plans to be in his lab." She said these words with an unconvincing laugh.

Kay eyed her for a second more. "Well, if you're sure you can afford the time?"

"Really," Clara insisted. "I couldn't think of a better way to spend a hot, beautiful summer."

"We might not find anything," Kay warned with a wave of her finger.

"But we *could* find something," Clara whispered back.

June 1812—The North Sea, off the coast of England

The ship creaked and groaned as it pitched up, then down, side to side. Waves battered, hissed, and then broke over the bow onto the deck. A chilling northeasterly wind made the sails smack, billow, and crack, and in the overcrowded cabin belowdecks, Mary cowered in a dark corner. Her knees were drawn up close to her chin, and with one hand she held on to a nearby wooden beam. Her knuckles turned whiter with each pitch of the boat. Mary's other arm was caught between her legs and chest and bound in a tattered sling. Her head was bowed and her eyes were squeezed shut.

Since this most recent storm began, Mary had dared not move— she dared not open her eyes. She was frightened enough when the seas were calm, but when the waves became violent, the winds howled, and water sloshed down the narrow stairs into the cabin, Mary was terrified. Keeping her eyes closed helped a little. Although she could still hear the ominous noises: the cracks, the groaning wood, and the whistling wind. Sometimes she would hum to herself in an effort to drown out these sounds. But then a big wave would hit and she would be rendered mute with panic. Her stomach was clenching, too, and she knew that if she looked up and saw with her own eyes how the boat was rocking so violently, she'd no doubt be sick. She'd been sick enough over the past three days since the ship set sail. She couldn't bear being ill another time.

Mary would be fifteen in a couple of months, and she knew that she should be braver than this. She was almost a woman, and cowering in a corner was childish and weak. She should be singing and talking, sleeping and playing whist, like the other passengers around her. No one but she seemed so frightened. Some were sick with the ship's stormy motion, but no one else was hiding, balled up like a beetle, as she was. Telling herself to be brave, though, and telling herself to grow up weren't helping. She was alone and she was terrified that she might not see land again, let alone any people she knew or loved.

"How could he?" she found herself muttering into the damp cloth of the dress that covered her knees. Another wave thundered over the deck, causing yet another stab of panic in Mary's chest. "How could he?" she murmured again through clenched teeth.

She was thinking of her father. It was he who had decided to send her on this voyage and to pack her off all alone to a family in Scotland she didn't even know. He sent her away last year, but that was different. A physician decided fresh sea air and a daily dip in salt water might help Mary's arm that, for some time, had suffered a curious skin condition, causing it to become weak and withered. She was sent to Ramsgate, on the coast not far from London, accompanied by her stepmother. During her six-month stay, young Mary missed home and yearned for her books and her father's study. But the stay in Ramsgate did help her arm a little, and there was no long, frightening sea voyage like this one to endure.

"Are ye awake?"

The whispery voice startled Mary and she looked up. It was the first time in more than an hour that she'd raised her head, let alone opened her eyes. In front of her a young woman was crouched down. She was probably only a couple of years older than Mary, but something about her expression and the way she was dressed made her seem decades older. The woman's muddy brown hair was pulled back off her pale face, but a few haphazard strands stuck to her shining forehead. Her dress was plain, coarse, and frayed at its edges. Mary had seen this woman before. She'd spotted her at the other end of the cabin sitting beside a young but gruff-looking man who Mary assumed was her husband. Mary noticed this woman, in particular, because she was reading. Mary desperately wanted her books, too, but they were buried in her trunk, and her trunk was stowed away in the dark and dank storage area of the ship. She was too scared of the stormy waves and the other passengers to go searching for it.

"I didna mean to scare you, lassie," the woman now said in her thick Scots accent. She reached out and gently laid a hand on Mary's, which was still gripping the wooden beam beside her. "Ye're frightened enough already, aren't ye?"

Mary nodded. At the same moment her eyes welled with tears. These were the first kind words she'd heard in days. On the dockside her father, clearly feeling a pang of guilt for sending his daughter away, asked a woman traveling with her own daughters to keep a watch over Mary, and although Mary saw no exchange of money, she suspected he paid the woman for the task. But as soon as they embarked on the ship, the woman told Mary not to bother her or her family again. Since then, no one had spoken to Mary except last night, when she was taunted by a group of men who were drinking and gambling nearby.

Mary had not uttered a word to anyone since the sails were hoisted, and now, still shocked by this woman's kind tone, she was finding it hard even to open her mouth to speak.

"These storms," the young woman said, shaking her head. "I've bin scared meself."

"You have?" Mary asked, finally finding her voice.

"Och, aye." She nodded. "I've ne'er known a voyage like it."

The woman's eyes darted away from Mary and looked around at the cabin. It seemed she was looking for someone, perhaps her husband.

"Reading helps," she said, turning back to Mary. Then, fiddling with the folds of her dress, she pulled out a book and held it out. "Tek it," she prompted.

Mary unfurled her fingers from the wooden beam and took the book. "*The Victim of Prejudice*, by Mary Hays," the cover read. Mary's mouth fell open. She knew this book. Not only did she know this book, she also knew the author. Mary Hays had been a good friend of both her parents. Indeed, she was the one who introduced William Godwin to Mary Wollstonecraft. Mary's father kept a copy of this very book in his study, and Mary had secretly read it just a few months ago—in spite of the fact that her father warned her that she was not yet ready for the content of Hays's controversial books.

Mary laid the book on her knees and stroked the cover. The book was like a piece of home and gave her immediate comfort. She then looked up to say thank you, but the woman was already standing up and looking away. Mary followed her gaze. The man whom the woman was traveling with was moving toward them. If the ship hadn't been rocking so violently, he would have been running. Instead, he zigzagged and stumbled to and fro. He bounced off beams and other passengers, and all the while, his eyes were blazing.

"What're ye doin', woman?" he barked at his wife when he finally reached her. "Get back over there!" He jerked his finger over his shoulder. "Ye want someone to tek our food?"

The woman said nothing. She simply bowed her head and started to move off behind her husband. But after a few steps, she raised her head again, checked to see if her husband was looking, and then glanced back at Mary.

Tek care, lassie, she mouthed.

Mary smiled for a second time and mouthed back, *Thank you.*

As she watched the woman leave, she shook her head a little. She might be young, but the irony of the woman's choice of reading was not lost on Mary. *The Victim of Prejudice* was the sorry tale of a woman mistreated, abused, and violated by the brutal Sir Osborne. It was a book about the pitiful position of women in a society where they made none of the rules. Mary once heard her father talk about the book as "controversial" and a "radical rebuke against those who believe that aristocratic men are the right and true rulers." At this memory, Mary's eyes slipped from the woman to her surly husband. He was no aristocratic Sir Osborne, but it was clear he was a bully.

When the couple was out of sight, lost amid the throng of other passengers, Mary's gaze returned to the book. She once again smoothed the cover with her free hand. The woman was right. Simply with the book in her hand and not yet having read one word, she felt better. Already the pitching and creaking ship didn't seem so bad, the howling winds and hissing waves were less ominous, and the crowd of strangers who surrounded her in the stuffy, dank cabin no longer felt menacing. All these things were backdrop now while the book in her lap became Mary's new world—a world she could lose herself in.

Mary carefully opened the book, and as she did so, she told herself she must take her time. In order to survive the next few days of the trip, she had to go slowly and savor every word. Luckily, the very first words caught her attention straightaway and she dwelled on them for the longest time.

> A child of misfortune, a wretched outcast from my fellow beings, driven with ignominy from social intercourse, cut off from human sympathy . . .

She read and reread these words. It was as if the book were talking right to her. *I, too, am a child of misfortune,* Mary thought. *I, too, have been driven from social intercourse and cut off from human sympathy.* As she read the passage again, Mary found herself thinking of her father once more, and anger, mixed with despair, resurfaced in her chest. She just couldn't understand why he treated her this way, sending her alone on the ship and casting her off with no one to protect her.

William Godwin raised her on books and ideas, intriguing arguments and radical philosophies. Yet the moment she started to have ideas of her own, the moment she started to express them, the moment she could put up with her nagging, ill-thinking stepmother no longer, he sent her away and dismissed her from his house. As Mary saw it, her father had created a child who could think great thoughts and appreciate great writing, yet he flung her away and turned his back on her as soon as she matured enough to fully articulate what he'd taught her.

Thanks to her father, all she had now was this book—a book about another young woman set adrift by a cruel man and a cruel world. And this book was going to have to save Mary from the fate her father forced upon her. She must endure yet more days alone on violent seas until she reached an unknown family in an unfamiliar land.

Mary bit her lip and blinked back a tear. She was a wretched outcast indeed. But she would not cry. Now that she had the book, she could be strong. As she thought this, she pulled the book in close, tucked her knees tighter to her chest, and then slowly continued to read.

Seven

Clara put down the piece of paper she'd just read and rubbed her eyes. Kay was right: Gerald Darrach's handwriting was spidery, tiny, and sometimes completely illegible. There was no rhyme or reason to the way his papers were collected. Old electricity bills could be found among notes on a Rembrandt painting. Drafts of Gerald's unpublished short stories sat between tax forms and letters from his family. Receipts for groceries punctuated journal entries. It was exhausting scouring this muddle of paperwork, and, as yet, Clara hadn't found one clue that might lead to Mary Shelley's childhood papers and to someone who might have them in a private collection.

But even after working through these boxes for the past two weeks and finding nothing, Clara was nowhere near giving up. She was a historian, after all. Trawling old papers, deciphering barely readable handwriting, and trying to find clues or put together a life through fragments and remains was what Clara loved to do most. Her academic work may not have soared like Anthony's, yet she never tired of the research. She reveled in it, in fact. The hunts and searches through history were exhilarating to her. But what she never liked so much was all the bureaucracy, pettiness, and fraught competition that went along with life as a professor. And her reluctance to enter the fray meant she got left behind in the academic rat race.

Clara was dwelling on none of this today, though. Only Gerald Darrach's papers mattered now, as she sat on the rug in Kay's living room with sunshine streaming in through a nearby window and bathing the Persian rug in a rectangle of light. One of Gerald's boxes was beside Clara, and in front of her were two piles of papers: read and unread. The unread pile was still dwarfing the read pile, even though she'd been hard at work on this box for two days now. Kay was close by, asleep in her wing-back armchair. She'd been napping on and off since Clara arrived a few hours ago. The last time she awoke, Clara asked whether she wanted to move to the bedroom, but Kay just shook her head and said, "I'm happy here." Clara liked her being there, too. Even if Kay was asleep, Clara liked the company and the hypnotic sound of her soft, slow breaths.

Giving herself a short break from the papers, Clara looked over and watched Kay as she slept. The rather austere-looking armchair probably wasn't the most comfortable place to sleep, and Kay's head was crooked awkwardly against one wing. Yet she managed to look serene. Her mouth, which was slightly open, seemed childlike and unguarded. Her eyelids were closed in a light and peaceful way.

In spite of Kay's seeming tranquillity, Clara couldn't help frowning. Kay's tiredness, these frequent naps, and her pale face reminded Clara of how ill she must be. She knew now that it was ovarian cancer. Kay told her this on their first day looking through Gerald's papers. But when Clara gently asked Kay for more details—Was the tumor removed? Had it spread? What about treatment?—Kay simply batted away the questions and said, "I am old, Clara. If cancer is how I'm going to leave this world, then so be it."

Although she didn't press Kay further, Clara was left with a sad, unsatisfied feeling. She wanted answers. She wanted to know how bad the cancer was and whether treatment could help. She wanted to know how much time Kay had left and how much time they had left together. She'd come to realize over the past few days that Kay's illness was like an hourglass hanging over them. Clara's own curiosity meant she was eager to find something among Gerald's documents. But because of Kay's illness, she was also desperate to find it fast. She didn't want Kay leaving this world, as she put it, without having an answer. In Clara's fantasy, she imagined her new friend holding Mary Shelley's childhood journals in her hands, staring excitedly down at them with her wise, inquisitive eyes. Clara then liked to think of her and Kay reading the rare pages together, discussing all the things biographers over the years had gotten right—or wrong—about Shelley's younger years.

None of this was going to happen, however, if she didn't get back to work. There were still four more boxes in Kay's bedroom, and at Clara's current rate it was going to take weeks, even months, to get through them. And did she have that kind of time? She wasn't sure. But, owing to Kay's increasing tiredness, the pain she was clearly suffering, Clara was beginning to doubt it.

"Come on, Gerald," she muttered under her breath as her gaze left Kay and returned to the papers in front of her. She reached for a page from the unread pile. "Give me a something. Just a little something."

But before she could settle back against the sofa with the fresh page in hand, Kay let out a series of small coughs and woke up.

"Are you okay?" Clara asked, springing up to Kay's side and offering her the glass of water that was perched on a nearby coffee table.

Kay took the glass, sipped the water, and then smiled. "Thank you, Clara." She waved her free hand and added, "Please sit. I'm fine. It was just a tickle."

"Are you sure?" Clara pressed. "Can I get you anything else?"

Kay laughed a light, raspy laugh. "Oh, just find out who owns Mary Shelley's diaries. That should do it."

Clara laughed, too. But then as she plopped herself back down on the floor, she said with a small frown, "It may take some time, Kay."

"I was joking, Clara," Kay said, pulling herself upright in the chair. "I'm in no rush."

But we are in a rush, aren't we? Clara wanted to say, looking at Kay's pale face. *We don't have all the time in the world, do we?*

"So, Clara, tell me about Anthony," Kay urged.

Clara wondered if Kay had read her thoughts and perhaps was changing the subject on purpose.

"Anthony?"

"Yes, Anthony, your fiancé. The man you intend to marry." Kay laughed. She hunched forward and asked, "You are going to marry him, aren't you? You said you've been engaged for a while."

"Five years."

"Five years?" Kay's sparse white eyebrows sprang upward.

Clara felt an unexpected heat flood into her cheeks. "Yes, five years. It's a long time, I know. But we will get married eventually. It's just, well, we just haven't found the time yet. Anthony is so busy with his work, and then we moved here and there, university to university. Stanford, Michigan, University of Chicago, UC San Diego, and now Manhattan U, to be precise. And then there's my work, too. . . ." She trailed off.

Kay searched Clara's face and said nothing for a while. Finally, she let her head drop back against her seat and said in a whisper, "A science widow."

Clara let out a disbelieving chuckle. "Did you say science widow?"

Kay nodded. "I had a wonderful friend once who was married to a scientist. He also worked very hard, very long hours, and that's what she called herself, the science widow." Kay was then silent for a beat and added, "Like poor Elizabeth in *Frankenstein*, left alone for all those years while her beloved Victor went off to Ingolstadt to make his monster."

"Only to be killed by the same monster on her wedding night!" Clara laughed.

"Well, let's hope that doesn't happen to you."

Clara shook her head. "Anthony isn't making any monsters."

"Or so you think!" Kay responded, grinning and wagging a finger.

"If I catch him robbing graves and sewing up dead body parts, I'll let you know."

The two women chuckled and then slipped into an easy silence. There had been a lot of exchanges like this one over the past few days: fun and smiling, sometimes teasing, and always familiar. Clara felt so surprisingly at ease with Kay, it was as if they'd been friends for years. There was something about the old woman that reminded Clara of her own mother, but also, strangely, of her sister, Maxie. Kay shared Maxie's spark, her ability to engage anyone who was in the room with her. Yet Kay also emanated a sense of consistency, goodness, and integrity that was more like Clara's mother. The retired professor was a fascinating and contradictory mix of the two women closest to Clara.

When Clara looked up again, she was about to speak but noticed that Kay's eyelids were fluttering and her breaths were getting slower once again. Clara's earlier smile began to fade as she watched her new friend fall into yet another sleep. She wondered, with an edge of panic, whether their one short exchange exhausted Kay that much. But then Clara caught herself; worrying simply wasted precious time.

She worked for another half an hour and got through a good chunk of Gerald's documents. Just after the clock struck four, she heard the front door to the apartment give a loud click. The noise was followed by a bang, a rumble of footsteps in the short hallway, and then Daniel was in the room. Clara looked up at him. From the floor, he seemed like a giant and she a Lilliputian. Her heart started thudding against her ribs at the very sight of him.

She'd seen Daniel just a few brief times since that first day, since his touch had provoked such an unexpected rush of desire. He came every day at lunchtime and sometimes late in the evening as well. But Clara was usually with Kay in the afternoon, between his visits. She didn't purposely avoid him. At least, she didn't think she did. But with Daniel now in the room, she realized how unnerved she felt in his presence and how she might have been avoiding him, at least on an unconscious level.

Clara could do little for a few seconds except take in Daniel's height, his intriguing eyes, and his soft linen clothes with their unusual collar and knotted buttons. As her eyes scanned over him, she wondered what it was about Daniel that made her feel so uncomfortable. Few people in Clara's life ever made her feel this way: edgy, nervous, her heart jumping in her chest.

"Hi," she finally managed to whisper.

Daniel gave a loose wave with one of his large hands. "Hey," he said. Next he looked from Clara to Kay. "Has she been asleep long?" he asked very quietly.

"On and off."

A silence followed as the two of them watched Kay sleep. When Clara finally looked back at Daniel, he was beckoning her, and with her heart rattling against her ribs, she got to her feet and followed him into the hallway. Once there, they stood opposite each other. Clara tried to press herself against the wall and as far away from Daniel as possible. The more distance between them, the less minuscule she thought she might feel. It didn't really work, though. She still felt dwarfed.

"I'm sorry to disturb you," Daniel was saying, while running a hand through his wavy hair. "I know you're hard at work on those documents. But I wanted to check on Kay. She seemed in a lot of pain this morning when I was here. . . ."

Clara nodded. "I think the pain's bad today. And she's so tired."

"She didn't get much sleep last night." He shrugged. "But if she's able to sleep now, the pain must be easing. Maybe the herbs helped," he added, more to himself than to Clara.

"Herbs?"

Daniel looked at Clara. "Taheebo. Some lobelia and ginseng powder. I brought them for her this morning. We tried five drops of the lobelia combined with . . ."

As Daniel talked, Clara found herself thinking about Maxie and the way she was always taking new herbs and spending dollars she really didn't have on aromatherapy and acupuncture. Anthony once heard about Maxie's alternative treatments and he laughed hard and said, "I thought even Maxie was smart enough not to be sucked into all that hocus-pocus, New Age stuff." Clara wasn't quite so dismissive. Even though she'd never tried any of these things herself (she couldn't bear the thought of Anthony's derision), she was always secretly curious. These healing practices claimed to take the whole human into account—and Clara liked that idea. It was so different from Anthony's science, the science she'd seen up close all these years, a science that broke down bodies into a million little pieces and attempted to cure and heal their infinitesimal parts. The entirety of a person was lost in modern medicine, Clara couldn't help thinking.

Nonetheless, as Daniel stood before her now, talking about the concoction of herbs he was supplying for Kay, Clara found herself growing panicked. She was curious about these treatments; it was true. But her years living with Anthony, hearing his unabashed confidence in today's science and its potential to rid the world of diseases like cancer, meant Clara couldn't quite let go. Maybe chasing the parts of the whole was the answer. Perhaps it was the only really effective way to help people like Kay.

"But will these herbs really help?" she finally blurted out.

Daniel looked at her, his dark eyes surprised by her forceful tone.

"I mean," Clara went on in a whisper, "this is cancer we're talking about. Not some minor ache or pain. Shouldn't Kay be taking some much more effective pain meds?"

With another surprised blink of his eyes, Daniel replied in a soft tone, "Not if she doesn't want those kinds of drugs. Or if she's not ready for them yet."

Daniel's coolness irked Clara. She couldn't tell if he was patronizing her with his quiet voice and calm manner. And not being able to read this man annoyed her even more.

"Well, perhaps she doesn't understand," Clara persisted. "Maybe it's time we got Kay to a doctor."

"She has a doctor, Clara." He shook his head, paused for few seconds, and then said, "Kay's a smart woman. She knows what is going on with her body. She's taking every day as it comes and dealing with her illness the way she wants to deal with her illness. I don't think it's up to us to take her—"

"But you're giving her these herbs?" Clara interrupted.

"She asked for my help. She's wanted to explore herbal treatments for her pain for a while now."

Clara's cheeks flushed. She felt chastised by this man, and thus embarrassed. In turn her embarrassment made her feel more irritated. She had no idea why he, almost a stranger, was bothering her in this way. Whatever the reason, she didn't like how it felt.

It was time to leave.

"I must get going," Clara said in a gruff whisper, and turned on her heel toward the living room.

In a matter of minutes, Clara tidied the papers, gathered her things, and was heading toward the front door. While she did all this, Daniel remained in the hallway fiddling with a shelf that had come loose on the wall. Clara couldn't tell if he was consciously keeping out of her way, or whether he really was intent on fixing Kay's shelving.

"Clara?"

Daniel's quiet voice stopped her as she reached the front door and was undoing the latch.

"Yes?" she said, without turning around.

"I'm sorry if I said something that offended you."

Clara said nothing for a few beats. Part of her wondered why she was so angry at him. After all, he'd done nothing but mention a few herbs. Yet, another part of Clara wanted, for no really good reason, to yell at him and pound angrily on his chest. But before she could respond in any way, she realized that Daniel had moved closer and was now standing right behind her. A voice in her head demanded that she just leave immediately, but in spite of herself she turned around and looked up, straight into Daniel's eyes. Once again she noticed how their darkness was a chimera. His eyes were actually a Pollock-like mix of green, brown, and even honey flecks.

When her gaze finally left his, she realized one of his hands was moving toward her face. Her heart jolted and then thumped into action. Was he going to kiss her? As much as she wanted to pull away from him, at the same time she could feel herself being pulled toward him. She had no idea what was going on or why Daniel had such an effect on her. Her body felt electrified in his presence. At the same time, though, she felt almost sick with guilt. She was an engaged woman. She was a loyal woman. She could not have these kinds of feelings—not for any man except Anthony.

But just as Clara thought his hand was going to touch her cheek, it stopped a couple of inches from the side of her head. She looked at his fingertips and then up at his face. She was confused and relieved, and also, deep down, she felt disappointment, too. Daniel's eyes, she now noticed, were thoughtful, and with a stab of embarrassment, she also noticed there wasn't one trace of lust in his gaze.

As her cheeks began to flush, Daniel spoke.

"You're holding on to something, Clara."

Clara instantly moved away from him, butting the back of her head against the door as she did so. "What?" she barked.

"You seem weighed down by something," Daniel said.

A flush of embarrassment returned to Clara's cheeks. "What are you talking about?" She then held up a hand, shook her head, and muttered, "You know what? I don't want to know."

With these words, she turned toward the door, opened it quickly, and moved out into the hallway.

"Clara, I—" Daniel was saying with a small, disbelieving laugh.

"I should go," she said, not allowing him to finish. Then, shooting him one last glare over her shoulder, she added, "Tell Kay I had to meet my fiancé."

A hasty flight downstairs followed. All the while, her cheeks burned and her mind raced as she wondered why on earth she'd made that last comment about Anthony. It was a lie. She had no plans to meet Anthony. She'd barely seen him in days, and the idea of having plans to meet him was laughable. But for some reason, mentioning Anthony to Daniel felt momentarily satisfying. It was like a small jab of revenge for the embarrassment he'd just put her through. Not that she expected Daniel to be jealous, of course. He clearly hadn't wanted to kiss her. He just wanted to touch her "heaviness" with those healing hands of his. Or whatever the hell he was trying to do. It had all been in her head; all the desire was hers. He wasn't interested in her. He never had been.

When she finally stepped out onto the front steps of Kay's building and pulled the front door behind her, Clara stopped and took a long, slow breath. Then another, and another. The warm sun shone down on her face, and at last the rush of panicked thoughts and tangled emotions began to ease and subside.

She moved down the stone steps and headed back through the sunshine to the park.

After a short while walking through Washington Square, Clara found an empty bench and sat down. She'd planned to go straight home, but the park was so lush and inviting, she couldn't help stopping for a while. She also needed time to clear her head. If she went back to the apartment, she'd get caught up with e-mails and phone calls and all the other things she'd put off in these past weeks while she was at Kay's. Luckily the semester was now over, so there was no teaching to prepare for, but there was still lots of outstanding grading and paperwork to get on with.

Before facing all this, Clara needed a little time now to process everything that had just happened. She was so frustrated and angry with Daniel, and there really was no explanation for it. And she'd felt that embarrassing and ridiculous rush of desire, too. She was clearly lonely. Clara hated this explanation, because she always liked to think she was strong and independent, self-sufficient and able to occupy herself. However, that was when Anthony was still sometimes around. Even if he worked long hours, he used to come home in the evenings with time for conversation and shared meals. Some nights, they even went out together. These days, though, the most she saw of him was his shadow beside the bed as he came in late at night, or his retreating back when he left their apartment in the morning.

Clara had tried to talk to him about it from time to time. She'd demanded to know when all these hours at the lab and the continual late nights might end. She'd reminded him of the deal they had once struck: the one that said that when his drug went into trials he'd work less and focus on their home life more. It was the same deal in which it was agreed that Clara and her career and maybe, eventually, starting a family would finally take precedence. But Anthony made vague, noncommittal responses when she spoke of their deal these days. He said indecipherable things about the drug being even "bigger" than he thought, and how great things were on the horizon: for his lab, for his scholarship, but also for them. Yet when Clara pressed for more details, Anthony simply tapped her nose and said, "All in good time, Clara."

It was frustrating. And, she would admit to herself now, it was lonely, too. She couldn't remember the last time they'd made love. She was even having a hard time remembering the last time they'd done anything more than a cursory good-bye kiss. It seemed they were drifting away from each other like a pair of unmoored, bobbing sailboats.

"Why? *Why?*"

The loud voice punctured Clara's thoughts and her gaze immediately snapped away from the leaves dancing above toward the bench beside her. A quarrel had struck up between two old men. By the state of their clothes, the wispy unkemptness of their hair, and the array of grocery bags and overstuffed carryalls at their feet, she could tell they were both homeless.

"Why? Why?" one of them kept shouting. "Why did you do it?"

The other man shouted something back, but Clara couldn't make it out. He was facing away from her. On top of which, his voice seemed slurred.

"Tell me, goddamn it, why did you do it?" the first man demanded once again.

Clara was about to avert her gaze, not wanting to pry into their increasingly heated exchange. But then the man who'd had his back to Clara jumped up, turned around to face his foe, and started flailing his arms and pointing at the sky. That was when Clara realized she'd seen him before. He was the same man she'd met coming out of the homeless shelter just a few weeks ago—the same homeless shelter she thought Anthony had disappeared into. He had told her his name, but now she struggled to remember it. Names reeled through her mind: Charlie, Billy, Bobby. Then it came to her.

"Georgie Worth," she said under her breath.

When she first met him, she'd thought how perfectly the name suited him. Georgie Worth was the kind of name that was given to kind old men in children's stories. Together with his ragtag clothes and battered fedora, his lively brown eyes and crooked smile, he was the perfect picture-book character.

Not today, though. Today his brown eyes showed none of the same sparkle and vivacity. They looked cold and hard, like small frozen clods of earth. His face seemed different, too. His skin appeared sallow, his cheeks sunken, and the lines on his face looked deeper and craggier than before. He was also shouting in a way Clara never imagined a Georgie Worth to shout. Georgie Worths didn't rant and rave like this; they didn't flail their arms and spit out angry, bitter words.

"Damn you," Georgie railed on as Clara watched from her bench. "You're a mean old bastard."

The other man started to laugh and wheeze and slap his thigh. This made Georgie even more infuriated.

"Don't laugh at me," he yelled, as a shower of spittle escaped his dry lips. "I had only two photos of her in the whole world, and now you let your damn dog eat one of them."

Georgie then plunged his hands into the pockets of his tattered pants, clearly looking for something. When he didn't find whatever it was, he grabbed one of the bags on the floor. He proceeded to toss out the contents, creating a puddle of old newspaper, ragged towels, and other assorted junk at his feet. Some kind of plastic container flew out during this furious rummaging, and it skittered across the pathway toward Clara.

Finally, Georgie found what he was looking for. He raised a photograph in his hand.

"Look," he roared. "Look at it! That's all I have left of her now. Just one picture of the woman I loved. The woman I still love. One picture!"

The other man didn't look. His head was lolling down toward his chest and he was still chuckling. Georgie stared hard at the man for a second, and Clara wondered if he was going to attack him. He looked angry enough. But then, through his haze of anger, he clearly thought better of it. Instead, he jammed the photograph into his pocket and swept up his bags with a flourish.

"Go to hell," he growled.

He then readjusted his hat, which had slipped out of place on his head, and stalked away. The man left behind on the bench slumped down, pulled up his feet, and proceeded to mutter and chuckle under his breath.

As Clara watched Georgie leave, she shook her head. It was so sad. She couldn't believe the change in the man with the twinkling chestnut eyes who had called her "beautiful lady." This was what life on the street clearly did to people. The hardships, the cold, the lack of food, the lack of dignity—it was enough to break anyone. If she were Georgie, she'd be angry, too.

A groan and then a loud snuffle made Clara look back toward the bench. The old man next to her was obviously settling in for a nap. It would be a long one, judging by the collection of empty beer cans poking out from his bags. Clara's gaze soon shifted downward to the smaller container near her feet, the one that had flown from Georgie's bag. She stared at it for a while and then found herself reaching over to pick it up.

It was a pill bottle, although the pills it once contained were now gone. She turned the bottle over in her hands and studied the label, which was strangely sparse. There was no drugstore logo, no name of the medicine, no patient's details. All it said in faded print was, SUB.—2. Clara had never seen a label like it before. Perhaps it was the way drugs were given to people with no fixed address and no health insurance. She had no idea, and this made her feel slightly ashamed. She had no idea, of course, because her life was blessed with good health, good insurance, and a home address.

Clara stood up and slipped the pill bottle into her purse. In that instant, she decided the small plastic container could remind her of how good her life really was. Every time she started complaining about Anthony and his late nights, or moaning about her narcissistic sister, or grousing about the slowness of her career, she would take a look at Georgie's bottle. It would be a reminder for her that things could be much worse, far worse. It would remind her of her wonderful fiancé, her beautiful apartment in downtown Manhattan, her good life, her blessed life.

As she started to walk toward the south side of the park, she vowed that the bottle with the ghost of whatever medication it once contained would be her elixir for contentment.

Eight

When Clara got home from the park just ten minutes later, she was shocked. She put her key into the lock, but it was already open. This surprised her, as she distinctly remembered locking it when she'd left that morning. But then, as she dipped the handle and pushed open the door, she was confronted with a wave of voices, music, and laughter. Anthony was home. She was stunned. Not only was he home, but he'd brought other people with him. Having visitors in the apartment was almost as startling as having Anthony home before midnight. Since they moved to New York last summer, they had invited guests over just once. They threw a small party right before Thanksgiving. It was their belated moving-in celebration, and most of the people who came were colleagues from Anthony's lab. Clara invited some neighbors, too—neighbors she barely knew and neighbors who, since then, she'd rarely seen again.

Clara moved down the hallway, which was cluttered with laptop bags, backpacks, a couple of bike helmets, and even a shiny new mountain bike. She dropped her own bag next to the assembled items and then headed into the living room. The place was packed. Every seat was taken, and people were standing in just about every space among the room's chairs, couch, and dining table. At first, she recognized no one and began to wonder whether her house had been invaded by a group of strangers and whether Anthony had had nothing at all to do with this party. But then she spotted the back of her fiancé's head, his thick hair gleaming in the late-afternoon sun that was spilling through the apartment's large picture window. He was standing near the table with a group of people surrounding him. They were all clutching plastic tumblers of wine and listening intently to whatever it was Anthony was saying.

Nodding brief hellos to the unfamiliar faces around her, Clara inched toward Anthony. She noticed, as she approached, that the dining table was covered with bottles of wine and what looked like hastily bought snacks. There was partially unwrapped cheese, open packets of chips, olives still in their jars, and loaves of fresh bread that were roughly cut with a large knife from the kitchen. Clara smiled a small smile. The thought of Anthony in a grocery store picking up these items seemed so incongruous. She couldn't remember the last time he'd joined her on the grocery run. For Anthony, food came from the refrigerator—which Clara stocked—or it came from the deli on the way to work. Grocery stores were a foreign land for him these days.

But then she shook her head, realizing her mistake. Anthony would have sent one of his postdocs or lab technicians out for these provisions. It didn't matter where Anthony was, whether it was in a lab at Stanford or New York, he was always admired and venerated by his junior colleagues. They adored him so much that they happily did any duty he requested or ran any errand he didn't have time to run himself. Clara knew that it wasn't uncommon for his acolytes to pick up his dry cleaning, fetch his coffee, and even sharpen his pencils. She used to tease Anthony a little and call his young colleagues his "slaves." But he would simply chuckle and say, "What can I say? They offer to do these things, and I can do with the help." He sometimes added with a wink, "And I sharpened a good share of pencils back when I was a grad student and a postdoc."

Anthony's most current crop of doting postdocs was swarming around him now. They were crowding in so tightly that for a few seconds Clara couldn't get close enough to get his attention and tell him she was home. Finally, though, a gap opened up as one of the postdocs moved to refill his wineglass and she was able to tap Anthony on the shoulder.

"Clara!" he exclaimed when he saw her. He leaned over and kissed her cheek.

She kissed him back and started to ask, "What's the celebra—"

Anthony was already answering her question, though. "Welcome to the party, darling." His blue eyes danced as he looked from Clara to the crowd around him. "We're celebrating! Bojing, here . . ." He tugged the arm of one of the postdocs standing nearby. "Bojing proposed to Lucy yesterday." Anthony then grabbed the arm of a small woman to his right. "And Lucy said yes!" He added with a laugh, "Love in the lab. Isn't it great?"

Clara recognized Bojing and Lucy from her occasional trips to Anthony's lab. They were a sweet pair, both bespectacled, shy, and fine boned. She'd seen them walking through Washington Square once, holding hands, both wearing fleece jackets and sensible walking shoes. Now the young couple were smiling, but they looked embarrassed, too. They were clearly delighted to have the praise of their beloved mentor but also surprised and awkward at the attention.

They weren't the only ones who were stunned. Clara was so shocked that for a moment she couldn't speak. She wasn't surprised Bojing and Lucy were getting married. What had her completely flummoxed was why Anthony was making such a big fuss about it. He was always politely interested in the lives of his colleagues and his staff. But his work and their work always came first. It was rare for Anthony to even mention to Clara anything about the lives of the people he worked with. He certainly never threw parties to celebrate an engagement. Indeed, the only time he ever threw impromptu parties like this was when he and whichever lab he was working at had some big breakthrough to celebrate. Positive research results were a reason for parties—not marriage proposals.

Clara's gaze flicked to Anthony and he looked back at her with his eyebrows knitted. He was clearly confused by her silence.

"Congratulations!" she finally blurted out, returning her gaze to Lucy and then Bojing. "What wonderful news."

Bojing and Lucy nodded and thanked her.

The partiers around them, who'd hushed a little while Anthony was telling Clara the news of the engagement, now started to chatter loudly again.

Amid the noise, Clara asked Bojing and Lucy, "So, when do you plan to marry?"

As the words escaped her, she regretted them, because Anthony was still standing close by. The question of their own wedding date was something they never spoke about these days. Years ago, they talked all the time about their future marriage. They would lie in bed and discuss all the wonderful places they could hold the ceremony, the friends they'd invite, the delicious food they wanted to serve, the dress Clara might wear. They would giggle as they made up silly vows to exchange on the day. But it never moved beyond these conversations. Thanks to Anthony's rocketing career, they were always on the move, always too busy, and always having to put off even the smallest of things, like hanging pictures or organizing closets in yet another new home. A wedding would just take too much time and sacrifice to organize.

When the topic of weddings came up these days, the air between Clara and Anthony always seemed to grow thick and heavy, shot through with awkwardness and a pinch of embarrassment. Indeed, Clara's small, twinkling engagement ring had become an elephant in the room, and in their lives. They both still wanted to marry each other; Clara had no doubt about that. But as the years ticked by, the ring on her finger was a mocking reminder of all they once dreamed of but never managed to realize.

Now, as Bojing and Lucy spoke about their own upcoming wedding, Clara flicked a glance at Anthony. She wondered if he felt as awkward as she did. She was surprised to see he was beaming.

"Such great news," he boomed out when the couple were through talking. "Such great news." Then, after giving Bojing a boyish slap on the back, he looked over at Clara. "Can I have a word, darling?"

The next thing she knew he stepped forward, took her arm, and was guiding her toward the hallway. Confused and curious, she allowed him to guide her through the crowd and out of the room.

"I have my own good news," he whispered when they were finally alone amid the gaggle of foreign bags and bike helmets.

"You do?" Clara asked, looking up at Anthony.

He was still smiling, but now she noticed there was something hard about his eyes. They weren't angry, but there was an intensity about them that could easily be mistaken for anger. She'd never seen his eyes look quite like this before.

"It looks like the start-up company is finally going ahead," he began. "I've got two big investors interested. I mean *big* investors." He raised his eyebrows for emphasis. "Sartrix will be launched later in the fall."

"Sartrix?" Clara raised her own eyebrows. She had no idea what Anthony was talking about. One thing that was clear, however, was that Anthony's good mood this evening had much more to do with this news, rather than the news that two of his postdocs were getting married.

"My start-up company," he whispered, his tone a little incredulous, as if she should have known what he was talking about. "The company that will get the pharmaceutical companies interested in my drug."

Clara had had no idea Anthony was planning a start-up. Indeed, when other colleagues launched such companies in the past, Anthony would scoff at them, calling them "sellout scientists with dollar signs shining in their eyes." Yet now here he was, talking of his own start-up. It didn't make any sense.

"But your drug hasn't even gone into clinical trials yet," she said.

Anthony rolled his eyes and let out a frustrated tutting noise. "The investors will help fund the trials, Clara."

Clara tried to process all this, but before she could say anything else Anthony was talking again.

"One of the investors is a Harvard alum. He wants to see the work come out of his old alma mater," Anthony whispered. He then waggled his eyebrows and nodded his head, as if prompting Clara to grasp what all this meant.

But she was clueless. She just stared up at her fiancé without saying a word.

Anthony rolled his eyes again, clearly annoyed that Clara wasn't getting it.

"Which means," he went on, "I'm moving to Harvard." His grin was so wide it seemed to cut his handsome face in two. He tapped Clara's cheek with one finger and said, "Clara, at long last we're moving to Cambridge!"

Nine

"Harvard has always been his dream, his holy Mecca of academic institutions. And then there's the fact that they didn't accept him when he was a teenager." Clara shook her head. "He admits that to no one, of course."

Kay shook her head, too. "You'd think it would make him determined to go to Princeton or Yale or Stanford instead."

"He was at Stanford for a while. But I think Anthony always wanted to prove to Harvard that they made a mistake. The best way to do that was to have them want him there; really want him. He always hoped that one day they would woo him, court him, and offer him his own laboratory."

"Well, it sounds like they're doing just that now," Kay replied.

"It does, doesn't it?"

The two women were sitting on Kay's bed looking out the long windows toward the trees beyond. Around them, Gerald's papers covered the bed. Kay didn't feel like getting up today, but she insisted on helping Clara nonetheless. Clara wasn't really achieving much, though. Since she'd arrived an hour ago, it was Kay who was doing most of the sorting and reading. She'd already worked her way through ten, maybe fifteen documents, while Clara had looked at only three. She just couldn't concentrate.

It was only yesterday that Anthony had announced his Harvard plans, but Clara felt like days, even weeks had passed. One sleepless night, coupled with a whole series of worries and confused questions chasing around in her head, had a way of drawing out time. The party at their apartment went on all evening and meant Clara didn't get to speak more to Anthony. Only when the last stragglers left and they were getting ready for bed did she finally manage to glean a few more details. She found out where his new lab would be, whom he was going to work with, which postdocs he intended to take with him, and a little more about the investors.

"When does it all start?" she'd called out as she brushed her teeth in the bathroom and Anthony idly flicked through TV channels in the bedroom. "When will the lab at Harvard open?"

"August," Anthony replied.

"This August?" she exclaimed, spluttering frothy toothpaste down her nightshirt.

There was a creaking of bedsprings and she heard Anthony saying, "Yup."

Clara stared at herself in the bathroom mirror, her toothbrush frozen midstroke in her mouth. This August. That was only a couple of months away. It was way too soon. It gave her no time to figure out what she was going to do next. Would she follow Anthony yet again? And if she didn't follow him, they would have to have an apartment in each city, and she wasn't sure if they could afford that. Or if they even wanted that.

Just a few months ago she might have been pleased to hear they were on the move again. She didn't settle into New York at first, and thanks to Anthony's reverence for Harvard, Clara had always harbored a desire to end up there herself. The university had the most prestigious history of science department in the country. Clara couldn't help romanticizing life at Harvard either. She imagined herself cycling through old streets, teaching in rooms with roaring fireplaces, dining in halls paneled in oak, and eating picnic lunches on college lawns.

Life in Cambridge, Massachusetts, would be just like grad school life back in Cambridge, England.

But with the news that this was happening so soon and so fast, a panic gripped Clara's chest. August would be upon them in no time, and she wasn't sure she was ready to leave at all. She'd come to like New York more and more—and now there was Kay, and Gerald's papers. They might not be finished by August, and surely moving, and all the work involved in packing up their home, would mean she'd have to cut short her time with Kay.

All these concerns made Clara feel slightly dizzy, and then angry as well. Anthony had sprung this on her at the last minute and now he just expected her to go along with it, to suck it up and be happy. But before the pulsing in her jaw and clenching in her chest could turn into a thumping rage, she spotted Anthony coming into the bathroom. With two quick strides, he was right behind her, pinning his body against hers and snaking his arms around her middle. Clara was too surprised to move. She had no time to consider what was happening—and what was about to happen—because Anthony was aleady lifting up her hair. Within seconds, he found her most sensitive spot, the place just above her shoulder and below her ear, and peppered it with light kisses. Clara couldn't help it: She melted backward into him without a moment's hesitation. It was so long since they were this close, and a very long time since she'd been touched in this way.

Anthony turned her around in his arms and tugged at her night-shirt. Soon they were both naked, pressed up against the sink, kissing each other urgently.

Between kisses, Anthony breathed hard and whispered, "It's going to be great, Clara."

She didn't know if he was talking about what they were doing now or if he was still thinking about Harvard. The thought quickly vanished as Anthony pushed his body harder against hers and then grabbed her hair in his hands and kissed her even more fiercely. She was surprised by his force. Anthony hadn't been like this in a long time. She wondered if he'd ever been so urgent or ferocious in his lovemaking.

These questions soon evaporated, too. Her body needed this. She needed this. She wanted Anthony and she found herself responding in kind to his rapid kisses. Their bodies moved together. Yet, in spite of the deep kisses and his body pushing up against hers, nothing happened. She moved against him and pushed her hands against his lower back, pulling him into her. But still nothing.

Suddenly their kissing came to an abrupt halt. Anthony moved away and looked down at himself.

"I had too much to drink," he muttered. "I can't. . . ."

Clara's forehead was beaded with sweat and her whole body was still tingling with anticipation. This had never happened to them before. Never.

"Maybe you just need more time," she whispered gently.

She moved to touch his cheek. But Anthony turned away from her before she could lay a finger on him and started walking out of the bathroom.

"I should go to sleep," he said without turning around. "I'm shattered."

Clara's immediate thought was to follow after him, to beg, to demand, to plead with him to try one more time. But, like a heavy rock falling in her gut, she felt the thud of disappointment. Whatever she said now, however hard she tried to convince him, it wouldn't change a thing. He was no doubt humiliated—and Anthony didn't like to be humiliated. Not only that, but once he made up his mind that he was too tired, there was no going back.

As she heard the springs squeak again and the sound of Anthony getting into bed, Clara gently kicked the bathroom door closed. She then slumped down on the floor. The tiles were cold on her naked skin. She didn't care, though; she needed something to cool the longing that was still pulsing through her body and burning her cheeks. She took a series of deep breaths and told herself to be calm. But just when she thought she was gaining control, an image of Daniel floated into her mind. She saw him in front of her, just as Anthony was a minute ago, his hair rumpled and moist, his big hands holding her body against his.

Clara immediately tried to shake the image, but it kept coming back. She imagined him kissing her softly and lightly and so unlike the urgent way Anthony had kissed her. She saw him staring down at her with his dappled eyes. She could feel his hands moving over her skin, gently lifting her hair. . . .

"Stop," she whispered to herself, as she pulled her knees into her chest and clung onto them. "Stop, stop, stop."

But she couldn't stop. She imagined his lips, so gentle, kissing the spot on her neck.

"Stop." She groaned the word this time.

Anthony was her fiancé, the man she loved. It was Anthony who got her feeling this way, so full of longing and desire and need. Not Daniel. And it was Anthony who was now lying in the next room, probably feeling both humiliated as well as tired. She shouldn't be here fantasizing about Daniel. She should be in there, consoling the man she loved.

With this thought, she pushed herself up from the floor, splashed water on her clammy cheeks, and headed toward the bedroom. She got into bed without bothering to put her nightshirt back on and curled up against Anthony's back. He didn't say anything; he didn't even stir. He was already asleep.

A day later, sitting beside Kay, Clara had an urge to tell her new friend everything. She'd already told her Anthony's news and about the party she walked in on the previous night. But now she wanted to tell her everything: about their failed lovemaking, about the disappointment that sat in her belly and prevented her from sleeping. She wanted to confess to Kay how this disappointment eventually waned, but how in the middle of the night her earlier anger and confusion re-emerged. Clara had watched the dawn arrive while wondering again why Anthony didn't tell her about the Harvard move—or the start-up company, for that matter. A few times, she thought about waking him and demanding to know his reasons. But then she finally fell into a fitful sleep, and a few hours later when she woke, Anthony was gone.

"Is everything okay between the two of you?"

Kay's question startled Clara. She jerked her head up, her gaze flitting away from one of Gerald's papers she hadn't really been reading, and looked across the bed at Kay. Kay looked back with concerned eyes.

"I don't mean to pry," Kay went on. "It's just that you seem a little sad, maybe angry, about Harvard. Am I right?"

Clara opened her mouth to speak, but then stopped. This could be the moment she let everything flood out: every worry, every thought, every flip-flop of her tired mind. Yet in the same second, out of the corner of her eye, she spotted her purse sitting on the dresser near Kay's bedroom door and was reminded of what lay inside: the pill bottle, Georgie's pill bottle. Just this morning, when she was getting ready to leave her apartment, she'd rediscovered the bottle and remembered the vow she made to herself in the park yesterday. Her life was good. Her life was blessed and lucky and healthy—and Georgie's bottle was a reminder of this fact.

"Everything is fine," she said to Kay. "Really. It's just hard to think about moving again, especially when I was finally beginning to settle in New York." She shook her head. "But Harvard . . . wow. I always dreamed of living there, teaching there. It will be amazing. I know it."

Kay didn't say anything in response; she simply gazed over at Clara, and Clara, sensing that Kay was expecting her to say more, carried on.

"I'm sure he's going to be really content when he finally gets there. Maybe he will stop working so hard because at last his biggest dream, his Harvard dream, has come true."

Kay studied Clara again, and after a short pause she said, "So it might be the end of your science widow days, you think?"

Clara let out a puff of laughter. "You like that 'science widow' expression, don't you?" But before Kay could reply, she went on. "I'm not sure if I really fit the bill. I mean, I'm not like Victor Frankenstein's Elizabeth, waiting patiently at home while my man goes off and makes monsters in his lab. No." Clara shook her head and pulled herself upright on the bed. "No. I have a full life, too: a career, books that I've written, friends like you."

"But widows can have full lives, too." Kay smiled. "Mary Shelley had a full life after Percy Shelley died. Indeed, I'm thankful to our dear Shelley for teaching me how to live alone. She taught me how to live, really live, as a widow."

Clara looked over at Kay. "You were married?"

"I got married just after college. Arthur and I were so young and in love. We were married only five years when he was killed in a car crash." Kay's eyes sparkled with tears.

"How awful." Clara gasped.

"It was. I lived like a zombie for three years." Kay paused and thought for a second. "I was in a fog: lonely, bereft, and completely despairing. Until I discovered Mary Shelley. That's when I went back to graduate school, using money that Arthur left me. And at grad school, I learned to live again. Mary Shelley gave me that. She gave me her books, which inspired a whole new passion for writing, research, and teaching, too. But her life was inspiring as well." Kay paused again.

"When Percy died she no longer toured Europe. Her life was relatively quiet, but she didn't fade away. And even when her later works didn't get the same attention as *Frankenstein*, she still found happiness. She still created and wrote and read and taught herself new things."

Kay reached over to the bedside table and took a sip of water. "Anyway, I couldn't help but draw similarities. Mary Shelley married so young, like me, only to lose her great love a few years later in a terrible accident."

Clara thought for a moment and then interjected, "My mother, too."

Kay looked over, her eyebrows raised. "Yes?"

"My father died when I was four—from a brain tumor, not an accident. I don't think my mother ever really recovered."

Kay shook her head. "I'm not sure if any young widow ever really recovers. But we learn, in different ways, to live with the scars that grief gives us."

Clara thought about her own mother and the quiet life she'd led, particularly after Clara and Maxie left home. She wondered if she ever found contentment, happiness, and purpose in her widowed life like Kay and Mary Shelley. Before now, Clara might have said no. Her mother's life in her rambling house in a sleepy town seemed so uneventful. Indeed, her mother's widowhood always frightened Clara a little and made her strive for a life that was very different. And, of course, different was what Clara got. Unlike her mother, Clara was constantly moving. She was always making new friends and new colleagues. She had to continually adjust to unfamiliar cities and universities across the country as she followed Anthony and his exciting rise to science-world fame.

Yet, as she thought about it now, Clara realized that maybe her mother's life wasn't so sad and lonely after all. Perhaps she did find contentment in her widowhood. The quiet, neighborly town, the small but cozy library where she worked, her two black cats who slept at the end of her bed—these were her ways of dealing with the "scar" of loss; these were the things that made her peaceful and happy. Perhaps.

Kay shifted on the bed and brought Clara back to the present.

"So that's why you've written so much about Shelley's widowed years?" she found herself asking.

"Exactly," Kay said. "I suppose the biggest lesson I learned from Shelley is that solitariness doesn't have to equal despair. Many of us are scared of being alone because we think being alone might kill us and sap us of our will to live. But Mary Shelley showed that through solitariness we can find great creativity and fulfillment."

Clara thought about this and then added, "I suppose she learned this when she was a girl. From what I read, it sounds like Shelley spent a good deal of time on her own. And it was during those times, like her solitary walks through the moors in Scotland, that she got her greatest ideas."

In perfect unison the two women then quoted the famous words from Mary Shelley's foreword to Frankenstein.

"'It was beneath the trees of the grounds belonging to our house, or on the bleak sides of the woodless mountains near, that my true compositions, the airy flights of my imagination, were born and fostered.'"

Clara and Kay followed these words with a long and joyous laugh.

"You're turning into a bigger Shelley geek than I am!" Kay joked, when their giggles began to subside.

"I hope so," Clara shot back.

After that, Clara and Kay resumed their work on Gerald's papers in silence, and much to Clara's surprise she found she could now concentrate. The exchange with Kay had soothed her. It caused the knot in her stomach to loosen. The news about Harvard, what happened in the bathroom last night . . . they didn't seem so bad now. Even if the move to Boston was tough, and if it turned out that Anthony worked even more hours at Harvard, she could still be happy. She would live a full and creative life, like Mary Shelley—and like Kay. While her fiancé was in his lab changing the world, she would be a happy science widow.

It was as if Clara's newfound calm made her vision more intense and clearer. Or perhaps it was just a coincidence. Whatever it was, a little while later, as Clara picked up a new paper from Gerald's box on the bed, the word "Shelley" sprang out at her.

"Oh, my goodness." She gasped.

"What is it?" Kay asked, looking up and over her half-moon glasses.

Clara didn't reply. She was too engrossed in the page in front of her.

"What is it?" Kay demanded again. This time she hoisted herself up against the pillows and leaned toward Clara. The movement clearly caused her pain, and she sucked in a breath.

"Are you okay?" Clara said, automatically reaching out and touching Kay's shoulder.

Kay batted her away. "I'll be okay when you tell me what you found."

Clara returned her attention to the small piece of paper in her hands. Her gaze hastily scanned over it once again. It looked like a misplaced page of Gerald's journal. She'd found many such pages before, fluttering loose amid all his other paperwork. It was as if his journals, handwritten on frail, wispy paper, were in the habit of falling apart. When she found these pages previously, Clara had wondered with a tinge of frustration why he did not choose sturdier paper or books that would more likely hold together.

"Jeez," she complained, feeling frustrated again. "No date, not even a day of the week. Nothing."

"Will you just read what it says?" Kay cried out with an incredulous laugh.

Clara apologized and began to read Gerald's scratchy handwriting.

"'At lunch, Teddy was telling me about a new collector in America. California, I suspect, as he's in the film business (one of these young chaps making a lot of money from cinema tickets and popcorn!). He keeps his collection very private, apparently, and even his family has not viewed everything he owns. Among other things, he has a Cézanne—Teddy didn't remember which—and some Mackintosh items. Last year, the collector made a Frankenstein movie and somehow acquired very rare letters by Mary Shelley. Some from her girlhood, Teddy believed.'" Clara then narrowed her eyes as she tried to read the last lines, which were bunched together at the bottom of the page. "'The man's name was Jonathan Maranto. Note to self: Look up Maranto. Might be interested in some incoming pieces.'"

"Jonathan Maranto." Kay whistled when Clara was finished. "Well, I'll be damned."

Clara dropped the paper into her lap and looked at Kay. "Jonathan Maranto? The director, right?"

"Of course. Maranto directed that Frankenstein movie back in the seventies. And," Kay said, pulling off her glasses and shaking her head, "the old devil interviewed me!"

"He interviewed you?"

"Uh-huh. He wanted more background on Shelley before making the movie." Kay shook her head again and wisps of her snowy hair fell around her face. "Not once did he mention any Shelley letters in his private collection. The old devil," she repeated.

"Maybe he didn't own them at that point."

"Maybe not. But you'd think he might have dropped me a line when he did." She let out a laugh. "After all, my Shelley insights were vital to his work."

Clara winked at Kay. "The movie would have been nothing without your insights, I'm sure."

She and Kay then slipped into silence. Clara looked back down at the paper and blinked a couple of times. They'd found what they were looking for. They'd finally found it. She was still in shock and couldn't really process it all. In just a few weeks, they had found what she thought, in her most pessimistic moments, would take them months to find. Suddenly it all felt a little unreal. Too good to be true.

"What now?" she said out loud.

Kay raised an eyebrow.

"I mean, what do we do now? Call up Jonathan Maranto and say, 'Hey, can we take a look at those Shelley journals in your collection'?" Clara laughed at the mere thought of it.

"Perhaps," Kay replied.

The two women were so caught up with their find that they didn't hear the apartment door opening and the sound of footfalls moving toward the bedroom. But they did hear the knock that followed.

"Come in, Daniel," Kay shouted.

Clara didn't know Daniel was coming by, even though Kay clearly did, and her heart immediately started thumping loudly in her chest.

"Hey," Daniel said as he pushed open the door and stepped into the room. He was smiling a broad smile, but when he spotted Clara his eyes darted away from her back to Kay and his smile waned. "Oh, I didn't realize you were still working. I'm sorry."

"Don't be sorry," Kay called out. Then she laughed and said, "Daniel, we have great—"

But Kay was cut off as another man walked in behind Daniel.

"You brought your brother!" Kay said, clapping her hands with delight. "This is your brother, isn't it? It has to be."

Daniel nodded and so did the man next to him.

"Yup, this is him. Paul Massey, my big brother," Daniel said while patting Paul on the shoulder.

Daniel then set about introducing everyone. Clara struggled to speak as she put out her hand to shake Paul's. She was too astonished. Daniel's "big" brother was in fact a good six inches shorter than Daniel. He was also a wiry man with neatly cropped hair and dressed entirely in black: black turtleneck, black slacks, topped off with heavy black-framed glasses. The two brothers could not look more different, except that there was something about them that spoke of their shared blood. Perhaps it was the dark eyes, or the pronounced jawline—she wasn't entirely clear. Looking from one brother to the other, Clara wondered whether anyone ever saw such a likeness between her and waifish, dark-eyed Maxie.

"I'm so delighted to meet you, Paul," Kay was saying, still beaming.

Paul smiled back. "I'm just sorry it's taken me so long to come and visit. Dan talks about you all the time."

Kay waved a hand. "I'm sure you have much more important things to be doing. Chasing drug barons? Bringing down billionaire businessmen and their Ponzi schemes?" She then turned to Clara. "Paul writes wonderful exposé pieces for the *New Yorker* and the *Times*. Even before I met Daniel I was one of his biggest fans."

It suddenly came back to Clara. Maxie had mentioned a "big-shot" brother. So this was him.

"You may be my only fan." Paul was now chuckling.

"I doubt that." Kay adjusted her glasses and stared up at Daniel's brother. "Now, I just read that last piece you did for the *New Yorker*. . . ."

Kay and Paul continued talking while Clara sat quietly listening. After a minute or so, her left cheek began to tingle. Somebody's eyes were on her; she could feel it. She turned to see Daniel looking down at her from his spot beside the door. His gaze was curious and intense. For a second, she locked eyes with him and her heart kicked in her chest once again. *Who are you?* she silently asked. *Why do you have this effect on me?* Then she remembered her fantasies last night in the bathroom and a flush rose up from her collarbone. She pulled her gaze away.

"Clara. Clara?"

Clara was so preoccupied she hadn't heard Kay calling for her.

"Can I tell them our news about Maranto?" Kay asked when Clara finally looked in her direction.

"Of course; yes, go ahead."

Kay proceeded to tell Daniel and his brother about their discovery. She read them Gerald's journal entry and told them about her own interview with Jonathan Maranto years ago.

When she was finished, Daniel's brother held up a finger and said, "There's a guy I know, a staff writer over at the *Nation*—he interviewed Maranto last year for a piece he was writing about the corporate takeover of Hollywood. . . ."

Kay's eyes flashed. "Do you think he still has contact? With Maranto, I mean."

"Perhaps. I will definitely give him a call and find out for you."

Kay looked at Clara and Clara looked back at Kay. They both grinned. They were clearly excited about the same thing: Shelley's lost journals might, just might, be within reach.

But when they looked back at Paul he was shaking his head. "You know, you shouldn't get your hopes up too high. Maranto's a tough nut to crack. Very private, apparently, and he doesn't do interviews often—hardly at all, in fact."

"He interviewed me!" Kay responded.

"True." Paul laughed. "He owes you."

"Too right," Kay shot back. "What do you think, Clara? It may be worth getting our hopes up just a little, right?"

Clara simply nodded. Her hopes were up already. She couldn't help it.

Knowing she shared blood with Mary Shelley was not enough, Clara now realized. She wanted to know so much more about the woman, her relative. She wanted to know what kind of child she was. She wanted to know what young Shelley really thought when she was shipped away from home by her father. She wanted to know exactly what those "airy flights of imagination" were as she wandered the barren moors of Scotland. She wanted to know much more about the young woman who would go on to write a tale of monsters and hubris and technology out of whack. Clara felt a connection to Mary Shelley and needed to explore it further. She wanted to know it all.

And perhaps knowing these things about Mary Shelley was no longer so very far out of reach.

September 1812—Broughty Ferry near Dundee, Scotland

There was a crispness to the air. October was still a week away, but with every breath she took outdoors, Mary could feel autumn coming. She loved this freshness, the bite in the earth and on the breeze. She also loved the deep reds and burnt oranges that autumn would soon bring to the trees around the Baxters' house—or "the Cottage," as the Baxters called their home. Even now, she could imagine the crunch and rustle of fallen leaves under her feet as she walked through the Cottage's extensive, rambling grounds.

But today, as Mary wound her way through these grounds considering the changing weather, she also felt a twinge of sadness. Winter would nip at autumn's heels and before she knew it snow, rain, and biting winds would put an end to her daily wanderings on the moors above the Cottage. Her trips to the beaches along the shores of the River Tay, which lay below the Baxters' home, would also come to a halt. The icy north winds wouldn't be as harsh as on the hills, but the bone-chilling breezes off the wide river could be.

On this cloudless September afternoon, however, it was still warm enough to stay out for some time. Mary had set off from the house a short while ago and was now climbing over the stone wall that divided the Baxters' grounds from the moors. Once over the wall, she patted down her skirts and began walking briskly up the hill in front of her.

"It won't be so terrible," she whispered as she tramped onward.

Being driven inside for the winter months wouldn't really be so bad, she reminded herself. She would miss her walks, but spending time with the Baxters was always a joy—an unexpected joy. The Scots family had turned out to be the most wonderful people, and in their home, over the past few months, Mary found great love and warmth and freedom. Indeed, from the moment she set foot on dry land, after her terrible sea voyage from Ramsgate, the family welcomed young Mary with a friendliness and kindness she'd never experienced before. Not even from her own family.

William Baxter, the master of the house, was like an indulgent uncle to Mary. He praised her young beauty, strong intellect, and sharp wit. He let her do whatever she pleased, including wandering these austere hills alone and pillaging his extensive library for books she desired. But most of all Baxter spoke often, and most highly, of Mary's parents. He respected and revered both William Godwin and the late Mary Wollstonecraft, and although still angry at her father for packing her off to sea all by herself, Mary delighted in hearing Baxter's praise for both of her parents.

"Up, up," Mary panted out loud for no particular reason, as she continued her climb.

She'd developed this habit of talking to herself on her trips to the moors. The sound of her voice had the curious effect of driving her onward and rallying her up the hills and across the craggy terrain. Her favorite spot lay at the very peak of a high hill where there was a small outcrop of rocks that overlooked the River Tay, the town of Broughty Ferry, and the grounds of the Cottage below.

As she reached the summit today, a light wind whipped around her, fluttering her skirts and flicking her loose hair across her face. She scrambled up the rocks, using her one free hand to grip and steady herself. Her other arm was still tied in a sling, even though her rash was healing and her ailing arm was much stronger, thanks to all the fresh air and her almost daily bathing in the river.

Mary sank down onto the widest and flattest of the rocks when she reached the top and took a few long, slow breaths. She allowed the wind to kick at her hair and face. The sun was bright but the sky was dappled with small white clouds that, every now and then, would float in front of the sun and soften its bright rays. Unlike some of the hotter days, when a haze hung over the landscape, today she could see for miles and miles. The river, the Cottage, Broughty Ferry, even the town of Newburgh across the Tay, were all in clear view.

A perfect day, Mary thought to herself, as she let out a small, happy sigh.

She then looked down to the valley below and spotted a fishing boat on the wide river. It was cutting slowly through the sparkling water, starting out on its journey east toward the North Sea. The boat was just a small vessel, but Mary was reminded of the stories that the Baxters recently told about the whaling ships that left from Broughty Ferry every April. All the residents of the town would meet at the harbor and wave them off. Not all the ships returned, though. Mr. Baxter spoke of one ship getting caught in the Arctic ice and the ship's crew freezing to death on board their trapped vessel.

A shiver traced Mary's spine as she remembered this horrifying story, but the chill didn't last long. Since arriving in Scotland, she'd heard many a frightening tale and she'd become hardened. Scary, startling, ghostly, and wondrous stories got told in the Baxter household all the time. In the first few weeks these stories would prompt feverish nightmares for Mary. But soon enough the dreams began to fade, and these days she looked forward to hearing the curious and sometimes terrifying tales told by her Scots hosts.

Isabel Baxter was Mary's chief storyteller. She was the youngest of Mr. Baxter's six children, but she was still four years older than Mary. Isabel would come to Mary's chamber late at night. She'd set her small candle down on a nearby table and, after slipping into bed beside Mary, Isabel would recount ancient Scottish legends, folklore about witches and evil eyes, tales of monsters, goblins, ghosts, and cloven-foot devils. Mary would listen, clutching the bedsheets with her heart pounding in her chest. Whenever Isabel got up to leave, however, Mary would always beg to hear more.

Mary smiled to herself again as she thought of these late-night visits from Isabel, her new and most beloved friend. It seemed ironic now that Isabel was the only member of the Baxter family whom Mary was wary of when she first arrived. Isabel was nothing like her other siblings. Where the other Baxters were pale, freckled, sturdy, and wholesome, Isabel was tall, wispy, and dark, with beautiful deep black eyes. She was intense and imaginative, playful and full of laughter. But sometimes, when upset, she would turn brooding and taciturn, and her black eyes would flicker with resentment. Her frown could sink ships; yet her smile could light the heavens. When Isabel found something she was interested in, she would immerse herself with a ferocious passion. She knew every detail of the French Revolution so well, for instance, that sometimes it seemed she was living among the revolutionaries in France.

Everything about the exotic Isabel intimidated Mary at first, and when she was in her presence in the first few weeks, she became tongue-tied and bashful. If she was completely honest with herself, Mary was also a little resentful. She was used to being the passionate member of the family in her own home back in London. She was the one who devoured books and spun tales to her siblings. She could make her father laugh and her stepmother fume and rage. But Isabel's intensity made Mary's passion, wit, and liveliness look tame.

Yet it didn't take long for the two young women to bond. A few weeks into Mary's stay, Isabel confessed her deep admiration for Mary's mother.

"What an amazing woman," Isabel said, when she first showed Mary the pristine copies of Wollstonecraft's works that she kept in her small bureau. "And she was your mother!" Isabel added with an appreciative sigh.

Still a little uneasy around Isabel, Mary replied, "Alas, a mother I did not know."

Isabel shook her head and her eyes flashed defiantly. "Aye, but you know her through her writings. She still lives with you." The fire then left Isabel's eyes and they immediately moistened with tears. "My mother, she didn't write . . . and now she is gone."

Six months before Mary's arrival Isabel's mother had died, and the family still grieved. It seemed that Mrs. Baxter's death hit Isabel, the youngest and most emotional child, the hardest. She was missing her mother with all her heart, and unlike Mary she had no papers, no books, and no lasting voice of her mother to hold on to.

It was in this moment, their moment of shared grief for their lost mothers, that Mary's wariness of Isabel evaporated. Isabel had once appeared so exotic and unreachable, but now, in Mary's eyes, she was

a young woman much like herself: vulnerable but passionate, suscep-
tible yet ardent, a loner who also craved a lost mother's love.

From that day on, Mary and Isabel were intimate friends. They
shared ghost stories at night and read poetry aloud to each other by
day. They bathed together in the Tay and scoured for shells together
on the beaches. Isabel was teaching Mary to ride and introducing
her to the basics of botany. Mary would delight Isabel with tales
about her life in London: the theater outings, the art exhibits, the
remarkable men and women who passed through her father's home,
the beauty and simultaneous squalor of the city.

Their friendship bloomed every day, and so similar were the two
young women that they also knew to give each other space. Both of
them reveled in their times together, but also treasured time alone.
When Mary would set off for the hills most afternoons, Isabel would
disappear on her own solitary adventures. At the end of the day, they
shared all the thoughts and dreams and flights of imagination that
their solitary time allowed.

Over the last few weeks, Mary had begun spinning a number of
tales in her head that she shared with Isabel when she returned home.
Isabel was impressed by Mary's unique, colorful, and sometimes wondrous stories, many of which were inspired by the legends and myths
that Isabel introduced her to. Just a few days ago, Isabel had pressed
a small leather journal into Mary's hands.

"You must write down your stories, dear Mary," Isabel said. "I in-
sist upon it."

And so today, still sitting on her perch high on the rocky escarp-
ment, Mary pulled the small journal from a pocket in her skirt. A tiny
pot of ink and a quill pen followed. She opened the book, scanned
over what she had written the previous day, and then thought for a
moment. She was uncertain whether to carry on with this story or
perhaps start something new. Her gaze then wandered back down the

hillside to the river and to the fishing boat that was now almost out of sight. Her thoughts returned again to the whaling boats stuck in the Arctic ice. She imagined the ship's crew huddled together in their futile attempts to keep warm. She could see their blue lips, their wide, frightened eyes, their hair tipped with shards of ice. She could hear the growl of their empty stomachs and the chattering of their teeth.

Mary's mind skipped and whirled as she imagined something even more frightful. She imagined a monster prowling the ice outside the ship. A monster that resembled a man, but so grotesque and ill formed that even the bravest of the crew could not look upon it. The horror of the image—the frozen men trapped in the hull of an unmoving ship with a monster lurking outside—made her shiver once again.

"How dreadful," Mary whispered, and at the same moment she dipped her quill in the ink and began to write.

Ten

Clara had not seen Maxie since the day she'd opened the test results. Her sister had called a number of times, but Clara was so caught up in the search through Gerald's papers that she didn't get around to calling back. However, just a couple of days after Clara found out about Jonathan Maranto and Shelley's journals, Maxie did get hold of her—and she sounded annoyed.

"I see you less these days than I saw you when you were living in San Diego and Michigan and all the other places you've decided to live over the years."

"That's an exaggeration, Max. . . ."

"No, it's not. You would think that two sisters living in the same city would see each other more than once a month," Maxie blustered down the phone line.

Moments like these always left Clara surprised. Before moving to New York, she'd thought her sister lived a life of constant parties and swarming friends, with never a spare minute. Indeed, when Clara arrived in the fall, she'd fully expected to see very little of Maxie. She believed that spending time with a bookish professor sister would be very low on Maxie's priorities.

But Clara was wrong, it turned out. Maxie did want to see her. She was always late, of course, and usually there was a drama for Maxie to share, a guy to analyze, or sometimes money to be borrowed. Nonetheless, Maxie kept calling, and Clara most of the time would agree to meet.

"What about the Maxie Tourist Trail?" Maxie was now demanding on this bright May morning. "We still haven't done the Statue of Liberty or the Staten Island Ferry."

This was another thing. Over the last few months, before Clara got sidetracked with Kay, Maxie had insisted on taking Clara on a grand tour of every tourist site and kitschy destination in town. They visited the Empire State Building, skated at Rockefeller Center, gazed at a sunset from a Circle Line boat on the Hudson, and even watched chimpanzees cavorting at the Bronx Zoo. Clara was a little baffled by this tour of Maxie's making, but she enjoyed it nonetheless. She also guessed that, in a way, the tour was Maxie's apology. Clara's sister was never good at apologies, but Clara knew that this goofy trail around the city was her way of saying, *I screwed up. I was late to our mother's funeral. Then every time we arranged to go to her house in Pennsylvania after she died, something more important came up: a callback, a double shift at the restaurant, an old flame in town. . . .*

With the phone still pressed to her ear, Clara smiled a wry smile at the thought of her sister ever actually saying these words. She then said, "Okay, Max, what about the Staten Island Ferry this afternoon? It seems like the perfect day."

And it was the perfect day. Just a few hours later, Clara and Maxie stood side by side on the deck of one of the boats. They missed two previous ferries because Maxie turned up half an hour late, even though she promised with all her heart that she would arrive on time. But her lateness allowed Clara to grab two cappuccinos from the café at the terminal. Now they sipped their steaming drinks as the wind blew fine droplets of salt spray in their faces, seagulls squawked above, and the engines chugged raucously beneath them. In spite of the noise and the wind, they were determined to stay outside. It was a beautiful afternoon; the sky was clear and the air warm but fresh. The view of the city was stunning, too. The sun, which was high in the sky, glinted in the windows of Manhattan's towering buildings, making the whole island look like one gigantic and twinkling jewel.

Clara watched the receding skyline as Maxie talked excitedly about a new guy she was dating.

"I think he really gets me," she was saying. "He's got this way of just looking right at me and then saying something really, I don't know, kind of profound."

Clara listened as Maxie talked on. Today, her sister's chatter didn't annoy her too much. Against the rumble of the boat's engine, Maxie's thoughts and musings about her latest guy were almost hypnotic.

"Have you told him about Mary Shelley?" Clara asked when her sister took a breath. "Have you told anyone?"

"Sure." Maxie shrugged. "I told him. I told some of my friends, too, and some of them heard the radio show."

"And that's it?"

Maxie narrowed her eyes. "That's it, what? What? Are you expecting me to be dancing on the rooftops singing, 'I'm related to the chick who wrote *Frankenstein*'?"

Clara rolled her eyes. "No," she retorted. "I just thought that maybe . . . I don't know . . . maybe . . ."

"You thought maybe I'd get fixated on Mary Shelley like you?" Maxie was now shouting in Clara's ear, as a strong gust of wind and sea spray battered their faces.

"No," Clara yelled back. "Of course not."

The wind suddenly dropped, offering them a chance to talk without shouting—yet neither of the sisters seized the moment. They were both brooding, clearly feeling judged by the other and a little angry. Clara had planned to tell Maxie about the Shelley journals and what she and Kay had discovered about the private collector. But now there seemed no point. What did Maxie care anyway?

Instead, Clara found herself saying the words that she knew would provoke and perhaps wound her sister a little. "We're moving to Harvard," she blurted out.

Maxie spun around, her long hair blowing and flicking into Clara's face. "What?"

"We're moving to Harvard." This time, as she repeated the words, she felt a trickle of guilt for the abrupt way she was breaking the news and so said the words more softly.

Maxie was glaring at her. "What do you mean, you're moving to Harvard? You only just got to New York; how can you be moving to Harvard?"

Clara opened her mouth to talk, but the wind struck up again and the ferry's engines seemed to roar even louder. She pointed to the ferry's cabin, and Maxie, who was still glaring at Clara, gave a quick nod. The two women made for the door. Once inside, they settled themselves on two adjacent seats near a wide window. The engines still chugged and clanked belowdecks, but without the wind and the gulls the inside of the ferry felt almost monastic in its relative quietness.

"Anthony has been offered a new position there," Clara said. She figured it was better just to launch straight into her explanation before Maxie could start asking questions. "It's an amazing opportunity. He's going to be able to test and develop the new drug with big financial and institutional backing. And, well, you know how much he's always wanted to be at Harvard."

Maxie gave a loud snort. "Ever since they rejected his sorry ass when he was a kid, right?" But then, clearly catching herself, realizing she must get back to the more pressing issue, she said, "But what about you, Clara? What does this all mean? Are you going to move with him yet again?"

Clara took a sip of her coffee and then shrugged. "I suppose I will. I don't want to do the weekend thing again. Remember, I tried that back in Michigan when he moved to San Diego. I hated it." She paused. "*We* hated it."

A few years before, Clara had decided to stay behind and not trail after Anthony when he was offered a new appointment. She loved her department at the University of Michigan and really didn't want to leave for California. For a year, she and Anthony spent their weekends flying back and forth across the country to see each other. On weeknights, Clara would stretch, flail, and fight the ache of loneliness as she tried to fall asleep without Anthony in the bed beside her. In the end, it was just too draining, too lonely, and too expensive, so when the academic year was over Clara packed up the apartment in Ann Arbor and headed out west.

Maxie's black eyes were burning into Clara's. "But is it what you want?"

"Harvard will be amazing, Max," she replied, pulling her gaze away and staring at the water rushing by outside. "I mean, think about it. It's the Ivy League. They have an incredible—I mean incredible—history of science department. If I got to teach there, I'd be made for life. I could finally get back to my next book on Darwin. I would have fantastic resources all around me."

"What if Anthony decides to move on again?"

Clara shook her head. "I'm sure this will be his last move. Where else would he go? Harvard has always been his dream."

"Maybe some big drug company will offer him beaucoup bucks and you'll find yourself moving to Zurich or someplace." Maxie wasn't joking. Her dark eyes were completely serious.

Her comment silenced Clara for a few moments. In the past, the idea of Anthony moving into commercial research was unthinkable. He was always ardent about his commitment to academic science and disdainful of any colleagues who supposedly "jumped ship." But now, with all this talk of his new start-up company and getting his drug on the market, such a move no longer seemed so unfeasible.

"But even if he does stay at Harvard"—Maxie was talking again—"is Harvard right for you? I mean, really, is it?"

Clara felt all the air leave her body. It was no good trying to pretend with Maxie. Her sister knew her too well. She couldn't lie or try to make it seem like she was happy or clear about Harvard. Maxie would see straight through it.

"I just don't know, Maxie," she said finally, as she shook her head. "I have no idea what I want anymore. But what choice do I really have? I can't stay in New York while Anthony is up in Boston."

Maxie simply looked at Clara, saying nothing.

"Anyhow, remember my and Anthony's deal?"

Maxie rolled her eyes. "You mean the deal"—she flicked her fingers as she said the words—"the deal where Anthony's drug goes into trials and he finally puts you first. That deal?"

Clara nodded. "It will happen," she insisted. "I'm certain."

"Yeah, right," Maxie scoffed. But then her voice softened. "But what if it doesn't, Clara?"

Clara said nothing for a moment. Then, avoiding Maxie's question, she said instead, "Relationships are hard work. That's what everyone says, right? And maybe Anthony and I just have to work harder than other people. And maybe when we get to Harvard and his drug goes into trial, things will get better for me—for us."

Maxie raised one eyebrow, but still said nothing.

Clara's thoughts, meanwhile, were all over the place. But now that she'd started, she couldn't stop. "I love him, Max. He's a great man; he's doing amazing work. I mean, for God's sake, if anyone's going to save someone like Kay, it will be Anthony, won't it?"

"Who's Kay?" Maxie looked confused. Then she tapped her forehead, clearly remembering. "Oh, yeah, that old Shelley lady. So what do you mean? Is she ill or something?"

Clara sighed. She'd told Maxie all this before. "She has cancer. I told you."

Maxie gave a small grimace. "Oh, yes, sorry."

"Even if Anthony can't help Kay, he could help people like her, and what kind of woman would I be if I didn't support him just as his career is going into this important new phase? He might be on the brink of developing a vital new drug that could save countless lives. I have to be there for him now."

Maxie shook her head. "But you don't have to follow his every move to support him, do you? You have a life and a career, too." She paused and added, "What do you want, Clara?"

Once again, Clara felt the air leave her body. "I always thought academia was what I wanted to spend my life doing. Remember how even in high school I wanted to be a professor? I ranted on and on about how great it would be to work at a university and how I'd have this big office full of books and a tribe of adoring students." She gave a puff of laughter and shook her head.

"I remember," Maxie said.

"But now I'm not so sure. I can't seem to find the enthusiasm for teaching anymore, and the thought of the summer ending and my having to go back to my department fills me with dread." This was the first time Clara had admitted this to herself, or to anyone, and it took her by surprise and caused a wave of panic in her chest.

"Why not quit?" Maxie asked, her face now dead serious.

Clara threw her head back and laughed—a loud, full-bellied laugh. "I'm thirty-four, Max. This is no time for me to quit my job, my chosen career. What on earth would I do with my life if I left? Work a cash register? Wait tables?"

"Like me," Maxie shot back.

Clara's cheeks flushed instantly. "I didn't mean—"

"It's all right," Maxie said with a wave of her hand. She sighed. "I wouldn't want to wait tables either. Not if I had a choice."

Clara looked over at her sister. Amid her dark beauty and effortless grace, there was vulnerability, and sadness, too. The urge to protect her burned deep inside Clara.

"How are things going, Max?" she found herself asking.

"Well, my sister is moving to Harvard, so that ain't so good." She shrugged and then went on. "I don't know. Like I said, Matt is great."

"Matt?"

"The guy I'm dating," Maxie retorted.

"Of course, yes." Guilt trickled through Clara as she realized she really hadn't been paying attention earlier.

"But work's work. You know, dull and exhausting."

"And have you auditioned for anything recently?" Clara pressed.

Maxie's face lit up. "I got a call from my agent yesterday. On Friday I'm auditioning for a new play at the Public."

"That's great."

Meanwhile, Maxie's smile faded a little. "Of course, there's a chance that they will say I'm too old for the part, but I—"

A sharp ringing cut across Maxie's words. Clara couldn't help letting out a small sigh as she looked down at Maxie's purse, expecting her sister to make a swift grab for her cell. But Maxie didn't move and the phone kept ringing. Clara looked over at her sister, bemused.

"It's not mine," Maxie said, half amused and half reproachful.

The phone gave out another chirp and Clara finally realized her sister was right. It was her phone that was ringing. In all the times the sisters had met up like this, Clara's cell never rang. She just didn't use it much, especially since she'd moved to New York and friends were thin on the ground.

"Hello," she said, after she pulled the cell from her own purse and snapped it open.

"Clara?" It was an unfamiliar male voice.

"Speaking."

"This is Paul Massey. Daniel's brother."

"Of course, yes," Clara replied.

Her heart skipped with excitement. She hadn't heard from Paul since they'd met at Kay's apartment a few days ago, but when they said their good-byes that afternoon he promised to call up his friend, the one who had interviewed Jonathan Maranto.

"I might as well cut to the chase," Paul continued. "I don't have too much to report."

Clara felt her stomach drop. "Oh."

"My friend did give me contact numbers for Maranto, but I'm not having much luck. I left messages with his agent, publicists, and manager, and so far I've heard nothing."

"Nothing at all?"

"Zilch, I'm sorry to say," Paul replied. "But my friend also gave me a few other numbers, friends of Maranto, that kind of thing. So I'm still working on it."

Clara's spirits rose a little. "Well, you did say Maranto was a tough one to crack. I'm sure the whole of Hollywood is always trying to pin him down."

Maxie, who was still sitting opposite and clearly listening, cocked her head as Clara said these words.

"I'm chasing some people in the art world, too," Paul went on. "There's some folks who are on the 'in' with art collectors; they know who's who and who owns what. Maybe they can confirm whether he still has the Shelley papers."

"You think Maranto might have sold them?"

"It's possible."

Clara felt her stomach give another disappointed tug. Even though Maranto was proving hard to contact, at least they knew who he was, where he was. He was here in this country, and it gave Clara a shred of hope that the papers were at least reachable. But if Shelley's letters and journals had been sold, who knew where they could be now?

"But I'll let you know as soon as I get some sort of lead." Clara was about to thank Paul, but he started to talk again. "There's another reason I called. . . ."

Clara wasn't sure, but his tone seemed tentative. "Yes?"

"Your full name is Clara Fitzgerald; is that right?"

"Correct."

"Are you the partner of Anthony Greene? Professor Anthony Greene, the geneticist at Manhattan University?"

Clara said nothing for a second; then her shoulders slumped. "Yes, that's me," she said quietly.

Paul didn't seem to pick up on the shift in her tone. He carried on: "I'm really hoping to get in touch with Professor Greene about a piece I'm writing."

Clara shook her head and let out a small sigh. She should have seen this coming. It seemed she was always going to live in Anthony's shadow, her dreams and desires always eclipsed by his work and success. She knew she was childish to resent it, but sometimes she just couldn't help herself.

"But I haven't had much luck getting hold of Professor Greene. I wonder if you could—"

"He has a publicist. You should contact her," Clara offered before Paul could finish. She then explained, "Anthony is always superbusy in his lab. He rarely picks up a phone. You're much better off trying his publicist." She then gave him the publicist's details.

"Well, um, thanks," Paul said after she was finished. He was clearly taken aback by Clara's sudden curt tone. "I'm sorry to ask. I usually never ask a family member like this."

"Don't worry about it." She tried to sound more upbeat. After all, Paul might be her only source of information on Maranto. "I understand," she added.

When they were finished, she closed her phone and slipped it back into her purse. Maxie was grinning over at her.

"Funny that it's your cell phone interrupting us," she said.

"I was about to say the same thing," Clara retorted.

She slipped into a brief silence as she thought about the conversation she'd just had. She wondered if Paul Massey was doing anything at all to chase Maranto or if he was just stringing her along so he could get to Anthony.

"So were you talking about Jonathan Maranto? The director?"

"Yes," Clara replied, still caught up in her own thoughts. But then her gaze settled on her sister, who was now leaning forward with her pointy elbows propped on her equally pointy knees. "And no," Clara added. "I can't get your résumé to him. We can't even—"

"I'm not that deluded," Maxie broke in. "Everyone knows you can't just send your head shot to someone like Maranto." She rolled her eyes and then plopped back against the ferry's plastic seat. "I'm just curious why you want to talk to him." She then waggled her eyebrows. "And you might be interested to know that I know someone who knows him."

"You do?" Clara almost yelped.

"I'm not telling until you spill your beans."

Clara was about to launch into her explanation when the ferry made a series of loud bangs and scraping noises. They were pulling into the dock at Staten Island and a crowd had already formed near the exits. The sisters got up and followed everyone down the clanking ramps and into the terminal.

*   *   *

"So it sounds like Paul didn't have much luck making contact," Clara said as they walked back onto the same ferry ten minutes later. "Not even a return call."

Maxie was nodding. "I doubt he will. Maranto doesn't speak to anyone. He's superprivate, apparently."

Clara turned to her sister. "So, come on, who is it? Who do you know who knows him? Or were you just spinning me a line?"

"Spinning you a line? Me?" Maxie laughed. But she shook her head. "No, it's the truth. I know this girl Jocelyn. She's not exactly a friend, but we see each other at auditions all the time. She's super-beautiful, but kind of a bitch, too. . . ." She trailed off as Clara pointed toward the ferry's inside seats and then to the door out to the deck. "Outside," Maxie decided, replying to Clara's gestured question. "I need a cigarette."

They headed out of the heavy metal door and Clara asked, "So this girl . . . ?"

"Yeah, like I said, Jocelyn's kind of bitchy. She's the type who looks at your belly after you've eaten a big lunch and says, 'Have we got good news? Are you expecting?'"

Clara looked down at Maxie's iron-flat stomach, an expanse of which was now showing above her jeans, and wondered how anyone would ever make such a comment to Maxie.

"So what does she have to do with Maranto?" Clara prodded.

Maxie was struggling in the salty breeze to light a cigarette. "Wait a minute," she said, the cigarette waggling in her mouth as she spoke. Finally the end glowed red as Maxie took in her first drag. She puffed out and said, "I am quitting. This is just one of the last packs I'm going to buy . . . ever."

Clara simply shrugged. She'd heard this many times before. "So this woman . . . ?" she prompted, trying not to sound as impatient as she felt.

"Oh, yes, so she's dating Jonathan Maranto's son."

"She is?" Clara coughed with surprise. She didn't expect this.

"That's what she told me." Maxie rolled her eyes. "She can be kind of full of herself, so I wasn't sure if it was true. But then I saw a paparazzi shot of them together on one of those crappy online celebrity Web sites. You know, those sites for photos that are too B-list to get into *Us* or *People*."

Clara was barely listening now. Her mind was whirring.

"Do you think we could talk to her?" she finally asked.

"Sure."

"You think she'd care if we asked her about Maranto? Or is she private about it?"

Maxie gave a low chuckle. "Like I said, she's full of herself. She pretends to be coy sometimes, but you know she's really itching to boast about dating a Maranto."

Clara was silent for a few seconds. "So can we call her? Could we arrange to meet her, perhaps?"

Through a cloud of newly blown smoke, Maxie looked at Clara. "What, now? You want me to call her now?"

Clara nodded as she waved away the smoke. "I know it's asking a lot, Max, but I'm running out of time."

"Because of Harvard, you mean?"

"No, because of Kay. She's pretty sick and . . . well . . ."

But Maxie was already pulling her slim cell phone from her purse. "Consider it done."

She threw the last of her cigarette over the ferry's railing, where it tumbled down into the water below, and then she headed back into the cabin.

Clara stayed outside and looked up at the white gulls flitting, coasting, and diving behind the boat. Every one of their movements seemed so purposeful, so flawless and unhindered. The birds knew exactly what they wanted and how to get it. Clara gazed up at them, admiring them. She found herself thinking of Maxie's question earlier: *What do you want, Clara?*

Now, as she looked up at the squawking gulls, what she wanted felt so clear. She wanted to find Mary Shelley's journals, and she wanted to find them soon, before Kay got too sick, before Kay . . . She wouldn't allow herself to finish this last thought. She could not think like that. Time was running out, but maybe with Maxie's help what she yearned for might not be out of reach. It could happen in time.

Clara then turned and looked in through the ferry's window. She saw her sister standing on the other side of the glass, speaking into her phone. Maxie caught Clara's gaze and flashed a smile. Clara smiled back. All the bad words and thoughts about her sister, the ones she'd felt and said so often over the years, seemed to evaporate into the swirling air of the New York Bay.

Eleven

When Maxie made up her mind to do something, she would follow through with tenacity and zeal unmatched by any hungry dog with a bone. Clara had a stubborn streak, too, of course. It was what made her search so persistently for that Darwin letter she never found back in grad school. Her obstinacy was returning again in this current seach to find Mary Shelley's journals. But Maxie's doggedness was much louder and more vivacious than Clara's, and it sucked in air and energy like a whirling tornado.

On the ferry ride home to Manhattan, Maxie didn't get hold of her friend. But it was as if a gauntlet had been thrown down and Maxie would not stop until she got in touch with the woman dating Jonathan Maranto's son. After five minutes on the deck alone, Clara headed back into the cabin to find out what was going on. She discovered Maxie pacing the boat, punching in numbers, and talking loudly to various friends, colleagues, and other contacts in the acting world.

"Can you get her to call me?" Clara heard Maxie demand into her cell. A few moments later, Maxie was saying in an almost-shout, "Yes, it is important."

When she finally got off the phone, Clara couldn't help looking surprised.

"Max, thanks. You didn't have to go to all that trouble."

Maxie shrugged. "Not a problem." She tapped her phone. "I spoke to a friend of Jocelyn's best friend and she said Jocelyn has moved to LA."

"Ah," Clara responded, her stomach giving a kick of disappointment.

"But," Maxie went on, waving the phone, "we're in luck. She's coming back into town tonight. Who knows? Maybe she will have her Maranto boy in tow. I'm going to try calling again later. Perhaps we can meet her tomorrow."

As she thanked her sister, guilt whisked through Clara. She remembered the manila envelope with Maxie's head shot and résumé that she never gave to Anthony. It wouldn't have been so hard to give Anthony that envelope. He might have scoffed at it and no doubt he would have thrown it in the nearest trash can. But Clara could have given it to him nonetheless. She might have tried to persuade him to help her sister out. It wouldn't have hurt her to do that much.

This guilt returned the next morning when Clara answered the phone and heard her sister's enthusiastic voice.

"Jocelyn says she'll meet us tonight at five o'clock," Maxie announced before even saying hello.

"Tonight? Seriously?"

"Seriously." Maxie then reeled off the address of a bar in SoHo and told Clara she would meet her there. "I won't be late," she added pointedly. "Jocelyn's on a tight schedule, apparently. She can only have one drink and then she's flying on to someplace else."

After she hung up, Clara stared at the phone for a few seconds. She was surprised and guilty, too, about her sister's continued gusto, but she was anxious as well. She knew she was building up hopes that would probably be dashed. Jocelyn was just some struggling actress dating the son of Jonathan Maranto. It wasn't exactly a free pass into Maranto's private collection.

"Take a look at this."

Anthony's voice made Clara almost topple from the kitchen stool where she was sitting. She thought he'd left the apartment already, and she hadn't heard his footfalls on the kitchen tiles behind her.

"What is it?" she asked as she spotted the papers he was now fluttering in front of her.

"My new lab!" Anthony beamed and his blue eyes glinted and danced. "At Harvard," he added.

She took the sheets and scanned the glossy photographs. The lab looked no different from any other lab that Anthony had worked at over the years: bright lights, slick surfaces, polished floors, white coats hanging on hooks by the door, and an array of slim laptops and otherworldly machines. She looked harder at the picture, knowing that Anthony wanted her to say something. Perhaps this laboratory did look bigger, slightly brighter and shinier, and the machines were more intricate-looking and imposing.

"Very impressive," she finally murmured.

"It really is, Clara," he said, slipping onto the stool next to her. "It's incredible."

Clara was about to respond, but Anthony kept talking. He told her about his new colleagues, the new equipment, and the imminent clinical trials for his drug. He told her about the start-up company and his plans to expand it and whom he intended to "bring on board" for his new venture.

"I'm so happy for you," Clara said when he was through.

Anthony looked at her for a second and then said, "But?"

"But what?"

Anthony's eyes narrowed. "It seemed like there was a 'but' coming."

Clara was about to shake her head, and then stopped herself. She remembered the conversation with Maxie on the ferry. She thought again of her sister's question about what she wanted and whether Harvard really was good for both of them.

"What about me, Anthony?" she exclaimed. The words came out with such force that it rustled the papers still in her hands.

"What do you mean?" Anthony looked genuinely bemused.

"Am I going to move with you?"

"Of course," Anthony said. He reached out and took the sheets from Clara's hands. "The history of science department is delighted to offer you a position on their faculty. Haven't you received the letter yet?"

Clara shook her head.

"You will soon." Anthony was beginning to get up, and the familiar look of preoccupation was creeping back across his face.

Clara's mind started spinning, somersaulting. She was going to slip into Harvard's history of science department just like that. How could that be? Surely there would be an interview, some sort of meeting, a call to talk about her work and her career? On the heels of these questions, another thought occurred to her. It was a thought that had passed through her mind a few times before, but she never allowed it to fully germinate.

"You didn't pay them off, did you?" she exclaimed.

Anthony, who was now standing, jerked his head back toward Clara. "What?"

"Did you pay the department to take me?" she said.

She couldn't help her accusing tone. Now that she'd let the thought surface, she couldn't push it under. So many of her colleagues had a hard time getting appointments at the same universities as their husbands and wives, yet it always seemed so effortless for Clara. Anthony was on the cusp of academic stardom; there was no doubt. But he hadn't won a Nobel Prize yet, and she knew the wife of a Nobel-winning mathematician who'd had to take a part-time position just so she could work at the same place as her husband. Spousal appointments weren't as easy as Anthony and Clara's experiences would seem to suggest.

Anthony tucked the sheets of paper into the inside pocket of his jacket. His eyes took on that hard look she'd seen a few times recently.

"And what exactly would I pay them off with, Clara?" His tone was saccharine but also biting. "We're professors. We're not exactly rolling in dough. Anyway, you know how these appointments work; if Harvard wants me, then they will take you, too."

Clara knew this all too well. It was her undeniable fate as a trailing spouse, but having it spelled out so blatantly by Anthony felt like a slap in the face, and right away, anger erupted inside her.

"Maybe one of your start-up investors paid them off," she spat out.

Anthony blinked and for the briefest moment looked shocked. But then he composed himself and said, "I have no idea what you're trying to get at, Clara. But whatever it is, most probably you have it all wrong. Your position at Harvard was secured just like all your last appointments were secured. There was no paying off." He rolled his eyes and added with a gruff laugh, "This is academia, not the mob."

With that, he turned on his heel and left the kitchen. Clara was left staring angrily at her morning coffee, which was now cold on the counter. She hated it when Anthony dismissed her like that. She hated it when he walked out, giving her no chance to respond. But before she could even consider getting up and pursuing him, he was back in the room.

"Oh, and, darling," he said in an upbeat tone. The hard look in his eyes had vanished. "I hope you're free tomorrow night. Professor Becker is in town. I said we would join him for dinner."

"He is? You did?"

Clara's anger was instantly replaced by shock. Professor Ernest Becker was the man who had introduced them all those years ago, back in England. Even though Anthony returned to the States after his postdoctoral year in England, Harold remained an important mentor to him. They wrote to each other frequently, and Professor Becker had been eager to know everything Anthony was doing in his skyrocketing career.

But then Professor Becker retired and in his retirement he wrote a book that shocked many of his colleagues—and completely disappointed Anthony. Clara hadn't read it herself but she knew that the book took a new and wary stance on genetic research. Anthony felt betrayed by his mentor's turnaround in views and even wondered whether Becker was "suffering early signs of dementia." The two men hadn't seen each other since the book came out.

Anthony was nodding. "We're meeting at a restaurant on Lafayette. I'm bringing along some colleagues and a couple of postdocs from the lab."

"Are you two talking again, then?" Clara couldn't take in the news.

Anthony gave an incredulous laugh and a wave. "Of course we're talking." He then flashed her a bright smile and said, "The table's booked for eight."

As Anthony left the kitchen—and then the apartment—Clara remained at the counter feeling wrong-footed and bewildered. One minute they were on the cusp of a row; the next minute Anthony was jovially announcing a dinner date with someone she thought he wanted nothing to do with these days. She looked up at the empty doorway and for a few seconds fought a strange giddy sensation. Did she even know who Anthony was anymore? The question ricocheted around her mind.

But then she shook her head, as if trying to shake away the question.

"Of course I know him," she muttered to herself as she stood up and began tidying her breakfast dishes.

*   *   *

It was six o'clock and Clara was standing amid a throng of happy-hour drinkers at a bar in SoHo. The laughter and chatter were deafening and fused with the hypnotic beat from nearby speakers; the resulting noise was almost unbearable. So, too, was the heat. The floor-to-ceiling doors of the bar were thrown open, spilling drinkers onto the sidewalk of Mercer Street, yet it was still impossibly hot inside. Today had been the first truly sultry day of summer, and this, combined with the jostling crowd, meant Clara was sticky and uncomfortable.

But worse than the heat and the noise was the fact that Clara was here alone—all alone. Maxie hadn't shown up, and as Clara didn't have any idea what this Jocelyn woman looked like she had no idea whether she'd shown up either. Clara had already made three calls to Maxie's cell, but each time she got the same "mailbox full" message. She was hot, clammy, and growing more annoyed by the second.

"Another drink?"

The barman yelled in order to be heard over the din. Clara simply shook her head and then slid her empty wineglass away from her. She looked at her phone again. The screen was blank.

"Maxie," she growled under her breath.

At six thirty, she gave up. She pushed her way out of the crowd and started moving up Mercer Street toward home. Her cheeks burned and her head pounded from the noise she left behind. She realized she was clenching her jaw, too. She felt as if something inside her were unraveling. Ever since the near row with Anthony this morning, she was feeling unsettled, on edge. But now this twisting agitation had bloomed into fury. Her anger, though, at this precise moment was directed more at herself than at Maxie. Waiting a whole hour and a half for her sister was insane, not to mention humiliating. She should have given up long before. But her persistence kept her there. She clung on, hoping that Maxie would show and then Jocelyn would show and they would all talk about Maranto and somehow Clara would find a way to bring up Mary Shelley and . . .

"Ridiculous," Clara muttered under her breath, cutting off her own thoughts.

She was now standing at the corner of Bleecker Street and Mercer. Left was home, but turning right would take her toward the East Village and Maxie's apartment. She knew she should probably just take the left turn and go back to her apartment, where she would sit in the air-conditioning, taking long, deep breaths, and cool off her body—and her anger. But the opposite direction was calling her. Her annoyance and frustration and disappointment were taking the lead. She couldn't stop herself from going right.

At Maxie's building on Seventh Street, Clara managed to get in by grabbing the door as another tenant was leaving. She didn't have to press the buzzer, which she was glad about. If there was no reply, she would never know if Maxie was simply out or if she was hiding (Maxie's front window overlooked the stoop and visitors could be checked out from above before they were invited up).

Clara climbed the six flights of narrow stairs and when she reached the door of Maxie's apartment, with its peeling paint and rusting peephole, she stood and caught her breath for a few seconds. Then she reached out to press the doorbell but at the last moment pulled her hand away. Instead, she sidled up to the door and pressed her ear against the painted wood. Sure enough she heard movement, voices, and the sound of footsteps. There was no denying Maxie was home.

Just as Clara pulled her head away, the door swung open and Clara found herself just inches from a man's chest. She stumbled back and let out a shocked and automatic, "Sorry."

The man looked down at her. "Not a problem," he drawled.

His hair was a mess of dark curls, and a pair of green eyes shone out from under his long eyelashes. He was beautiful, in spite of his frayed

Levi's and white T-shirt punctuated with holes around the neckline. He was exactly Maxie's type: disheveled yet handsome, skinny but not scrawny, tall yet not towering. As Clara took him in, anger reignited in her chest. This was the reason Maxie hadn't shown up.

"Clara?"

It was Maxie's voice. She was standing in the doorway behind the guy wearing nothing but a washed-out I ♥ NY T-shirt that barely reached the top of her thighs.

"Maxie," Clara responded, her tone cutting the air like a knife.

The smile on Maxie's face disappeared.

"I'd better get going," the man said. He then turned and kissed Maxie on the forehead. "Speak to you later, babe."

Clara stood aside as he moved past and she kept standing there as he lollopped down the stairs and out of sight. Finally, she turned and looked at her sister. Maxie was looking down at the ground.

"I screwed up, didn't I?"

Clara scowled. "You did." She moved toward her sister. "Are you going to let me in? I don't want to have this discussion in the hallway."

Maxie stepped back and pushed the door open farther so Clara could come in.

"Thanks," Clara muttered with a bitterness that surprised even her.

Maxie's studio apartment was in more disarray than usual. Empty pizza boxes crowded the work surface in the tiny kitchen area, clothes were strewn all over the floor and the back of Maxie's tattered love seat, a pile of junk mail teetered on the edge of a green Formica table by the window. And the bed, of course, was a muddle of tangled sheets, pillows, and cushions. Clara could see an imprint on the mattress from where two people recently lay. She snapped her eyes away.

"Why do you live like this, Max?" The words flew from her mouth.

Maxie looked startled for a second, but then she slumped down onto her love seat and let out a sigh. "So you've stopped by to criticize how I live?" Her tone was as icy as Clara's.

"I stopped by," Clara retorted, flicking her fingers in a quotation sign, "I stopped by to see where the hell you got to." She paused and stared down at her sister. "You said five o'clock. You promised you wouldn't be late."

Maxie was looking sheepish again. "I forgot," she mumbled. "I ran into Matt and one thing led—"

"You forgot?" Clara's shout cut across her sister's words. "We made the plan this morning. This morning. How could you forget that fast?"

Maxie didn't look up. Instead she curled her long bare legs beneath her and then studied her fingernails.

"And what about your friend Jocelyn?" Clara persisted. "You stood her up, too, you realize."

Maxie still didn't say anything, which just made Clara more furious. She wanted to reach down and grab her sister by the flimsy T-shirt, haul her to her feet, and then shake her.

"Haven't you got anything to say for yourself?"

A laugh erupted from Maxie. "You sound like Miss Greeble. Remember her?"

Every vein and muscle in Clara's body was now pulsing with anger. "You remember your fifth-grade teacher, but you don't remember a date that you set up this morning." Her voice was low and tight, pinched by her fury.

"Clara, I think it's time to calm down and put this in perspective. . . ."

"Put this in perspective?" Clara was shouting again. "Okay, Max, I'll put this in perspective. You're an unreliable flake who cares about no one but yourself." The words tumbled out and as she said them

Clara felt, all at once, nauseous and liberated and on the verge of tears.

Maxie didn't say anything for a few seconds. Instead, she leaned across the arm of the love seat and picked up a packet of cigarettes from a nearby shelf. She then set about lighting one and taking a long, slow drag. She seemed poised and calm, yet Clara could see her sister's fingers trembling a little.

"That's what you think of me," Maxie finally said in a calm but frosty tone. "That's what you have always thought of me."

Clara opened her mouth to respond, but Maxie carried on.

"Just like Mom."

"What?" Clara thought she misheard.

"That's exactly what Mom always thought of me, too," Maxie muttered.

"That's not true. Mom's heart was too big to ever think that about you."

Maxie blew out another puff of smoke and simply shook her head.

Clara went on. "In fact, it was probably because Mom was so unconditional with her love that you ended up . . ."

"So unreliable and self-centered?" Maxie retorted. "That makes such a neat theory for you, doesn't it? Mom spoiled me with love, so I ended up a spoiled brat." She shook her head. "You're so blind, Clara. You always have been. You think you're so observant. You think you see everything, but you really don't."

"I see that you can't keep a date that you arranged this morning. I see that you can't make it to your own mother's funeral on time." Clara was spitting out the words now. "I see that you're thirty years old and you still live like an eighteen-year-old college student. I'm definitely not blind, Maxie."

Maxie looked up, her dark eyes suddenly furious. She stabbed at the air with her cigarette. "You call me self-absorbed, but you live in your own self-absorbed bubble, too. It used to be the Mom-and-you bubble. Then it was the Anthony bubble. Now it's the Mary Shelley bubble."

"What are you talking about?" As Clara asked this, she slumped down onto one of Maxie's folding bistro chairs. Her legs felt weak from the strain of the conversation. Clara always hated confrontation, but she'd waded into this and now there was no way to get out.

"You and Mom always lived in your happy bubble together. You were so alike. In the summer, when kids like me were riding bikes or swimming at the old quarry, you followed Mom to the library and as she worked, you sat there for hours reading your books. On the way home, the two of you would gawp at flowers, stare at the sky, and chatter away to each other like a pair of little birds." Maxie's eyes were still fixed on Clara, but now they looked more sad than furious. "I just didn't fit in—and you never saw that."

"I am . . . was more like Mom; it's true," Clara said quietly. "But she never judged you. She always loved you."

"Ha!" Maxie let out a bitter laugh. "Never judged me? If I had a dollar for every time she told me I should be more like you, or that I should study hard like you, that I should dress like you, date guys like the guys you dated . . ."

Clara was stunned. "She didn't—"

"She did," Maxie snapped. "You were away at college when it was at its worst, but you came home for the holidays. You saw the fights." Maxie stubbed out her cigarette in her ceramic ashtray shaped like a pair of glittering lips. "But you clearly didn't hear them," she added.

Of course Clara saw the fights, and heard them, too. But they always passed quickly enough, like storms in the night, and Clara dismissed them just as fast. Maxie was just being a difficult high schooler, more interested in guys and drinking than settling down to her studies and thinking about a college career. Maybe their mother was tough on Maxie, tougher than she'd ever been with Clara. But Clara didn't need a strong hand, did she? Maxie did.

Clara looked over at her sister now and said, "But Mom meant well, didn't she? She only wanted the best for you."

"Whatever she 'meant,' it was hard to live with that kind of judgment. It sucked to be the daughter who didn't live up to what she expected." Maxie looked down at her legs and scratched at an invisible blemish. "It sucked being in your shadow all the time, too."

Clara was reeling. In her mind, her mother was a kind woman who loved her girls and would do anything for them. She wasn't a woman who would mess up her beautiful but free-spirited daughter by laying judgments and criticism on her. That just wasn't the mother Clara knew.

But maybe it was the mother Maxie had known.

"Is that why you never went home? To visit her, I mean," Clara asked, her tone still strained and disbelieving.

"It was hard enough having agents and theater directors and movie scouts telling me I wasn't quite good enough. The last thing I needed was to go home and hear Mom tell me the same things." Maxie's eyes were hard still, but there was a glassiness now, too, a suggestion of tears.

Clara studied her sister for a brief moment. She always thought her sister didn't go home because the uneventful small town where they grew up bored her. Clara assumed that Maxie couldn't face the quiet and solitariness of their mother's widowed life. But it wasn't their mother's life she was avoiding. It was their mother.

"But Mom wasn't so bad, was she? I mean, she didn't beat you or starve you or . . ." Clara trailed off, not really knowing where her thoughts were going. Her mind was still reeling.

Maxie was lighting another cigarette. "And I'm not so bad either, am I?" Her tone still had an edge of bitterness.

Clara said nothing. Her sister had inadvertently reminded Clara why she was here in the first place and how Maxie had let her down.

"Kay, my friend," Clara said finally. "She's really sick and I wanted to find those journals and letters before she . . . before, you know . . ."

"She dies," Maxie offered.

Her sister's nonchalance stung. "Yes, before she dies," Clara snapped.

Maxie shook her head and her high forehead furrowed. "Talking to Jocelyn was always going to be a long shot. You realize that, don't you?"

"But a long shot was better than no shot at all," Clara retorted.

She glared over at Maxie, who was back to picking at her bare legs with one hand and puffing on her cigarette with the other. Then, startling them both, a cell phone gave out a loud warble. It was Maxie's and it was juddering and chirping on the Formica table. Maxie did not hesitate. She uncurled her legs, rested her burning cigarette in the ashtray, and then got up and reached for the phone.

"Hey, Gwen," she said, her face breaking into a smile. "No . . . Yes . . . You're kidding. . . ."

And she was off, chattering to her friend as if Clara weren't in the room. Watching Maxie, Clara felt as if something were opening up and then sinking deep inside her. It was as if a large trapdoor were snapping open and swallowing up her hope—not just the hope of finding Shelley's childhood papers but also the hope that she would always be able to tolerate her unfathomable and unreliable younger sister.

She stood up. "I have to go."

But Maxie didn't hear her. Nor did she say good-bye when Clara let herself out of the apartment. As Clara headed down the stairs, her head pounding and her chest clenched, she realized there was another word her sister had not brought herself to utter.

The missing word was "sorry."

Twelve

The next afternoon Clara visited Kay. She found her friend in bed, but in good spirits and evidently not in too much pain. Kay's happy face made Clara instantly regret calling her the day before and telling her about the meeting with Jocelyn. Now she had to break the news that nothing came of it and that her sister didn't even show.

Kay, however, took the news in stride. "Ah, well," she said, with a wave of her hand. "It was a long shot, wasn't it?"

Clara frowned. "That's what my sister said."

Kay searched Clara's face. "You're mad at her, aren't you?"

"Of course I am." Clara sighed. "How couldn't I be? I mean, one minute she was calling everyone on earth to try to get hold of Jocelyn and the next minute her new guy shows up and she forgets all about it. She's so . . . so . . ."

"Inconsistent?" Kay offered.

Clara gave a sharp nod. "Inconsistent, yes." She then fell into a forlorn silence for a few seconds. She wanted to vent more about her sister. But to do so would be childish. Kay didn't want to hear about their squabbles.

"I suppose we're all inconsistent," Kay was saying. "We're all a mass of contradictions. We think we make sense, yet a lot of the time what we do, what we think, how we love, how we feel—all these can fly in a million different directions and make no sense whatsoever. Take me," she said, pointing at herself. "I always loved to teach my students. I was confident and at ease in the classroom. Even if I was lecturing to a hall of three hundred students, I never wavered. I didn't feel one butterfly in my stomach. But put me in a room full of other professors and I became a bag of nerves. A veritable jelly!" she added with a laugh.

"I can't believe it . . ." Clara began.

"Oh, yes, you'd better believe it." Kay smiled. "It took me years and years to find the confidence to give conference papers or to chair committees in my department."

"But you found the confidence in the end, right?"

"Oh, yes, but it took time and work, self-reflection and practice." Kay paused. "All I'm saying is that our inconsistencies are who we are. Sometimes we can iron them out, sometimes not." Kay raised her finger as a thought occurred to her. "Think of young Mary Shelley, too. She was so bookish and good and quiet in many ways, but she had a whole wild streak also. One that made her argue with her step-mother and run off with a married man, an effusive and daring poet called Percy." She waved her raised finger. "So, you see, even if we are inconsistent, does it matter? Aren't contradiction and inconsistency what make the world so interesting? A world without Mary Shelley's inconsistencies would have been very different."

Clara gave a shrug. "Yes, but . . ."

Kay reached across her bed and took hold of Clara's hand. She gave it a gentle squeeze.

"The other thing I have learned over my many years . . ." She smiled as she said this. "I've learned that you can't change people. You certainly cannot iron out their contradictions. You can help them, you can love them, you can enjoy them for who they are. Or, if they are impossible, you can choose not to know them at all." She paused and then nodded. "But you really can't change them."

"I don't want to change Maxie," Clara replied. "At least, I don't think I do. I just wish . . . I just wish this time she came through." She looked at Kay. "She knew how much this meant to me. She didn't even apologize. She hasn't called me since we argued yesterday either." Clara realized she was beginning to sound querulous, so she added, "I just want to find those journals and letters, Kay. I really do."

"And hopefully we will," Kay countered. "Maybe Daniel's brother will still make contact with Maranto for us."

Clara just frowned. She wasn't holding out much hope for Paul Massey. Since his call, she'd convinced herself that he cozied up to her only to get in contact with Anthony.

"I'm sure we'll get hold of Maranto somehow," Kay added.

"But we're running out of time," Clara said without thinking.

Her cheeks then flushed as what she said sank in, but before she could try to backpedal Kay started to chuckle lightly.

"You're worried about me dying, aren't you?"

"I . . ." Clara began, but she couldn't finish. She had no words to respond.

Kay stared at her for a few beats, her face now serious. "I'm dying, Clara. That's a fact. I may die tomorrow or it might not be for a few months, but I'm definitely dying."

As she said this, she squeezed Clara's hand tighter. The skin on Clara's bare arms prickled into goose bumps and tears jabbed her eyes.

"But," Kay went on, "I'm living now, in this moment, and in this moment you and I are still on our journey. We are still searching for Shelley's papers and thinking about different ways we might get our hands on them."

"And what if . . . ?" Clara started, her voice croaky with her effort to hold back the tears.

"What if I die?" Kay replied. "Then you will continue the journey without me." She gave a smile.

Clara watched her friend and words escaped her. She was floored by how Kay could be so calm and so accepting.

As if reading Clara's mind, Kay continued, "Perhaps my life, my path, my role is to lead you to those Shelley papers, and if that is my path, then it makes me truly happy." Kay squeezed Clara's hand again.

Clara squeezed back, as a tear trickled down her cheek.

"How are you so brave?" she finally whispered.

"I'm not always so brave," Kay said with a light laugh. "In the middle of the night, I sometimes lie awake trembling in fear." She stopped and waved over to some books on her bedside table. "But some of these have really helped me in those moments."

Clara's gaze focused on the books. The top one read, *The Tibetan Book of Living and Dying*. She could see the spines of a couple of others. One said *There's More to Dying than Death: A Buddhist Perspective*. Another read, *Be Here Now*, by Ram Dass.

"These books remind me to breathe, to be in the moment, to enjoy the life and breath I still have in me. They have taught me the great beauty of living and dying and about how illness and pain and fear can teach us so much, if we only embrace them and look them in the face. . . ."

Kay continued to talk, but Clara began to tune her out. Her thoughts were on the books. She wondered if Daniel brought these for Kay, and this caused a push and pull of feelings. She was glad that he provided something that brought Kay relief and comfort in those dark, fearful moments in the night. Yet, Clara couldn't help being slightly irritated, too. These books, with all their talk about the beauty of dying, were taking the fight out of Kay. They were making her accept her death too readily, at least as far as Clara was concerned. Clara couldn't help thinking of her own mother, whose stroke was so severe it killed her in less than a week. She didn't have the chance to fight, and that, to Clara, seemed so sad and unfair.

Clara didn't ask about the books, though. Instead, when Kay was finished talking, she looked at her friend with a determined stare and said, "I am going to get us those papers, Kay, and I'm not going to do it without you."

If Kay wasn't going to fight, Clara resolved, she would do the fighting for her. She would will Kay into living a few more months, or until they got access to Maranto's collection. It shouldn't just be Kay's path to lead Clara to the papers. Kay should be there, too. She should see them for herself.

In response to Clara's declaration, Kay said in an almost ethereal tone, "You will never be without me, Clara."

When Clara left Kay's apartment later on, she ran into Daniel in the stairwell. He was carrying two brown grocery bags.

"Let me take one," she said, offering her hands.

Daniel shook his head. "If I can't carry one lettuce, four apples, and a few boxes of Kleenex up two more flights of stairs, then I have no right to call myself a man."

A laugh escaped Clara. "Well, I won't rob you of your masculinity."

Daniel laughed, too. "That's kind of you."

Clara looked up at Daniel and he looked down at her, and for a few seconds they said nothing. The silence felt comfortable at first, but then it turned awkward.

"I must get going," Clara said, snapping her eyes away from his.

"Me, too. These boxes of Kleenex are getting heavy."

Clara couldn't help letting out another laugh. She looked back at Daniel and studied him for a moment. She really knew nothing about this man. He was utterly unknown to her. Yet, as she found herself looking into his speckled eyes, there was something deeply familiar about him, too. It was eerie. But then she remembered what Kay said earlier about inconsistency, and for a moment, just a brief moment, she found herself accepting the contradiction that Daniel posed. And as she accepted it, she felt completely peaceful—the most peaceful she'd ever felt around him. In fact, she felt more peaceful than she had in a long while. For a short, blissful time, the row with Maxie, the near row with Anthony, Kay's sickness—they were all shut out. They were held away at a comfortable and muted distance for a few moments.

"I really should go," she said finally.

Daniel nodded and then, pretending to buckle and strain under the weight of the paper bags, he said with a chuckle, "Yup, like I said, me, too."

He headed up the stairs, and she headed down.

Anthony had reminded Clara of the location and told her that dinner with Professor Becker would start at eight sharp, so she kept the time in mind as she walked home and started getting ready back at the apartment. But just after her shower she accidentally kicked a stack of books on the floor beside her bed and found herself staring down at a biography of Percy Shelley. She sat on the bed, reached for the book, and then spent a minute or so studying the portrait of the poet on the cover. He was a beautiful, unusual man with wide, almost feminine eyes, high moon-shaped eyebrows, and a shock of curly hair. Clara found herself wondering when exactly it was that Mary first set eyes on this face.

Clara headed to the study with dripping hair and just a towel wrapped around her. She leafed through the stack of biographies and articles on her desk, only to find that the jury was still out about the first sighting between the lovers. Percy Shelley became acquainted with Mary's father when she was living in Scotland with the Baxters, and it was commonly believed that Percy and Mary met when Mary returned from Scotland for a short visit in 1812. Other biographers said this was speculation and the two young lovers in fact met when sixteen-year-old Mary returned home for good a year and a half later.

Clara sat in her office chair contemplating this. It was incredible to think that such a moment was not recorded—the moment when two burning comets of writing and thought, love and poetry, collided for the very first time. It was the vital moment when Mary met the great love of her young life, the man who would sweep her away from her humdrum life in London and off to Europe for adventures and excitement and, in the end, heartache, too. He would be the father of her children and the person who encouraged her to write *Franken-stein*. He would make her heart soar—and he would break it, too. Yet, in spite of all this, no one knew for sure when Mary first saw him.

Of course, the moment probably was recorded at the time, perhaps in a letter to her friend Isabel in Scotland or on the pages of Mary's own journal. But those papers were lost now. Or maybe not lost, but locked away in a private collection in a high-walled mansion in Los Angeles, unreachable to the people who yearned to see them.

With this thought in mind, Clara fired up her computer and punched Jonathan Maranto's name into Google.

"Come on," she murmured.

She wasn't just urging the search engine to work faster; she was also urging it to find something, anything, that might lead her to Maranto. A tip, a clue, a way in, a fortuitous coincidence, that might lead to an introduction and a way of getting access to this man who owned something she so desperately wanted to see.

Her searching turned up nothing, except a whole list of random facts about Maranto and his movies. It also made her late. By the time she reached the restaurant it was nearly eight thirty, and when the maître d' showed her to the table, Anthony shot her a questioning and slightly annoyed glare. She chose to ignore it, though. She wasn't in the mood for apologies. She was still feeling angry at Anthony after their conversation about Harvard yesterday. Furthermore, what she thought was going to be a small dinner party was in fact a gathering of at least a dozen people. Postdocs and colleagues from Anthony's lab were crammed along each side of the restaurant's long table, all of them chattering in animated loud voices and pouring themselves large glasses of red wine. She really wasn't in the right frame of mind for a big party.

Clara sat down in the last empty seat at the table and smiled briefly at Anthony, who was opposite. She then noticed that beside Anthony was Professor Becker. She breathed a small sigh of relief. She instantly remembered what she loved about the professor back when she was a young grad student in England. There was something so kind and grandfatherly about his demeanor. Yet, with his bright hazel eyes, wild silver hair, and quiet, astute voice, he also exuded great intelligence and gravitas. If she had to sit near anyone at this dinner, she was unquestionably pleased it would be him.

"It's wonderful to see you again, Professor Becker," she said to the old man as she caught his eye.

"Clara!" he exclaimed. He clapped his hands in clear delight. "So wonderful to see you, too."

Clara's mood lifted a little. Professor Becker seemed genuinely delighted at her presence. She was also heartened to see that his eyes bore the same vivacity that they always had. Anthony had been so sure that Becker's recent book, which he'd disagreed with so tenaciously, was a product of an aging mind. But the man who sat opposite Clara seemed far from a man on the wane.

"How are you and your Darwin studies coming along?" Before she could answer, he added, "I still have a copy of *Watch and Listen* on my shelf. What a wonderful and important book."

Clara's mouth nearly dropped open in shock. This man's mind was definitely not on the wane. He remembered her book and its title. He even had a copy on his bookshelf.

"Don't look so shocked." Professor Becker chuckled. "Some of us scientists read more than textbooks and journals, you know."

"I'm glad you enjoyed it," Clara said, finally finding her voice.

At the same moment, she also felt a flush of guilt. This eminent professor of genetic science had read her book, yet she could not respond in kind. Not only had she not read his latest book, but she'd never read any of his earlier works either.

"And are you deep into a new project?" Professor Becker pressed.

"I am."

It wasn't a complete lie. She did have half a book written on her computer at home and folders upon folders of research data on her office shelves. But she hadn't written a single word on the project since her passion for Shelley took root, and she was reluctant to share this fact with Professor Becker. He was a prolific man, even in his retirement, and he'd no doubt be mystified by someone who stalled out on their own writing.

Luckily, she didn't have to elaborate on her work, because the waiter arrived to take her order, and when she was finished looking at the menu and selecting her entrée, she managed to shift the conversation away from herself and onto Professor Becker.

"And what about you?" she asked. "Are you busy working on your next book?"

"Of course, yes." He then leaned into the table so he could get a little closer to Clara and, with a hand up against his mouth, clearly shielding his words from Anthony beside him, he whispered, "I have a confession."

Clara raised her eyebrows.

"I'm obsessed with tomatoes."

Clara's eyebrows arched even higher.

"I never grew anything in my life until I retired," he announced. "But I've discovered the joys of gardening, and tomato plants are my absolute favorite."

"They are?" Clara said, not really knowing how else to respond.

Professor Becker nodded enthusiastically. He then went on to regale Clara with stories of all the different varieties of tomato he was growing and the joys of noticing their differences and tasting their unique flavors. He talked of learning as much in his garden, and from his tomato plants, as he'd learned in all the years in laboratories. From the soil, the compost, and varying weeds, to the changing of seasons and the ripening of his fruits, he'd come to understand the interconnectedness of the natural world and how wondrous it all was. His eyes danced as he spoke and Clara found herself unexpectedly fascinated by all that he had to say.

"And what's most amazing . . ." Professor Becker said, after taking a sip of wine, "is how meditative gardening is. I always find that after a good session in my garden, I can concentrate much better on my writing. It's as if the soil and the plants and the time outside settle my mind. Gardening brings the world into sharper relief. I'm certain I've done my best writing since I've been growing my tomatoes." He winked as he said this last part.

Clara smiled and then her gaze slipped briefly to Anthony; she was curious to see whether her fiancé was listening to any of this. He wasn't. He was deep in conversation with his neighbor. But if he had been listening, she was certain that the professor's passionate talk of tomato plants would have been grist for Anthony's mill about the old man's state of mind. No doubt Anthony would take it as more proof of Becker's diminishing faculties and of a once brilliant brain beginning to wither.

But it wasn't what Clara saw when she looked across the table at this old man. Professor Becker, she realized now, had the same spark, the same liveliness and intensified wisdom that she saw and felt in Kay—at least, in Kay when she wasn't tired or suffering the pains and aches brought on by her illness. As she considered this, she wondered whether it was only those in their older years who could possess this kind of intensity and vivacity of spirit and mind. She certainly had never really seen it or felt it with those who were younger.

As her thoughts turned to Kay, Clara felt her stomach lurch with sadness. She was having a good time talking to Professor Becker, but she couldn't help thinking of her friend. She realized now that Kay had filled her with unexpected happiness and hope, and the prospect of losing the old woman was too much to bear. Kay could try to convince Clara that she would be with her in spirit after death. But this didn't console Clara. Once Kay was gone, she was gone. Just like her own mother was now gone and completely unreachable, so Kay would be, too.

"Now, Clara," Becker said, interrupting her thoughts. "Enough about my tomatoes; tell me about Mary Shelley. I heard through the grapevine that you share DNA. That must be quite something, no?"

"It certainly is."

Glad to be distracted from thinking about Kay's illness, Clara settled back against her seat, nursed her glass of wine, and proceeded to tell Professor Becker the whole story: finding her mother's old copy of *Frankenstein*, her search for family ties, the DNA test and its results. She even told him about Kay and the papers they were looking for.

"You know, it's funny," the professor said when she was finished. "I often find myself coming back to Mary Shelley these days. In fact, in my last book, I wrote a whole chapter that used *Frankenstein* as a springboard for my discussion." He paused. "It's ironic because when I was younger, I despised the book. I saw it as a big, fat albatross weighing around the neck of modern science, particularly modern genetics. It always seemed that you couldn't have a serious talk about genetic science or genetic engineering without some shrill antiscience folks screaming the words 'Frankenfoods' or 'Frankenbabies' at you." He rolled his eyes. "And I held Mary Shelley responsible for this."

"But now you've changed your mind?" Clara asked.

He nodded. "I've now come to understand and truly respect her novel. She looked at the advancing technologies of her age and asked, 'What if?' She dared to wonder what would happen if man tried to create life. She allowed herself to imagine the consequences of 'pursuing Nature to her hiding places,' as she put it so eloquently."

Professor Becker took a sip of his drink and then continued. "Her book may be dated now, but it is an example of how we scientists need to think deeply about what we are doing and about what we ought to be doing." He shook his head. "I'm not saying we should stop our scientific pursuits, but we should really think about what we study, why we study it, and the possible consequences." He gave a short chuckle. "For instance, do we want a world where all tomato plants bear exactly the same fruit just so big food corporations will make a lot of money? Or where all cows grow to the same height, live to the same age, and produce the same milk, so the dairy company's task is a no-brainer?"

"Or," Clara said, joining in, "a forest of straight trees just so the lumber companies have an easier time of it?" She thought back to an article she read a while ago on this topic.

"Exactly." Professor Becker clapped his hands, clearly delighted she was getting his point. "And if Mary Shelley were writing today," he continued, "she would have dared to think about what it means for our world that modern science is becoming so embroiled with profit and corporate interest. She would surely try to imagine the consequences of a scientific community more interested in making money than doing good, solid science."

"And you believe that is what's happening?" Clara asked.

Becker nodded. "I've seen it for myself."

"But what about science that helps people?" Clara asked him. Her forehead furrowed a little. "I mean, does it matter if they make money while they're developing vaccines or new medicines?"

She thought of Anthony and his new start-up company. If he made profits developing a cancer drug that might help people like Kay, then that didn't seem so bad.

"Here's the thing, Clara. When you add money into the equation, it changes things. It means that those drugs that make the most money will be pursued above all others. Drugs that are taken every day, like antidepressants or blood-pressure tablets, they are where the real money is. We need those drugs, of course, but do we need a whole slew of them? Do we need all the copycat antidepressants?" He paused for a second. "It's a fact that less research money is going into the vital development of antibiotics, simply because they are not so profitable." His eyes were flashing with deep passion.

Clara considered this for a second. "I'd never thought about that, but I suppose it's probably true."

"If we don't take stock and think deeply about our actions," Professor Becker added, "science, including medical science, will soon be too busy pursuing profits, and not its own goals."

"I think that's somewhat of an overstatement."

The voice was Anthony's. Neither Clara nor Professor Becker had realized he was listening. They both turned their gazes toward him, and Anthony was looking back at them with a winning smile.

"I mean," Anthony continued, "not all scientists are out to make a quick buck, if that's what you're implying."

"Maybe not now," Professor Becker responded. "But might we

soon be in a situation where only profit-hungry scientists survive? Or where only those happy to appease stakeholders will have labs and research grants?"

Anthony chuckled. "I think you're getting ahead of yourself, Ernest. I really don't think that will be the case."

"No? But what if it were?"

Anthony's mouth twitched in a way that Clara knew meant he was getting angry. But then she watched as he shifted in his seat and pulled his mouth back into a smile. He was clearly trying to rein himself in. Clara thought she was the only one to notice this, but she wasn't.

"He's holding back." Professor Becker laughed, looking at Clara but waving toward Anthony. "He wants to challenge me, the way he used to when he was a live-wire, upstart grad student. But he won't dare."

Anthony looked momentarily shocked. "I—" he began.

But Professor Becker cut in. "He wants to be in my good favor."

Clara was confused. She looked from Professor Becker to Anthony and back again.

"I've been invited to talk to a new government ethics panel," the professor explained. "The panel is looking into the practices of biotech start-up companies and their place in university laboratories." He tapped Anthony's arm and, in a tone that was still jovial and teasing, he added, "Indeed, it might be because I'm speaking to this influential panel that I'm here tonight. Could that be right, Anthony?"

Anthony had been caught out. The trace of pink on his cheeks made it abundantly clear. Clara was shocked, too, by Professor Becker's words. He seemed to know about Anthony's start-up company, when she had only recently heard about it herself—and she was pretty sure Anthony had been keeping it secret from most of his colleagues at Manhattan U.

While Clara considered this, Anthony had already regained control. He gathered his composure back as quickly as it was lost.

"Don't be absurd, Ernest. You're here tonight because it's been too long since I last saw you. Plus, I wanted my team"—he waved around at the table—"to finally meet you."

Professor Becker sat back in his seat and raised his glass. "Of course, of course," he said with a wink.

Anthony took this as his cue. He tinkled his knife against the bottle of wine in front of him and soon everyone at the table had hushed and turned to look at him.

"Thanks, everyone," he started. "Before our food arrives, I just want to introduce all of you to Professor Ernest Becker. All of you know his work, of course. But many of you haven't been fortunate enough to meet him in person." Anthony then turned to Professor Becker and raised his glass. "Thank you for coming, Ernest. We're honored to have you with us."

Professor Becker nodded, flashed a wry grin, and raised his own glass.

When dinner ended and Anthony and Clara helped Professor Becker get a cab back to his hotel, the two of them walked home to their apartment just five minutes away. It occurred to Clara as they made their way along Fourth Street that she could barely remember the last time she and Anthony had walked anywhere together. If they did go out on a date, which they hadn't in a long while, they usually took a cab. They certainly never spent their Sundays browsing around parks and antiques stores or hiking in the country, like they did when they were first in love.

Tonight Anthony wasn't exactly walking either. He drank almost two bottles of wine at dinner and now, with his arm thrown over

Clara's small shoulders, he was leaning heavily against her. His foot-steps were erratic, his voice was a little slurred, and he was grinning merrily. Clara wasn't angry, even though taking his drunken weight was proving awkward. She drank a couple of glasses of wine herself and the maudlin thoughts and worries about Kay were now numbed by the cabernet buzz. She also had to admit she was enjoying Anthony's goofy mood. She hadn't seen him like this in so long, and it brought back memories of earlier days.

"Harvard," Anthony was saying—singing, almost. "Harvard. Harvard. Harvard. Here I come, Harvard!"

Clara laughed. "What are you saying, you idiot?"

Anthony stopped in his tracks and pulled Clara around to face him. He was trying to pull his face into something more deadpan.

"It's going to be incredible, Clara," he said. "So fricking incredible."

Under the light from a nearby streetlamp, she could see his blue eyes sparkling. In spite of his drunken swaying and the half-silly, half-serious expression, he looked so handsome. She realized as she studied him that she had gotten so used to his looks over the years that she stopped seeing their beauty.

"We'll have lunch at the Harr-varrd Faculty Club," Anthony slurred in a mock Brahmin accent. "We'll ride around on bikes with big college scarves flowing like this." He did a ridiculous fluttering gesture from his neck up into the sky.

Clara laughed again. She laughed harder as he jiggled around, pretending he was cycling. When he finally stopped, she studied him once again, and suddenly something deep and hard clutched at her chest. It was guilt: guilt for all the uncharitable things she'd thought about him recently; guilt for all the doubts she had about following him to Harvard; guilt for bemoaning his long hours and constant working; and guilt also for those thoughts, those brief feelings, about Daniel.

Here he was, her Anthony. He was such a brilliant man: idolized by his young colleagues, teased but clearly still liked by Professor Becker, one of the most esteemed minds in genetic science. And, as she could see now, the goofy, overenthusiastic young man whom she once fell in love with still lurked beneath the new polished exterior that Anthony had crafted for himself over recent years. This revelation made her smile.

"Tell you what." Anthony laughed, grabbing her hand. "Why don't we get married in the Harrr-varrd Faculty Club?"

Clara's mouth dropped. She was flabbergasted. This was the first time in years one of them had mentioned the possibility of an actual wedding.

"What's the matter?" Anthony asked, still slurring a little. "You still wanna marry me, don't you?"

"I . . . Of course . . . but . . ." she stammered. She then paused, trying to gather her thoughts. The only thing she could think to say was, "But don't you have to be a Harvard grad to get married there?"

Anthony hooted with laughter. "Oh, Clara," he said, "don't worry about those kinds of small details."

He plopped an arm back over her shoulder and clumsily pulled her into him. He placed a long, wet kiss on her lips. When he finally drew back, he said, "No one is going to stop us if we want to get married at the faculty club. I'll make sure of that."

All Clara could do in response was giggle. Anthony's giddy mood was infectious, and the talk of a wedding made her suddenly, unexpectedly, and overwhelmingly happy.

November 1812—Skinner Street, London

Everything in London seemed so much dirtier, louder, and more frantic when Mary returned from Scotland in late autumn. Compared to the barren hills above the Baxters' house, or the gentle rush and flow of the river below, anything would seem loud and bustling. Yet Mary was convinced that in her six-month absence London had changed. The air seemed thicker with smoke, the voices outside her window were noisier and more urgent, the whinnying of horses and the clatter of passing carriages was almost deafening.

The fifteen-year-old had been home only a week, but already she was yearning to return to Scotland. She missed the wide-open views of the Grampian Mountains that she awoke to every day over the summer. She yearned for the crisp Scottish air, the chirp of birds, and the rustle of leaves in the wind. The change of locale wouldn't have been so dramatic for Mary if her family home were still in Somers Town: the small village just outside London surrounded by green fields, babbling streams, and dreamy churchyards. But now they lived in the heart of the city, where her father and stepmother ran a dingy and unprofitable bookshop. The stench from a nearby abattoir never failed to infiltrate their home above the store, and when some unfortunate soul was being taken to the gallows a few blocks away, the cries of the bloodthirsty crowds would rattle the windows.

Mary could have endured all of this if Isabel were by her side. But her beloved friend remained in Scotland. It was decided that Isabel's sister, Christy, would be the one to accompany Mary. Christy was the elder of the two sisters and therefore she was deemed the most suitable travel companion. Although Mary was glad not to travel alone, as she had when she first went to Dundee, she considered Christy a poor substitute for Isabel. Christy was serious, sensible, and staid. There would be no late-night ghost stories with Christy during their trip to

London, no giggling or speculating on visitors to the household. The two young women would not share daydreams about the men whom they might one day marry, as Mary and Isabel often did; neither would they talk about all the changes they hoped to bring to the world.

Christy might not have been a romantic or a dreamer, but she was a willing escort. Luckily the hardy Scots woman wasn't scared to accompany Mary out into the city, and even though the bustling London streets weren't where Mary really wanted to be, they did provide an escape from the drab home at Skinner Street and the constant interferences from Mary's stepmother. With Christy by her side, Mary had already visited a number of exhibits, taken in a new play, and explored some new buildings dotted around the city.

On a cold and damp Tuesday in late November, the two women were headed out again to see some paintings by Joshua Reynolds. Their bonnets were pulled tight against the London drizzle and they walked quickly and carefully, avoiding the steaming piles of horse manure and the puddles of sewage that patchworked London's cobbled streets. Children wearing nothing but rags and dirtied faces would stop them now and again and ask for help, and Mary, as always, would dole out pennies or the scraps of food she gathered from the Skinner Street kitchen before she left. It wasn't that her family had much to spare, but Mary could never walk past these hungry children without offering something and so she always came prepared.

"It only encourages them," Christy hissed, after Mary stopped for a fifth time and handed out her last piece of bread.

"So?" Mary retorted. "What are the poor mites supposed to do? Hope that angels deliver food to their bellies? The poor do not choose to beg, Christy; they are forced into it by circumstance and the greed of the rich."

Christy rolled her eyes. "You sound like that Shelley fellow," she scoffed.

Mary instantly bristled. If she had a penny for every time Christy mentioned "that Shelley fellow" in the past week, she would be as wealthy as the French aristocracy. The only reason Christy mentioned him was because she had met Shelley and Mary had not. Percy Bysshe Shelley was her father's new young friend and acolyte, and he and his wife paid a visit to Skinner Street the night after Mary and Christy arrived home from Scotland. Mary was pale and weak from the sea voyage and her stepmother insisted she must stay in her room to recover.

"You are not a pretty sight," Godwin's wife pointed out with her usual lack of tact. "You cannot receive company in such a state."

Christy was in characteristic good health following their journey and was perfectly able to join Mary's family and guests for dinner. After the meeting was over, Christy reveled in telling Mary every detail, every joke, and every twist and turn of the conversation during the "delightful evening" with the "enchanting guests." What Christy did not know, what no one knew, was that Mary was there. She saw the guests and she heard some of the conversation—albeit from her hiding place in the gloomy hallway outside the parlor.

Mary heard the guests arriving while she was still in bed, and after giving enough time for predinner drinks and for everyone to get settled, she threw back her bedclothes and stole quietly from her room and down the stairs. She was still shaky after the trip, but curiosity burned bright within her and made her forget her fragility. In his letters to Mary in Scotland, her father had written such fascinating and wondrous things about this young man Shelley. He was a writer and a poet and quite the radical, apparently. Only a year ago, he wrote a pamphlet about atheism for which he was expelled from Oxford University. Mary also knew that Shelley had eloped with the sixteen-year-old young woman whom he rescued from the oppressive and cruel boarding school she attended. He sounded such a daring and romantic man, and she was desperate to set eyes on him, if only for a moment.

The door to the dining room was ajar, Mary soon discovered, and she pressed herself against the wall outside so that the shadows would hide her and so she could get the best view of the party assembled inside. Her father sat at the head of table and beside him was a young woman in a purple satin dress. This had to be Shelley's young wife, Harriet, Mary surmised. She was beautiful; there was no doubt. But there was something lackluster and uninspiring about her, too. Although she was pretty, her eyes were glassy, distant, and without any sparkle of curiosity or question. Mary did not hear her voice because the young girl spoke only once or twice and each time in a volume so soft that it did not reach the door where Mary stood.

At first, Percy Shelley was facing away from Mary, talking to Mrs. Godwin beside him. But she could see his shock of curling chestnut hair and the gentle slope of his unusually delicate shoulders. And even though his face was turned in the other direction, Shelley's liveliness and passion were obvious to Mary in every one of his movements and gestures. His long, thin hands waved as he spoke. His head bobbed and shook and he seemed unable to stay still for even the shortest of moments. When conversation elsewhere in the room would ebb, she could hear him, too. His voice was much like his countenance: delicate and soft around the edges, yet at the same time brimming with life and enthusiasm, force and fire.

Finally, Shelley turned away from her stepmother and faced Christy, who was sitting opposite at the dining table. For the first time, Mary saw his eyes. They were crystal blue, wide, and astonishingly pronounced. Like his voice and his movements, they were slightly feminine, yet they also shone with a fiery intensity and vigor. Like a cobra in front of a charmer, Mary found she was enthralled. She could not take her gaze away from those eyes, and every few moments she would inch a little closer to the door, trying to get a better look.

Mary was so deep in her trance that she did not realize at first that Shelley's eyes had shifted from Christy and were now looking up and over toward the door. It was only when his head cocked to one side and small smile tweaked the corners of his mouth that she realized he was looking at her—directly at her. She froze in panic, but then as Shelley continued to gaze up at her, saying nothing to the people around him, she began slowly to smile back. They remained like that for a few moments, the two of them simply staring, smiling, watching, searching each other's eyes.

"Shelley, my good man."

Mary's father broke the spell and Shelley looked away.

"You are newly wed," William Godwin said with a chuckle. "Pray, tell us your philosophy on love."

The room fell silent, waiting for Shelley's response. Mary held her breath, too, and pushed herself as close as she could to the open door.

"Shakespeare's Lysander captures it best, I believe," Shelley began.

But he was interrupted by Mary's stepsister, Jane. "'The course of true love never did run smooth,'" she piped up with a giggle.

"Indeed," Shelley said with a nod. "But he also says, 'Or, if there were a sympathy in choice/War, death, or sickness did lay siege to it.'" He looked around the dining table. "Even if lovers are a good match, the great yet common forces of war and death and sickness may ruin it."

Mrs. Godwin tapped his arm and gave a nervous laugh. "You are most pessimistic, I fear, Mr. Shelley."

Shelley gave an emphatic shake of his head. "Love is fleeting, like lightning or a dream, as Lysander says, or like a swift shadow"—as he said these last words, Shelley's eyes flicked to the door, where

Mary remained hidden in the gloom of the hallway—"and it is precisely because of love's ephemeral nature that it lends us such intensity and joy."

Mary did not hear the rest of Shelley's speech. Footsteps clattered in the hallway behind her and she realized that the maid was bringing more food for the table. So as not to be discovered, she darted with small, quick strides toward the stairs. It was only when she got back to her room that she realized she was shivering from head to toe. The hallway outside the dining room was chilly, and her nightdress quite flimsy. But really it hadn't been that cold. These shivers came from somewhere else, somewhere much deeper inside of her. They were, although she didn't know it yet, the first tremors of this fleeting yet beautiful thing called love.

A week later, out on her walk in London with Christy, Mary found herself asking a question she'd asked a number of times already.

"And you say Shelley's wife was quite charming?"

Christy gave a precise and serious nod. "Yes, I have told you before, Mrs. Shelley was most charming. Well read and beautiful, too."

Mary did not reveal that she saw Shelley's wife. Nor did she tell that in her brief inspection of Harriet Shelley she found none of the charm that Christy spoke of. Mary saw someone fair of face, with sweet manners, but not the kind of woman who could ever match the energy, vibrancy, and intellect of her husband. She was no more than a fair moon, while he was a brilliant and glistening star.

Tramping onward through the damp streets of London, Mary thought again about Shelley. She remembered his eyes upon her that night and his words, "swift shadow," spoken in his soft yet vigorous tone. He'd spoken of love and looked right at her, and the memory of this sent a hot thrill rocketing through Mary once again. Yet the thrill was followed by a fleeting and inexplicable clench of cold fear.

"Oh, my goodness!"

Christy's sudden and startled cry made Mary jump. She looked up and followed the direction of Christy's horrified gaze. A horse was passing beside them and on the cart it was pulling lay a young man. He was covered with blood. Before Mary could look away, she caught sight of his scalp; it was hanging in a mess of tangled hair and clotted blood from the rest of his head.

"Oh, my . . ." Mary muttered, as she slapped her hand to her mouth and removed her eyes from the nauseating sight.

But she could not stop herself from hearing the man's whimpering noises as he writhed on the cart in pain. It was the most bone-chilling, animallike noise she'd ever heard, and Mary knew she'd never, in all her years, forget its low, guttural, and tragic tone.

"What happened?" she heard Christy ask a man who was walking alongside the cart and trying, clearly in vain, to tend to the man's wounds and to move passersby away from the cart.

The man did not reply, but a woman nearby called out, "It happened at the mint. He was cleaning the floors under the new machines."

Mary looked back at the cart. She couldn't help herself. She'd heard about the new steam-powered machines that were recently installed at the Royal Mint. Many of her father's guests talked of them and described the efficient, powerful, and incredibly fast way these machines could press coins.

"Steam power is moving man into a new age," she remembered one of her father's companions saying after he described the new coinage machine. "Steam is revolutionizing every single way we live."

No one had spoken of this, however: the way these machines could eat off a young man's scalp.

"Are so many coins worth a poor boy's head?" she muttered.

But no one heard, not even Christy. Mary's stomach rolled and sank. Man was moving into a new age; her father's friend was right.

But it seemed the cost of this new age was going to be high. Too high, perhaps.

Mary stood motionless with the image of the boy's torn scalp imprinting itself forever in her mind. Christy, who was never usually a tactile person, looped her arm through Mary's.

"Let us keep moving," she said in a whisper, as she gave Mary's arm a coaxing tug.

Mary allowed herself to be pulled away, but the horror of what she witnessed lingered long after. The image of the bloodied boy would resurface again and again in the weeks, months, and even years to come.

Thirteen

For two nights and almost two days after the dinner with Professor Becker, Anthony was sick—wildly sick. It started in the middle of the night and Clara at first thought it was the wine. He drank much more than he usually did these days, and perhaps his body just wasn't used to that quantity of alcohol anymore. Back in Cambridge and in the early years together that followed, they could finish a couple of bottles of cheap red wine together and suffer merely a headache the next day. After they left their twenties behind them, however, their drinking had gotten more moderate.

Anthony's sickness continued into the next day, and when the chills and sweats began, Clara started to suspect it was food poisoning instead. But this explanation wasn't wholly satisfying. She'd eaten the fish, too, and felt fine. Other colleagues chose the same appetizer as Anthony and they weren't sick. She called to check.

The next night, Anthony didn't get any better. He sweated through two sets of bedsheets, and when he wasn't shivering, he was constantly reaching for the plastic red pail Clara placed by the bed. He was delirious, too, and on a number of occasions, Clara heard him mumbling the words "adverse effects." She had no idea what that might mean. In the end, she decided it must simply be the product of fever.

By noon of the second day, Clara was exhausted. She'd gotten little sleep and she'd changed sheets, washed towels, and emptied pails for nearly thirty-six hours. She was also worried. Regular food poisoning rarely went on this long. Salmonella was looking like a possibility. She was about to call their physician when Anthony appeared in the kitchen. He looked like death with his matted hair, his skin almost translucent, and purple crescents underlining his dulled eyes. But he was on his feet and that was more than he'd been in many hours.

"Hey," Clara exclaimed, both in surprise and relief.

"Hey," he whispered before slumping down on a stool at the kitchen counter. Then, after rubbing his face with his hands, he summoned up a weak smile and said, "I think I might be hungry."

Clara set about making him dry toast. As she flitted around the kitchen, she speculated aloud about what it was that had struck him down.

"Perhaps it was the fish," she said as she slid the bread into the toaster oven. "Maybe there was just something off about your fillet."

Anthony simply muttered, "I don't think it was the fish."

"What do you think it was then?"

"I don't know," he snapped, his voice still weak but also with a hardened edge.

She looked up, shocked. He glared back at her for a second, but then shook his head. "I'm sorry," he said. "I'm not one hundred percent yet."

"I can see that."

She didn't press him further. He clearly wasn't up to it. She wouldn't bring up the other matter that had been on her mind during his sickness either: namely, their wedding. She wouldn't bring it up until he was better. Maybe she would never bring it up again. He'd probably forgotten everything he said anyway.

Clara hadn't forgotten, though. While Anthony endured his fevers and vomiting, she milled around him trying to focus on the present and what she could do to help him. All the while, however, her mind kept coming back to what he'd said about their wedding and the Harvard Faculty Club.

She'd stopped fantasizing about her dream wedding long ago, of course, and it wasn't that she wanted some huge affair. Ornate gowns, grand speeches, truckloads of flowers, and wedding cakes like skyscrapers weren't her style. All she wanted was something simple where she and Anthony would be surrounded by friends. Together they would eat good food, drink champagne, and laugh and celebrate into the night. The most appealing part of their wedding, she realized now, was the idea of being the center of Anthony's world for a day. She would walk toward him wearing a pretty dress, a flower in her hair, and with her red-gold curls falling around her face, and he would gaze back at her with an adoring, focused, and undivided gaze.

The toast popped from the toaster and shook Clara from these thoughts. She grinned to herself as she put the bread on a plate. It was ridiculous to even entertain ideas about a wedding that might never happen.

She sat down at the counter and placed the toast in front of Anthony. He reached out and took her hand.

"You were amazing," Anthony said in a weakened voice. His blue eyes had settled on hers. "While I was sick, I mean. I'm so lucky to have you, Clara."

His words were kind and seemingly genuine, but Clara felt awkward. His hand on hers felt strange, too tight and curiously unfamiliar, and she could think of nothing to say in response.

"I haven't forgotten," Anthony added. "I'm serious about the Harvard Faculty Club and our wedding. Let's do it soon. How about this summer?"

Clara, who was about to take a sip of her coffee, almost dropped her mug.

"This summer?" she croaked out, her eyes wide with surprise.

Anthony laughed. "Why not?"

Clara set her drink down on the counter. Her hands, she realized, were shaking a little. She eyed Anthony for a few seconds.

"Are you serious?"

He let out another laugh. "Of course I am."

She was silent again. This was all too sudden, too astonishing, to take in. A wedding this summer on top of everything else—Kay, the move to Harvard, a new job—it just seemed unfeasible. But then the idea began to penetrate a little. Perhaps this was what she and Anthony needed. Things hadn't been so great between them recently. She wasn't a fool; she knew that. They'd grown distant, removed from each other. But a wedding could change all that. They would have to work together to make plans and arrange the big day. They'd become partners again, as they used to be. And as a married couple things might be different for the long haul, too. A stronger commitment would tie them together and perhaps renew everything between them.

"Okay," she said finally. "Let's do it."

The next week passed in a blur. With a wedding now on the horizon Clara realized it was time to prepare for the move to Harvard. The first task was to talk to her new department. The conversation with the department chair was friendly, and she found herself agreeing to go to Boston in the next few weeks for a visit.

"Not many of the faculty will be around, as it's the summer," the chair warned. "But we can have lunch and I can have someone show you around."

"That would be wonderful," Clara replied with genuine enthusiasm.

Now that the move was becoming a reality, she found she was excited about the new job. Just as she hoped the wedding would kickstart her and Anthony's relationship, she hoped that the move to

Harvard would kick-start her academic life, too. She pushed to the back of her mind all the concerns about how she got the appointment in the first place. Instead she thought about how much she was going to get done in her new Harvard office and how she would set about finishing her next book on Darwin. The best news of all was that her new chair told her she wouldn't be expected to teach in the fall, which meant she had a whole semester to devote to her writing.

In short, and in spite of the rush of activity, Clara felt decidedly happy. She made time for Kay each day, and her friend was having a good week, too. Seeing Kay in less pain and with her eyes sparkling lifted Clara's spirits even further. They discussed the Shelley documents now and again and even penned a letter to Maranto's publicist. They both new it was another long shot, but Clara didn't let this dampen her mood.

There was one thing, though, that niggled at the back of Clara's mind: Maxie. The sisters hadn't spoken since their row. Not one phone call or e-mail or text message. At first, Clara was resolute. She would not contact Maxie until her sister found it in herself to apologize. But as the week wore on and Clara heard nothing from Maxie, her resolve began to dwindle and worry slowly replaced her annoyance. In the past when she and Maxie argued, even if there were no apologies and no real makeup moments, they always found a way back to each other soon enough.

After a week hearing nothing, Clara decided it was time to make a call. She wouldn't be friendly, she definitely wouldn't offer any apologies of her own, but she would just check in and make sure Maxie was okay. She dialed Maxie's cell but the phone didn't even ring. It went straight to the mailbox, which, as usual, was full. Clara tried again a few hours later and the same thing happened. She kept calling every hour or so into the evening, with the same result every time. She shot off an e-mail and some texts, too, but they prompted no reply either.

As the summer night turned to darkness outside, Clara's concern was beginning to mount. Her mind kept spinning back to Maxie's disheveled apartment and the beautiful yet equally disheveled guy she was dating. She couldn't help but think the worst—Maxie passed out amid her empty pizza boxes while the boyfriend disappeared to peddle drugs to some other beautiful but lost woman. Of course, Clara never had any reason to believe that Maxie was into drugs. She'd never even entertained the idea before. She also knew she was jumping to conclusions just because her sister liked to live in a pit and the guy she was dating had a few holes in his shirt. But drugs might explain a lot about Maxie, now that she thought about it. Her inconsistency, her forgetfulness, her flightiness, perhaps they all added up to some kind of addiction—and Maxie was definitely an addictive type. Look at the way she could never quit smoking.

And then there was Maxie's constant lack of money. Even after their mother died and Maxie received the same modest but decent inheritance check that Clara received, Maxie still seemed to be constantly broke. At the time Clara just assumed her sister was blowing the money on nights out, new leather purses, a river of new shoes and designer jeans, and no doubt her cell phone bills were hefty each month. But it would take quite a few pairs of shoes and nights out to run out of their mother's money entirely. Drugs, on the other hand . . . drugs could drain the same money fast.

Clara's mind spun onward and soon she was wondering whether their row had pushed Maxie over the edge. Perhaps her sister took a large hit of something in order to forget the fight and everything Clara had said to her. Clara swallowed hard as the image of a passed-out Maxie returned like a tidal wave into her mind: the pizza boxes, Maxie's hair stuck to her face, vomit by her side, a crumpled and fragile heap in the middle of a shabby apartment.

What if she was . . . ?

Clara didn't allow herself to finish the next question. Instead, she scooped up her purse and keys and headed straight for the door.

There was no answer at Maxie's apartment. Clara pressed the buzzer a number of times, only to hear silence through the intercom. Finally, a neighbor buzzed her into the building, but banging hard on Maxie's door yielded the same result: silence. Clara hung around in the stairwell for a little while. A group of twentysomethings in uniforms of skinny jeans, Ray-Bans, and tight plaid shirts came bustling out of the neighboring apartment. She asked them if they'd seen Maxie.

"Nope," was the single reply she received from a girl with stringy blond hair.

The rest filed past, saying nothing. She listened to their footfalls on the stairs and the thud of the front door closing behind them and then Clara checked her watch. It was just past ten. She should head over to the restaurant where Maxie worked. Clara had considered going there first, but she was sure that Wednesday—which it was today—wasn't Maxie's usual work night. But shifts might have been switched. It was worth trying.

The restaurant was a few blocks from Maxie's apartment. Clara hurried the whole way, and with every step she tried to quell the panic that was beginning to bubble in her chest. She peered in the restaurant's large glass windows when she arrived and did not see her sister among the night's waitstaff. But the place was crowded and Maxie could be anywhere, perhaps out back smoking a cigarette.

Clara wove her way through tables and chattering diners, and eventually through the crowd at the bar. She spotted Jack the bartender, who was also Maxie's friend and someone Clara had met a couple of times, too. He was busy shaking up cosmopolitans and didn't spot Clara. The other bartender, whom Clara didn't recognize, noticed her first.

"What can I get you, Red?" he asked, looking at Clara's hair more than her face.

"Jack," she replied, pointing toward the other end of the bar.

The bartender rolled his eyes. "Story of my life." He chuckled. "All the beautiful ones want Jack." He headed down the bar, and when he reached Jack he nudged him and jerked his thumb in Clara's direction.

"Maxie's sister," Jack said when he reached her. "Claire, right?"

"Clara," she corrected. "Good to see you again, Jack."

People were crowding in behind her, trying to get Jack's attention. Clara knew she had to get straight to the point.

"Have you seen, Maxie? Is she working tonight?"

Jack jerked his head back, clearly surprised. "No . . ." he said, shaking his head. "She's out of town. Didn't she tell you?"

Now it was Clara's turn to look shocked. "Out of town? Where? For how long?"

Jack shrugged. "She didn't say."

Clara's mind was reeling. Maxie just didn't go out of town. She never had the money, for one. And even if she did, she would always tell Clara where she was going, and how many bathing suits she was packing, and how many men she intended to seduce.

"Did she go with Matt?"

Jack began to shrug and then a thought clearly occurred to him. "You mean that creep she's dating?"

Something clutched at Clara's heart. "He's a creep? What do you mean, he's a creep?"

"He's just one of those too-cool-for-school jerks, that's all," Jack responded with a sniff.

The clutching feeling eased a little as Clara remembered that Jack once had a crush on Maxie. Perhaps it was just his jealousy talking.

"But you don't know whether she's gone away with him? Matt?"

Jack shook his head. "Nope. Sorry."

Someone farther along the bar was calling his name, and after giving Clara a two-fingered salute, Jack moved off to serve the customer and didn't look back.

Clara was left standing amid the jostling crowd.

"Maxie," she growled under her breath, as she turned to leave.

She hated that her sister had put her through a whole roller coaster of emotions once again. But when she got outside and stared down at her cell phone, which still showed no new messages, panic continued to tug at her. Maxie probably wasn't in some drug-induced coma, which was good news. But she'd gone away and Clara had no idea where, or when, or for how long.

As she moved off down Second Avenue, her thoughts shifted to the wedding. Surely Maxie would return from wherever it was she'd gone in time for the wedding. It wouldn't be until the end of the summer, after all. But the bigger questions were whether they would be talking by then, and would she ask Maxie to be her bridesmaid—and would Maxie accept if she did. Regardless of everything that had happened between them, Clara wanted her sister at the wedding—her sister who would no doubt upstage her in some tiny, slinky dress, and who'd get astoundingly drunk at the reception and then sleep with some school friend of Anthony's at the end of the night. Maxie would be outrageous and embarrassing and she would make the wedding a day everyone would remember.

And in spite of this, and because of this, Clara knew she could not get married without Maxie being there.

Fourteen

Clara hadn't taken the car out of the parking garage in months. It was absurd that she and Anthony even kept a car in the city, considering how infrequently they used it. Nonetheless, today she was happy that she paid the excessive parking fees and had the car at her disposal. It was the only way the trip she'd planned was possible.

Kay had done amazingly well over the last week: no pain, lots of sleep, and even the gray pallor on her cheeks was replaced with a soft hint of pink. Seeing the improvement in her friend made Clara believe a trip out was feasible. Kay had been shut up in her apartment for a long time now, and it seemed like a change of scene might buoy her spirits—and her health—even more. Clara had thought of New York's central library and the manuscript room that housed a number of Mary Shelley's writings. It would offer the perfect venue for a trip out. In the library, Kay would be protected from the bustle of the city, and seeing the manuscripts might ease some of the disappointment of not finding the lost Shelley papers. Kay had gone to the library numerous times during her career, but Clara was certain that she'd relish the chance to see the precious manuscripts again.

There was one flaw in her plan, though. Clara wasn't sure she could manage taking Kay on her own. Getting the frail woman down the stairs of the apartment building would be the first of many tasks that Clara couldn't do unassisted. Anthony was back at his lab now that he was fully recovered, and of course he was too busy to help. She'd still not heard from Maxie, who was off on her trip to who knew where. That left Daniel.

It turned out asking him wasn't as bad as she'd anticipated. She'd caught him coming into Kay's apartment just yesterday, and as her plan tumbled out, she noticed that she no longer felt awkward in his presence. It seemed her crush—or whatever it was—had abated. Around him she now felt surprisingly normal. Relaxed, almost.

"Of course," Daniel responded when she finished explaining. "When do you want to go?"

"Tomorrow. I figure we need to do this while Kay's doing well."

Daniel nodded and then the two of them talked logistics and times. When they said their good-byes and Clara headed out the door, she smiled and twisted the engagement ring on her finger. The prospect of the wedding, she realized, had brought her peace in more ways than she could have imagined. Now it seemed that Daniel could be a friend instead of the subject of her lonely and desperate fantasies.

The next morning, Clara pulled up in front of Kay's apartment building in her car. A wheelchair sat on the top step outside the building. Daniel must have brought it down a few minutes before. Clara hopped out of the car and went to retrieve it, and as she did so she pushed Kay's buzzer—a signal that she'd arrived and Daniel should now come down with Kay. Clara set about carrying the wheelchair down the steps, folding it up, and then putting it in the trunk of her car.

A few minutes later, Daniel appeared at the front door with Kay in his arms. Both of them were laughing.

"Hey, you guys," Clara said, bounding up the stairs to meet them. "What's so funny?"

Kay's eyes were glimmering. "I'm laughing at all the grunts and groans poor Daniel was making as he carried me down here."

Daniel laughed again, his dark eyes glimmering, too. "In fairy tales, carrying the damsel in distress down from the tower always sounded so easy."

As Daniel proceeded to carry Kay down the last few steps toward the car, Clara noticed the sheen of sweat on his brow and the twitch of his biceps under Kay's weight and from the strain of carrying her in a way that didn't hurt her frail body. Something kicked inside Clara. It was desire trying to take root again. She immediately pulled her gaze away. She must smother these sparks before they ignited once again. She was going to be married by the end of the summer, she reminded herself, and Daniel was her friend—just a friend.

In the car, Kay chattered excitedly. Daniel sat in the back, staring out of the window, with his long body folded into the seat behind Clara. Only when Clara looked in the rearview mirror and caught a glimpse of him was she reminded of his presence. When they finally drew up in front of the library, she was certain she'd extinguished the sparks she felt earlier. The guy in the back of her car was just another person—a friend, hopefully, but nothing more.

The curator in the manuscript room awaited them. Knowing that Kay would tire quickly and that their time would be limited, Clara had called ahead and arranged for a number of manuscripts to be out when they arrived. The curator had done a great job. She'd found every manuscript Clara requested and laid them all out on a long reading table where Kay, in her wheelchair, could look at them easily. The curator had even set out a small box that contained the same lock of Mary Shelley's hair that Anthony's lab used for the genetic test— Clara's test. A strange giddy feeling rippled through Clara when she spotted the box. Anthony's precise tests and instruments confirmed that she and Mary Shelley shared DNA, yet it was still so hard to believe.

For the next hour, Kay perused everything on the table. Clara did, too, and she was surprised to see that Daniel was captivated by

Shelley's handwriting as well. Occasionally one of the three would whisper a comment or point to a passage, but for the most part they remained silent in their reading and their thoughts.

"Thank you, Clara," Kay said eventually. Her voice sounded choked and her blue eyes glistened with tears. "Thank you for bringing me here."

Clara studied her friend's face. She couldn't quite read her expression. There was great happiness in Kay's eyes, but also sadness, and where one emotion started and the other ended, Clara couldn't tell. In the end, she simply reached over and took Kay's small, fragile hand.

"It's my pleasure; you know that," she whispered.

Kay's gaze then moved over to Daniel, and Clara's eyes followed. Daniel leaned deep into the table with his face only a few inches from the paper he was studying. Clara noticed how his wavy hair, which fell onto his forehead while he read, was as multifaceted as his eyes. Brown and gold streaks tangled together and were punctuated here and there by a few strands of gray. Daniel was oblivious to the fact that he was being watched. A fleeting pulse of desire kicked once again and Clara almost groaned aloud in frustration. She hated the way her body and her emotions betrayed her like this. It seemed like just when she had everything in check, she would take one look at Daniel and something would unfasten inside her; something would break loose and try to whip up a storm.

Luckily, Kay's voice broke into her thoughts.

"Thank you, too, Daniel," Kay said when he looked up. "I can't thank you both enough for arranging this."

Daniel winked. "Not a problem."

After a beat of silence, Kay let out a laugh and said, "I know how I can thank you." Her gaze flicked from Daniel to Clara. "I'll buy you both a hot dog."

Clara's eyebrows arched and then she laughed. "What?"

"If you drive me to Coney Island, I'll buy you two a hot dog . . . with all the trimmings." She then explained, "I've always loved Coney Island. When I was young, my father—he was a professor, too," she said as an aside. "He worked for a year at Columbia University. My mother and I came along with him. It was the highlight of the year when my parents took me to Coney Island for the day. I rode every ride at the amusement park at least five times, until I was almost sick." Her eyes were dancing as she spoke. "All those Nathan's hot dogs didn't help. I ate two when we arrived and, as soon as I got over the queasiness, I ate two when we left."

Kay fell into silence when she was finished. Meanwhile, Clara looked over at Daniel and he nodded.

"Okay. Next stop, Coney Island," she said with a chuckle.

The drive out of Manhattan and through Brooklyn was long and hot. The traffic was heavy and the summer sun blazed through the windows. Even with the air-conditioning on, the car still managed to get sticky and uncomfortable. At first they talked as they rode, but then the stop-start driving and the heat made Kay tired, and by the time they finally reached Coney Island, she was sound asleep in the seat beside Clara.

Clara managed to find a parking spot not far from the Nathan's hot-dog booth. She figured that when Kay woke up at least they would be close by. So she got out, smoothed her crumpled sundress, and moved toward the front of the car. Once there, she leaned against the hood and looked out over the crowded beach and twinkling ocean. Daniel came around and joined her.

"Do you want a hot dog?" he offered.

She shook her head.

"A soda?"

She shook her head again. "I'll wait for Kay."

They remained silent for a few minutes, listening to the gulls squawking above and the shouts and excited laughs from children in the water. Music from the nearby amusement park floated on the ocean breeze toward them. It was an oddly perfect moment, Clara thought, as she felt her body beginning to cool off and relax after the heat and tension of the city driving. The salt air was fresh, the sky vast and iridescently blue, and the sound of the crashing waves reassuringly methodical.

"What you did for Kay today was amazing." Daniel's soft voice broke Clara's trance.

She turned to look in his direction. "I couldn't have done it without you."

He shook his head. "Lots of times I wanted to take Kay out. She's been cooped up in that apartment for too long. But I was never brave enough to do it. I was scared—scared that she'd get hurt or that it would just be too much for her. But with you . . ."—he flashed a small smile and for the first time Clara noticed a small scar above his top lip—"I knew it would be okay."

This confession surprised Clara. Daniel didn't seem as if he would be scared of anything. He always appeared so in the moment, so comfortable in his skin. She couldn't imagine him fretting or being scared of anything.

As if reading her mind, he explained, "When my wife first got sick, I pushed her too hard. I didn't want to believe she was ill, I suppose."

Clara's mouth dropped open. "Wife?"

Once again, Daniel read her mind. "She died," he said in a whisper. "Five years ago. It was cancer."

Clara let out a quiet puff of air. "I'm so sorry."

Daniel nodded and then looked out toward the ocean. His eyes twinkled with a glaze of tears. As Clara watched him, she realized suddenly that she had this man so wrong. She dismissed him at first as some sort of New Age hippie. She'd gotten angry at him for those unwelcome feelings and desires he'd provoked within her. She avoided him and then tried to convince herself they were friends. But all along, she never bothered to really know him. She overlooked that he was a human being with a past, and a life, and with happiness and dreams, sadness and despair, all of his own.

"It wasn't perfect." Daniel started talking again, but he continued to look out at the water. "Before she was sick, I mean. It's strange when someone dies; it's like the past gets retold. 'You were such a wonderful couple,' people said to me at her funeral." He shook his head. "But we weren't so wonderful."

"No?" Clara prompted.

"We were kids when we met, juniors at Stanford. For some reason we decided college was too dull for us. We bought an old car, packed our lives into the trunk, then left Palo Alto for Las Vegas to get married." He gave a small chuckle. "Our parents despaired."

Clara chuckled, too. "I bet. Ivy League to Vegas . . ."

"Then we grew up and things were tough. No college degrees, no real support from our families, and no real home anymore. We moved from city to city, taking bar jobs, waiting tables, things like that." Daniel frowned. "We held on to each other because that's all we had, and all we knew. But we fought a lot. It turned out that we were very different people; we wanted really different things out of life."

For a fleeting second, Clara thought of Anthony. She thought about how different they were, too: his ambition and her dreaminess; his drive and professionalism, her endless procrastination and her desire to chase Mary Shelley rather than do her own research. If one of them were to die, no doubt people would talk about them as a "wonderful couple," and whether that was a fair assessment was debatable.

"Then she got sick," Daniel went on. "And I was terrified. I was scared of losing the one person who, for all our differences, really knew me." He paused and sighed. "The treatments she underwent were experimental and aggressive. Her father was a physician, and even though they were estranged after our wedding, when he heard she was sick, he hooked her up with one of the top oncologists in the country." Daniel shook his head. "I could tell the treatments made her miserable, though, and, if possible, they made her even sicker. But I held my tongue. The treatments were what she wanted and I wasn't going to try to contradict her, not when she was so ill."

Clara's gaze flicked from Daniel back toward the car. Kay was still sleeping in the front seat, her face pale and her head slumped against the window.

"Is that why you're helping Kay with all these herbal remedies?" she asked. "Is that why you think she shouldn't get treatment?"

Daniel flinched a little. Clara didn't mean her words to be so accusing, although it appeared they came out that way.

"I don't think Kay shouldn't get treatment," he countered, his tone shocked and hurt. "I never said that."

"I just thought . . ." Clara tried to backpedal.

"Kay is a smart woman, Clara," he said, his eyes now blazing. "She's doing what she wants to do with her illness. I'm just here as a friend and someone who will help her when things get rough. I admire her bravery and I think the way she is confronting her own mortality is incredible." He softened his tone. "But I'm not here to push alternative remedies on her just because my wife took a more medical route, if that's what you're thinking."

"I wasn't thinking that." Clara blushed.

Daniel smiled. "Yes, you were." She was about to argue, but he held one of his large hands up to stop her. Then he paused before saying, "That day—the day when I said that something seemed to be weighing on you? I didn't mean to offend you. I'm sorry if I did."

Clara thought back to that day in Kay's apartment and how he lifted his hand toward her face, and how she fled from him like a deer skittering from a truck's headlights.

"I thought you were going to kiss me."

Clara had no idea why she blurted out this confession. But it was done; she'd said it, and now it was out there, bobbing between the two of them like a giant balloon. Daniel looked over at her. His expression was shocked but there was also a twinkle of something else in his eyes.

"And if I had?" His gaze leveled with hers, and once again, as she looked into his speckled eyes, she felt that kick, that loosening feeling inside her chest.

Heat flooded Clara's cheeks. "I . . . well . . ." she stammered. She then jerked her left hand into the air and flashed her engagement ring toward Daniel. "I'm engaged," she said, the words sticking awkwardly in her throat.

Daniel looked at the ring and then back out at the ocean. "Of course, yes." The light in his eyes went out in an instant.

The silence that followed was uncomfortable, and Clara kicked herself for blurting out those words. Their topic before was somber, but she liked being here, talking with Daniel. His soft voice, his tender thoughts, his sad memories were as melodic as the sound of the gulls above and the crashing waves nearby. It all felt so peaceful and now she'd ruined it.

"When are you getting married?" Daniel was the one to break the silence.

"Soon," Clara replied.

He was looking back in her direction and she saw something flicker across his face. It looked a lot like disappointment, and as this occurred to her, she had an almost irrepressible desire to lean toward him, cover his lips with her own, and kiss him slowly and deeply and without end.

But then she caught herself and pulled her gaze away. As she stared down at her sandaled feet, she said, "We're moving to Harvard in the fall and we plan to get married before the new semester starts."

"You are?"

Clara spun around and saw Kay looking at them through the windshield. She'd woken up and rolled down her window without either Clara or Daniel noticing. Clara immediately walked around to Kay's side of the car and crouched by the window.

"You're awake," Clara said. "Do you want that hot dog now?"

Kay shook her head. "First, tell me about this wedding. When did all this happen?"

Clara wanted to tell Kay about Anthony and his drunken declaration that he finally wanted to get married. She wanted to tell her about the new job and her upcoming trip to Harvard. She wanted to describe the dress she'd seen in a boutique on Greene Street just a few days ago—a dress she thought might be perfect for a summer wedding in Cambridge. But none of this she wanted to share while Daniel was just a few feet away.

So instead, she said, "I'll tell you all about it soon, but first we should get you some food."

Kay shook her head again. "You know, I think I might have to take a rain check on the hot dog. I'm feeling a little groggy." Her gaze traveled to Daniel. "Why don't you two go get yourselves something and I'll wait here?"

It was in this moment that Clara took her first good look at Kay's face and realized how the ominous gray pallor had returned to her cheeks.

"You're in a lot of pain, aren't you?"

"It's coming and going." Kay nodded. "I think if I don't rest, it might get worse."

Daniel moved around the car and stood next to Clara.

"We should take you home, Kay," he said.

"I . . ." Kay started to protest, but she was silenced by Clara and Daniel shaking their heads. "Okay, you're right," she conceded. "I probably need my bed."

The ride back to Manhattan was quick, although for Clara it felt impossibly long. In the seat beside her, Kay writhed and fidgeted and every now and then she sucked in a shaky breath or let out a small moan. It seemed like the pain was intensifying with every block they traveled. Kay took some pain medication when they left Coney Island, but it clearly wasn't strong enough.

As she negotiated the traffic back into the city, Clara gripped and released the steering wheel and chewed on her lower lip. She couldn't help thinking about what Daniel said earlier, about pushing his wife too hard when she got sick. Clara's dragging Kay across Manhattan and Brooklyn on a scorching summer day had set her on a downward spiral. And it was all Clara's fault for thinking of the plan in the first place. Kay suggested Coney Island, but Clara should have refused. It was clearly insane to drag someone with late-stage cancer across two boroughs in eighty-degree heat.

When they got back to the apartment, Daniel carried Kay upstairs and as he eased her into bed, she was nearly passed out with pain. Against her plump pillows, she looked minuscule. Clara wondered if it was really possible that her friend could actually diminish in the course of one day. Kay's pallor was more pronounced, nearly matching the snowy whiteness of her sheets.

Clara wanted to stay and help out, but her car was double-parked outside. Before she left, she leaned over and kissed Kay's dry fore-head. Like a mother with a child in pain, Clara hoped the touch of her lips might heal her friend.

Kay stirred and her eyes flicked open. She then fumbled for Clara's hand.

"Don't blame yourself, Clara," she whispered. "I know you will, but don't. Today was wonderful. Truly wonderful. The only thing you have done for me today is to make me happy, unquestionably happy."

Clara smiled and nodded, but as she turned to leave her eyes were full with tears. How could she not blame herself? If Kay was now going to get sicker and sicker, she could only blame herself.

As she began moving out of the room, Daniel was coming in. He'd gone to fetch Kay a glass of water. Clara blinked heavily to try to dis-guise her tears, but he clearly spotted them. He didn't say anything, though. Instead, he laid one of his large hands on her shoulder. It would have been an odd gesture from anyone else, but from Daniel it felt right. For a moment, Clara felt soothed.

But when she finally left Kay's bedroom, she overheard Kay saying to Daniel in a raspy whisper, "I think it's time to call the hospice nurse."

It was the final straw for Clara. She fled the building, just like she had from Daniel that day, but this time she was blinded by hot tears. When she got to her car she knew she should move straight off and get the car back to the garage, but she couldn't. She slumped onto the steering wheel and let out a series of loud sobs. Her whole body heaved with the effort and it seemed every ounce of air in her lungs was expelled with each cry.

It was the jangle of her cell phone that finally halted her tears. She pushed herself back from the steering wheel, pressed her palms against her wet cheeks, and then reached over to retrieve her phone from her purse.

MAXIE'S CELL, it read on the screen.

Clara let out a sharp laugh. It wasn't a laugh of surprise or relief. It was a laugh of bitterness. How ironic that Maxie chose this moment of all moments to finally return her calls.

She snapped open her phone and could already feel her sadness turning into anger. But before she could speak, Maxie's voice was singing out something in her ear.

"Have I got news for you!"

Clara was discombobulated by her sister's chirpiness and for a moment didn't speak.

"Did you hear me, C?" Maxie said with a laugh.

"Whatever it is," Clara growled finally, "now is not the time."

"But Clara—"

"I'm serious," Clara retorted. Her voice was still a little shaky with tears.

Maxie let out a sigh down the phone line. "C'mon, Clara, listen. I'm sorry I didn't call before now, but there's a reason, and, well, something exciting has happened. . . ."

Clara didn't listen to what came next. Instead she pulled the phone away from her ear, eyed it for a second, and then gently closed it and placed it back in her purse. She knew she was being harsh, but she really didn't have the strength to listen to another word from her sister. She didn't want to hear that Maxie had run off to Vegas and married her new guy. She had no interest in knowing about the great deal Maxie might have gotten on a pair of designer jeans. If her sister had landed a bit part in some underfunded independent movie, it could wait. Whatever it was, she didn't want to hear it. Not now.

Turning the keys in the ignition, she looked back up at Kay's building and tears brimmed in her eyes once again. But then she sucked in a deep breath.

"Stop," she scolded herself. "Pull yourself together. Kay needs you."

Fifteen

Clara didn't head straight to the parking garage as she'd planned to. Instead, she headed a few blocks west; then, as a thought occurred to her, she about-faced and drove back east in the direction of Anthony's lab. She wanted to be near him, she realized. With everything going on, Clara knew she needed grounding. She must see Anthony, hear his voice, watch the intensity of his blue eyes, and think again of their upcoming wedding. It would soothe her; she was sure of it. It would repress all those panicked feelings she could sense bubbling so close to the surface.

The hallways of Manhattan U's Biological Sciences Building were eerily quiet when Clara arrived. It was getting close to seven p.m. and most of the technicians and postdocs had cleared out for the day. Clara knew that Anthony would still be in his lab, however. He always claimed that his best work was done when the lab was deserted.

Sure enough, when she got to the fifth floor and peered through an internal window to his lab, there he was. He was standing at a bench, peering intently at an electronic scale in front of him. The metal tray on the scale contained a collection of small pink pills. After taking the reading on the scale, Anthony made a note in his lab book and then funneled the pills into a small bottle. Afterward he scribbled something on the bottle's label.

He repeated this routine a few more times, and Clara, who'd chosen to just stand and watch instead of bustling in and interrupting his flow, found herself relaxing. Just as she expected, the very sight of him grounded her and made the knot of panic in her chest loosen a little. Years ago, she used to come to his lab and watch him. Just like this, he'd be standing at a lab bench, his blue eyes fixed on his instruments, completely absorbed in his work. His remarkable concentration and focus enthralled her. He had an intensity but also an attentive grace that were captivating to watch.

When they first fell in love, he used to look at her with the same focus and fascination. She was his specimen on a microscope slide. He wanted to know every inch of her and understand every pulse of her body, every flush of her skin. She found it both flattering and also completely sexy. These days, though, his eyes were always too distracted. They rarely looked at her with such fascination anymore.

A ripple of sadness coasted down Clara's body as she watched Anthony some more. She yearned for his eyes on her now. She needed his gaze—that old fascinated and loving gaze of his. She wanted him to comfort her and to shut out all her worries and sadness about Kay. With his arms around her and his gaze upon her, she would feel safe and steady and moored again. All those ridiculous and unwanted thoughts about Daniel would be erased, too.

Clara found herself moving toward the door of the lab, but as she pushed down on the handle, she hesitated for a second. The ocean breeze had tangled her hair and chapped her lips. Her pale yellow sundress was creased from the time in the sweltering car. She was a mess and she suddenly felt a pang of unfamiliar nerves about being under Anthony's studious gaze.

She shook her head and told herself she was being ridiculous. Anthony would not care about how she looked. She was the woman he loved, the woman he wanted to marry. Clara then pushed the handle again and gently opened the door. Anthony didn't look up. He was still engrossed in his work and clearly didn't even hear the door opening.

Clara was about to open her mouth to speak, but was silenced by what Anthony did next. After jotting another note in his book, he looked at his watch. Then he reached toward the pills on the bench in front of him and popped two into his mouth.

It was when he picked up a nearby bottle of water to wash the pills down that he finally noticed Clara.

"Clara!" he exclaimed. As he said her name, he blinked and wiped his mouth with the back of his hand in an awkward and obviously flustered gesture.

"Hi," was her whispered reply.

"What are you doing here?"

Clara found herself gazing at the water in Anthony's hand and then the pills on the bench. Her eyebrows dipped into a confused frown.

"What are *you* doing?" she asked, ignoring Anthony's question. "Why are you taking those? What are they?"

The strangeness of what she'd just witnessed finally hit home, and as she started to move toward him, she began to wonder whether her eyes had deceived her. Perhaps he was taking an aspirin, not one of these pink pills. Maybe she was mistaken. But as she got close to Anthony, he shuffled the remaining tablets into a large plastic container and thrust on a lid with a decisive whack. His movements seemed guilty and anxious.

"What are they?" Clara repeated her last question.

His gaze soon met Clara's and he was silent for a few seconds. It was obvious he was figuring out his next move. He was deciding whether to confess or to lie, and it shocked Clara to see how clearly this dilemma was written across his face.

"It's SRT254," he said, finally opting for the truth.

Clara blinked. "Your drug? Why are you taking it?" Before he could answer, Clara blurted out, "Is it even safe?"

Anthony waved a hand. "Of course it's safe, Clara. I wouldn't put it into trials if I didn't think it was safe." As he spoke, Anthony began to smile. He was regaining his usual poise.

"But why? Why are you taking it?"

"Why not?" Anthony shot back.

"You're not ill. You don't have cancer."

As Clara said this, a seed of doubt entered her mind. Maybe he was ill. She thought back to his days of sickness last week and worry kicked in her gut.

"You worry so much, Clara." Anthony chuckled. "Of course I'm not sick. This . . ." he said, waving one of the pills, "this isn't just a drug for people who are sick."

"It's not?"

Clara was confused. Anthony had said himself this was SRT254, his beloved compound that in lab animals had inhibited the growth and spread of tumors. It was the drug he was getting so much kudos for and the reason people like Charlie Rose wanted to interview him. Anthony and his drug were waging the war against cancer, or so she always thought.

Anthony slid onto a nearby stool. "As all my research has shown, SRT254 can help prevent cancer. It can stop the tumors from form-ing. In laypeople-speak, it's anticarcinogenic."

Suddenly something clicked in Clara's brain. "So it can also be taken as a preventative?"

"Exactly!" Anthony clapped his hands. "She finally figures it out!" he added with a grin.

He meant it as a joke, but Clara couldn't help prickling at his words.

"But why didn't you tell me you were taking it?" she found herself snapping.

"Since when have I told you everything I do in the lab?" Anthony snapped back, the smile now gone from his face.

"But this isn't some new experiment or some new process. This is different. This is . . ." Clara trailed off for a second. She couldn't quite find the right words. "This just seems risky."

Anthony got up and moved around the lab bench so he was next to her. He then put an arm around her shoulder and pulled her toward him.

"I'm fine," he whispered. "I've been taking small doses of the drug for a few months and everything is fine. It's completely safe." He laughed, moved away from her, and threw out his arms. "Look at me. I'm a picture of health."

Clara did look at him, and he was right: He did appear the picture of health. Through his pressed blue shirt, his chest and torso were lean and toned. His face looked healthy, lithe, and handsome as ever. His hair was thick and glossy. Yet his eyes were different, she noticed. He always had an intense gaze, but a few times recently this intensity could almost be mistaken for anger. Today his eyes bore the same almost manic gleam they had when he told her he was moving to Harvard.

"I'll just pick up some papers from the office," he was saying as he jerked his thumb over his shoulder. "Then why don't we go grab something to eat?"

"Okay," Clara muttered while he retreated to his office at the far end of the lab.

She was still feeling discombobulated, though. Anthony was taking his own drug. It seemed so strange, so unexpected, and the fact that he'd never told her just made it all the stranger. She wondered if other people in his lab knew he was doing this, and if they did, were they doing the same? If the drug was safe, which it clearly was, and if it could help prevent cancer, Clara could understand why Anthony might want to take it, but she just couldn't understand his keeping all this from her.

Clara could hear Anthony in his office, rustling papers and banging filing cabinet drawers. Her eyes slipped back to the plastic container of pills. All of a sudden, she was thinking of Kay again. Could these . . . ? Immediately she shook her head, cutting off her question. But it was no use. She couldn't stop her mind from going there. She couldn't help thinking about the pills and whether they might help Kay. Maybe they could ease her pain and slow this terrible downward turn she'd taken today. Even if they could only help her for a while that would be something; it would give her more time. It would give them both more time.

After glancing in the direction of Anthony's office, Clara lunged forward and grabbed the plastic container. She struggled for a few seconds with the lid, but finally it popped off and she reached inside and grabbed a handful of pink pills. She heard the office door swishing open, so she hastily smacked the lid back on the container with one hand and poured the pills into her purse with the other. The pills would be scattered amid all the junk in her purse, but she could deal with that later.

Anthony was now back in the lab and moving toward her. It was only when she looked up at him that she realized her heart was pounding in her chest. She was crazy, utterly crazy. If Anthony ever found out, he would be disgusted and furious with her. To take something from his lab was bad enough, but to take a handful of his precious drug was beyond forgiveness.

Yet Clara had done it; she'd taken the pills, and there was no going back. The pills were in her purse and she knew that, whatever the consequences, she would take them to Kay and hope and pray they could do something for her friend.

"Shall we go?" Anthony said.

Clara simply nodded and then, pulling her purse tight under her arm, she followed Anthony out of the lab. As she walked, her heart continued to thud in her chest, but whereas she had felt guilty a few moments ago, now a new and unfamiliar exhilaration raced through her veins. She was going to help Kay, even if it meant risking so much to do so.

June 1814—St. Pancras, England

The summer sun was beginning to wane in the sky and the willow trees cast long shadows over the churchyard. Mary slowed her pace and allowed Shelley and her stepsister to walk ahead. She did this now and again, let them move in front of her. It wasn't because she wanted Jane to have time alone with Shelley—of course not. Shelley was here to be with Mary and Mary to be with Shelley. But in the name of decency, they would always bring Jane along to these meetings. A young woman and a married man walking out together alone would cause too many tongues to wag.

Although Mary could rarely pull herself from the spell of Shelley's gaze and conversation, she loved to simply watch him, too, and therefore she would sometimes allow him to move away from her like this. Just for a short while. His frame was slight, his shoulders narrow, yet there was something forceful and energetic about the way he moved. She'd seen it that night in the dining room and she saw it again now. She loved how the late-afternoon sun was glinting off his wavy brown hair, and although she could not see his eyes, she knew their blue irises would be twinkling in the evening light.

Mary's own eyes then settled on his hands, which were waving and pointing as he spoke. She spotted a few ink stains on his fingers. She imagined him hunched over a small table, his eyes intense, and his hand etching words across a curling sheaf of paper. The image prompted her heart to thud in her chest and she found she was smiling yet again.

Mary was still smiling when, up ahead on the stony path, Shelley turned and looked back toward her. He was smiling, too, and as their eyes met, it felt like a bolt of lightning sparking through her body. There was something between them, so strong, so unfathomable, and so true. She could hardly find the words to express it. Every time they met, every moment like this one, left her breathless and floating, giddy and oddly exposed. Whatever it was, it felt magical. But there was a tang of danger, too—and that made it all the more exciting.

"Miss Godwin," Shelley finally shouted. "We are speaking of Napoleon once again. Please join us. I wish to hear more of your thoughts."

Mary nodded and then picked up her pace. Within a few seconds, she was beside him again, back under the warmth of his gaze and wonderfully close to his energy and intensity. Mary began to speak about the recent deposing of Napoleon. Yet even as her mouth moved and intelligent thoughts spilled forth about the disappointments and trials of a return to monarchist rule in France, only half her mind was really on the subject. The other half could think of nothing but the man beside her.

Mary had returned from Scotland in early March, and just like when she returned with Christy over a year before, her old home on Skinner Street seemed drab and impossibly humdrum. Mary had been in Broughty Ferry with the Baxters for almost two years, and her life there, between the Scottish mountains and the wild North Sea, had been exciting and fresh, inspiring and invigorating. It was full of friendship, freedom, and laughter. Her ailing arm healed, thanks to the brisk air and clear waters, and she blossomed into a firm-minded and radiant young woman. The world seem filled with endless possibilities when she boarded the ship back to London dressed in a bright plaid dress with her wild golden hair dancing in the sea breeze.

Yet the hardships of Skinner Street quickly made her vibrancy and rosy cheeks fade. William Godwin and her stepmother were struggling more than ever, and it soon dawned on Mary that the life she imagined for herself as an independent woman and a writer wasn't going to happen. Her father could not help support her beyond his home, and it would be another four years until she would receive money from Mary Wollstonecraft's estate. Moreover, she was lacking the usual feminine skills that may have gained her employment and given her an escape from Skinner Street. Mary's time in Scotland was spent fencing rather than learning needlepoint; reading literature and telling ghost stories rather than perfecting her French and Latin. London promised little except working in the family's struggling bookstore and missing her dear friend Isabel, whom she left behind in Scotland.

In May, however, everything changed with the arrival of Shelley. She had not seen him for a year and a half, since he spied her lurking in the shadows outside the dining room. But a few weeks ago he visited Skinner Street again, and it was like a bright, burning star bursting into Mary's dull life. This time she got to meet him properly, and because he was offering money to help her father, his visits to their home grew more frequent. He would come alone, and even though he would spend time with Godwin, whom he admired greatly, with every visit he would spend more and more time with Mary, too. They would sometimes read together in the schoolroom. Other times, they would share political views over the counter in the bookstore. Mary awaited his visits with the utmost impatience. Shelley's vibrant hues, his sparkle and magic, lit up the drab grays and somber tones of her London home, and she soon found the time between their meetings insufferable.

There was no sign of Shelley's young wife, Harriet, and although nothing was said between them, Mary suspected his marriage was in trouble. She was curious to know more, but too embarrassed and aware of her manners to actually do so. Furthermore, with his elegant words and captivating looks, his unhindered intensity and his praise for her parents, she was caught under his spell, and it was hard to think of him married to that silent and unexciting young woman whom she'd seen only once at the Skinner Street dining table.

Today, though, in the shade of the churchyard willows, Shelley's silence about his wife would finally be broken. Jane had discreetly wandered away after the discussion about France ended, leaving Mary and Shelley to sit alone together at Mary's mother's grave. The couple spoke in pleasantries for a short while, and Shelley once again praised Mary's parentage. But then, as the sun began to slide down behind the St. Pancras church, Shelley began to speak of himself.

"All my life my heart has been filled with warmth, yet cold, hard hearts have surrounded me," he told Mary.

He went on to describe his childhood, his schooldays and college days, when his passion and intensity, his search for love and understanding, were always met with "falsity." He talked of his father, who did not appreciate him and at times thought his son was insane.

"He wanted me taken to the madhouse," Shelley said with a tear glinting in his eye.

Mary shook her head now and again as Shelley spoke and made soft tutting noises with her tongue. When he talked of his father and his threats of the insane asylum, tears sprang to her eyes. She searched his elegant, interesting, and boyish face as he spoke. She tried, but failed, to imagine anyone wanting to be wicked and cold to such a man.

When Shelley was finished talking, Mary cleared her throat and finally asked what had been on the tip of her tongue for so long.

"And what of your wife? She has a good and warm heart, I trust?"

He said nothing for a moment. He simply stared deep into her eyes.

"She does not love me," he said finally, with a sigh and a shake of his head.

Mary shook her head, too. "That cannot be so . . ." she began.

"She loves another."

Mary gasped. "No."

"It is true."

"Harriet is with child again, and I fear this time it is not mine."

Mary gasped again but was at a loss for what to say next. Instead she reached out and touched one of Shelley's hands that rested on his knee. As their fingers made contact for the first time, Shelley flinched with clear surprise. But then, after the briefest of pauses, he turned his hand over and clenched her small fingers in his. Both of them looked down at their entwined hands, and for a few moments they said nothing. The pulsing warmth around their joined skin, the electricity jolting up and down Mary's arm, said everything.

"And I love another, too." Shelley's words broke their silence.

Mary looked back up at Shelley. His eyes were glassy with tears and his gaze was bearing down into hers once more.

"But," he went on, his voice thick and faltering, "I fear she cannot be mine. An unloving wife, a false marriage on my part, stands between us."

Mary felt her body beginning to tremble. The breeze in the churchyard had turned a little cooler now that the sun had set. But it was not the breeze that was causing her to shiver. It was Shelley's words. He was talking about her—his love for her, the love between them. He seemed unable to say it outright, but she knew it anyway.

Before Shelley could utter another word, Mary leaned forward and placed her lips over his. Her heart pounded in her chest. She was taken aback by her own boldness. But never in her young life had she felt so alive, so pure and so right. This moment, she realized, was all she'd been waiting for from the moment she first set eyes on this man. He'd captured her heart in a way that only the finest and greatest poets could ever describe. And now, with Shelley returning her kiss with great ardor and appreciation and longing, she felt utter and complete joy.

"Convention cannot stand in our way," Mary whispered, when she finally pulled back. "Convention is but vulgar superstition. This love is too great, too powerful and true." She paused for a second, took a breath, and said, "I love you."

Shelley's eyes danced and twinkled in the last embers of the summer sunset.

"At last. Great love has been delivered to me."

With that, he took Mary in his arms. Their lips pressed together once again. Before long they tumbled onto the grass, and as the moon emerged from behind a cloud in the indigo sky, the two lovers entwined their arms, their bodies, their legs, and their hearts right there under the willow tree and in the ghostly presence of Mary Wollstonecraft's grave.

Sixteen

Overnight Kay's bedroom was completely transformed. By the time Clara got to the apartment at eleven the next morning, the hospice nurse had arrived with a team of helpers. A new hospital bed, a bedside commode, and an array of unmarked bags, equipment, and stacks of towels and sheets now filled the bedroom. Kay's old bed and dresser had been moved into the living room and hallway to make way for all the paraphernalia.

Yet, in spite of the changes, in spite of the medical clutter that signaled so graphically Kay's deterioration, the bedroom felt fresh and serene. The windows were open, letting in a light summer breeze. Around the room were vases upon vases of daisies, and although the apartment was crawling with busy people, the whole place seemed calm. Someone had turned on a radio and classical music burbled throughout the rooms, and the smell of freshly cooked pancakes wafted out from the tiny kitchen.

Kay was asleep in the new bed when Clara arrived. She looked peaceful in her sleep, yet Clara could see the pain and her recent decline etched on her face. Clara sat in a chair beside the bed and watched her friend for a few minutes. She laid her hand over Kay's, too, and its frailness prompted tears to prick at Clara's eyes. She sucked in a breath, though, determined not to cry. *This is a time for action*, she told herself, *not tears*. When Kay woke, she would tell her about the pills; she would describe how they might offer hope, time, possibility.

"Pancakes?"

The whispered voice came from behind her. Clara swiveled around in her seat and saw Daniel in the doorway. He was holding a spatula in one hand. She didn't see him on her way in earlier, but since she'd stepped into the apartment, she'd known he was here. The smell of pancakes, the daisies in their vases, the music playing—she was sure they were all Daniel's doing. As she looked at him now, she realized how he embodied calmness and tranquillity. There was a looseness about him, a composure that was almost intoxicating—especially when everything else seemed so uncertain, fragile, and grave.

"You want some pancakes?" he whispered again.

Clara blushed a little, realizing she was staring rather than replying.

"No, thanks," she whispered back, and, at the same time, she got up and walked toward him. "I just had breakfast," she lied.

When she got close to Daniel, she noticed a streak of flour across his cheek. She was caught by an urge to dab it away with her fingertips. But then she scolded herself for thinking of such a thing.

Daniel must have seen the annoyance flicker across her face and immediately asked, "Are you okay?"

"Of course, yes," she blurted out a little too forcefully. She noticed the shadows hanging under his dark eyes. "Did you get any sleep?" she demanded. Once again it came out with more vigor than she meant.

"A little," he responded. He then shook his head. "Okay, none."

Clara frowned and searched his tired face again. "You must sleep, Daniel," she whispered, then asked, "So it was a rough night, then?"

Daniel nodded.

"You should have called me," Clara said.

With a small smile, Daniel replied, "One of us needed to sleep." He added, "The nurse showed up at dawn and brought all this." He waved around the room. "And things got a lot better."

Both Daniel and Clara looked over at Kay for a few seconds.

"She looks so peaceful," Clara said, more to herself than to Daniel.

"The morphine really helped," Daniel responded. "She tried to do without it, but then the pain got to be too much."

The thought of Kay in so much pain made tears sting Clara's eyes once more. "But how . . . how," she began, trying to hold her voice steady, "how did it happen so fast? This time yesterday, she was doing so well."

Daniel didn't reply at first. He simply reached up and laid a hand on Clara's shoulder. It was the same thing he did last night, a gesture that seemed so formal, yet with Daniel's warm hands, it felt intimate and comforting. His touch was so full of understanding and sympathy, it made a sob rise up in Clara's throat. She managed to hold it back, though.

"It was the same with Dana, my wife," he clarified. "Some days she seemed so full of life, so young and vibrant. You would never have guessed she was sick. Except for how much weight she lost. Oh, and her hair, too. Her hair was gone."

Clara turned to look at Daniel as he continued to talk.

"But she had life in her eyes, and strength." He shook his head. "But then the very next day, she couldn't even get out of bed. Sometimes she could barely open her eyes."

Clara paused for a moment and then asked, "She would rally sometimes, though? Your wife would get sick like this"—she waved toward Kay—"and then get better and then worse again? Is that how it was? Up and down?"

She'd never known anyone close to her to have cancer. Her mother's death was brutally quick. There were no dips and rebounds; it was just one speedy and unhindered slide downward. But from what

Daniel was saying it seemed that the tide could—might—turn for Kay. Maybe tomorrow she would be strong again.

"It was up and down for a good few months. But then it was down all the way at the end." Daniel grimaced a little, clearly recalling his wife's last days.

Clara reached up and laid her fingers on top of Daniel's hand that was still on her shoulder. They remained like that for a few quiet moments, the tips of their fingers touching.

Daniel finally broke the spell by giving her shoulder a squeeze and whispering, "Come on; I'm sure you could eat just one pancake. My pancakes are world renowned, you know."

Clara started to reply, "They are, are—" when a raspy noise came from the bed.

Daniel and Clara both turned to see Kay with her eyes open. She was coughing a little, but also trying to smile.

"Clara," she finally managed to say in a hoarse whisper.

Clara moved quickly toward the bed and resumed her seat. "Hey, you," she said in a soft tone. "I'm sorry; did we wake you?"

"No, no." She then searched Clara's face for a few seconds and brightness flickered across her tired eyes. "You are such a beauty, Clara," she said. "And I can see the Mary Shelley in you."

Clara laughed. "Really? I always tried to see it, but then I thought I was deluding myself."

"It's there." Kay nodded slowly. "You have the golden hair, the same shape eyes. . . ." She trailed off as she winced with pain.

Clara blurted out, "Should I get the nurse?" As she said this, she glanced toward the door and noticed that Daniel had disappeared again. Panic rose in her chest.

Then she felt Kay's cool fingers on hers.

"I'm okay, Clara. The pain comes and goes. I'll let you know if I need the nurse." Kay then said in a lucid, upbeat tone, as if the moment of pain hadn't just happened, "Did you ever hear back from the National Archives in England? Did you learn any more about the Dickson link between your families?"

Clara shook her head. "No, not a thing."

"Well, are you going to follow up?"

"Maybe," Clara muttered.

The truth was, she sent one letter to the archives office in London a while ago, before the genetic test results came through. But she heard nothing back and never got around to following up. It wasn't that Clara wasn't interested. Even though science told her she was related, she was still curious to know exactly how her bloodline snaked back to a shared one with Mary Shelley. Yet, over the summer, she was so preoccupied with Kay and Gerald's papers that the Dicksons were shelved in her mind. But not entirely forgotten.

"Ah, you poor dear, you haven't had the time," Kay said, reading her mind. She frowned a little but then her eyes flickered briefly. "You have a wedding to plan! Tell me, do you have a dress yet?"

"No." Clara laughed.

She'd done a lot of thinking about her upcoming wedding, but hadn't really managed anything concrete. She picked out some invitation stationery and flicked through some bridal magazines, but that was it.

Kay searched Clara's face for a few more seconds. It seemed she wanted to ask something, but then she said, "Well, I have my outfit for the big day all picked out."

Clara laughed at first, but then fell silent. She hadn't even really thought about the possibility—or not—of Kay being at her wedding. It was as if her mind purposely blanked out the whole question of whether Kay would still be alive.

"Oh, come on." Kay was now chuckling. "Don't look like that. I was joking."

Clara quickly tried to pull her glum face into a smile, but she knew she wasn't very successful. So she stopped fighting it. "I wish you could be there, Kay," she said in a soft, sad whisper.

Kay patted her hand. "I wish I could be, too." She paused and then added, "I'd love to see you happy, Clara, truly happy."

It was as if Kay were asking Clara if she would be happy on the big day. Clara opened her mouth to respond, but then Kay winced, closed her eyes, and shifted in pain. Clara fought the panic and the urge to call out for the nurse or Daniel. Instead she reached for her purse. Inside was the small bottle of Anthony's pills. Last night in the bathroom, she'd picked them out of her bag, where they lay scattered, and poured them into an old aspirin container.

Now she slipped her fingers around the plastic bottle and was about to pull it out when Kay let out a long, exhausted sigh. The pain had ebbed away and she lay against her pillows with her eyes shut for a few seconds. Clara looked on, studying her friend. Once again, she moved her hand to bring out the pills, but then she stopped. Doubt began to trickle and flow in her mind. Was this really the right thing to do? Anthony said these drugs were safe, and if he was taking them, and he was in such good health, then they must be. But Clara's mind reeled back. She thought of the hard look in his eyes. She remembered the night he got so sick not long ago. Maybe the drugs had nothing to do with these things. But what if they did?

She looked over at Kay again and heat began to flow to her cheeks. She was suddenly embarrassed by her deluded fantasy that she could fix Kay with these drugs. Even if they were safe, they could probably do little for her friend now. Clara realized that she was trying to hold on to Kay so desperately that she was acting like a fool.

"What is it?" Kay's quiet voice made Clara jump. "You look upset."

"It's nothing . . ." Clara began. But then she shook her head. She pulled the bottle from her bag and her shoulders slumped. "I had a plan to give you these," she confessed. "I thought they would help you."

Kay raised an eyebrow, but said nothing.

"Anthony has been working on a drug for a while now. SRT254 is the lab name, and it's had proven effects in diminishing cancer tumors."

"I know, I saw him on *Charlie Rose*," Kay whispered. "It sounds like he's doing some groundbreaking work."

Clara nodded and then blurted out, "I stole them. From Anthony's lab."

Kay gave a chuckle. "For me?"

Clara could feel the heat rising in her cheeks again as she gave a nod. "I know, I know. It was a foolish thing to do—"

"You are so kind, Clara," Kay interrupted. Her voice seemed thick and tired again. "You weren't foolish. You want to help me; I know that. You want to keep me alive. Nobody likes to let go of a friend, especially one they have just found."

"I . . ." Clara tried to interrupt, but Kay lifted her head from the pillow and turned to look at Clara.

"But here's the thing, Clara. I'm dying." Her blue eyes shone out with a sudden intensity. "But I am at peace with that. I'm ready—almost ready, anyway—to move on from this world. And you must find a way to make peace with that, too," she added.

"I know," Clara whispered while tears jabbed at her eyes. "But it's so hard. I just wish we had a little more time, a little more time to fight this thing." She waved toward Kay as if her cancer were lying like a hungry beast on top of her.

"Sometimes acceptance takes even more courage than fighting.

You are fighting, Clara. You are fighting in so many ways. I think you're fighting your own happiness. Is such a fight a good thing? It's time to move on, Clara."

Clara's brow furrowed. She didn't understand what Kay was getting at. But before she could ask, Kay was talking again. This time her voice was even more whispery.

"I know you wanted to find Mary Shelley's journals with me. I'm sorry I can't continue the journey with you. But remember, Clara, we always have her writings. And I will go into the next world with her words forever here." Kay slowly pressed her hand to her heart. "Her writing contains so much beauty but also so many lessons—lessons we can learn if only we open our eyes to them." She gave a tired cough. "Go back to *Frankenstein*, Clara. Go back to *Frankenstein*."

These last sentences exhausted her, and when she was finished, she closed her eyes and almost immediately her breathing became heavy. Kay was asleep once more. Clara looked on while her heart thudded in her chest. There was so much more she wanted to say to Kay. There was so much more she wanted Kay to ask her. She needed this old woman. Clara knew she was weak, but she wasn't ready to accept such a loss yet. She wanted the fight to continue. She wasn't ready to let go.

Clara stayed at Kay's apartment for a couple more hours, reluctantly eating a couple of Daniel's pancakes and helping the hospice nurse clean up. But it was soon clear that there was little else she could do. Kay continued to sleep, the nurse had everything under control, and even Daniel left to go home, have a shower, and take a much-needed nap. So, after making a sandwich and fresh pot of coffee for the nurse, Clara headed home herself.

As she entered her apartment, a stack of flattened boxes confronted her. They were delivered a few days ago, but she still hadn't put any of them together yet, let alone made any inroads into packing. The Harvard move still felt like a distant dream. One day soon she was going to realize she'd left everything to the last minute and she would have to pack in a haphazard and hurried manner, which she would no doubt hate. Still, even this thought hadn't prompted her into starting the arduous job yet.

She scooted into the living room and saw the barely touched bridal magazines lying on the coffee table. The wedding, too, felt like a far-off dream. Anthony told her a few nights ago that he'd booked the Harvard Faculty Club for the last Saturday in August. But this didn't make it any more real for Clara. She still couldn't bring herself to settle down and start making concrete plans.

Clara soon slumped onto the couch and picked up one of the magazines. In a distracted trance, she started to thumb her way through. Photographs on every page showed white satin, ivory silk, delicate ruffles, and intricate veils fluttering under brilliant blue skies. Women with pearly white teeth and glistening eyes stared out at Clara. She began to flip more quickly through the pages. Every photo, every ad, every saccharine headline made her feel irritated, uneasy, and mostly sad. Her friend was over in that apartment dying, and this magazine, with all its plastic smiles and white lace, just seemed so fake and meaningless and pointless.

She slapped the magazine shut and threw her head against the back of the couch. Tears gathered in the corners of her eyes and then trickled quietly down into her hair. It was so unfair. Last fall it was her mother. Now it was Kay. How was she supposed to face this? A sob rose from deep inside her, an untamed kind of sob. Then more followed. The tears began rolling down the sides of her face and matting her wet hair against the top of the couch.

After a few minutes, her body gave up. It was completely spent from crying. She dabbed at her eyes with the back of her hand and then stared up at the ceiling. As the fog of sadness and grief began to clear a little, her mind reeled back to what Kay had said earlier. *Go back to* Frankenstein, *Clara.* Clara rocked her head from side to side, still confused about what Kay was trying to say. She blinked a couple of times and said aloud, "Where is it?"

She lifted her head and in one fluid movement got to her feet. She hadn't seen her copy of *Frankenstein* in a while. It was the copy she'd found in her mother's house and the one that kick-started her passion for Mary Shelley. She'd tidied some of the books in her study just a few days ago but didn't remember seeing it there, and it definitely wasn't on her bedside table. Panic rose in her chest and Clara moved quickly from the living room to her study and then the bedroom. There were shelves bursting with books in every room, but she couldn't find *Frankenstein* on any of them. After checking the last and lowest shelf in the bedroom, she stood up and looked around. Perhaps she took the book with her someplace and accidentally left it behind. She shook her head. There was no way she would be so careless. Not with that particular book.

Clara started to search the closets and drawers throughout the apartment. Anthony never liked clutter, at least not where his eye could see it. He had a penchant for throwing anything that he deemed unsightly into any available storage spaces. This meant Anthony's and Clara's drawers and closets were always in a state of disarray and filled with hidden clutter. When it came time to move from one home to the next, the task of trying to sort through the higgledy-piggledy mess always fell to Clara—and it always annoyed her.

It annoyed her now, too, as she went from closet to drawer, drawer to closet, unearthing all kinds of junk on her way. She found her favorite woolen hat that she'd searched for all winter scrunched up at the bottom of the broom closet in the kitchen. In the living room, at the back of the cabinet under the television, she found a draft of a paper she had been working on in the fall. In the coat closet by the front door, high up on a shelf, she found a stack of old photographs.

When she found the photos, she stood very quietly and just looked down at them for a few moments. Not long after her mother died, Clara decided to work her way through some old family photo albums. She picked out a number of photographs and intended to compile them all into one book, a book that would help her remember her mother. But she'd chosen to do the task too soon, and every time she started work on the book her heart would ache and the tears would fall. The project was abandoned and somehow the stack of pictures ended up here, in the coat closet.

Clara was clean out of tears now. Instead she just stared down at the photo on the top of the pile. It was an old black-and-white picture of her mother. She was sitting on a plaid picnic blanket, smiling and squinting into the camera. Wisps of golden hair stuck out from under a flowered scarf tied under her chin. She looked happy, youthful, and slightly embarrassed. It was probably taken before Clara was even born. Here was a woman Clara never knew, a woman younger than Clara was now. She had love and sadness, joy and despair, motherhood and widowhood all awaiting her, but she knew none of that then. Not on that carefree sunny day.

Clara shuffled the picture to the back of the pile, and the next one that stared up at her was a photo of Clara and Maxie with their mother. Clara was probably eleven when the shot was taken and Maxie just seven. The three of them were standing in front of an overdecorated Christmas tree in a shopping mall and already the differences between the two sisters were apparent. Maxie's straight dark hair reflected the light of the camera flash, while Clara's wild red-gold curls obscured half of her face. Their poses spoke of their differences, too. Maxie's hands were on her hips and her hips were jutted forward dramatically and defiantly. Her grin was missing two front teeth; nonetheless it was wide, beautiful, and mischievous. Meanwhile, Clara was hovering close to her mother and smiling and squinting behind her curls. Her expression was uncannily similar to her mother's expression in the first photo.

Pulling the picture closer, Clara studied it more. She'd seen this photo a thousand times, but for the first time ever she noticed her mother's gaze wasn't straight at the camera. Instead, her eyes were cast slightly to the left, looking toward Clara. Even in this sideward glance, they seemed to speak of love and unmediated pride. Clara sucked in a breath as she noticed this, and everything that Maxie said the day of their row came tumbling back.

Their mother loved them equally, or so Clara always thought. She was too good, too honest and loving to put one daughter on a pedestal and let the other one live in her shadow. Helena Fitzgerald wasn't the kind of woman who judged her boisterous, beautiful, and tempestuous younger daughter so much that she drove her away.

Or was she?

Clara blinked hard and looked at her mother's gaze again. It was all there, written in the photograph. A preferential look caught and immortalized by the camera. There was no denying it, and as Clara realized this something snapped and twisted and unraveled inside her.

"Maxie," she said in a whisper.

She had judged her, too, hadn't she? Clara was just like her mother, always expecting Maxie to be someone different, wanting her to be the kind of person who was more worthy of her love. But Maxie was Maxie: hips forward, smile wide, almost too beautiful and larger-than-life to be real. It was this Maxie whom Clara—and her mother—should have loved. Not some idealized version of Maxie she could be if only she tried harder.

Clara patted the photographs back into a neat stack. It was time she called her sister. She felt bad for the way she'd cut Maxie off and even worse for not listening to the messages Maxie left last night and this morning after Clara hung up on her. It was time to start making things right between them. It was time to start making things better and more honest and healthy.

She was about to shut the closet door and head for the phone in the kitchen when Clara noticed something on the lowest shelf. Amid the snow boots and old sports bags, light was glinting off something small and shiny. She reached down, pushed away the strap of a bag, and soon found herself grasping a pill bottle. She pulled it into the light.

"Georgie," she said, her eyebrows raised.

It was Georgie's pill bottle, the same one she picked up that day in the park, but she had no idea what it was doing here. The last time she looked the small container was still in her purse. She never took it out, and even if it dropped out, how did it get into the closet? Clara spun around and saw her purse hanging on the hat stand where she always left it. She moved quickly across the hallway and retrieved the purse. She then turned it upside down and emptied its contents onto the small table by the door. Keys, her cell phone, tissues, loose change, and a couple of pens clattered onto the wood.

Georgie's pill bottle rolled out, too.

"What?" Clara gasped, as she picked up the second container.

She put the two bottles side by side. They were exactly the same. The labels were the same size and color. The typed font on the labels was identical. The only difference was the numbers. On Georgie's bottle, in Clara's right hand, it said, SUB.—2. On the other bottle, in her left, the label read, SUB.—1.

Clara began to feel the palms of her hands turning moist under the bottles' plastic. A stream of questions started colliding, swirling, and clattering into her mind. Then the image of Anthony disappearing into the homeless shelter slammed into this whirlpool of thoughts and her heart began to hammer behind her ribs.

"I must find Georgie," she said in an urgent whisper.

Without another thought, she shoved her keys, wallet, cell phone, and the two pill bottles into her purse. She turned and unlatched the door.

Seventeen

"I'm not asking you to tell me where he is. I don't need to know anything personal about him. I just want to know whether Georgie Worth
stayed here recently," Clara said with an edge of frustration creeping
into her voice.

The woman behind the glass simply sighed, shifted in the plastic
seat, and shook her head.

"It's not happening, lady," she responded. "Unless you are his case-
worker or a cop, I can't give you that information." She turned back to
the old PC on the right side of the cluttered counter. Her nails started
to *click-clack* across the plastic keys.

"Can I talk to the manager?" Clara persisted.

The woman didn't say anything, and so Clara leaned closer to the
holes in the glass.

"Can I talk to the manager? Or whoever it is who runs this
place?"

Without looking up, the woman replied, "He's not in today."

Clara sighed and slumped her forehead against the glass. She'd
been here ten minutes and still she was getting nowhere. She'd found
the homeless shelter again easily enough and thought finding Georgie
would be easy, too. But getting even the most basic information was
proving impossible.

The woman continued to type, unbothered by Clara's presence
on the other side of the glass. So after a few more seconds, Clara

pulled back, shook her head, and turned away from the counter. It was probably best just to move on to her next plan: She would head to Washington Square Park. Maybe she could find the man whom Georgie argued with that day. If she didn't find him, maybe some of the guys who played chess under the oak trees would know about Georgie and his whereabouts. Then she sighed and shook her head. Perhaps chasing Georgie around the city was just a ridiculous idea altogether. Heading straight over to Anthony's lab and asking him about the pill bottles made more sense. He was sure to have some logical explanation. Yet, she felt reticent about doing this, too, and she couldn't put her finger on why.

Clara was about to move toward the front door when the sight of an old woman sitting on the bench opposite stopped her in her tracks. The woman wasn't there when Clara arrived. The shelter's lobby was empty, in fact. And while Clara was talking and pleading with the receptionist, she didn't hear anyone come in. Yet here she was: an old woman in a straw sun hat that had clearly seen better days, a thick pair of spectacles held together with Band-Aids, and a turquoise sundress with spaghetti straps that looked like it belonged on a fifteen-year-old, not on this shrunken, bony woman who was clearly into her seventies, maybe even her eighties.

Clara realized she was staring and therefore walked quickly toward the door. The sunshine outside meant that Clara didn't keep up her fast pace, though. She'd thrown her sunglasses into her purse on the way in, and now she had to stand in the glaring sunshine on the steps to the shelter, scrabbling to find them again.

She was still groping in her bag when she felt the tap on her shoulder. She turned around to find the woman in the sun hat staring up at her through her thick, smudged spectacles.

"I saw Georgie this morning," the woman said in a raspy voice.

"You did?" Clara's tone was urgent, excited.

The woman nodded. Her face was lined with deep wrinkles, and her hair, which poked out from under the sun hat, was white, thin, and straggling over her shoulders.

"Was he here?" Clara pressed.

"No, no. I saw him in the park." She then leaned closer to Clara and said in a whisper, "He was very upset."

Clara's eyebrows arched. "Upset?"

The woman nodded, her sun hat bobbing up and down in front of her small face. "And angry, very, very angry. He was pacing and yelling, pulling at his hair. He even punched a tree and made his hand bleed, real bad. He kept shouting that he had to find the professor."

In her chest, Clara's heart leaped and thudded hard. "The professor?"

The woman nodded.

"Which professor? Did he say the professor's name?" The questions came out like gunfire.

"He's probably talking about the professor who comes here," the woman replied, jerking a crooked thumb over her shoulder.

"Do you know his name?" Clara's heart was beginning to hammer.

"Everyone just calls him the professor," the woman said with a shrug. But then one of her bony fingers shot in the air. "Wait. Today Georgie called him . . . now, what did he call him?"

Clara sucked in a breath and then, with trepidation, asked, "Greene? Did he call him Professor Greene?"

The woman gave an emphatic shake of her head. "No, no, not Greene."

Clara felt a lightness wash over her until, just a moment later, the woman spoke again.

"No, no, Georgie called him something else. A funny name . . . let me see. . . ." She scratched her chin, which was sharp like a pixie's.

"Acton! That was it." The woman flashed a smile, revealing a set of teeth that were surprisingly white and straight. But then the smile disappeared and she gave a frustrated frown. "No, no, that isn't it . . . It was Ack-something. Ack . . . Ack . . . Ackson. Maybe that was it."

Clara looked on. Her heart was pounding at her ribs again. Finally, she found her voice and asked in a strained whisper, "Ackerman? Was it Ackerman?"

The woman's head jerked back and she stared through her thick lenses up at Clara. "That's it. Yes!"

It felt as if someone had taken a running kick at Clara's gut. She exhaled a deep puff of air and then shook her head. "Anthony?" She gasped.

The woman cocked her head. "Anthony? I'm not sure about that. . . ."

Clara waved a hand. "No, no, I was just . . ." She trailed off and shook her head again.

She wasn't going to stand here and explain to this woman that Anthony was her fiancé and that the last name Ackerman was his mother's maiden name, and that maybe . . . maybe "Professor Ackerman" was the name her fiancé was giving as his own.

"Are you all right, dear?" the old woman was now asking, as she reached out and laid a hand on Clara's arm.

Clara nodded. "Yes, yes, fine, fine."

She wasn't fine. She felt dizzy, nauseated, as if she were standing on the edge of a precipice with a vast canyon swirling and gusting beneath. Everything she knew about Anthony, her Anthony, seemed to be shaking, cracking, on the verge of falling apart. If it was Anthony who was the professor who came here and used his mother's name, why?

"I'd better go," she finally managed to say. "Thank you for your help."

The woman nodded. "You're welcome," she said, and just as Clara was about to step away, she added with a rolling chuckle, "Seems like a lot of people want to know about the professor these days."

Clara froze in her tracks. "Who else wants to know about him?"

The woman didn't answer. Instead, she started to rummage in the overstuffed straw bag that was hanging on her arm. She pulled out wads of Kleenex, pencils, a plastic flower, a bag of Cheetos, and set them on the low wall outside the shelter. She then continued to rifle through the large bag.

Clara looked on, her jaw pulsing with momentary impatience. "Who else—" she began to ask again.

But she was interrupted by the woman pulling something out of the bag and exclaiming, "Here it is."

A crumpled business card was thrust into Clara's hand. She turned it over and read the front. For the second time in less than five minutes, she felt winded, breathless.

PAUL MASSEY, the card read. JOURNALIST. Underneath, both his phone number and e-mail address were neatly printed.

"When did he give you this?" Clara asked, giving the card an urgent flick with her fingers.

"A couple of days ago." The woman spoke as she loaded her junk back into the bag. "A real nice man, so kind and friendly."

"Why was he looking for the professor? Did he say?"

The woman looked up from what she was doing. "He said something about the program. Georgie and the others are always talking about the program. But I don't know what it's all about. No one ever tells me anything," she added, pulling her face into a small grimace. "They think I'm too dumb to understand."

Clara studied the woman for a few moments. She wanted to fire at her all the questions now reeling through her mind. But it was clear just looking at the woman's old yet paradoxically childlike face that she was telling the truth: She knew very little.

In the end, Clara asked, "So why did he give you this? If you know nothing about this program, I mean?"

"He told me to call him if I saw the professor." The woman gave a chuckle. "Like I have a cell phone, or even a quarter to put in a pay phone."

This gave Clara an idea. She delved into her own purse and found a pen and her wallet. First, she scribbled her own number on Paul Massey's card. Then she opened her purse, scooped out all the quarters she could find, and plucked a twenty-dollar bill. She pressed all of this into the woman's hands.

"Please call me, too," she said, pointing at the card. "Call me if you see Georgie."

The woman looked a little confused but also delighted. She pocketed the money and then threw the card back into her bag. Clara wondered whether the woman would just take the money and run. But then she realized it didn't matter. Twenty bucks and some change seemed worth it for a shot. More than ever, she wanted to know where Georgie was.

After she thanked the woman again, Clara walked quickly eastward. Her heart still fluttered in an unsettled way behind her ribs. She was confused and worried, and a deep foreboding weighed heavy in the pit of her stomach. She'd seen Anthony with her own eyes disappearing into the shelter not so long ago. And now there were the pill bottles linking him to Georgie. But what "the program" was and whether the pill bottles had anything to do with it was uncertain.

But her mind couldn't focus on figuring all this out because her thoughts kept coming back to the woman's first words: Georgie was really, really angry and wanted to find the professor. Clara had seen the intensity of Georgie's rage that day in the park, and if that rage was turning against Anthony now, she couldn't imagine what might happen next.

Clara picked up her pace even more. It was time she found the professor, too.

Eighteen

By the time Clara got to Washington Square and just a few blocks from Anthony's lab, she'd calmed down a little. A thought occurred to her on the brisk walk over: Georgie might be looking for the professor, but he would be looking for a Professor Ackerman, not Professor Greene. Even if Georgie was after Anthony, he was going to have a hard time finding him.

She slowed her pace as she entered the park and, in light of her ebbing worry, she decided to take a small detour and loop around to the southwest corner. There she would ask the chess guys whether they knew Georgie and, if they did, whether they'd seen him recently. Maybe he would even be there. After all, it had only been that morning that the woman from the shelter saw him at the park.

It was just after five thirty now and Washington Square was bustling with people enjoying the balmy evening. Clara had to skirt her way around men in business suits, nannies with strollers, groups of young guys playing drums, and dogs bounding and yapping on their leashes. Amid the life and buzz of the park, Clara felt her mood lighten even more. There had to be a logical explanation for all of this. Perhaps everything Anthony was doing—the pill bottles, the homeless shelter, everything—perhaps it was all completely aboveboard.

Clara finally approached the chess tables, which were a hive of activity and chatter. She was about to press forward into the crowds to see if there was anyone she might talk to when her cell began to warble in her purse. She stopped and pulled out the phone, hoping it might be Anthony.

It was Maxie.

"At last you decide to pick up!" Maxie chirped as soon as Clara flipped open the phone and put it to her ear. "Why did you cut me off last night?"

"I'm sorry, Max, I—"

But Clara didn't get to finish. Maxie was talking. "Your phone went dead or something. I bet you forgot to charge it again."

Maxie only saw the good in Clara, never the bad. This realization hit Clara like a slap. For her, it was the opposite. If the phone went dead at Maxie's end, she would assume that her sister hung up on her. She would not make the assumption that something so innocent as an uncharged phone was the reason. Clara judged Maxie, just like her mother did.

"Anyway, did you get my messages?" Maxie's voice was breathless and excited.

"No, I didn't. . . ." Clara paused. "Things have been crazy, Max. But listen, where are you? I went to the restaurant and they said you—"

"I know, I know, I'm sorry," Maxie broke in again. "I'm sorry I just disappeared like that." Her voice sounded more serious now. "I just had to do this."

"Do what?"

"Come to LA."

"LA?" Clara blurted. "Why? How? Is it an audition? For a movie? What?"

Maxie gave a chuckle. "I wish." She sighed. "No. I came to find Jonathan Maranto."

Clara's mouth dropped open. She was speechless.

"Clara? Are you there? Did you hear me?"

Clara blinked a couple of times. Maxie's voice, the bright sunshine, the noise of the chess players, and the sound of a cheap plastic radio blasting out from a bench nearby made her feel suddenly giddy.

"Clar-ra?" Maxie singsonged down the phone line.

"Yes, yes, I'm here," Clara finally stammered. "What do you mean, you went to find Maranto?"

"Just what I said." Maxie laughed. "And you know what? I found him!"

"What?"

"Yup. I called you last night to say I had a meeting scheduled with him this morning."

Clara was silent again, as her mind tried to make sense of everything Clara was telling her. "So you met him? Today?" she finally managed in a tight whisper.

"Uh-huh. We drank cappuccinos together. Can you believe that?"

"I can't." Clara half laughed, half gasped. "But how? I mean, no one gets to talk with Maranto. No one. Did Jocelyn help you?"

Maxie gave a loud laugh. "Jocelyn turned out to be useless. I don't think she's even dating his son anymore."

"Then how—"

"Ellen Smythe," Maxie cut in.

"Ellen Smythe?" Clara responded, but as she said the name, she remembered "You mean, Ellen Smythe 'with a y'? The NPR woman? The one who interviewed us?"

Maxie laughed again. "The very same."

"But . . . how . . . when?" Clara was stammering and making no sense.

"Let's just say that I made a good impression on Ms. Smythe. She was more than happy to help me. I will tell you the full story when—"

Clara's mind was reeling and somersaulting. She couldn't concentrate on Maxie's words. "So what was he like? Maranto?" she exclaimed.

"Did you ask about the Shelley stuff? My God, Maxie, how did you do it? How did you afford to fly out there in the first place?" The questions were tumbling out in an illogical torrent.

Maxie was laughing again. "Whoa, hold up there, sister! There's plenty of time for me to answer all your questions. But first off, you have to get your tiny ass on a plane to LA. Pronto!"

"What?" Clara barked out, causing a few people nearby to turn and stare.

"Yes, he has the documents in question, and yes, he will let you see them."

"Are you serious?" Clara was practically shouting now, and the people around her were frowning and shooting scathing looks in her direction. Clara simply ignored them. "This is incredible." She laughed.

"But you have to get here soon," Maxie warned. "He's only in town for the next week. Then he's off to Florence or Rome or someplace. Anyway, you have to get to LA soon."

The proposition that she fly to LA brought everything else flooding back. She couldn't go anywhere. Not now. No way. She had to find Georgie. She had to talk to Anthony. And then there was Kay, who was getting sicker by the minute. There was absolutely no way she could travel now. But if she didn't, Maranto might go back on his word.

"Clara?"

"I'm here, I'm here." Clara felt her pulse beginning to race again. "Maxie, I just don't know if I can leave right now."

"What?" Maxie shouted. "You have to, C. We have to do this now."

Clara thought for a moment and then said, "Listen, Max. I have to go. There's something I have to sort out before I can figure out LA."

"Okay," Maxie said, although her tone suggested she wasn't too sure.

"I can't believe you did this, Max," Clara then said. "I can't believe it. Thank you."

After their call ended, Clara decided to head over to Kay's. Georgie and Anthony would have to wait. She'd pretty much convinced herself that she was overreacting anyway and that Anthony probably wasn't in any imminent danger. Although she still wanted to get to the bottom of the pill bottles and the homeless shelter, she had to tell Kay about Maxie and Maranto. She couldn't wait. She was bursting with the news and had to share it straightaway.

Clara weaved her way back through the park. A short while ago her heart raced with anxiety and confusion; now it pounded with excitement as she considered the possibility of flying to Los Angeles soon, just for a few days, to see the documents. Kay would not be well enough to join her, but Clara could make copies and bring them back to New York. She imagined the two of them sitting on Kay's bed deciphering Shelley's words and piecing together the parts of her early life that, until now, were known only through secondhand sources or through Shelley's reminiscences in later life. Finally, they would know how Shelley really felt about her stepmother. They would learn for certain when she first spied Percy. Through Shelley's own words, they would see how she coped when her father disapproved of their union and what young Mary was thinking when she packed her bags and planned her escape to France.

Clara rounded the corner of Kay's street with a smile beginning to tweak the corners of her mouth. The evening sun warmed her face, and for the first time today her steps felt light and eager. The good feelings disappeared immediately, however, as she spotted up ahead, right outside Kay's building, a somber black truck. She squinted through the yellow light and saw two men, dressed in equally somber dark gray suits, at the back end of the truck. They were collapsing a gurney, on top of which was the unmistakable and lifeless mound of a body bag. A small crowd of onlookers was gathered on the sidewalk nearby.

Something twisted, tugged, and rocked deep inside Clara. It felt as if everything within her were imploding.

"Kay?" she whispered as she broke into a trot. "Please, not Kay, not now." She repeated these words over and over as she made her way down the block.

When she reached the truck, she saw what she prayed she would not see. She saw Daniel amid the huddle of people, his handsome face gray and sad and fraught.

"Daniel?" The word came out as both a desperate question and a sob.

He looked up and stepped out of the crowd toward Clara. Without a word, he took her in his arms and pressed her to his chest. Clara's legs buckled beneath her, but Daniel held her up.

"No, no, no," she repeated into the clammy fabric of his T-shirt. "How? No . . . this can't be happening."

Daniel lifted a hand and stroked Clara's hair. She let out a low guttural sound and her whole body began to shake. After a few moments, she found the strength to pull away and look up at Daniel. The questions began to tumble out of her.

"How? When? She wasn't that bad, was she? I thought she had more time. How can she be gone? Why didn't anyone call me?"

Daniel reached up and stroked her hair again. "Shhhh," he soothed. "Sshhh."

A clanking noise came from the truck and both Daniel and Clara turned to look. The two men shut the back doors and were now heading toward the front. The hospice nurse, whom Clara hadn't seen before this moment, exchanged whispers and nods with the driver.

Then the suited men climbed into the cab and before long the black truck was disappearing into the distance.

Clara's head flopped back against Daniel's chest. She closed her eyes tight and tried to hold back the tears that were threatening to come. But the image of the disappearing truck would not go away, and then, unexpectedly, the image fused with a memory of the hearse at her own mother's funeral. There was no holding back after that. Clara's tears flowed in a torrent.

July 1814—Skinner Street, London

In the dim light of his study, William Godwin's face was a patch-work of shadows. His sparse hair was ruffled from where he'd clearly been raking it with fretting hands, and in spite of the bad light, Mary could see the twitching in his jaw that signaled his frustration and anger. Mary hated seeing her father this way; yet she loved Shelley, too. Since that day in the churchyard, since she and Shelley declared their love and devotion to each other, Mary felt as though her whole body, her whole spirit, her whole life, were filled with warmth and grace and fulfillment. Shelley's radiance had poured itself upon her and turned her once drab world into one of sparkling and dazzling colors. She could not lose such a love now that she'd found it, and she had to do everything in her power to keep, cherish, and follow it wherever it would take her.

At least, this was what she'd decided as she made her way to her father's study earlier. She knew what awaited her would not be ami-cable. Two days ago, Shelley and Godwin took a very long walk and Shelley told her father of his great affection for Mary and how the young couple intended to start a new life together in Europe. Shelley and Mary were hoping for Godwin's blessing. Instead, the older man was furious, and when he returned from the walk he told his daughter that her plans with Shelley were "utter insanity." He ordered Mary to her room, where she'd stayed for the last two days working on all the arguments and pleas she would make to her father.

The talk had finally arrived, and as soon as she entered the room and seated herself in the wingback chair opposite his large desk, Godwin told her in a flat, solemn tone, "Mr. Shelley is not welcome in this house again."

Her father's grim but cool voice unnerved Mary a little. She'd expected more fiery anger. Nonetheless, she jumped in with the words, "I love him, Father." Her chest was tight and her pulse raced as she said this, but she willed herself onward. If her father would only listen, then he might understand. "He loves me. . . ."

Godwin raised a finger and shook his head at her. "Shelley feels only the basest, shallowest kind of love if he pursues you in this way. If he truly loves you, my dear, he would leave you be. He would not bring such disgrace and ill repute on you and your family."

"No, no," Mary cried out while her cheeks flushed hot and pink. "He is a good man. His love is pure. I know it. I know in my heart that his love is noble and good and pure."

Godwin raised an eyebrow. "As his love for his young wife is noble and good and pure?"

Mary shook her own head furiously. Gold wisps of hair stuck to her hot cheeks. "His wife does not love him; she loves another. It is a wretched marriage and soon it will be over."

"And what of the child?" Godwin asked, cocking his head to one side. "You wish to take a father from his child?"

"I . . ." Mary tried to speak.

"Think of your own mother," Godwin said, his tone lower and more solemn than ever. "Before I met her, your mother was left by such an excitable young man. She was left with a young child, your sister Fanny—"

It was now Mary's turn to interrupt. "But it's not the same. Imlay was dishonorable. Shelley is different. He is . . ." Mary cast her eyes around the room. She found it hard to find the words to describe him. He was, she thought, beyond any words. "He is everything," she finally whispered, knowing it didn't make much sense, but it was all she could find to say.

Her father stared at her for a few seconds, while the lines in his forehead deepened. "If you choose to go with him," he said in a quiet voice, "I cannot stop you. I will leave it to you, and your good sense, to give up on this preposterous idea." He glared hard at his daughter. "If you decide to go, know that you are bringing ruin on your family."

"Shelley is still going to help you, Father," Mary said, her tone whispery and soothing.

Godwin glowered. "With only half of the money he promised, I will be ruined."

Mary swallowed hard. She knew her father wasn't happy that the money Shelley pledged to him was going to be cut in half. But she and Shelley had thought it would still be enough to help him. Her mind began to reel with questions. If they left for Europe, would her father indeed be ruined? Would his business be lost? Might he end up destitute and hauled off to debtors' prison? And what would become of her brother and sisters? For the first time since she and her lover talked of their elopement, doubt began to gnaw in the pit of Mary's stomach.

"But even if my ruin does not sway you," her father went on with a grimace etching deep lines across his forehead, "then think of the infamy and disgrace you will bring on yourself, our family, and, most of all, your mother's memory." As he said these last words, he turned slightly in his seat and flicked his eyes up at the portrait of his dead wife.

Mary tried not to follow Godwin's gaze at first. Even though she was desperate to leave her Skinner Street home, she was not desperate to leave this picture. It was, and always had been, her lifeline to her lost mother. It was one of the few things she yearned for during her days of freedom and happiness in Scotland, and no doubt she would yearn for it again when she left with Shelley for Europe.

Hard as she tried, though, Mary could not keep her gaze from turning to the portrait, and immediately she began to wonder what her mother would think about her elopement. Mary Wollstonecraft was a very liberal, strong, and open-minded woman. But, from everything Mary had heard, she was intensely loyal, too. She would not have left her family in financial ruin. She would not have intentionally brought ill repute on those she loved. She was too good a woman.

Hot tears sprang into Mary's eyes and her heart felt as if it were being tugged in two. Shelley was her great love, the love she'd waited for all her young life, and surely no love would ever surpass it. But then there was her father, and his finances; her mother and her good name. How could Mary leave behind such ruin and scandal?

Mary's gaze left the picture of Wollstonecraft and moved to her father again. His worry lines were deeper than ever. His jaw continued to twitch. And as she took in this sight, a sad and sickening weight thudded deep inside her. She wouldn't be able to follow her great love. She could not be the instigator of such hardship and infamy. She let out a small, almost inaudible sigh and let her chin drop downward.

Shelley, she mouthed silently, as one tear trickled slowly down her right cheek.

He could not be hers.

A few days later, Mary was slumped in a low chair in the corner of Skinner Street's schoolroom. Her stepsister was looking down at her.

"Mary, I beg you, let us leave the house now," Jane pleaded. "The day is beautiful and a walk is exactly what you need."

Jane's right hand was on her hip, the other pointed out of the small attic window at the blue sky beyond. Her dark eyes glimmered with both frustration and determination.

"Look at you," Jane went on, her tone sharp and reprimanding. "You have not left this room in days and days. You are deathly pale, your hair is bone dry, and your eyes are so swollen from the endless tears that you can barely see."

Not long ago, Jane's lack of tact would have provoked a fiery response from Mary. Not now, though. Today, the words of her stepsister were like a fly buzzing too close to her ear: annoying but innocuous.

"We could walk to St. Pancras," Jane persisted.

Mary knew she must respond; otherwise Jane would keep at this all afternoon. Buzz, buzz, buzz.

"I do not wish to go out, Jane," she said finally, sounding resolute but tired and defeated all at the same time. "Please, Jane, let me be." She sighed.

True to her melodramatic nature, Jane flicked her bouncing curls over her shoulders and cried out, "I despair of you, Mary. I despair!" She flounced across the room and took a seat at the small desk with her back to Mary.

Mary sighed again as she watched her stepsister. Later on, she would have to make peace. Jane could be an irritation much of the time, but she was a willing conspirator and a source of much-needed information about Shelley—and for that Mary must be both grateful and appeasing.

Since the day of the talk with her father, Mary had seen nothing of Shelley. Under her father's instruction, she wrote to Shelley and told him they could not be together; their plans to escape to Europe must be relinquished immediately. Hot tears fell onto the paper and smudged the ink.

However, it seemed that Shelley had not received the tearstained letter, or if he did he was choosing to ignore it, because every day he would smuggle a note, via Jane, to Mary. These notes would profess his undying affection and implore Mary to not give up on their love. On one occasion he even sent a gift: a copy of his own work, *Queen Mab*. The narrative poem had been written and published a year ago, and in its opening pages it bore a dedication to Harriet, his young wife. But in the copy he sent for Mary, he scribbled a note below this dedication that talked of an unloving woman leaving her man in his hour of need.

When the book first arrived, Mary simply sat with it in her lap, occasionally feeling its pages and turning it over in her hands. It felt as if a piece of Shelley were right there with her, and that made her heart ache all the more.

It was only yesterday morning, two days after the book arrived, that she finally managed to hold back her tears long enough to actually open it and read the words within. It wasn't the first time she'd read *Queen Mab*, of course. Nonetheless, she relished every word, every image, and every note that accompanied the text, as if it were her first time. Once again, as Shelley's words echoed through her mind, she felt as if he were there with her. She could hear his voice and imagine his lively eyes dancing to the beat of his own verse.

Late in the afternoon, she smoothed open the back cover and scribbled a note on one of the end pages. She wrote that Shelley's book was sacred to her and that she loved its author beyond all powers of expression. With tears welling once again in her eyes, she also wrote the words, *Although I may not be yours I can never be another's*. She then quoted lines from a poem by Lord Byron that she'd recently read:

The glance none saw beside
The smile none else might understand
The whispered thought of hearts allied
The pressure of the thrilling hand.

When she was finished, she blew on the wet ink. By marking the book with her own words, it was as if she'd sealed their love and made it permanent. On paper they were now eternal lovers and kindred spirits.

A day had passed since she wrote in her copy of *Queen Mab*, yet still the book was close beside her. And now, while Jane still sulked on the other side of the room, Mary contemplated picking up the beloved book once more. She reached out her hand to do so, but then faltered. Perhaps appeasing her stepsister should come first, she thought. After all, if there were more notes from Shelley to come, she would need Jane.

She opened her mouth to offer her apologies, but she was halted by a loud clattering sound coming from somewhere below in the house. The clattering was followed by some shouts and a rumble of feet. Both Mary and Jane looked up and exchanged confused glances. The footsteps got louder and louder, and it was clear they were nearing the attic and the schoolhouse where the two young women were sitting.

Mary started to get to her feet, anticipating a knock at the door. But before she even stood upright, the old wooden door to the room was flung open and in the opening stood Shelley. His hair was wild, his eyes even wilder. The clothes he wore were rumpled and looked as if he'd been sleeping in them for days.

"My love?" Mary said in a breathless whisper, as she collapsed with shock and surprise back into her seat.

Shelley was about to move toward her when Mrs. Godwin, Mary's stepmother, appeared in the doorway beside him. She was wheezing and red-faced, but this did not stop her from lunging forward and grabbing Shelley's elbow.

"I told you, young man," she cried out between pants, "Mr. Godwin forbids your presence here. . . ."

With a nudge and then a firmer push, Shelley released himself from the woman's grasp. He then marched onward into the room while Mrs. Godwin, who was reeling behind him, cried out, "How dare—"

She was cut short by Shelley's words that were directed at Mary. "They wish to separate us, my beloved; but death shall unite us."

He pulled a small bottle from his pocket and held it out. Without thinking, Mary reached out to take what he was offering, but then halted as Shelley spoke again.

"By this you can escape from tyranny, and this . . ." He paused as he pulled something from his other jacket pocket. It was a small silver pistol. Mary immediately slapped her hand to her mouth and every trace of color drained from face. Across the room, Jane stood and let out an ear-piercing scream.

Brandishing the gun, Shelley continued, "This shall reunite me to you."

Jane continued to wail, Mrs. Godwin gasped and swooned, and Mary stared at the pistol in Shelley's hand.

"What are you . . . ?" she began. But then, as she looked up from the gun to her lover's wild and bloodshot eyes, she blinked and realized she must end the situation immediately.

"Be calm, my love," she entreated. "Please be calm."

Shelley gave another wave of the pistol that caused Jane to shriek again and Mrs. Godwin to let out another gasp and groan.

"You must take this," he cried out, while pushing the small bottle toward Mary.

Mary did not take the bottle. Instead, she got to her feet and moved cautiously toward Shelley. Her cheeks were now stained with tears. "My dear Shelley," she said in a shaky but soft voice, "I won't take this laudanum; but if you will only be reasonable and calm, I will promise to be ever faithful to you."

Shelley said nothing, but continued to stare with a fixed intensity at Mary. Meanwhile, Mary's heart hammered in her chest, and out of the corner of her eye she could see the glint of the gun's metal.

"Be calm," she repeated in a whisper.

His intensity began to wane. It was as if Mary's words threw a spray of water on his once raging fire. In front of her, he seemed to buckle a little and deflate. His knuckles, which had been white as they grasped the laudanum, now turned pink.

More footsteps sounded on the stairwell, and before Mary could say anything more, James Marshall, a friend of her father's, was in the room (he'd been downstairs waiting to lunch with Godwin, who was still running errands in town). Marshall strode past the swooning Mrs. Godwin and grabbed hold of Shelley from behind. Shelley didn't struggle or resist, however. The fight had already escaped him. The pistol slid unhindered from his hand and thudded onto the floorboards.

"It's time to leave, good fellow," Marshall boomed.

Shelley did not respond. He simply crumpled against Marshall and allowed himself to be half carried, half marched out of the room.

Jane sobbed hysterical sobs after the men departed. Mrs. Godwin prattled on and on about what they had all witnessed. Meanwhile, Mary sat quietly back in her seat. She took long, slow breaths and stared out the open doorway to the tiny hallway at the top of the attic stairs. Her heart still beat with heavy thuds in her chest, and a burning nausea now gripped her throat. *Oh, poor Shelley*, she thought, *how could it have come to this?*

He'd been calmed this time, but maybe not the next. Left alone, he might hurt himself. Maybe he could do much worse. *Please, no*, she begged silently. *Anything but that.* A world where she and Shelley were separated was insufferable enough. A world with no Shelley was too awful for Mary to contemplate.

Mary looked over at the small table beside her. Then, with Jane's sobs still echoing around the room and Mrs. Godwin's chatter nagging at her ears, Mary picked up her copy of *Queen Mab*, pressed it to her heart, and mouthed the silent words, *Wait for me, my love. Wait for me.*

Nineteen

Clara and Daniel sat side by side on Kay's velvet couch, saying nothing. A grandfather clock in the corner of the room ticked methodically, and from the open window, noises of the warm city night flooded in. It was beginning to get dark, but neither of them stood up to flick on a lamp. Instead, they were slumped against the couch with their elbows touching, their thighs grazing. Daniel's eyes were closed, although he was awake. Clara pressed her palms together and stared out the window at the indigo sky.

They had been like this for a few minutes now, just sitting alone but together in their respective silence. When the truck first left, Clara sobbed hard, raked her hands through her curls, and paced the sidewalk. All the while, questions poured out of her. Daniel soothed and listened and tried to answer as best he could. No, he hadn't thought it would be so soon. Yes, it was peaceful: Kay simply didn't wake from the nap she fell into when Clara was still there. Yes, he tried to call, but he found only Clara's landline number scribbled on an old piece of paper beside Kay's bed. Yes, the hospice nurse was there. No, she probably could have done little to save Kay.

Now, though, Clara's tears and pacing and demands for answers were over. Numbness and shock had settled upon her like a heavy, immobilizing cloud. It just didn't seem possible that Kay was gone. Even when Kay was at her sickest, she still appeared so full of life.

That she could just disappear—here one minute and then gone the next—was too much for Clara to fathom.

She couldn't help but think of her mother again. Her mother's sickness was so much quicker than Kay's, but in those last days, when the ventilator rasped and wheezed beside her mother's hospital bed, the journey into death seemed, paradoxically, more gradual and more fluid than Kay's. As Clara sat and held her mother's hand, she watched the life drip and ebb out of her. Her mother faded, breath by mechanical breath, into the night. But with Kay, Clara hadn't seen that. Not in the same immediate way.

"I can feel her," Daniel said in a whisper, finally breaking their silence.

Clara said nothing. She simply raised her eyebrows and then flicked her gaze sideways to look at him.

His eyes were open now. "I feel Kay in this room."

"Really?" Clara hadn't meant the question to come out in such a condescending tone.

Daniel smiled a small, sad smile. "I take it you don't."

Clara shook her head and pushed her palms together even tighter. She really didn't want to get into a discussion about afterlives or universal spirits or karmas or rebirth. Daniel no doubt believed in all that stuff—all that "moneymaking, New Age mumbo jumbo," as Anthony called it.

As far as Clara was concerned, Kay was gone. Gone, gone, gone. She was not in this room. She was not in this apartment. She would never be here again. Kay was in the back of a black truck on its way to some cold and echoing funeral home. Her body would soon be prodded, moved, sewn, and prepared by people who stared death in the face every day—people who'd learned to distance themselves from the corpses in front of them on their embalming tables, people who trained themselves not to reflect on the lives that had so recently danced under the cold skins they now handled.

Once again, an image of her mother sneaked into Clara's mind. She saw her body lying in the funeral home. Her face was gray, her eyes shut, her hair splayed out across the coffin's velvet interior. There had been a tiny speck of dirt on her mother's cheek, and Clara had stared at the blemish, wanting to wipe it away but also recoiling from it at the same time.

Daniel's voice broke the silence again. "Last night, in the middle of the night when Kay was so sick, I made a promise to her."

Clara turned her body toward Daniel. "What did you promise?"

"She was in real pain, but somehow, through the fog of it all, she demanded I make a promise: the promise that I would start living my own life again." He pulled a hand through his hair and gave a small laugh.

"What did she mean by that?" Clara asked.

"She said . . ." He smiled again, clearly thinking of Kay's words. "She said I gave away too much of my own energy to others, through my hands and my heart, and that one day I would have none left for myself." Daniel looked away and shook his head. "I'm not sure—"

"No?" Clara cut in. "Maybe she was onto something."

More than once it had struck Clara as odd that Daniel spent so much time with Kay. She knew he had massage clients in the city, but he rarely talked about his work. Indeed, except for when he shared the story of his wife's illness, he gave little away about himself.

Daniel looked back at her. "Maybe." He then searched Clara's face for a few seconds.

She felt a now familiar heat rising from her collar to her cheeks. The same urge to kiss Daniel consumed her, just as it had at Coney Island. Before she could act on the impulse, before she could even chastise herself for entertaining the thought in the first place, Daniel's next words halted her.

"I'm going to do what I promised her I would do. I'll take the job in California and start . . ." He flicked his fingers. "I'll start living my own life."

"A job . . ." Clara began, but her throat seemed to close in panic over the words. She tried again. "A job in California?" she croaked.

Daniel nodded. "It's an amazing opportunity. It's a place I always dreamed of working. But I kept putting it off." He looked down. "Because of Kay, because of a lot of things." He paused and then went on. "But now I'm going to go. I will keep the promise and make the leap."

Clara could not say anything else for a moment. Tears jabbed at her eyes, but she bit her lip and held them back. The news left her winded. She'd lost Kay, and now Daniel was going to move to the other side of the country. She couldn't bear it.

"Good for you," she finally said in a quiet voice.

Daniel was still looking at her, and it was as if he was waiting for her to say something more. But she didn't. She couldn't. She couldn't even begin to put words to what she was feeling right now. There was a deep-seated urge to beg him not to go, to demand that he stay. But that would be ridiculous. She barely knew him. She wasn't even sure if they were friends.

"I made Kay another promise," Daniel said, getting to his feet.

Clara raised her eyebrows, but Daniel didn't see, as he was already heading toward Kay's bedroom. He came back a few seconds later with a book in his large hands.

"She wanted you to have this. When she passed," he added.

Clara reached out her hands and took the book. It was an old copy of *Frankenstein*, a lot like the one from her mother's attic. The synchronicity made Clara struggle to compose herself. The book also reminded her of Maxie's phone call earlier and the reason she was on her way to Kay's apartment in the first place. Kay died at almost the same moment that Clara was told they could finally see the Shelley papers. The irony was too painful, and Clara swallowed hard. She smoothed the book and tweaked a pink piece of paper that was protruding from its pages.

"I think she wrote something in the front for you," Daniel said as he lowered himself back onto the couch beside her.

Clara carefully opened the book and moved through the first pages to the title page. Underneath *Frankenstein, or the Modern Prometheus*, and in small, feathery handwriting, it read, *Dear Clara, We may never discover the secrets of MS's childhood, but we will always have her books, like this one. Through* Frankenstein *we can learn so much—if only we open our eyes and our hearts to her words.* The inscription then ended with the words, *Shelley's lessons will live on—as I will in you, Clara. Yours most lovingly, Kay.*

Sucking in a breath, Clara read the inscription again.

"Are you okay?" Daniel asked.

Clara nodded without looking up. She then flipped to where the Post-it stuck out. She wondered whether Kay put this marker in for her or whether it was from another time. On the pink paper, there was more of Kay's handwriting, this time in pencil.

Hubris is hubris, even if it is in the name of science and progress, read the first sentence. Another scrawled sentence was underneath. *Progress shouldn't take us away from who we are, our pleasures, and those we love.*

Below these words was an arrow pointing to the text below. Clara peeled back the sticker and read the passage.

If the study to which you apply yourself has a tendency to weaken your affections, and to destroy your taste for those

*simple pleasures in which no alloy can possibly mix, then that
study is certainly unlawful, that is to say, not befitting the
human mind. If this rule were always observed; if no man
allowed any pursuit whatsoever to interfere with the tranquillity of his domestic affections; Greece had not been enslaved,
Caesar would have spared his country; America would have
been discovered more gradually, and the empires of Mexico
and Peru had not been destroyed.*

Clara read these lines a few times. She had no idea when Kay
highlighted them or for whom she'd done it. Yet, each time Clara read
the passage, she found herself thinking of Anthony—his ambition, his
gradual disappearance over the past few years from their home to his
lab, his up-and-down moods, his increasing distance from her, and
their lack of intimacy. A deep, unsettled feeling began to churn inside
her. The passage warned of not allowing your ambition and pursuit of
knowledge to get in the way of "simple pleasures" and "domestic affections." But that was not all. The passage also suggested that great
ill could come from such ambition: Countries could be enslaved and
empires could be destroyed.

Anthony wasn't about to jeopardize nations, but perhaps he was
playing with fire. Maybe his ambition, his pursuit of knowledge, was
putting him in danger. Clara thought of the pill bottles, Georgie, and
what the old woman at the homeless shelter said. Her stomach turned
over and panic clenched in her chest.

"I must go," she said as she slapped the book shut.

Daniel looked over at her. He opened his mouth to say something,
but then seemed to think better of it.

Studying him, Clara had an urge to confess everything. To tell
him of her worries about Anthony, about what she suspected might
be going on. She even wanted to tell him about those moments,

those guilty moments, when she wanted to cover his lips with her own.

In the end, she thought better of it, too. She leaned over and kissed his cheek instead.

"You're a good man," she found herself whispering. She wasn't entirely sure why, but in that moment it felt like the only right thing to say.

She then got up and left.

Twenty

Anthony rarely picked up a phone. He was always too involved in his work to mess with answering calls. If Clara wanted to talk to him while he was at the lab, she had to call one of the technicians or postdocs and ask them to pass on a message. He owned a cell phone, but he hardly ever turned it on. He used the phone only to check messages or to call someone himself. It was Anthony's theory that if anyone really wanted to get in touch with him they would find a way, and, in the meantime, his work was too important to be interrupted by "unnecessary calls."

So when Clara left Kay's apartment, she didn't bother calling ahead to Anthony's lab. It was almost nine o'clock, but she was positive Anthony would still be there. After all, it wasn't common for him to be home before eleven p.m. these days. She was surprised, then, when she got to the lab and was told by a postdoc who was working late that Anthony wasn't around.

"I was out of the lab this afternoon," the postdoc said as he looked up at Clara through heavy specs. "But when I got back here around seven, Professor Greene was gone."

"Really?" Clara asked.

Her mind whirred, trying to think whether Anthony had a dinner date or a function scheduled. She was pretty sure he didn't.

"Yup." The postdoc nodded.

"Do you have any idea where he went?"

"No, sorry," he replied. "The lab was like this when I got in." He waved around the room. "Empty." Then he scratched his head. "I think some of the other postdocs were planning to go see a movie at the Film Forum. Maybe he went with them?"

Clara shook her head at his question.

The postdoc laughed. "I don't know why I said that. Professor Greene at the movies with some postdocs? Not very plausible." He blushed. "I'm sorry, I didn't mean to suggest—"

Clara waved her hand and cut him off. "It's fine. I know what you mean." Then, after a pause, she said, "I'm just going to duck into his office."

The postdoc had already lost interest and was back to scribbling in his notebook. Clara made off to the far end of the lab and toward Anthony's office. She wasn't entirely sure why she needed to go in there. The postdoc already told her Anthony was gone. But she figured there might be clues to his whereabouts left in the office. If his gym bag was gone, she'd know he was working out. She would check his desk calendar, too, and see if there was a dinner date he'd forgotten to tell her about. And while she was at it, she might poke around and see if she could find something that would explain the whole pill bottle mystery.

As she pushed the door open and peeked in, Clara's mouth dropped. The carpet in Anthony's office was scattered with loose papers. From his desk, a pot of pens, pencils, and scissors had fallen to the floor, and the pretty shade on his standing lamp—the one they'd picked out together years ago—was knocked askew. Clara's gaze traced the disarray and her heart skipped and thudded. Something was wrong, very wrong. Anthony's office was usually neat; at least, on the surface it was neat. Just like at home, where he would clutter up their closets for the sake of clear countertops and unencumbered hallways, his office always looked sparse and tidy to the unfamiliar eye. His mess, meanwhile, was hidden away in the filing cabinets, desk drawers, and the coat cupboard behind the door. Anthony's filing system was terrible, and within drawers and hidden spaces in this room, Clara knew, was a hodgepodge of cardboard folders, lab books, papers, and knickknacks.

Clara moved forward into the office, carefully picking her way over the strewn papers as she went. She headed for Anthony's desk. In spite of the disorder in the rest of the room, his desktop looked as it always looked: sparse, organized, a few envelopes neatly stacked in a wire-mesh tray, his phone and his flat-screen PC monitor and keyboard dusted and shining. She lowered herself into the bouncing desk seat and looked around at the office.

"What's going on?" she whispered to herself.

Clara leaned forward and picked up the phone. She dialed his cell phone number first but, as she expected, it was turned off, and clicked immediately over to his voice mail. Clara then punched in their home number. Even if he was at the apartment, she doubted he would answer. But perhaps if she left a message demanding he pick up, he might. After a few rings, the machine's greeting message kicked in.

"Anthony? Are you there?" she said loudly, so that if he was in the next room he would hear. "Anthony? Please pick up if you're there." She paused and then tried again. "Anthony. Please. Pick up now. I'm at your office looking for you." But in spite of her pleas, there was no reply. She tried one more time. "Anthony, pick up. Please."

Finally, she gave up and replaced the phone in the cradle. As she leaned back in the chair, wondering what on earth to do next, she noticed the standby light on the computer monitor was winking. She reached out and clicked the mouse. The dark screen immediately awoke from its slumber and Clara found herself looking at an open Microsoft Outlook window. The cursor flashed on a half-written e-mail. Her first impulse was to look away. She couldn't read his e-mails. That was something she would never do. Privacy was too important to her, and to Anthony. Nonetheless, a word caught her eye.

The word was "Sartrix," the name of Anthony's start-up company.

Anthony hadn't spoken much about the venture since the night he announced his Harvard move. When Clara asked him to elaborate a couple of times, he offered little except to say he was talking to the investors and everything was moving forward smoothly. Clara's curiosity was now piqued. She had to read the e-mail. Unfortunately it said very little.

Thank you for your interest in my work, Anthony began. *I am unable to comment on Sartrix at th—* It stopped like this, midword and midsentence.

Clara noticed that the message was a reply to an incoming e-mail, and so she tapped at the down arrow to read the original message. She was about to flick past the header information, but then noticed the sender's e-mail: pmassey@gmail.com.

"Paul Massey?" she said aloud.

She pounded again on the down arrow, with her gaze following quickly to the bottom of the message. *Yours, Paul Massey,* she read. Her eyes popped open wide. She then headed back up to the top of the message and began to read.

Dear Professor Greene,

I have left a number of messages on your machine and with your colleagues, but to no avail. I'm trying to contact you to see if you will talk with me about your work and your start-up company, Sartrix. I am a freelance journalist and write for the *New York Times,* among other publications. You can contact me at either of the numbers below.

Yours, Paul Massey

Clara stared hard at the screen. She thought back to the woman at the shelter and the card Paul Massey left with her. This guy, it seemed, was almost more eager to find Anthony than she was. The e-mail made his interest in Anthony sound innocuous. Yet he was chasing around to shelters, giving his cards to homeless women, which didn't suggest a mundane financial report on biotech start-ups.

Clara looked from the screen around at the room and worry re-ignited in her chest. She remembered Kay saying that Paul Massey wrote hard-hitting exposé pieces for the *Times* and the *New Yorker*. But the idea that he was doing some kind of exposé on Anthony and Anthony's company just seemed laughable. Anthony was Anthony, not some villain in a *New Yorker* feature.

As she considered this, Clara noticed something on the floor, peeking out from behind a chair. It looked like a hat. She stood up and moved fast around the desk. This time she did not pick her way over the papers. Instead she walked straight across them and toward the chair. Once there, she swooped down and picked up the hat. But as soon as its rim was between her fingers, she dropped it again.

The hat was Georgie's. She recognized it instantly. It was tattered and torn on its peaks and it had the same forlorn feather stuck in its green band. It was definitely Georgie's. Clara's knees buckled and she slumped down into the nearby seat.

To the empty office, she whispered, "Georgie was here?"

July 1814—Skinner Street, London

The messenger came in the middle of the night. The rest of the house was silent and slumbering, but Mary was wide-awake. She'd slept little since Shelley burst into the schoolroom a few days before, brandishing his gun. Tonight was no different. She'd been staring up at the gloomy ceiling for the past few hours, while clutching her copy of *Queen Mab* to her chest and thinking of nothing but Shelley. Even before the rattle at the front door, a strange, panicky feeling churned deep in her stomach. It was as if she could sense the gathering storm.

A rush of feet and voices followed the messenger's arrival, and Mary sat up in bed, straining to hear what was going on. It was no good, though; she was too high up in the house to make out what was being said. But before she could even get out of bed, loud footfalls thudded on the stairwell and her stepmother flew into the room. The flickering light from the candle that Mrs. Godwin was holding lit her agitated face.

"What is it?" Mary pleaded, before her stepmother could say a word.

Mary was now on her feet and moving toward Mrs. Godwin. Her heart thumped at a frightening pace in her chest.

"Girls," Mrs. Godwin said, addressing Jane, too, who was only now beginning to wake up and rub her eyes. "It's Mr. Shelley," she announced in a grave tone.

Everything inside of Mary turned to ice. Her heart, which had been beating so fast, now seemed to stop dead behind her ribs. For a second, she could do nothing but stare at her stepmother, this woman whom she felt nothing for and who now, it seemed, was going to deliver the worst news Mary could ever bear to hear.

"Tell me he is alive. Tell me." The words escaped Mary as a staccato yell. Their ferocity and urgency shocked everyone in the room, including herself.

Mrs. Godwin reached out and patted Mary's arm. Her touch was not unkind; nonetheless, it was cool and stiff, and Mary couldn't help pulling away.

"Be calm, Mary," her stepmother snapped, clearly annoyed at the way her stepdaughter had recoiled from her. "He is alive." She then sucked in a breath and added, "Just."

Mary's head was spinning. Her blood was flowing again, but it was now coursing through her veins in a way that made her utterly dizzy. "What . . . ? How . . . ?" she stammered. She could not form a sentence.

Luckily, Jane was now beside her. "What do you mean 'just,' Mother?" she was demanding. "Is Shelley well or not? What has happened?"

Mrs. Godwin raised her thin eyebrows. "What a capricious and excitable young man he is!"

"Mother," growled Jane. "I beg of you, tell us what has happened to Mr. Shelley."

"Just this night he has attempted to take his own life with laudanum," she declared.

Both Mary and Jane gasped. Then Mary felt her legs buckle beneath her. Like a statue slowly crumbling, she sank to the floor. Her stepsister and stepmother looked down at her, but, seeing she had not fainted outright, they continued their conversation.

"But he is alive?" Jane asked.

Mrs. Godwin nodded. "But very sick. Mr. Godwin is on his way to Shelley's quarters this minute. We are to follow." She waved toward her daughter. "Go. Get yourself prepared."

Although almost delirious from shock, Mary heard these final words and began to push herself from the floor. Her body felt lifeless, but she knew she must get up. She must get dressed as quickly as possible and be at Shelley's side right away. His lodgings were a mere stone's throw away, but his situation sounded grave. She had to be there. . . .

"Not you, Mary," Mrs. Godwin said, holding up her hand.

"But I . . ." Mary started to protest.

Her stepmother glared hard through the candlelight. "You shall stay here. Your brother is asleep downstairs. You must be here for him should he awake."

Mary was speechless for a second. But then, as Jane bustled beside her pulling her housedress over her nightgown, she found her voice and cried out, "Jane will stay with her brother, not I." She shook her head and turned toward the armoire. "I must go to Shelley now."

Mrs. Godwin didn't allow her to get more than a few paces, however. She grabbed Mary's arm and said in a low voice, "Mr. Godwin will not allow it."

The next few hours passed so slowly that it seemed to Mary as if each second were a lifetime. It was the dead of night, but she'd moved down to her father's dark and empty bookstore on the first floor. It was easier to wait here for the messengers sent by Jane who brought news of Shelley's condition. At first Jane's scribbled notes were sparse. *He is very, very pale, but his breathing is more regular.* But as the night wore on and Shelley slowly began to improve, Jane wrote more. *He has taken some sips of water, but his skin is still gray. Mr. Godwin allowed the physician to retire to the next room.*

Mary held tight to these notes, reading them over and over by the light of a nearby candle. She also brought with her the notes and letters Shelley had sent her secretly. As Mary reread his words now, she berated herself over and over. Right here, in his own ink, he'd spelled out what he was about to do. He said on a number of pages that unless they could be together, unless they could be partners for life, he would destroy himself. At the time the words panicked and frightened her, but she never thought he would actually do it. Even when he came and waved the pistol, she talked herself out of believing he would seriously harm himself. Her beloved was too full of life and love, she thought; he could not possibly yearn for death.

But he had done it. He'd opened the vial of laudanum and swallowed it down, all because of his love for her and his despair over their separation. Every time Mary thought of this, her eyes would fill with hot tears. She wanted to chastise Shelley for his foolishness. She wanted to berate him for nearly leaving her alone in this world. Yet, at the same time, she wanted nothing else but to have him in her arms, to pepper his damp, sickened forehead with her kisses. She yearned to tell him she loved him, and only him, for life.

Finally, as the morning light began to creep into the store's front window and Jane's notes reported a clear improvement in the patient, Mary's fluctuating emotions congealed around just one feeling: anger. She continued to hold her letters from her lover, but her thoughts were now with someone else, namely her father.

She was furious with Godwin: furious that he had refused her union with Shelley in the first place, furious that it was his disapproval that had led to tonight's terrible events, and, even more, she was furious that her father had forbidden her from seeing her love in his hour of greatest need. If Shelley's health had not improved, if he'd died tonight, she would not have been there with him. He would have gone to his grave thinking she didn't care enough to disobey her father. He would not have known the great love and passion she held for him in her heart.

With anger now pounding in her chest, Mary got up from the hard wooden seat where she was sitting and moved to the window. She looked out at the golden-orange morning sky and whispered to herself, "I will not endure Princess Charlotte's fate."

Just a few weeks ago, the prince regent banished his daughter Charlotte to Windsor Park after hearing about her meetings with a secret love. He hoped his daughter would one day marry Prince William of Orange, thereby ensuring an alliance between Great Britain and the Netherlands. But the prince regent's daughter showed no interest in the Dutch prince and dallied with another young love. Her father was furious.

Although no royalist, Mary felt a powerful affinity for the head-strong young Charlotte, who was second in line to the throne. But now, Mary knew, her path could not follow that of the princess. She would not allow her father to keep her under lock and key the way Charlotte's had. Godwin could no longer keep his daughter from Shelley. Mary was the daughter of Mary Wollstonecraft, after all. Her mother was an outspoken advocate for the rights of women—all women. Mary Wollstonecraft's daughter could not, and would not, give in to a father's tyranny.

"Never," she finally mumbled under her breath, as she turned from the window and headed for the stairs.

Back in her room, she would start a fresh letter to Shelley. Everything was going to change, she would tell him. Their love was not going to be held in check any longer. It was their time—their time to be together. Forever.

Twenty-one

After finding the hat by the door, Clara could do nothing but sit and ask herself panicked questions about where Anthony might be and how Georgie found him in the first place and whether Georgie might hurt Anthony. Finally, though, she realized she must act. She wasn't sure what the action would be. Nonetheless, she got to her feet and headed in purposeful strides toward the desk to pick up her purse. As she pulled on the short strap, the purse caught the computer keyboard and caused it to clatter against the desk. The noise made her pause and look from the keyboard to the computer monitor. A thought then occurred to her.

Clara hurried around the desk and sat down at the computer once again. Paul Massey's e-mail was still on the screen. She grabbed a pen and a Post-it note from a nearby drawer and scribbled down his number. Then, without stopping to shut down the computer or close the desk drawer, she stood up and clamped the Post-it between her lips. She made for the door while rummaging in her purse for her phone.

Back out in the laboratory, she found her cell, took the Post-it from her mouth, and was poised to punch in Paul Massey's number. But she spotted the postdoc from earlier still sitting at the bench and lowered the phone.

"Sorry to disturb you again," she said, moving toward him.

He looked up.

"So you really have no idea where Anthony—I mean Professor Greene—might be?"

The postdoc shrugged. "Nope. Like I said, the place was empty when I arrived."

Clara cocked her head. "Has anyone else come in this evening?"

"Not as far as I know. I went out for about five minutes to get a soda, but I doubt anyone came in then." His brow furrowed above his glasses. "Is there anything wrong?"

"No, no," Clara replied. "No, I was just wondering where Anthony might be. I can't get hold of him at the moment." She hoped she sounded breezy and calm.

"If I see Professor Greene, I'll let him know you were looking for him," the postdoc offered.

Clara nodded. "That would be great. Thanks."

She then turned on her heel and left the lab. She waited until she was down the hallway and out of earshot before she raised her cell phone again and tapped in the number from the Post-it.

Paul picked up after just two rings.

"Paul Massey," he said in an abrupt tone.

"Hi, um, yes," Clara stammered, surprised that the phone was answered so fast. She hadn't really gathered her thoughts and felt unprepared and a little foolish. "This is Clara Fitzgerald. I . . . ."

"Of course. Clara. Hi, how are you?" His tone warmed immediately. "I've been meaning to call you. I heard back from Maranto's publicist, but—"

"I'm calling about something else," Clara cut in. She didn't have time for his apologies. Maxie had, miraculously, found a way to Maranto. They didn't need Paul Massey's connections anymore.

"Oh, okay. Of course," Paul responded.

"I wanted to talk to you. . . ." She hesitated, wondering where this all might lead and whether she was doing the right thing. "I'm wondering if you've seen Anthony." Before Paul could answer, she added quickly, "I know you are trying to talk to him, and, well, I'm not sure where he is, and I was wondering—"

"I've been trying to set up a meeting with him, yes," Paul said. He sounded surprised and a little confused. "But he never responded. So, no, I haven't seen him."

"Have you seen a man called Georgie Worth?"

There was silence on the other end of the line. "I saw Georgie last week, but I haven't seen him since. I have been looking for him. . . ." He trailed off but then added, "Can I ask what all this is about?" His question was not accusatory—more probing in a careful way.

Clara sucked in a breath. She wasn't sure if she should trust this man. She would trust Daniel, his brother, in a heartbeat. But she wasn't sure about Paul. She needed answers, though.

"Are you writing a story about Anthony?" she blurted out.

There was another silence. Then, after clearing his throat, Paul replied, "Not exactly."

A spark of anger shot through Clara. She'd seen the e-mail on Anthony's computer, and Paul himself told her he wanted to talk to Anthony about an article he was writing when they last spoke. But before she could say anything, Paul was talking again.

"I am writing a story on a large pharmaceutical company," he said. His voice sounded cautious. "A company I think Anthony's start-up might be involved with."

"Oh," was Clara's response.

She had no idea Anthony was working with a pharmaceutical company. But then, it seemed she knew very little about what Anthony was up to these days.

"I'm worried about Anthony," she blurted out, as she stepped into the elevator. "I think Georgie Worth might be angry with him and he might have found Anthony at his lab."

"What makes you think that?"

"I met a woman today at the homeless shelter in the West Village, a woman you talked to also."

Paul grunted to acknowledge he had.

"She told me Georgie was angry at a professor and I think that professor might be Anthony."

"I see," Paul responded, his tone quiet and unreadable.

"I was just in Anthony's lab, looking for him." The story was flooding out now and Clara couldn't stop it. "It was a mess, which isn't like Anthony. And then . . ." She took another breath. "Then I found Georgie's hat."

"His hat? The one with the feather?"

"Exactly."

Both Paul and Clara said nothing for a few beats. The elevator rumbled down toward the ground floor.

"Okay, Clara," Paul said, breaking their silence. "I'm going to be honest with you. I'm investigating Maerco Pharmaceuticals. I believe they're up to some pretty questionable practices. One of these is backing a series of illegal and undocumented drug trials on homeless people." He paused and then added in a somber tone, "And I have a hunch that Anthony may be conducting these trials and it is his drug they're testing."

Clara pressed the phone tighter to her ear and a lump formed in her throat. She then voiced something that she hadn't allowed herself to think, let alone say, since she found the pill bottle in her bedroom.

"I think your hunch might be right," she said in a whisper.

Then, as she stepped out of the elevator into the foyer, she told him how she saw Anthony that day at the shelter. She explained about the pill bottles: the one Georgie threw in the park, and the matching one she found in the apartment.

"But," she said finally, as she left the Biological Sciences Building and headed south. "But what I don't understand is why. Why would he conduct these unofficial trials when his drug is going into official phase-one trials so soon?"

Paul responded straightaway. "My guess is Maerco wants to know if the horse it's going to back is a good one. Phase-one trials are very expensive, and if they come to nothing it would be a huge waste of money for Maerco."

"So you're saying they are doing preliminary trials to see if they want to invest in the drug longer term?"

"Uh-huh," Paul said, and then added, "Of course, there are such things as official phase-zero trials."

"Phase zero?" Clara had never heard of such a thing.

"They're also called microdosing studies, and they're used to speed up drug development. Basically, these trials are used to get early data on a drug and see if it acts in humans like it did in the lab on test animals. They basically allow drug companies to make decisions about which drugs they will help develop and which they won't bother with."

Relief washed over Clara. "So Anthony's doing these phase-zero trials, then? It's all completely legitimate?"

"Far from it. The trials Anthony is conducting have not been made official." He paused and then said, "And this is one question I'm trying to figure out. Why isn't he doing phase zero?" Paul went on: "My suspicion is that Maerco Pharmaceuticals wanted to cut to the chase. In phase-zero trials the drug dosing is really low and therefore the studies can't give really accurate data on safety or whether the drug completely works in humans."

"So Maerco thought if they just gave the correct higher dose to some homeless guys," Clara said, beginning to understand what Paul was getting at, "they would get all the data they needed."

"Yup," Paul replied. "At least, that's what I'm guessing."

Clara was walking through the warm city night. Cars and taxis honked around her, people pushed by her on the sidewalk, yet she felt as if she were walking in a bubble: a floating and surreal bubble. Her mind was turning over and over, tumbling and spinning, trying to make sense of everything Paul was suggesting.

The old Anthony, the one she fell in love with at grad school, would never have done such an unethical thing. In those days, he was ambitious, but he was also righteous about scientific ethics and dismissive of anyone who ever stepped over the line. These days, though, who knew? He'd changed in the last few years. He'd become harder around the edges and more driven than before. Then there was the fact that he spent almost every waking hour in the lab, working on his beloved drug. His whole life was so invested in its development, maybe he would do something unethical and over-the-line to ensure its success.

These thoughts spiraled around in her mind and seemed to suck the breath out of her. Then, to top it off, she found herself thinking of Kay and wishing she could talk it all over with her friend. In the instant that followed, she remembered Kay was gone. Gone.

"Clara. Are you there?" It was Paul. She'd almost forgotten she was still holding the phone.

"Yes, yes," she said, her voice shaky. "I'm here. Sorry."

"You know, the one thing I really can't figure out," Paul continued, "is why Maerco is so interested in Anthony's drug."

"Why wouldn't they be?" Clara responded. "I mean, the results in the lab have been amazing. The drug consistently reduced cancer tumors in test animals." Clara cringed a little, realizing how much she sounded like Anthony.

"I know, but Maerco is the maker of big blockbuster drugs like Zorack, the antidepressant. They rarely develop cancer drugs because cancer drugs are so expensive and, in the end, they're taken by only a few people."

"Cancer drugs don't make enough money, you mean?"

"Exactly."

Clara paused for a second and then an image of Anthony taking his own pill floated into her mind. She stopped in her tracks. "But if the drug could be marketed as a preventive, as a drug every person might take whether they are healthy or not, then it could make a lot of money, right?" she said, her tone fast and urgent.

"Well, yes—" Paul began, but she cut him off.

"And a drug that prevented cancer and stopped you from aging would be even better." Clara's heart was now racing behind her ribs; her mind was spinning.

"What are you getting at, Clara?" Paul asked.

She took a breath before saying, "His drug works by manipulating genes associated with aging. The drug activates, or turns on, a longevity gene, a gene that can help you live longer and stops you from aging."

Paul made a sound like a surprised cough. "Are you saying what I think you're saying? That Anthony and Maerco Pharmaceuticals are developing an antiaging drug?" He was half laughing, half whispering. "Some kind of elixir of life?"

Clara said nothing for a few seconds. She was standing on the sidewalk just a block from her apartment building. "I know; it sounds ridiculous, doesn't it? Especially because Anthony has always been so adamant that this is exactly what his research is not. He always called those scientists who wanted to find a way to live forever kooks."

"But when a big pharmaceutical company comes knocking and waving lots of money and promises of spanking-new laboratories, it might be hard to resist," Paul suggested.

Clara thought of Harvard and what Anthony said about the investors who wanted him to have a lab there. She thought about how Anthony always yearned to be in Cambridge, and how, until now, he'd never attained it. She knew that offers of money from a pharmaceutical company wouldn't have been enough to lure Anthony. But maybe the lure of Harvard was great enough. The promise of a Harvard lab might make him step over the ethical line.

In a quiet voice, Clara finally said, "Yes, you might be right."

Paul was about to say something else, but his words were cut off by a beeping on Clara's phone. Another person was calling her.

"Sorry, Paul. Can you wait a second? I have another call," she said in a rush, wondering if it might be Anthony.

She pulled the phone from her ear and looked at the display. The number was unfamiliar, but she answered it anyway.

"Hello?"

There was a silence, a strange rustling noise, and then a shaky, whispered voice came on the line. "Clara?"

"Speaking."

"This is Daisy." The voice was female and she sounded elderly. "From the shelter."

"Oh, yes, yes. Of course," Clara replied.

"You said to call if I saw Georgie—"

Clara cut in. "Yes, yes, I did. Did you see him?"

The old woman coughed and said, "Well, no. But"—she coughed again—"I thought you should know he's in a lot of trouble."

Clara blinked. "Who? Georgie?"

"Bob says that Georgie killed his dog."

"What?" Clara gasped. "Who's Bob? What dog?"

"Bob is one of the guys at the park. He used to be a friend of Georgie's, until they fell out, that is."

Clara thought of the old man she saw in Washington Square that day, the one Georgie was arguing with.

"Bob says his dog disappeared yesterday, after him and Georgie had another fight. Then Bob goes to his usual spot in the park this morning and there's his dog, you know, dead. It looked like its neck was clean broke. That's what Bob and the other guys said."

Clara gasped again. "But . . . Georgie? Would Georgie really do that?"

"Not the Georgie I used to know." The woman sighed. "But he's not been himself these days. He's always so mad." Daisy coughed again.

"So does anyone know where he might be? Is Bob looking for him?"

The woman gave a raspy laugh. "He sure as hell's looking for him. He's a mean one, that Bob, but he loved his dog. Any kindness inside him, he gave it to that old mutt."

Clara's stomach rolled as she thought of Georgie and the dog with the broken neck. It didn't seem possible that he could do such a thing.

"If you hear any more, if they find him, will you call me?"

Daisy said she would. "You seem a nice lady, Clara. Such kind eyes," she added, before hanging up.

When Daisy was gone, Clara flicked back to Paul's line.

She didn't apologize or explain her last call. Instead, she hurriedly said, "Tell me what you know about Georgie."

"Georgie?" Paul replied, clearly surprised by Clara's renewed urgency. "Well, I only met him once. Another old guy in Washington Square tipped me off and said Georgie might be part of the trial. But when I caught up with Georgie, he didn't give much away. He just wanted to talk about some boats down at the Seaport."

"Boats?"

"Yeah, those old sailing boats by Pier Seventeen near Water Street. Apparently, he loves the boats and in the summer he sometimes sleeps down there on a bench looking out over the ships and the water." Paul went on: "He talked a mile a minute about those boats and I didn't get anything out of him. But then, a couple of days ago, I saw him. I saw him near Anthony's lab."

"You did?" Clara's eyes opened wide.

"It was just fleeting. I tried to follow him, but he was gone as fast as I spotted him. But I swear it was him." Paul stopped for a second. "That's why I tried to find him again. I thought if I pressed him one more time he might give me information."

Clara wasn't really listening anymore. She was thinking of just three things: the hat in Anthony's office, the old dog with its broken neck, and the boats by the Seaport.

"You said Water Street? That's downtown on the East River, right?"

There was a silence on the other end of the line. "You're not going to go down there, Clara?"

She said nothing.

"Clara, it's late. I don't think you should go there now—not alone."

"Meet me there in fifteen minutes, then."

Paul paused and then said, "I promised to meet Daniel. . . ." He trailed off. "Listen, Clara. I'm sure this could wait until the morning. I mean, Georgie seemed pretty harmless. I'm certain nothing could—"

But Paul didn't get to say anything more. Clara had already shut her phone and was hailing a cab.

Twenty-two

The cab screeched to a halt beside Pier 17. Clara leaned forward and gave the driver the two twenty-dollar bills she'd promised him if he drove quickly. Then she stepped out into the warm night. As she shut the cab door behind her, she looked over at the pier and felt momentarily foolish. She fretted all the way here about coming alone so late in the evening. Maybe Paul was right to be concerned. But looking around now, she could see that the pier wasn't a dark or dangerous wasteland. There weren't many people around, but the city roared and honked close behind, and the river, up ahead, was still alive with late-night tour boats and cruisers.

Clara kept her cell phone in her hand just in case, but as she moved across the pier, she felt her shoulders relax. She would be fine, she told herself. She would just take a quick look around, and if she didn't find Georgie or Anthony, she would go straight home.

"Anthony is probably at home right now," Clara whispered, although she wasn't entirely convinced.

She stayed close to the South Street Seaport mall at first. The stores and restaurants, which were crowded on the left-hand side of the pier, were all closed now. But their glowing signs spilled a reassuring light across the wooden slats of the pier. Every now and again, Clara would stop and peek behind a pillar or an empty hot-dog stand or in a nook between two storefronts just to check whether Georgie or Anthony was hidden in the shadows.

She continued moving toward the water, and as the stores receded behind her, the shadows started to get longer and wider. Still clutching her cell, she rubbed at her shoulder with her free hand. Even though the night was warm, as she got closer to the river a cool wind blew over her bare skin and flapped at the light sundress she was wearing.

Up ahead, she could just make out some benches, and on one she could see the shadowy outlines of two people. Her heart began to thud in her chest. Could this be them? She prayed it would be, as there was no sign of confrontation or argument between these inert figures. If this was Georgie and Anthony, everything looked calm—mercifully calm.

Clara upped her pace, and in just a few short moments she was behind the bench.

"Anthony?" she blurted out, her heart now in her throat.

The figures turned around fast and the whites of two pairs of eyes glinted up at Clara. But these were young eyes, teenage eyes. They were also now wide, shocked eyes. She'd disturbed two young lovers during a quiet moment out by the river.

"Oh, I'm sorry," Clara stammered. "I was looking for . . . for . . ." She shook her head and trailed off.

The young couple stared at her for a second, clearly bemused. Then, without saying a word, they shifted back around and resumed staring out at the river. Meanwhile, Clara turned on her heel and moved quickly away.

She retraced her earlier steps while trying to calm herself. As she walked, Clara looked over toward the old ships and boats on the other side of the pier. She should have gone in that direction in the first place. After all, she knew it was the ships that drew Georgie to the seaport. But it was much darker on the southside, away from the glow of the mall, and just a few lights, strung on the masts and ropes of the boats, lit the area. She couldn't give up now, though. She'd come this far, and it would be ridiculous to run back home without checking the whole pier. She sucked in a breath, pulled her spine straighter, and moved in the direction of the boats.

The first ship she reached was vast, with four high masts and its sails tightly wound. She looked up at the boat for a second or two and then moved along beside it, in the direction of the river. Clearly no one was around. Except for the occasional creak from the big vessel, there were no sounds, no movement, no voices. She came up along-side the boarding bridge to the boat that was closed off to the public by a small metal gate. She stopped and tested the gate, but of course it was locked.

She decided to continue walking, and when she finally passed the bow of the big boat, she found herself next to a similarly old, but much smaller sailboat. She came to a halt and watched the vintage schooner bob gently on the water.

For a few seconds, Clara felt peaceful. The air was rich with salt, and the sounds of the city were replaced with the sounds of water slapping against wood, the jangle of buoys, and the snap and slow creak of wet ropes. No wonder Georgie liked to come here. These boats and this pier were just a short walk from downtown Manhattan, yet if you closed your eyes it seemed like another world—an ancient and seafaring world. And for Clara, whose day was frantic and sad and utterly perplexing, the out-of-time feeling of this place was a wel-come relief.

But then she heard voices and her calm evaporated in an instant. They were coming from the small boat in front of her, and for the first time, she noticed a ray of light shining out of a cabin window.

"You conned me," the first voice bellowed. "You said it was safe."

"I . . ." began the reply, but the rest was lost amid the noise of a passing cruiser on the river.

Clara's blood turned to ice. She recognized the bellowing voice as Georgie's and she knew—she just knew—that Anthony was on the boat with him. She immediately started to move toward the boat's small boarding bridge. Her heart pounded and her mind somersaulted with worry, but she kept moving.

The bridge was narrow and bobbed gently in time with the boat. Clara tiptoed, not wanting her low heels to clank on the metal underfoot. She held her breath, too, scared that any sound she made might disturb what was happening on board. After no more than four or five steps, she reached the open deck of the boat. She paused for a second. The boat bobbed up and down and a heady scent of gasoline and sea salt hung in the air. Quickly, Clara ducked down low, realizing that she would be in full view if anyone was to suddenly emerge from the cabin. Then, in her crouched position, she awkwardly pulled off her sandals one at a time and started creeping slowly toward the cabin, trying to make the boat move as little as possible. The wooden deck felt slick and wet under her bare feet, so she took care with every step.

The sounds of passing cruiser boats still hummed loudly from the river, but as she neared the front of the boat, once again she could hear the conversation coming from within.

"What do you want, Georgie?" she heard Anthony ask. His voice sounded irritated yet panicked too.

Clara inched closer. She could now see in through the cabin window, just about. She didn't want to be seen, so she remained a pace or two back, just enough for the night shadows to conceal her. Inside the small round window, she could make out the back of Anthony's head, and beyond Anthony stood Georgie. He was waving a small pill bottle in Anthony's direction, and even from where she was standing, Clara could see the wildness and anger in Georgie's eyes.

"I want you to get me off this stuff," he was now saying.

Anthony's head began to shake. "As I keep telling you, it's not addictive. . . ."

"Not addictive, Professor Greene?" Georgie spat, using Anthony's real name. "When I take these things, my mind races, I'm mad, I'm excited, I can't sleep. . . . I . . ." He pushed his free hand through his hair. "I'm bouncing off the walls." He then sighed and shook his head. "But when I don't take them, it is worse. My poor old body shakes and aches; my skin crawls. I want to curl up and die." His voice cracked as he said these last words.

Clara watched as Anthony leaned forward a little. "As you well know, Georgie, I've been taking them, too, and I've had none of these side effects—"

Georgie cut him off. "But you said yourself that when you first started taking them you felt focused and, and . . . What was the word you used?"

"Euphoric," Anthony offered.

"Yes, euphoric. That's it."

"I did. I do. Since I've been taking them, I feel alive and young and focused. It's like I'm a teenager again. I can work for hours, days at a time. But I haven't experienced any of the side effects you describe, Georgie." Anthony was trying to sound calm and appeasing, but there was still the edge of fear in his voice.

Georgie was silent for a few beats and then he lifted his eyes skyward. "But I took more than you did. Three tablets a day wasn't enough. I started to take five, then seven. . . ."

Anthony shook his head again. "Seven? You shouldn't have done that."

Georgie paced away from Anthony, but then turned on his heel and reared toward him.

"I couldn't stop myself," he bellowed. "My body needed more. My mind kept telling me I had to have more."

Anthony jerked his head back. He was clearly terrified. And no wonder, thought Clara. Georgie was terrifying. He looked so utterly different from the smiling old man whom she first met outside the shelter. He was even different now from the Georgie she saw in the park. His rage today was a thousand times more intense. It was manic, ferocious, and unyielding.

"Listen, Georgie," Anthony said, holding up his hands. "If you think it's the drug, I believe you. I can help you get over all this. I know people who can help you." His voice was fast and he sounded rattled. He waved a hand around at the cabin. "Just let me off this boat and I will help you."

Georgie made a low roaring noise. Anthony flinched and so did Clara, who remained in the shadows outside. She'd managed to stay perfectly still as she listened to all that had just been said, but her heart continued to thud heavily in her chest. She was scared for Anthony. She was panicked and dismayed at what she was hearing. In just one short exchange, all her fears were confirmed. Anthony was testing his drugs on Georgie—drugs that hadn't even been put into phase-one trials yet. It was unbelievable, insane.

"I'm a damn junkie now. A junkie to your drug." Georgie spoke in a bitter growl. "All these years on the streets and I've always, always been clean. I don't even need booze. It's been tough, but I did it. I stayed off all that stuff. And you know why I did?" He looked hard at Anthony and then fiddled clumsily with the pocket of his shirt. He pulled out a photograph. "Drugs killed this woman. The only woman I ever loved."

Georgie held up the crinkled picture for Anthony to see. Clara was certain it was the same picture he took from his pocket that day in the park, the picture of a woman who Georgie loved. Clara remembered now that he was furious because the other man's dog destroyed his only other picture of this woman. The man must have been Bob, and it looked like Georgie was probably the one who killed his dog. With this kind of rage, anything seemed possible.

"She was beautiful, Professor, beautiful. Just look at her." He waggled the photo furiously and then turned the picture to himself and frowned the saddest, most haunted kind of frown. "She was beautiful inside, too. Kind, sweet, and honest." He paused for a moment, as if collecting himself, and then added, "But she was vulnerable— vulnerable to evil people. She got sucked in. She couldn't help it. She was shy, and a man gave her something that made her feel not so shy anymore. She thought he was helping her, but really he was slowly, slowly killing her. That pusher had an expensive smile and a smart suit, just like you, Professor Greene."

Clara could see tears gathering in the old man's eyes.

"Georgie," Anthony said, "I swear I can help you. Just give me a chance—"

"It's not only me!" Georgie cut him off again with another yell. The tears in his eyes disappeared as quickly as they had appeared, and he was angrily shoving the photo back in his pocket. "I don't care about just me."

"Then what else do you want?" Anthony's voice was almost inaudible now.

"I want you to stop making this stuff." He shook the bottle another time, now just inches from Anthony's face.

There was a silence and then Anthony said, quietly again, "I can't do that. This drug is going to save many lives. Many lives. It will be at the forefront of the fight against cancer. It will reduce all kinds of tumors. It will prevent tumors in the first place—"

Georgie interrupted again with another bitter laugh, but this time it wasn't so long or loud. "I know, and you know, that is not why you're making this drug or why you're testing it on guys like me."

"Of course it is," Anthony tried to protest.

Waving the pills again, Georgie stepped even closer to Anthony. "I know what you're up to," he growled. "I might be a bum, I don't have a home, but I'm not stupid."

"I didn't say—"

"I am not stupid," Georgie repeated. "You plan to sell this drug to everyone. You want to make everyone young with these pills. And, in the process, you want to become a very rich man."

"That's not—"

Georgie put his hand up to halt Anthony's words. "I know that's what you're up to, Professor Greene. I'm sure you started out on the right path. You wanted to save lives. But then dollar signs flashed in your eyes, and now you want to make a drug that every fool in the world will buy, thinking it will keep them young."

He paused for a few moments while he stared hard at Anthony. His eyes were filled with unabashed rage and frustration.

Outside, Clara held her breath. She couldn't imagine what was going to happen next. Surely this old man couldn't hurt Anthony or force him to do something he didn't want to do. But he had brought Anthony here, onto this boat, and how had he done that? He must have threatened him somehow or blackmailed him.

It was then that Clara noticed the glint of metal. There was something sleek and heavy poking out from the left pocket of Georgie's baggy pants. A gasp caught in her throat. A gun? Maybe. A gun would explain a lot. But just as she squinted harder to try and see for sure, Georgie turned away, just enough to conceal his left hip and the ominous object in his pocket.

"Listen, Georgie. Listen to me." Anthony was talking again. "This drug is my life. It's all that I have worked for. It could do a lot of good in this world." His voice was shaky. "And it could be good for you, too. If you let me go, if you let me press ahead with the drug's development, then I promise you will be rewarded—handsomely.

You have my word. I will make you a wealthy man—a more than wealthy man."

Clara sucked in a sharp breath. She couldn't believe what she was hearing. She stepped backward in shock, and as she did so, she slipped on the boat's slick deck and caused the small ship to shift and bob. Panicked by the sudden movement, she quickly crouched very low down and pressed her back against the cabin wall. She could no longer see in the window, and underneath her, the ship still tipped and bobbed gently. Clara felt suddenly queasy. The movement of the boat, the heady smell of gasoline and salt air, coupled with the shocking things she was hearing, turned her stomach over and over again. She shut her eyes tight and prayed for the boat to stop rocking.

"What was that?" she heard Anthony say, and when Georgie didn't reply, he said, "Are you going to go out there and see? Maybe someone's on the boat."

"You really do think I'm dumb, don't you?" Georgie said, clearly through gritted teeth. "I'm not going anywhere until you agree to what I want."

"But, Georgie," Anthony pleaded, "you're not hearing me. I'm offering you an incredible opportunity."

Georgie let out a loud sigh. "That's exactly what you said when you first put me on these damn things. 'An incredible opportunity,' those were your words, 'an incredible opportunity to play a part in one of the greatest medical breakthroughs of the twenty-first century.'"

"And it was a great opportunity then, just as it is now," Anthony insisted.

There was a silence. Clara couldn't stay back from the window any longer. She had to see what was going on, so she pulled herself up and inched forward again. Careful to remain in the shadows, she peeked inside the cabin and saw Georgie in front of Anthony; his eyes continued to shine with rage. Meanwhile, Anthony was waving his cell phone.

"Georgie, listen to me," Anthony said. "I can call my contact at Maerco Pharmaceuticals right now, and we'll figure out a deal. We'll make sure you're written into our contracts and that you're rewarded for all your efforts."

"Efforts?" Georgie cackled. "Is that what you call them?"

"I'm serious, Georgie," Anthony carried on, in spite of the old man's bitterness. "I have the number right here. Just let me step outside and I can make the call."

Georgie shook his head. "You're not going anywhere." His face then contorted into a wry and foreboding grin. "Plus, I wouldn't want you hurting yourself on that deck. It's very slippery out there, you know." His eyes flashed. "Thanks to all the gasoline I poured on it earlier."

At these words, Clara's gaze snapped down to her own feet. She'd felt the wetness of the deck and assumed it was water. But now it was all startlingly clear: the powerful smell of gasoline, the slickness of the wood. Georgie had laced the deck—and maybe the cabin, too—with gasoline. It would take only one match. . . .

Without another thought, Clara raised her hand that was still gripping her cell phone. She flipped it open and her shaking finger hovered above the number pad, preparing to punch in 911. But the phone's screen didn't light up. She punched the "on" button, but nothing happened.

The phone was dead.

"I tell you what you're going to do with that phone of yours," Georgie was now saying in a low growl. "You're going to call that journalist who's been snooping around and tell him what you've been up to. You're going to tell him that your drug is no longer going to be made.

And you're going to confess what you've been up to with me. You're going to tell him these pills are unsafe."

Clara looked up from her useless cell phone and back in the window. Her heart was pounding so hard she could hear it in her ears.

When Anthony didn't say anything, Georgie reached into the pocket of his ragged pants and pulled out a box of matches. He waggled it in the air.

"If you don't make that call, Professor Greene . . ." He finished his sentence by gesturing upward with his hands and muttering, "Poof."

"But you will kill yourself, too!" Anthony exclaimed, his voice almost hysterical with fear.

"Yes, I will. It's the price I'm prepared to pay," Georgie said with an eerie calm. "The things we feel most passionately about are those we are most willing to die for."

Twenty-three

Clara was unable to move, and from her place in the shadows, she stared through the small cabin window. She was rigid with terror, and now that she knew that gasoline was laced across the small ship, she could smell nothing but its rich, bittersweet odor. Inside, Georgie still held the matches in his hand and he continued to eye Anthony with a look of defiance and fury. Anthony was saying nothing, clearly frozen in fear himself.

Finally, though, he found some words.

"Georgie, listen," he said, starting quietly. "I will make that call. As soon as you get us off this boat, I'll make that call."

Georgie shook his head. "You will make the call now."

Anthony hesitated for a second, but then Clara saw his shoulders slump and he pulled up his cell phone in front of him. The small screen lit up as he jabbed at one of the small buttons. But then he stopped.

"I don't know his number," he blurted out.

"Well, I do," Georgie shot back. He started reeling a number off to Anthony and Anthony slowly punched it into his phone.

Clara watched the whole thing, barely able to breathe, but as Anthony finished with the number and held the phone to his ear, she took a deep gulp of air. Tentative relief flooded through her. He was doing what Georgie was asking. He was going to save himself. He was going to ensure that he and Georgie—and herself, for that matter—would get off this boat alive.

At this last thought, Clara suddenly averted her eyes from the cabin window and looked around at the ship. She hadn't really considered her own safety up until now. She was terrified, but terrified in a removed way, as if she were watching some surreal and awful movie where someone she actually knew was about to be hurt. But now it sank in that this boat really was a deathtrap. She should get off. And fast.

But then she thought about Anthony and her gaze flicked back to the cabin. He was still listening silently to his cell phone. She sucked in another breath and told herself it would all be okay. This phone call would put a stop to all this craziness. Georgie just wanted to frighten Anthony, and once Anthony confessed everything to Paul, this would all be over.

Clara quickly noticed Anthony's knuckles turning white as he gripped the small phone, and a sudden and unexpected pang of anger stabbed inside her. He'd gotten himself into this awful situation. What was he thinking? She thought about his ambition and his desire to be a leader in his scientific field. It was those things she once found so compelling about him. He was so different from her, with her own quiet dreams. He was so driven and motivated and eager to change the world. But now it had come to this. His ambition had congealed into something cold and hard like steel—into something ruthless and unethical. He was endangering lives in the name of his work and his desire for profit. His own life was in danger now, too.

"He's not picking up."

Anthony's voice shook her from her thoughts.

Georgie let out a growl of frustration. "Leave a message," he ordered. "Then you can try again in a few minutes."

Anthony did as he was told, leaving a short message in which he said he needed to speak to Paul urgently. He then prodded at the phone to end the call. Meanwhile, Clara sat outside, paralyzed by fear and anger and indecision. She should get off this boat and go find help. But if she slipped or caused the boat to rock, if she were found out there by the raging Georgie, who knew what would happen next? But only a fool would just sit there on a boat laced with gasoline with an angry, bitter man holding a box of matches.

Clara looked away from the cabin toward the pier, trying to make up her mind. Go or stay. But just as she was about to look back to the cabin, she did a double take at the dark pier. In the gloom, two figures were moving in the direction of the boat. At first, they were just two murky shadows, but as they got closer, it was clearly two men, one tall and one much shorter. As they got closer still, Clara gasped. The taller of the two men was Daniel. She was certain of it. She'd never studied the way he walked before. But now, even in the poor light, she knew that this long, slow, but purposeful gait was his. She knew those large shoulders and long frame.

Their voices began to pierce the night air as they approached.

". . . probably one of these . . ."

Clara instantly recognized the voice as Paul's.

". . . Georgie said it was the old ships he loved best."

"Do you really think Clara's here?" The question came from Daniel. "Alone?"

The realization that they were here, and heading her way, finally sank in, and Clara had the sudden urge to wave and scream out to them. She fought the urge, though. If they saw her, if they heard her screams, no doubt they would run to the boat and come aboard. Their lives would be at risk, too.

In a split second, her next move was decided. Rather than call out, she had to keep them away. Far away. She sprang like a coil onto her feet and bounded, with a few light, quick steps, back to the boarding ramp. There, she unhitched the small ramp from the side of the boat and pushed hard. But the boat moved only an inch or two, as it was still tied by a couple of ropes to the pier.

Panicked, she looked up. Daniel and Paul were still far enough away that they could not see her in the shadows, but they were getting closer. She sprinted down the side of the boat and knelt beside one of the ropes. She scrabbled at the coiled twine with shaking hands. It wouldn't unravel fast enough, so with all the strength and might she could muster, she simply pulled the whole tangle of rope off its steel holder and let it slowly fall into the water. She then darted to the other end of the boat, slipping and sliding on the slick, gasoline-laden wood as she went, and did the same with the other rope. She sprinted back to the boarding bridge and gave it another hard shove. The bridge remained on the dock, fixed by heavy bolts and supports, but at last the sailboat began to bob away.

"You idiot!"

Georgie's cry made her stop dead. She'd been caught. Of course she'd been caught. Bounding up and down the boat like that was insane. She flicked her head around, expecting to see Georgie standing on the deck, his wild eyes zeroing in on her. Instead, there was no one, just darkness.

"This is not the number I gave you." Georgie was screaming now, clearly still inside the cabin. "You are a foolish man, Professor Greene. A liar and a fool. You think you can outsmart me? Well, you can't."

As Clara's mind reeled, trying to make sense of what was happening, a shout came from the pier.

"Clara?!" It was Paul. "What's happening? Was that Georgie?"

Her eyes darted back to the pier, which was now receding away from her. Paul and Daniel stood behind the wooden railing. Paul was waving his arms above his head.

The next thing she heard was a muffled thud and a loud cry from the cabin.

"Don't. Don't do it!" screamed Anthony.

Then, before she could even look back in the direction of the cabin, Daniel was hollering from the pier, "Clara! *Jump . . . now!*"

Clara hesitated for a second. She flicked her gaze toward the cabin and saw a ferocious orange blaze coming from the small doorway. A deafening crackle and bang followed. Without another thought, she climbed up on the boat's edge and threw herself upward and outward and as far away from the small vessel as her strength could take her.

She landed in the cool river with a splash. She tried to push herself up for air, but was forced down by a surge of waves. She flailed her arms and kicked her legs furiously, but she still could not surface. *This is how I am going to die. This is how I am going to die.* The mantra kept repeating over and over in her mind as she struggled against the waves and commotion of the water. *This is how I am going to die.*

She flailed even more and managed to push herself above the water for the first time, but as she tried to breathe, she took a mouthful of the foul river water and was dragged under again. *This is it. This is it.* Her mind shifted to a new mantra. Her arms and legs burned with the effort of her struggle. But just as she thought she couldn't go on, and that all her strength was used up, something powerful encircled her and pulled tight around her chest. Before she knew it, she was dragged upward and her head popped out of the water. This time she was able to take a gulp of air. She then coughed and spit and found herself almost fainting against whatever it was that was holding her from behind.

"I've got you," a breathless voice said into her ear. It was Daniel. "Just breathe."

Clara took another big gulp of air as Daniel's grip tightened around her and he began dragging her through the water. Her face was covered with her wet hair. Her eyes were blurred with water. But she could tell that Daniel was pulling her toward the pier—toward safety. Pull, swim. Pull, swim. Against her back, she could feel his whole body straining with the effort. She tried to kick her own legs to help him, but they felt like deadwood beneath her. All her strength was spent. Finally, after what seemed an eternity, he stopped. They'd reached the dockside.

"Thank you." Clara gasped. "Thank you."

She lifted a weary hand and pushed her hair from her face and blinked heavily. In front of her, no more than thirty feet away, the small boat bobbed up and down on the river.

It was engulfed in roaring and spluttering flames.

July 1814—Skinner Street, London

Mary crept around her bedchamber. A bright moon shone outside and its bluish light spilled across the floorboards, making it easier for Mary to find what she was looking for. Before retiring to bed last night, she'd prepared everything for a swift departure. Yet she was also careful not to let anyone see the evidence of her packing. All that she intended to travel with was stored in hidden places where she could gather the items quickly, but also tucked away from the prying eyes of Mrs. Godwin and her stepsister, Jane.

The wooden floor creaked now and then as she flitted back and forth across the gloomy room. These creaks seemed almost deafening to Mary. Although, across the room and still in her bed, Jane did not stir. Mary was almost finished. Her dress was laced, her bonnet secure, and her old leather valise nearly full. She had one last item to collect: her precious box of letters and personal writings that she'd placed at the back of her armoire last evening.

Holding her breath, she crouched down and fished around in the darkness of the old cupboard. Her fingers passed by shoes that she would leave behind, some long-ago-discarded books, and an old shawl that she'd used to hide the box. But, in spite of the work done by her probing fingers, she could not find the small wooden box.

Her heart began to skip and panic gripped in her chest. She could not leave without her letters or her writings. Everything was contained within those pages: her life, her thoughts, the words of family and friends addressed to her. Also within the box were the seeds of her many writing ideas: first pages of books she would one day write and fragments of thoughts that would one day be essays. They were the seeds of writings that, when finished, she hoped would make her deceased mother proud.

She pushed and groped with more fury, and still the box did not materialize. How could this be? Her mind raced. She'd left the room only once last night after she stored the box in this hiding place. How could it be gone?

The answer did not take long to come.

"Are you looking for this, Mary?"

Jane's voice cut through the room like a knife, and Mary, utterly shocked, toppled backward from her crouched position on the floor. She looked up and over to Jane's bed, where, in the moonlight, she could see Jane was sitting up and holding something in her outstretched hands. It was Mary's box, of course.

"Don't make too much noise, dear Mary. We do not want Mother to hear you thudding about." She said this in a low, giggling whisper. But as Mary gathered up her skirts and scrambled to her feet, Jane's tone changed. "Take me with you."

"Jane, I . . ." Mary began, as she shook her head.

But Jane was already out of bed and moving toward her. "You are leaving with Shelley for the Continent, I know," she said, not letting Mary finish. "If you take me, I will speak French for you. I will be a willing and able travel companion, I assure you. Please, Mary, I beg of you. Take me with you."

Mary was about to open her mouth and let her remonstrations spill out, but at the final moment she stopped herself. She looked hard at Jane's face, which was shadowy and indistinct in the purple light. She thought about how her stepsister so often vexed her, yet how she was also an important accomplice over these last few months. She willingly chaperoned Mary on those delightful trips out with Shelley to St. Pancras and beyond—those trips that now seemed so long ago. Jane also helped deliver letters and notes between the lovers when they were banished from each other's sight. If Mary left without her, she would be denying Jane the chance of escape from this dreary Skinner Street life.

As Mary mulled this over, Jane started to giggle again. "Think how furious Mother will be to find me gone, as well as you."

Whether intended or not, this final detail clinched it for Mary. She could think of nothing more satisfying than the image of Mrs. Godwin's face upon finding that her impertinent stepdaughter and her beloved real daughter had both fled in the middle of the night.

"Get dressed," was Mary's simple and whispered command to Jane.

While Jane pulled on her dress and gathered her possessions, Mary left their room. She stole her way through the house and out the front door. She then ran a few blocks south to where Shelley would be waiting. Even though she'd made up her own mind to bring Jane, she realized she must ask him, too. Could they afford another mouth to feed? Could another person's travel expenses be covered? She had no idea. Only he could tell her that.

As she rounded the last corner, she spotted him. He stood just where he said he would be. The chaise and horses were ready. She drew closer, and even in the half-light, she noticed his changed countenance. He was always slight of build, but now he was even slighter. The episode with the laudanum had clearly taken its toll.

"My darling," he called out upon spotting her.

He threw open his arms, but she did not run into them, as much as she wished to. She had to save that moment, the moment for which she'd yearned for so long now. She had to wait until she had fully escaped before she surrendered herself into his arms.

Shelley sensed her reticence. "What is it, my love?" His wide eyes then darted downward. "Where is your valise? You're not having doubts. Pray, let it not be so."

Mary reached out a hand and touched his arm. "No, no." She almost laughed. "Never. Be calm, my love," she added.

In a hurried whisper, she told him about Jane. He nodded as she spoke.

"Of course. Jane shall come," he said when she was finished. "No young woman should be left to fester in that house."

Mary was then on her way, speedily retracing her steps back to Skinner Street. The house was still quiet when she arrived, and she tiptoed quietly up the stairs to her room. Inside, Jane was tying the ribbon of her bonnet under her chin. Just like Mary, she was dressed in a heavy black silk dress.

"Are you ready?" Mary asked in an urgent whisper.

Jane nodded.

"We have no time to lose," Mary said under her breath.

The two of them gathered up their heavy valises, looked around one more time, and then moved out of the room without hesitation. The rustle of skirts was their only noise. Just as Mary was about to close the door behind them, however, she remembered two things: her box of papers and the letter she wrote for her father. She scooted back into the room and lifted the box from the small table where Jane set it down. She lodged it under her arm and immediately her heart lifted. This box was who she was, and who she hoped to be, and thus it must remain ever close to her.

She then turned to her bed and reached down. Jammed between

the heavy wool mattress and the bed's hard frame she found the letter. She pulled it out quickly and looked at it. In the moonlight, she could see that the ink of her handwritten *Father* had smudged. The lightness and excitement in her chest abated a little. Her father had exasperated her in the last few weeks, and forbidding her from seeing Shelley nearly destroyed her. But still he was a good man and a good father, and she hated to disappoint him. This letter, she was sure, would break his heart.

Yet she knew she must go. Godwin made her the young woman she was today. He instilled in her values of freedom, independence, and thinking for oneself. And it was now her time to act on those values. She could not stay here, tied to the man who created her. If she did, she would turn bitter and stagnant and no doubt mean. It was time to break free and follow her love and her dreams. In her new life, she would write and live and flourish and be cherished by a man of great talent and vitality. Thanks to this new and beautiful life, she would make her mother proud—but also, one day, her father, too.

With the letter in hand, Mary turned on her heel and headed back out of the room. She led Jane down the stairs, and before they left the house, she propped the letter on a dresser, where her father would not miss it. Then, in the early-morning gloom, the sisters fled the house, and like two floating shadows in their black silk dresses, they chased through the streets toward Shelley and their carriage.

This time when she saw him, Mary fell into Shelley's waiting arms.

Twenty-four

Clara stayed on the pier, wrapped in a paramedic's blanket, until every flame was doused and until the burned-out carcass of the small boat was pulled back to the dockside. Daniel didn't leave either. He sat quietly beside her, clearly aware that words could do little at this moment. When he spotted her shivering, however, he would pull her close and rub her arm and back with a gentle hand. Clara wasn't cold anymore, though. The blanket was plenty warm enough in this summer night, in spite of her wet clothes. Instead, she was shivering in shock—complete and utter shock. Every bone, every blood vessel, every nerve ending in her body seemed to be pulsating in disbelief.

Anthony was gone.

The firefighters arrived only minutes after Daniel dragged Clara from the water, but still they were too late. The flames ate up the boat in seconds, and according to Paul, who was still milling around talking with the cops, there had been a small explosion, too. It was the explosion that caused the swell in the river that dragged Clara under. She jumped from the boat, it turned out, just a second before the blast.

As she sat beside Daniel, Clara listened in a vague way to the people talking around her. She heard their theories and questions about the blast. "A gas tank in the cabin, perhaps?" "Did the homeless guy bring it aboard?" "How did he get in the boat in the first place?" But only a thorough investigation would give the final answers. She'd told the police the essential information: who was on the boat, what was happening, and why Georgie had done what he'd done. But the cops were granting her some time and space before they started their full questioning. For now, all she could do was sit and watch and let her body respond to the shock.

"Professor Fitzgerald?"

It was an unfamiliar voice that finally broke her trance. She looked up to see one of the plainclothes detectives she spoke to earlier standing over her. His already downcast eyes looked even more melancholic.

"I'm sorry to say, the bodies have been found."

Clara flinched and then, after a few moments, she nodded numbly. It wasn't like she was expecting any other news. After all, there was no way Anthony or Georgie could have escaped the inferno or the blast. She escaped by only a hairbreadth herself, and she wasn't trapped inside the cabin. But still the news set off a fresh round of shivers and muted shock.

"Maybe it's time we left," Daniel whispered as the detective walked away. "The paramedics still want to make sure you're okay, and both of us need to get out of these clothes." He tugged on his own damp shirt as he said this.

Clara turned around and looked at him. For a while, she said nothing. Under the bright lights shining from the police vans and fire trucks, she could see his eyes. They were so rich and varied, a palette of dark shades and intricate colors. They were the kind of eyes that seemed to suggest answers—answers to deep and infinite questions. She wanted to ask his eyes why this happened and whether she could have stopped it and how on earth Anthony ended up in this mess. She also wanted to know what would happen next. Anthony was gone. Kay was gone, too. Clara was now a boat whose anchors had been ripped away in just one day. Where would the current take her? Would she be swept out to sea, or drift like deadwood upon some shore? Would she sink into the murky river before she even reached the ocean?

She didn't ask any of these questions. Instead, she said in a quiet voice, "I'll come in just a minute."

She then got to her feet and moved past Daniel. She pulled the blanket tighter around her and walked slowly to the easternmost end of the pier. Over the buildings of Brooklyn on the opposite side of the river, a pinkish golden glow was growing in the sky. A few wispy clouds hung in the air and reflected the predawn light. Clara stopped at the wooden railing and looked out. A group of seagulls circled above, letting out the occasional squawk, and in the distance a tugboat chugged rhythmically downstream.

Anthony was gone. The thought sucked every molecule of air from her body, as she stood looking out over the river. It was unbelievable. And what was even more unbelievable was who he'd become and everything he'd done. He'd forsaken his own life, and Georgie's, for his beloved drug and for greed and ambition. Clara wanted to shout at him, demand a thousand answers to the questions that burned within her. But she never would be able to. Not now. She would never even know the answers to the smaller questions, like whether he really did want to marry her this summer in Harvard or had he just said it to appease her. Now she would never know. Never.

He was gone.

Clara just stood for a while and let the shock and confusion spiral around her. Her body was numb and cold and shivering. Yet after a few minutes, and as the first golden rays from the rising sun began to permeate the sky, warmth trickled very slowly into her veins. It would take a long time for this cold shock, the utter disbelief and grief, to work its way out of her body, if it ever completely did. But this warmth was new and it was coming from a gradual realization that she was not alone. In this sunrise, in the scudding clouds and squawking gulls above, she could feel Kay's presence. She'd scoffed at Daniel earlier for saying he could feel Kay around him. But now she understood. Kay was here with her. She was everywhere. So, too, was Clara's mother. And also the ghosts of Mary Shelley and all the other women throughout history who'd endured great losses, yet found the strength to live—and found the strength to survive.

She would survive like they did. She had to.

July 1814—English Channel, a few miles from Calais, France

The voyage started well when they set off. There was nothing but quiet seas and a gentle breeze. Then, halfway between the White Cliffs of Dover and the waiting shores of France, a ferocious squall hit the fisherman's boat that Shelley had hired for the trip. Huge waves pounded against the small vessel, rain lashed the deck, and lightning cracked in every direction. The boat pitched and rolled and, at one point, almost capsized. They were traveling at night, and the blanket of darkness made the events all the more terrifying.

Mary was never a good sea traveler, but this storm surpassed anything she'd experienced before. So scared was she, she couldn't move. She could not even scream or talk, and through the pounding, pitching, and deafening thunderclaps she clung silently to Shelley's legs. She was convinced they would all die, and in her panicked mind, she apologized over and over to her father. This storm, she believed, was punishment for her flight.

The journey from London to Dover was arduous enough. The clattering chaise made her sick to her stomach and they stopped many times en route for her to recover. But on the furiously rocking boat, she was too scared to even feel ill. Terror transformed her into a mute and unresponsive statue. She was rigid in life, as she assumed she would be in her imminent death.

But as fast as the storm came upon them, it receded just as quickly. The waves flattened, the skies cleared, and the winds died back to a breeze in a matter of minutes. Mary, Shelley, and Jane were left breathless and shocked. They climbed out on deck and found that, above them, the stars were twinkling innocently again in the wide indigo sky. Like a nightmare that felt so intense in its midst, the storm disappeared in the blink of a waking eye.

Jane soon retired back to the tiny cabin to try to sleep. But Mary and Shelley remained on deck. In the east, a morning glow began nudging its way into the sky, and the two lovers stared out at the emerging dawn. Shelley held his arm around the small of Mary's back. They said very little, but the intimacy between them was palpable. They were together at last, and their new life was about to begin.

As Mary watched the reds, pinks, and golden hues unfurl into the sky, she thought of this: their future. The storm that just passed was a sign, she realized. There would be more storms to come; there was no doubt. With such a passion and intensity between the two of them, storms would inevitably chase them and engulf their lives. But like the iridescent rays of morning sun now forking out from the horizon, there would also be great love, great moments, and great joy.

Mary's hand slipped down to her own middle. One of these rays was within her. She was carrying Shelley's child; she knew it now. The swelling, the sickness, and the quickness of her emotions in the last weeks, they were all signs. But only now, as she stood in front of the new dawn, did she know the truth with such unfettered clarity. Soon she would become a mother. Soon she would feel all the joys and pains of motherhood.

She and Shelley had created something new, something all their own. Storms would batter them; hardships would hamper them. There would be places where their unconventional love would draw stares and rebuke. In many foreign lands, they would be strangers, outsiders. But together, with their child and their words, their writings and their passion, there would always be bright new dawns, too.

Epilogue

One Year Later

Clara woke up with a jerk. She hadn't meant to fall asleep out here on the grass, in the shade of an old oak tree. But the sound of the Pacific Ocean pounding against the rocks below, the sweet salt smells, and the soft early afternoon breeze encircled her, and before she knew it her eyelids grew heavy, her breathing deep, and pretty soon she was asleep. Her dreams were peaceful. In the last few months they'd become this way. But every now and then, a nightmare like the ones that plagued her almost every night after Anthony's death would sneak up on her again, leaving her panicked and sweating and gasping for breath. Today, though, her dreams were vague, shimmering, and beautifully calm.

Now, as she woke from these dreams, she blinked hard against the bright sun and crystal blue sky. Her eyes finally adjusted, and for a moment she watched a small blue jay circle and land on the tree above her. She listened to the ocean continuing its rhythmic pounding not far away. This place was heavenly, just as she was told it would be. She'd never been to Big Sur before. She'd certainly never been to this green, wooded retreat and spa that hung on the side of California's rugged cliffs.

A rustling of paper interrupted her trance. She turned on her side and looked over at Daniel. He was in the exact same position he had been in before she fell asleep—cross-legged, his hair fluttering in the breeze, and his eyes staring down at the stack of papers in his lap. Clara's heart gave a small kick. It was still hard to believe she was here—here with him, here at this place where he now lived and worked.

Until yesterday, when he met her at the airport, they had not seen each other since that night—that awful night at the seaport when he pulled her from the water and the two of them watched the burned-out wreckage of the deadly sailboat being brought to shore. They'd spoken, of course, and in the last few months, their phone calls became almost daily. They wrote e-mails, too, a whole slew of them. And when she traveled to England in the early spring, they even wrote lengthy letters, like correspondents of a long-ago age. Those letters were with Clara now, tucked away in her purse where she always carried them.

"Hey," she whispered.

Daniel didn't notice her waking up, but she wanted his eyes on her. Those intoxicating, complex eyes had not changed one bit in the year that had passed, and now, in this quiet California paradise, she was reveling in all the uninterrupted time she was going to spend with them.

Daniel turned toward her. "Good nap?" he asked, his eyes glistening in the sunlight.

She nodded.

He held up a long, broad finger. "Just one more minute," he said. "I'm nearly done."

She grinned and nodded again, and as his gaze returned to the papers, she flopped back onto the grass. The smile on her face did not disappear. He was reading her manuscript. He was reading the book that poured out of her in the last year. The book she'd given up her professorship at Manhattan U to pursue. And the book that, just a month ago, had sold to one of the biggest publishing houses in New York.

The day she sold the book was incredible. But nothing felt quite like this, being next to Daniel: the man she'd thought so much about of late, the man who'd begun to appear in her peaceful, shimmering dreams. It felt so indescribably good and right and true. Anthony never read anything Clara wrote back in her academic days. He was too busy with his own work. But since the moment she started work on this book, Daniel was with her every step of the way—cheerleading for her with the research, demanding drafted chapters be e-mailed, listening to every related conversation with agents and publishers. And today, only their second day together, he insisted on reading the latest version of the manuscript. He'd read almost half before lunch, and now he was finishing up.

"It's incredible, Clara," Daniel said finally.

She flopped her head to one side and looked over at him. "You think?"

He placed the manuscript down on the grass and set a stone on top so the loose sheets would not float away on the breeze. He then scooted over and stretched himself out next to Clara. He propped himself on one elbow and looked down at her. For the thousandth time since she arrived, she felt a glow in her chest and that unfamiliar yet beautiful feeling of safety and wholeness.

"Mary Shelley is in you and she's in these pages," he said. "It's a book about her, her childhood, her first love, yes. But it's like you're channeling her, too." He paused and then added, "Kay would be so proud."

Clara swallowed. "I hope she would," she whispered.

Daniel was right. It was as if she channeled Mary Shelley when she wrote the book. But, in a way, she was channeling Kay, too, and Kay's love and enthusiasm for Shelley. The book flowed out of Clara without effort, without hesitation or doubt. It was as if Mary and Kay were cheering her from beyond the grave, willing her onward, and helping her tell the story.

After Anthony's funeral last summer, after the investigation was complete, and after she managed to haul and scrabble her way out of the pit of shock and grief, Clara headed to Los Angeles to stay with her sister. Maxie decided not to return to New York after going to find Maranto. She needed a fresh start, she told Clara, and instead of dismissing the move to California as another harebrained Maxie scheme, as she would have in the past, Clara simply smiled and told Maxie she loved her. She'd lost Kay. She'd lost Anthony. She was determined not to lose her sister, too.

Maxie, it turned out, was amazing in the aftermath of Anthony's death. She flew in for the funeral and didn't leave Clara's side until she knew she was ready to be alone. Somehow, with her wiles and charms, she also managed to keep in good favor with Jonathan Maranto, and in early October of last year, on a balmy LA afternoon, the two sisters headed up to his mansion in Beverly Hills. Maranto was nothing but kind and warm, they were surprised to discover. He even set aside a small room in his house where he invited Clara to come as often as she pleased to view Mary Shelley's old journals and letters.

In that white-walled room, which overlooked Maranto's vast swimming pool and collection of swaying palm trees, Clara spent days and days poring over every page, every word, and every punctuation mark. As her gloved hands traced Shelley's inky handwriting and as she gently thumbed through the pages of the two-hundred-year-old journals, Clara could feel new life breathing into her. She was ready to live again, these pages taught her. And she was ready to live again in a whole new way. In that room, in front of Shelley's papers, she decided she wouldn't go back to a job she felt only lukewarm about. Instead, she would draw from her savings, take a gamble, and write. She would write a book about Mary Shelley and she would tell the childhood and teenage stories that for all these years had been told only through the eyes of others.

This decision took her from the sun-drenched room in Beverly Hills to the misty countryside of England and the bustling streets of London. She visited the places she read about in Shelley's journals. She researched Shelley's life and times in the huge collections of newspapers and books in the British Library. She took a trip to the National Archives offices in Richmond, where she picked up the search through her own family history. Anthony's DNA test once told her, in all its cold and scientific certainty, that she was related to Mary Shelley. Yet, as she traced her own ancestry and discovered exactly how her family connected with Shelley's, at last she felt truly connected. The old birth certificates and death certificates finally made it real, and it was after those days in the archive offices that the book really began to flow out of her.

"Of course, you need to start working on the sequel," Daniel was now saying with a chuckle.

Clara laughed, too, but her laugh was interrupted by a sharp ring from her cell phone.

"Sorry." She cringed at Daniel.

"Answer it," he said with wave.

She sat up and pulled out the phone. She grinned when she saw the name on the screen and flipped open the phone.

"Maxie!"

"Hey, you," Maxie replied. "How's California?"

Clara laughed again and looked toward Daniel. "Just perfect."

"So tell me about Daniel. I want all the details."

"I can't, Max; he's right beside me."

Daniel smiled up at Clara as she said this.

"Get rid of him later and then call me, okay?" Maxie demanded.

"I will," Clara said. And she would.

The two sisters talked for a short while. Clara told Maxie about her trip. She described the jagged cliffs and the iridescent skies of Big

Sur. Maxie asked her about the book and Clara filled her in on the latest conversation with her new editor.

"I've got some news, too," Maxie said.

Clara didn't frown. She didn't shake her head and expect some excited chatter about a new guy. Instead, she simply asked, "What is it?"

"I'm going back to school."

Clara's eyebrows shot up. "What?"

"Yup, it's all decided. I'm going to get that degree I never finished when I was twenty."

Clara was speechless for a second. "Are you serious?"

"Totally."

"That's amazing, Max." She paused. "Maxie, you know school is expensive." She paused again. "But if you need any help—"

"Oh, stop," her sister cut in with a loud chuckle. "I have the money."

"You do?" Clara was confused.

Maxie had moved to California a year ago, and although her life was going well, she hadn't landed any high-paying acting gigs. Tips in the new restaurant in Santa Monica where she now worked were good, but surely not enough to put her through college.

"Mom's money," Maxie stated. "I never touched it."

Clara was speechless again. A shadow of guilt clenched somewhere inside her, as she remembered how she once suspected that Maxie blew her inheritance on drugs. She'd been so wrong and blind about her sister. She was blind about a lot of things.

"I couldn't," Maxie went on. "I felt, I don't know, too guilty or something. I was so distant from her. I never visited her—"

"Oh, Maxie," Clara broke in. "She did still love you. You know that, right? She was tough on you, but she did it because she wanted the best for you."

Maxie was silent for a beat and then said quietly, "I know. I think I've come to realize that now." She paused. "And that's why I decided to use the money. Her money. It would make her proud, don't you think?"

"It would," Clara replied, nodding. "But, you know, that can't be your only reason. . . ."

"It isn't. I promise. I'm doing this for me. I really am."

Clara looked out at the sparkling, dancing waves. "I'm proud of you, Max. But mostly," she added, "I'm happy for you."

When their call ended, Clara slipped back down onto the grass and, propped on one elbow, she faced Daniel again.

"So, the sequel?" he said, poking her gently in the ribs. "You can't get out of my question that easily. Are you going to write one?"

"I'm not sure. . . ."

"Because," Daniel went on, "I want to know what will become of this wonderful Mary Shelley. I want to hear about her writing *Frankenstein*, and all her other books, for that matter. I want to know what happened with Percy and their travels. Her children, her next books."

Clara gave a wry laugh. "Well, let's see. Their journey through Europe had some high points, like when she met Lord Byron and when she conceived *Frankenstein* in a 'waking dream.'" Clara flicked her fingers to make quotation marks. "But generally their travels were really tough. She and Percy were broke most of the time. Their first child was born too premature to survive, and their next two children died as well. Mary's stepsister, Jane, was rumored to have had an affair with Percy, and Percy had a bunch of other affairs. Then, to top it off, he died at sea when Mary was just shy of twenty-five years old. He left her with their one remaining child, penniless and heartbroken." She chuckled again. "Not exactly a happy sequel."

Daniel laughed, too. "But then she went on to live a successful life as a widow. Isn't that what Kay wrote about? The strong and independent Mary Shelley as a widow?"

Clara nodded, and after a pause, she said, "I miss Kay."

"I do, too," Daniel whispered.

The two of them were quiet for a moment. Birds squawked high up in the vibrant blue sky. The waves crashed and receded on the cliffs below. The ocean breeze kicked at the leaves and circled Clara's golden hair.

"But Kay brought me to you," she finally whispered.

"And me to you."

Then Clara and Daniel stared at each other for a while, saying nothing. She loved these moments. It was as if they were going to kiss, wanting to kiss, but neither of them was prepared to submit to the longing. It was too pleasurable to keep looking at each other, to keep taking each other in. Everything was so delicate and fresh and new between them, like a snowflake in early winter, or like the glowing pink horizon at dawn. She wanted to stay in this moment forever. Yet, at the same time, she wanted to move onward, just as Mary Shelley always did. Clara yearned for all the new moments yet to come.

Photo by Phil Treble

Joanne Rendell was born and raised in the United Kingdom. She has a PhD in literature and is married to a professor at New York University. She currently lives in faculty housing in New York City with her family. Visit her Web site at www.joannerendell.com.

OUT OF THE SHADOWS

Joanne Rendell

This Conversation Guide is intended to enrich the
individual reading experience, as well as encourage us
to explore these topics together—because books,
and life, are meant for sharing.

A CONVERSATION
WITH JOANNE RENDELL

Q. Why did you decide to write a book about Mary Shelley?

A. I've always loved Mary Shelley's *Frankenstein*. It's a wonderful gothic novel, but it's very thoughtful, daring, and extremely prescient, too—even now, two hundred years after it was written. *Frankenstein* has had a huge cultural impact. It has inspired numerous novels, countless movies, and the name Frankenstein is known throughout the popular imagination. Newspapers talk of "Frankenfoods," kids dress up as green-skinned monsters with bolts in their necks on Halloween, and Broadway audiences line up to see Mel Brooks's musical *Young Frankenstein*.

In spite of this, many people don't know that a nineteen-year-old woman called Mary Shelley wrote the original book. Fewer people still know anything about this woman who led a rich yet tragic life, who married the daring romantic poet Percy Shelley, and who was the child of two radical writers, William Godwin and Mary Wollstonecraft. In *Out of the Shadows* I wanted to bring Mary Shelley out of the shadows of the monster she created!

Q. How did you research the book?

A. For details on Mary Shelley's life and writing, I referred to a number of very comprehensive biographies and literary studies, including Emily W. Sunstein's *Mary Shelley: Romance and Reality*; Miranda Seymour's *Mary Shelley*; Anne Kostelanetz Mellor's *Mary Shelley:*

Her Life, Her Fiction, Her Monsters; and John Williams's *Mary Shelley: A Literary Life*. I drew on a number of sources to understand the field of aging genetics. Lenny Guarente's *Ageless Quest: One Scientist's Search for the Genes that Prolong Youth* was particularly useful. Carl Elliott's *New Yorker* article "Guinea-pigging" (January 7, 2008), which offered an eye-opening exposé into the world of drug safety trials and the human "guinea pigs" who take part in them, was a big inspiration for Georgie's story. The recent memoir *Go Ask Your Father: One Man's Obsession with Finding His Origins Through DNA Testing*, written by my friend Lennard Davis, was invaluable, too. Lenny's book tells of his own journey to find out whether his father really was his biological father using DNA extracted from an envelope used long ago. Reading about the exciting yet terrifying moment when my friend opened the genetic test results both inspired and informed one of the key moments in *Out of the Shadows*.

Q. How much did you fictionalize about Shelley's story and how much is true?

A. Mary Shelley was in all of the places at the times I mention in the book and she was with the people I depict her with. The key elements to every Mary Shelley scene are true: As a child she heard all kinds of thinkers, poets, and scientists speak in her father's parlor; she struggled to accept her stepmother; she was sent away to Scotland, where she often wandered the barren moors alone; she first kissed Percy Shelley at her mother's gravestone; and when she eloped to France her childhood journals and papers were left behind (unlike in my novel, however, the journals and papers have never been found).

What I did fictionalize was dialogue, and I had to guess at Mary's feelings. Also, as it says in the novel, it is still undecided when Mary

Shelley saw Percy for the first time. My depiction of their first meeting came from my imagination—and what a fun scene it was to imagine!

Q. In Out of the Shadows, *you alternate between Mary's and Clara's stories. Why did you decide to narrate the book like this?*

A. In many ways, Clara's and Mary's stories are so different. Mary is a young girl growing up in early-nineteenth-century London, while Clara is a thirtysomething professor who lives in modern-day New York City. But there are many similarities and echoes, too. For one, Clara's story resonates with Shelley's most famous book. Clara's fiancé is not unlike Victor Frankenstein in his ambition, his desire to extend life, and his creation of something so dangerous that it eventually causes him great troubles.

I think the stories of the two women speak to each other on other levels, too. Mary and Clara are both on the cusp of finding themselves. They are searching for a way out of the shadows of those around them. For Mary, it is the shadow of her mother's death, her father's protection, and the life that doesn't yet fulfill her. For Clara, she must find a way to live for herself, to pursue her own dreams, and not just follow her fiancé's career.

Q. Do you see your novel as a warning about genetic science?

A. As a character in my novel says, Mary Shelley dared to ask "what if?" in *Frankenstein*. She looked around at the rapidly emerging technologies of her time and she considered their darker sides. She wondered what the price of "progress" might be (she lived during the Industrial Revolution, of course, when steam power, modern machinery, and medicine were all taking off). She dared to imagine how technology and science might change us and lead us in potentially dangerous directions.

Technology and science are still advancing rapidly today, and in *Out of the Shadows* I wanted to carry on asking this important question: What if? Professor Greene is developing a drug that might fight cancer. It also has the potential to reverse the effects of aging and extend life—and thus make a lot of money. In the book I wanted to ask what the consequences might be when science is mixed with the desire for profit.

Q. Your books always include a literary theme. In The Professors' Wives' Club *it is Edgar Allan Poe. In* Crossing Washington Square *it is Sylvia Plath, and, of course, in* Out of the Shadows *it's Mary Shelley. Why do you include these literary elements?*

A. I can't help it! Literature has always been my love, my inspiration, and my life. I have a PhD in literature, and even when I moved from academia to fiction writing I never stopped reading, or reading about, books. I've enjoyed including these literary themes in my novels, both as a way to pay homage to these writers but also as a way to keep their works alive, loved, and thought about.

Q. What do you like to do when you're not writing?

A. I have a six-year-old son whom I'm homeschooling—although "homeschool" is something of a misnomer, as we spend a relatively small amount of time schooling at "home." We live in New York City, so we are lucky enough to have an amazing array of fun and educational places on our doorstep. Benny and I, together with his homeschooled friends, are always out on trips to the Metropolitan Museum, the Museum of Natural History, aquariums, zoos, galleries, libraries, and parks. When we're not out and about, Benny and I love to read—either together or separately. I'm so thankful he loves books as much as I do.

QUESTIONS
FOR DISCUSSION

1. *Out of the Shadows* alternates between Clara's and Mary Shelley's stories. Did you like this narrative style? Did you find that the two stories echoed and spoke to each other? Did you enjoy the mix of historical and contemporary fiction?

2. According to the character Kay, "Losing our mothers. It's the hardest thing. But it can change us, too, sometimes in profound ways. It can shape our direction and who we will become." Both Clara and Mary have lost their mothers, although at different points in their lives. How did these losses shape and change them?

3. Have you lost your mother? If so, how did it change and affect your life?

4. Attention-seeking and inconsistent Maxie seems to be the antithesis of her bookish and steadfast sister, Clara. But do you think the sisters have more in common than either would care to admit? Did you feel sorry for Maxie toward the end of the book? Did you agree that, in some ways, she's been living in Clara's shadow?

5. Almost two hundred years separate the lives of Clara and Mary Shelley. How have women's roles changed from the eighteenth century to the twenty-first century? What about their opportunities and obligations? Do women still have to struggle to find their way out of the shadows?

6. Anthony allows his desire for profit and status to get in the way of his professional ethics. Did *Out of the Shadows* make you think about the potential downsides of mixing profit and medical science? Is Anthony just a "bad apple" or do you think it is likely that more scientists and drug companies are cutting ethical corners to get drugs on the market?

7. If the story had been told from Anthony's perspective, how would it have been different?

8. How are Kay and Kay's story a counterpart to Anthony and his desires to extend life?

9. Was the end of the novel shocking to you? How else do you think it could have ended?

10. Knowing what you now know about Mary Shelley's childhood, why do you think she wrote *Frankenstein*, a story of a man who tried to create life but ended up creating a monster? How do you think the loss of her mother, the tumultuous relationship with her father and stepmother, her love for the wild-eyed Percy Shelley, and her time in Scotland factored into the writing of her most famous novel?

11. If you've read Shelley's *Frankenstein*, what similarities do you see between Victor Frankenstein and Anthony in this novel?

Printed in the United States
by Baker & Taylor Publisher Services

Printed in the United States
by Baker & Taylor Publisher Services